SVETLANA'S GARDEN

For Antonia and Duncan

I hope you find enough Russian intrigue in here!

With best wishes

Ivan

SVETLANA'S GARDEN

By Ivan Britanov

Nyet Books

Nyet Books

SVETLANA'S GARDEN

Copyright © Ivan Britanov 2012

All rights reserved. This book is sold subject to condition that it shall not be lent, re-sold, hired out, used or reproduced in any manner whatsoever without the publisher's prior written permission except in the case of brief quotations embodied in reviews and articles.

The right of Ivan Britanov to be identified as the author of this work has been asserted in accordance with sections 77 and 78 of the Copyright Designs and Patents Act 1988.

A catalogue record for this book is available from the British Library.

Originally published in the United Kingdom by Nyet Books in 2012.

All characters and events in this book are fictitious and any resemblance to real persons, alive or deceased is coincidental only.

ISBN 978-0-9572417-0-1

For Anna Politkovskaya, and all those like her, who have passed or will pass in pursuit of the truth.

When the truth is not convenient to its master in the Kremlin, an investigative reporter needs to understand one thing at the start of every day – truth has consequences.

Prologue

The click of his stopwatch broke the silence as Sergeant Arkady Leontev stepped forward to draw back the door bolt and release another bunch of hapless conscripts from the gas training chamber. They tumbled out, these men, more boys in reality, and wrenched dark green gas masks from their faces, coughing, some vomiting, all desperate for fresh air to drive from their lungs the disgusting contaminant the masks had not held properly at bay.

Left behind in the doorway, its wooden outer frame rotten with neglect, lay Andrei Petrov like the runt of the litter, face down on the concrete, twitching for a while before he became still, his frightened eyes wide open. There was just time for a final thought to pass through his mind. He'd hoped it would be of the happy day he'd spent in the forest as a child, his mother and father holding hands, his sister giggling the way she always did, soldiers of sunlight standing to attention between the trees to salute them; a special day before drink and poverty overwhelmed them. But it was not to be. That final thought was not a golden memory to be held for a moment like a babe in arms and lovingly admired. Instead, it was of Major Victor Rebikov, a ruddy-faced giant of a man nose to nose with him, screaming at the top of his voice.

'I said put that fucking mask on and fall in line!'

With that order, Andrei Ivanovich Petrov fell in line for the last time.

'Get yourselves cleaned up and report to the parade ground in camouflage uniforms at eleven hundred hours. Fall out!' barked the Major.

Svetlana's Garden

They were perhaps unlucky that day, for the night before Rebikov had been drinking heavily, boasting about his murderous exploits in Chechnya before pronouncing to his subordinates that the very next day he would show them how to lead properly. Now here he was, demonstrating his leadership. The conscripts, still in need of time to recuperate, dared not defy him. The strong ones managed hateful glances in his direction, careful not to make eye contact. One by one they dragged themselves to their feet, lifted their burdens of resentment and shuffled away through long grass stained with vomit and bile to find some temporary sanctuary.

A heavy grey sky framed the chamber building, which was now clear of gas. This structure of crumbling concrete and corroded metal, long since in need of renovation, had staged its daily play of disdain, with unwilling and bewildered young men as the actors. Behind it, tall pine trees watched on as they had for many years, their branches folded like the arms of disgruntled elders, a brooding and difficult audience. The door swung gently in the breeze, its progress halted by hinges in one direction and the lifeless body of Andrei in the other, nudging him, gently prompting him to wake, the only thing that day to show him any hint of tenderness.

'Another one, Major; another set of paperwork and explanations,' said Leontev, looking on.

'Fuck the paperwork, Sergeant, this was a simple accident. You can see where he fell and hit his head.'

'Where, sir?'

Rebikov stepped back, measured a short run up and then landed a vicious crunching kick with his toe-capped boot on the temple of the pale, pathetic Andrei, his head recoiling from the blow.

'There, Sergeant, right there! Report it as an accident. That's an order!'

Chapter 1

Svetlana Dorenko had just enough fame for members of the Moscow public to take her seriously but not enough for the FSB to pay her too much attention. She was on their radar, naturally, but most of the time they had bigger targets to concern themselves with. The stories she investigated for the weekly *Search for Truth* newspaper were mainly about low-level bureaucratic corruption. Muscovites knew about it; they lived with it daily but she gave them additional insight into some of the more unusual cases. She had enemies, of course, but those enemies generally knew that she had her own protection, her 'roof', provided by the Dubnikov gang. She knew it was a deal with the devil: they protected her and she never wrote about them. As a result, publicity usually avoided them and she stayed alive, which she reckoned was a better bargain than the price paid by some of the principled but now deceased members of her profession. Right now, she was running late while trying to hurry her fourteen-year-old son to be ready for school.

'Ivan, will you please get a move on. Every day it's the same story. Pack your books and don't forget your lunch. It's on the top shelf of the fridge.'

Ivan emerged from his room and strolled across the modest sparsely furnished living room of their fourteenth-floor apartment, not bothering to acknowledge her. She had hoped his adolescent behaviour might have been delayed a year or two yet but no, he was starting early. In a way, it was like having her husband back, all dark and unpredictable moods, although Ivan, she hoped, was not yet drinking, or if he was, not in the spectacular way his father had. She watched him head for the kitchen, his blue shirt hanging out from the waistband of his trousers, his dark hair as unruly as it was when he'd lifted his head from the pillow that morning.

'It's your granny's birthday tomorrow. I've put a card on your desk so can you write her a nice message later and I'll take it when I go to see her.'

She knew Ivan was fond of his grandmother but that he'd also be mindful she always had a few rubles for him, each time he visited.

'I'll take it. I'm going to Misha's tomorrow after school, so it's on my way.'

'Okay, but don't forget.'

'I won't,' said Ivan.

She looked at her watch, the one her mother had given her. It was not expensive but the pearlescent pink of the face had always fascinated her, as though it shouldn't really be like that. As she moved her wrist, the lamplight danced around the oval surface, her eyes following it for a few lingering seconds, wondering where it would rest. Then, she took in the time.

'Shit,' she said, under her breath, realising it was now touch and go as to whether she'd catch her usual train or stand impatiently waiting for the later one, and on a day she'd promised to meet her editor to go over her research into the Orlov bribery case. The trains from Babushkinskaya metro station were like brother and sister to her, depending on how her day was to unfold. She didn't think of them as trains but instead by their pet names of Early and Late even though only a couple of minutes separated them.

'Bye, Vanya! See you later.'

Ivan ignored her as she swept up her keys, opened the front door to the apartment and set off for the lift at the end of the corridor.

'Come on, come on!' she urged the sliding steel doors. They ignored her too. Had they been taking lessons from Ivan? Eventually, with a hiss and a mechanical groan she was enclosed and descending to the exit onto Lenskaya ulitsa and her five-hundred-metre walk to Babushkinskaya.

It was early but the traffic was already heavy as she made her way along the sidewalk of the wide Eniseyskaya ulitsa, lanes of cars jostling for position, fleeing the bad-tempered buses as if swatted away. It was cold, even for late November. The snow was white in the centre reservation, marking out a privileged route for the trams gliding by but she and her fellow pedestrians struggled through brown-stained slush, slithering gingerly to their destinations. Needlessly, a horn sounded next to her as somebody's self-appointed contribution to that day's hustle and bustle of the city.

'Ignorant pig!' she muttered.

Noise wasn't her thing and life was hectic enough at the best of times. Why couldn't this creep keep his hand on the bloody steering wheel and off the horn? He probably had a tiny dick anyway, she decided.

Yep, it was Late who would take her to the office that day. Early was cheekily wagging its arse at her as it disappeared from the end of the platform into the dark tunnel leading south to the city centre. She knew it was her fault really, but it seemed that the gods were conspiring against her. Gods? What was she thinking of? There weren't any. She knew that for sure. Lenin had said so, her teachers had taught her so, *Pravda* had printed so and therefore there were no gods.

'You've let me down here, God, I really needed to catch Early,' she said, oblivious to the school children giggling at this woman who talked to herself.

Why couldn't Babushkinskaya be a more interesting station? This one, with its plain oval roof was all function and no form compared to some of the magnificent structures, with their works of art, elsewhere on the network but at least the lack of benches kept the sleeping rough count down.

*

By the time she reached her office on ulitsa Pravdy, Gregoriy Demochev, her editor, was already on his second cup of coffee and his third cigarette. He was on the phone but beckoned her in as she looked through the clear glass pane of his office door.

'I don't care what the Prosecutor's office says, he did it, we know he did it and we're printing it anyway!'

Demochev, known to his friends as Demchi, put the receiver down, sat back in his old leather chair and took a long drag on his cigarette. He was actually quite tall but the oversized desk seemed to make him shrink, in comparison. His pugnacious character was emphasised by features of receding hair greying at the temples and his nose, swollen and bent to one side, a legacy of a short undistinguished career as an amateur boxer.

'Thanks for showing up.'

'Demchi, I'm sorry it was –'

'Skip it! Okay, let's review your evidence. I want our arses covered on this one. That was Gurevich on the phone. He says the Prosecutor's office is getting heat again from the FSB because they've had a call that no way is Koulikov to be prosecuted.'

'But he did it, everybody knows he did it.'

'Sveta, you know how it is; we can do what we can do. When you learn how to stop the tide coming in, let me know and we'll pick this conversation up again. Now, let's go over the Orlov stuff.'

She took a deep breath and fixed her eyes on him but it was clear their short debate had ended and she would indeed now have to move to the Orlov file. Svetlana spread the papers and photographs out for him. Her hands danced over the text and images, spinning here and there, pointing for emphasis with long slender fingers, complemented by smooth even nails, lingering a little longer on the really important items. While she was attractive, at work, she didn't dress to impress although her mother had always taught her to take care of her hands, to moisturise them against the Russian winter, to wear gloves when she could and to keep her nails manicured.

'Beautiful hands point to a beautiful heart,' her mother used to say. 'One day those hands will carry the ring given to you by the man you love.'

Well, she'd lost the man she once loved but kept her beautiful hands. As for a beautiful heart, at thirty-seven and in her line of work she wasn't exactly moving in circles where she was going to encounter a prince charming.

'Okay, you've convinced me. Good work,' said Demochev, taking another cigarette to replace the one he'd allowed to burn down. 'We'll run it in the next issue.'

This had gone better than she had hoped for. Demchi was no fool and he often challenged evidence that was put before him, but once he was onside he'd back you, unlike his two-faced predecessor in the post. Svetlana admired him, not from any sense of attraction but as a proper man. Yes, he could be short tempered and often impatient but, unlike so many of the men she encountered, skilled at ducking and diving as was the Russian way, he strode through life arm in arm with principle.

She picked up her voicemail messages and made a start on the Orlov copy. By twelve-thirty, she was hungry. She glanced at her watch and then looked up to see her assistant, Vasiliy Telyanin, strolling back from the photocopier. He was a good kid, hard working and committed. One day he'd be a good journalist and, she thought, a distinctive one as he had no idea of dress sense. That day, for example, he'd chosen to wear an orange shirt and a purple jumper. Had he not looked in the mirror before he walked out this morning? She smiled and gently shook her head.

'Vasiliy, I'm going out to buy some lunch. Do you want anything?'

'Thanks, Sveta, can you get me some pelmeni and a carton of milk?'

'Sure, no problem.'

'Here, I'll give you the money.'

'It's okay. We can sort it out, when I get back.'

Rising from her chair, Svetlana went to collect her winter coat and fur hat from the stand in the corner of the journalists' open-plan office.

She stepped out onto the street and set off for her favourite deli. It was only two hundred metres away but the wind had become stronger through the morning and she wrapped a scarf around her face to protect herself from the sleet, dusting the sidewalk as it fell. In the distance, lines of traffic on Leningradsky prospekt seemed to fuse together, like a giant snake sliding slowly but purposefully through the urban undergrowth. She did drive but what was the point in a city with traffic as bad as this? Anyway, her old Lada needed love and attention to keep it running and the stop-start of city centre Moscow would probably finish it off, for good.

Olga, short and stout with flushed cheeks and the deli's proprietor, was not noted for her chitchat but, as Svetlana approached, a smile crossed her face.

'Svetlana Yuriyevna, how are you today?'

'Pretty good, thanks, Olga. How's business?'

'Surviving, but no thanks to those criminals in the mayor's office. I'm really glad there's somebody, like you, who'll take them on but see if you can do something about the roof situation. It's not like it used to be and soon they'll be advertising prices on the radio!'

'I'll see what I can do,' replied Svetlana.

'What can I get you?' asked Olga.

'*Pelmeni* for Vasiliy and I'll have some Moskovskaya salami and *bliny*.'

'Of course. How is Vasiliy? You know, every time he comes in here he looks thinner. Doesn't his mother feed him?'

'I think he's one of those naturally slim types.'

'Huh, that will change,' snorted Olga.

'Oh, a carton of milk and a fresh orange, as well,' added Svetlana.

She was almost blasé about orange juice these days but when she was a young girl growing up in Yaroslavl, north of Moscow, there were no oranges. They simply weren't available to ordinary people. However, her father was owed a favour by the quartermaster of the local army barracks, and one day after work he came home with a bunch of bananas and two oranges. She'd been fascinated by the colour and texture of this rare and, to her, exotic fruit. When she'd peeled off the first segment and savoured its delicious sharp taste, she had decided then and there that this would be her favourite food for all time, this forbidden fruit, this orange. Later, she'd seen a documentary film at her school showing Spanish agricultural workers picking oranges. She'd sneaked back to see it a second time when it was shown later to the older pupils. One day, she'd promised herself, she'd have a house in a sunny place far from Yaroslavl, where she'd plant seeds and grow orange trees; her own garden. A paradise. As she stepped out into the spiteful sleet she was rudely reminded that paradise was a distant dream of innocent childhood. This was what real life had in store for her: cold, damp, and a looming confrontation with a corrupt official called Orlov.

'Svetlana Yuriyevna, are you a mother?'

Svetlana, shielding her face from the wind, looked up to see what she thought was just another *babushka* selling this or that on street corners to supplement her meagre pension. She looked again beyond the first impression to see a woman, probably not much older than herself, to whom life had obviously not been kind. The clothes were functional not fashionable and the hole in those knitted gloves, well, that would do her hands no favours at this time of year. Was she a Muscovite? Probably not.

'Svetlana Yuriyevna, I'm Katia Petrova and I'm a mother. Are you a mother?'

'Yes, I am. I have a son, fourteen,' she replied.

She shepherded Katia to shelter in the office doorway.

'Is he a good boy?'

'Sometimes.'

'My boy's a good boy. I visit him every day.'

'Oh, where does he live?'

'He doesn't live any more. I visit him in the cemetery.'

'What?'

'They killed him. I know they killed him but they won't give me answers.'

'Who killed him?'

'The army, the army killed him. Can you help me?'

Svetlana didn't do military stories. It was one of Demchi's rules: stick to what you knew. What they knew about was officials, mafia and cops on the take but the military was outside their comfort zone.

'I don't work on military stories. I'm sorry, it's just not my area.'

Katia looked deep into her eyes. Svetlana could not avoid her gaze and was forced to look back at her. She shivered as if an unwelcome ghost had stepped forward and embraced her. This was no Moscow *babushka* selling matches, no eccentric pulling at the frayed edges of notoriety to seek attention as sometimes happened, but instead a mother in excruciating, unremitting pain at the loss of her son. Svetlana hesitated but thought of what Demchi had said: 'Stick to what you know. The world's full of hard luck stories and you can't save the entire world.'

'I'm so sorry, Katia, but it's not my area of work. I really can't help you.'

Katia sank to her knees and bowed her head as she tightly gripped the hem of Svetlana's long fur coat.

'I am nothing to this country. It has discarded me as if I was litter in the street. But my son, my only child, was truly something to me and he served this country, this Russia, which turned on him. I carried him in my arms as a baby and now I carry his troubled soul, wandering from place to place, looking for the answers that will allow me to explain to him and to lay him down to rest. He deserves to rest.'

Svetlana had listened to so many stories, many of them untrue, that she thought she could distinguish genuine from false as easily as black from white. This was heartfelt and as genuine as it got but still it wasn't her line of work. Maybe there were no sinister facts at the end of it, just a story of bad luck and grief.

'Svetlana Yuriyevna, help me, please! Will you help me?'

Chapter 2

'Hey, Nick, JF said he wanted to see you when you got in,' called out Victoria Santos, twenty-two-year-old, raven-haired PA to Nick Mendez, International News Network's Madrid correspondent, for the last five years.

'What's it about?' asked Nick.

'I don't know, he wouldn't say but it sounded *muy urgente.*'

'Huh, it's always *urgente*. Okay, wish me luck.'

'Good luck.'

Nick spread his arms like make-believe wings and swivelled round to head in the direction of Jack Freeman's office. Victoria watched him as he went. She thought he moved well and he did have a cute butt, especially in the black cotton pants he wore that day. She gave him a quick once-over. He was handsome, well sort of, and in good shape: tall and dark were plus points. On the other hand, he was only just the right side of forty. Did that make him an older man? She guessed it did. It wasn't really her thing but as she concluded her debate, on balance and with that butt of his, she'd make an exception for him if the moment presented itself.

'Hi, Jack. You wanted to see me?' asked Nick, leaning into Freeman's room.

'Yeah. Hi, Nick. Come in and take a seat.'

You had to be careful with JF, director of European operations. He could be light and breezy but if there was something pressing on his mind, you knew to let him speak first. Nick had even considered making it a routine to sweep by the nearby weather desk to get the JF forecast, before entering his room.

'How's your Russian, Nick?'

'I'm sorry?'

'Your Russian?'

'A little rusty, I guess, but I'm sure it would come back with a little practice.'

Nick, a US national, had a Russian mother and a Cuban father but they'd lived so long in the States, they spoke English more or less all the time these days. The triangular conversations they'd had while he was growing up, seamlessly shifting between Russian, Spanish and English, were now things of the distant past.

'Good, because you're gonna need it.'

'Yeah?'

'I need you to go cover for me, in Moscow.'

'Moscow! Hey, it's winter. Do you know what it's like in Moscow at this time of year?'

'It's interesting, that's what.'

'It's interesting here.'

'No, it's just sunny here. There's plenty of people who can cover for you and who speak Spanish but right now, I need you in Moscow. Kyle Hughes has broken both legs and his pelvis in a car crash so he's out of action there for months and that bastard Trent, the only other fucker on the payroll who speaks Russian, has defected to CNN. I had to put him on six months' gardening leave, so that leaves you.'

'When?'

'Tomorrow.'

'Tomorrow! But I was going down to the villa for a few days on Thursday!'

'Rent it out. The officials are working out the strategic arms reduction details, starting Thursday, for the two presidents to announce at their summit next week. So, I need you on a plane.'

Nick pulled the door to JF's office closed behind him and made for his desk.

'Vicki, you're not going to believe this but I'm going to have to let you go.'

'What?'

'Well, not really but it's *hasta la vista* for you and me. JF's just posted me to Moscow. I've gotta go, tomorrow.'

Victoria sat back in her chair and looked up at him.

Nick saw something in her face he'd not seen before. It wasn't just professional disappointment, for he knew she enjoyed working with him. Did she have a bit of a crush on him? Was that what it was? If it was, how had he missed that, with his antennae attuned to pick up undercurrents of stories? Maybe he needed a bit more quality personal time away from the job to polish his other senses. No point going there. It would have been complicated and time had just killed it off anyway.

'Vicki,' he said, trying to gain her attention.

She didn't respond.

'Vicki!'

'Huh? Oh, sorry, Nick, I was just thinking...'

'Can you organise a flight for me and a hotel for tomorrow night? If Kyle's in hospital for a while, I guess I'll be able to use his apartment, but can you check for me?'

'Sure,' she said, her focus apparently restored.

'Oh, and can you get Ramon to sort out the visa situation?'

'No problem.'

*

Why is it when you're in a hurry, you can never find a fucking thing? he thought, as he packed.

The trouble with not living out of suitcases for five years was that he'd lost the art of storing and packing, everything in its place. He paused, sat down on the bed and for a moment, let his confidence dip. In Madrid he was at the top of his game, confident, incisive in his work and, above all, well connected. People who knew him knew his number and they used it. Now, he was a fish off to swim in an unfamiliar pond and it unnerved him. He drew breath and shut his eyes. When he opened them, he chastised himself for being so timid. This was a new challenge. Everybody needed a new challenge from time to time and who better to take it on than him?

*

He was surprised, at Madrid Barajas check-in, to find his Aeroflot flight was scheduled to leave on time. Why was he surprised? Old prejudices, he supposed, carried with him from his mother's tales of collective inefficiency and the generally complacent diet of western-produced news he'd absorbed over the years. It was time to re-set his objectivity compass. He was a pro and this was a new game, with new rules. He was ready, he told himself.

'Your flight boards at twelve-fifty, sir. Have a pleasant trip,' said the pretty check-in clerk, her severely tied-back hairstyle contrasting with her practised but nevertheless warm smile.

'Thanks very much,' said Nick, as he took his passport and boarding card.

He cleared security faster than he'd expected so had time to make it to the business class lounge to collect his thoughts and make a couple of calls. He signed in and ordered a café Americano before sinking into a comfortable leather armchair.

'Hi, Vicki, what's new...? Okay, that's great. Tell Kyle I owe him a drink. I'll call you when I get a chance, to tie up the outstanding leads. *Hasta pronto.* Be good.'

He put his phone away in his jacket pocket, sat back and followed the few bubbles gently circulating on the surface of his coffee.

'Nick... Nick Mendez?' asked a British voice.

He looked up to see a man he didn't recognise coming towards him from the reception desk, hand outstretched. Before the stranger had covered the five or six paces between them, Nick had checked him out. He had a medium build, sharp haircut, okay suit and expensive silk tie, probably bought for him. It looked like his shoes could do with a polish and the briefcase was fake leather. Before Nick could reach a conclusion on these conflicting signals the guy was shaking his hand firmly.

'Peter Hubbard. We met at a reception at the British Embassy a couple of years ago, the one when the Picassos were being leant to the National Gallery in London, for a season.'

Nick remembered the reception but he didn't remember this guy, at all. He hesitated, then decided it was probably better to play along than not.

'Oh yes... yes, Peter, how are you?'

'Fine, fine, thank you. Where are you travelling to?'

'To Moscow.'

'Moscow?'

'Filling in for the regular guy.'

'Well, there's a coincidence. I'll be in Moscow next week, although I've a little business to take care of in Berlin first. Perhaps we could meet up for a drink, if that's okay with you? Where are you staying?'

'Well, I'm staying in the Metropol tonight...'

'Ah good, a journalist with a sense of history.'

'But after that I'm moving to an apartment I've borrowed, but I don't have the phone number on me.'

Nick lied about the number. Victoria had prepared him a note with all the details he needed but he wasn't sure about this apparent acquaintance, at all, and he didn't need a new drinking buddy, not yet anyway.

'Tell you what, if you give the INN office a call when you get to Moscow, they'll be able to give you the number, I'm sure.'

'Thanks, Nick, I will.'

'Good... well...'

A short, awkward silence followed. Nick managed a weak, insincere smile as he attempted to hide his irritation that his longed-for coffee moment had been so interrupted.

Faced with the prospect of making small talk or leaving, he decided to go. Comparing prices of cologne in Duty Free would be preferable to this. He glanced past Hubbard at his coffee with a stolen look, like catching the eye of another man's wife when he wasn't noticing. As with those encounters, it wasn't to be and he abandoned the now still but rich-smelling drink.

'I'd better be going, Peter. I've a couple of things I need to buy before my flight is called.'

'Absolutely, old chap. Look, great to see you again and I'll be sure to look you up in Moscow,' said Hubbard, clasping Nick's hand once again.

'Great,' said Nick, with as much enthusiasm as he could muster before he turned for the door. He reached out to push it open.

'When were you last in Moscow?'

Nick looked back over his shoulder.

'As a child.'

'It's changed a lot, you know.'

This was not news. He was a bloody journalist and the world was a small place, these days. It had actually dawned on him that Moscow might have changed a bit. Hubbard was starting to irritate him. He nodded and left.

One piece of news that had amused him was that Aeroflot had announced it was only going to recruit attractive, slim flight attendants as it felt it had an image problem. From where he was sitting, it looked like they'd made a rapid start, in business class at least. Walking down the aisle of the plane was a tall blonde badged Lyudmila, her make-up immaculate, her skirt gently swishing as it rode up and down her slim hips. She reached gracefully to shut the overhead lockers as she passed by.

Do they all have cheekbones like that? thought Nick, as she glided past him.

He must have been on hundreds of flights and so far, apart from a little pushy queue-jumping by an over-excited Russian couple returning from a shopping expedition, he'd not noticed any significant difference from other airlines. Then he heard the squeak of metal rings on a rail as the curtain dividing business class from economy was pulled back and closed again. Muffled voices nudged his journalist's curiosity to look back and see, under the curtain, a hairy male hand pass a small roll of dollar notes to an elegant female hand. It looked like the bottom half of a puppet theatre but this was the part of the show the public was not meant to see. The curtain was swept open and the lovely Lyudmila swished by, followed by the overweight owner of the hairy hand, the armpits of his shirt stained with sweat. She led the man to a seat in the vacant row in front of Nick. Body odour reached him almost immediately. *When had this guy last had a shower?* As for this goddess, well, Nick stopped constructing in his head the pedestal he'd been in danger of putting her on. She looked flawless but it had come as such a disappointment to see beneath the physical perfection, the ease with which this slob who was not fit to walk in her shadow had procured his grubby upgrade. He would limit his admiration to her beauty and body, as the inner vision was now tarnished.

Was an Aeroflot aircraft technically Russian territory? Nick thought it probably was but he didn't know for certain. He had researchers who did that sort of thing for him. He looked forward and sideways to survey this little piece of Mother Russia. To his right a bald, bespectacled man was accompanied by a pretty young girl, auburn-haired with a short skirt and tight T-shirt. She could not have been more than nineteen and he was definitely old enough to be her father although, thought Nick, suppressing a faint smile, there was no apparent resemblance. No doubt she was his niece, as Nick had noticed a number of Russian businessmen in Madrid and in the holiday areas of Spain, accompanied by such a relative. Ahead, an expensively dressed mother scolded her young son and daughter for continually baiting each other while the thin nervous-looking man in the row behind them made his excuses as he stepped past on his way once again to the toilet.

Nick heard the curtain rings on the rail again and there was Lyudmila standing next to him, handing him his in-flight meal. She was gorgeous, no doubt about it. Her perfume raced up his nostrils, leapt into his cranium and shook his brain. Her exquisite cleavage was momentarily exposed to him, offered up by the white lace bra within her cream satin blouse, as she bent over with his tray. The assault on his senses mercilessly continued when the rustle of that skirt delivered a final aural blow as though a breaking wave had swept over him. Temporarily disorientated, he missed the first words she spoke to him.

'I'm sorry?' he muttered, unconsciously responding in Russian.

He looked up. She had him fixed with her piercing blue eyes, a steely look bordering on malevolence. Nick, his senses returning, realised that she knew that he knew about the upgrade transaction and she was having a definite sense of humour failure about it.

'I've seen you on the TV, in Madrid. You won't be reporting any secrets, will you?' she asked.

'There's nothing to report,' he assured her.

Her look softened slightly, but only slightly. He knew that she knew. He had the message.

'Enjoy Moscow but don't make enemies.'

'I've had no chance to make any.'

'You will,' she said, as she effortlessly stepped out of sight and closed the curtain behind her.

Chapter 3

In the small, scruffy staff lounge at *Search for Truth*, Katia sat at a wooden table, painted pale green but stained with the memories of a thousand cups and a hundred ash trays. She clasped trembling hands together, her old gloves consigned to her coat pocket. She was all alone.

Svetlana entered, carrying clear, strong tea for them, a spoon standing up in each cup. She looked at Katia. She'd spent a lot of time waiting alone, thought Svetlana. She put down the teas and sat to face the informant she had unwisely allowed to breach her journalist's outer defences.

'Thank you, Svetlana Yuriyevna. You're very kind.'

Katia reached out to squeeze Svetlana's hand. The tips of her fingers were rough. As Svetlana had suspected, these were not city hands. The texture was dry and uneven but the touch was gentle, reassuring.

'Call me Sveta, please.'

Her technique with informants was not intended to be over-familiar but to put them at ease, instead.

'I don't know where to start,' said Katia.

She looked up at the single unshaded light bulb hanging from the centre of the ceiling, as if she was looking for inspiration. A long silence followed, before Katia's faltering words began.

'I have carried my sadness from one official to another, for the past eighteen months and now I've found somebody who'll listen, I can't speak.'

'Where are you from, Katia?'

'From Gorokhovets – well, nearby. We have a cottage about five kilometres from the town.'

Svetlana knew this town, on the Klyazma River in the Vladimir Oblast, east of Moscow. She'd been there several times for work and once for a few days' holiday. It was quite a pretty place, she recalled.

'And your husband?'

'No longer alive, I'm afraid. He was killed in an industrial accident when Andrei was twelve.'

'I'm very sorry, it's just that you said "we" and I assumed –'

'"We" means Andrei and me. It's a habit. I talk to him all the time as if he was still here. I ask him what he'd like for breakfast and whether he'll be going to the stream to see if he can catch us a trout for supper. I know he's not there physically but I feel him all the time and if I talk to him, it's as if I have company. When I go to the cemetery I take some breadcrumbs and a jam jar of water for him so he won't be hungry or thirsty. He was skinny but he always liked his food.'

She looked at Svetlana, who tried to disguise her unease and suppress the lump arising in her throat. This gentle, genuine woman was as if shipwrecked, quite lost in life's sea and in danger of drifting for ever if somebody did not throw her a lifeline. Nevertheless, Svetlana had resolved to explain to Katia at more length about the difficulty of looking into military stories and how her editor would be furious with her if she departed from the areas of work she knew. She would help her as far as she was able but digging into military issues was beyond what she could offer.

'Katia, my editor has a policy about the military.'

'Is your boy always hungry, Sveta?' interrupted Katia.

'Yes, he is.'

'They all seem to be similar, at that age.'

She paused and looked at Svetlana, but without eye contact, before continuing.

'You have beautiful hands. I used to have beautiful hands when I was a girl. Andrei had lovely hands. You should have seen him play the balalaika. His grandfather taught him and gave it to him as a present for his sixteenth birthday. He was so proud and used to practise all the time.'

Her brow furrowed.

'They bullied him. He wrote to tell me how they kicked him, spat at him, called him sparrow legs because he was thin. But he told me he was all right; he was just treating it as part of the training and they would not get to him.'

'Look, Katia, my editor, Mr Demochev, is very strict.'

'They did kill him, you know,' said Katia, this time looking Svetlana straight in the eye.

'How do you know that, Katia? What did they tell you?'

'They told me he had a fall and hit his head.'

'Well, it happens. I'm so sorry for your loss but accidents do happen.'

Katia picked up her scuffed brown handbag, reached in and took out a folded piece of paper before handing it to Svetlana. The writing on it looked like that of a child, barely legible. She studied it and held it under the light to see more clearly. *Andrei was poisoned*, it read.

'Was there anything else, Katia?'

'No.'

'Well, this doesn't really prove anything. Anybody could have written that. Somebody with a grudge, somebody wanting to make trouble.'

'That's what I thought, too.'

'So what makes you think the army killed him?'

'I'd asked to see his commanding officer; didn't know his name.'

'And?'

'They told me he was on leave and wasn't available.'

'Well, they are allowed leave.'

'They said Andrei fell and fractured his skull.'

'Did he have a skull fracture?'

'The undertaker said he did when they received the body... he was in quite a mess with the delay and everything.'

'I'm sorry but this still doesn't prove anything,' said Svetlana.

Katia narrowed her eyes, scolding her for interrupting. She had found her voice and apparently wanted to finish. Svetlana, chastened, averted her gaze and followed the steam still rising from her tea.

'Then, I received the note. I went back to see the commanding officer and they told me he'd been transferred to another regiment in the far east. I asked which one and they said it was confidential.'

'Go on.'

'They treated me like an insect, a nuisance. I was grieving. I'd lost my son and they wanted me to shut up and go away. I sat at home day after day, only going out to visit Andrei. I could not sleep. Why would somebody say Andrei had been poisoned, just to make trouble? Who would do such a thing to a mother?'

'What did you do?'

'I went back, asked them if Andrei had been poisoned. They told me he'd had an accident and I should mind my own business. I said it was my business, it was my son. They told me to go away.'

'Who else have you spoken to?'

'I went to the *politsiya*, in Gorokhovets. They told me it was outside their jurisdiction and I was upset. I spent two weeks at home crying, hardly sleeping.'

The door opened to show Vasiliy in his garish clothes, a notebook in hand. He was about to speak when Svetlana raised her hand to him and gently shook her head. He withdrew, gesturing his apologies and closed the door behind him. Svetlana, a pinched smile on her face, turned her head back to Katia and nodded to indicate her attention was entirely back in the conversation.

'I was exhausted and frustrated. I began to debate whether I was making it all up. I spoke to Andrei...'

Katia closed her eyes, fighting, it seemed, to keep in place the dam holding back the reservoir of pain which drove her. It was no use, as tears flowed down her face. Svetlana stood, stepped over and knelt to embrace her. She was surprised to be held so tightly in return by Katia, as a frightened child might cling to a parent preparing to leave the house. Tepid tears seeped into the foundation and blusher on Svetlana's face as cheek met cheek.

They held each other for what seemed an age to Svetlana, until there were no tears left and the whimpering cries subsided. Then, in little more than a broken whisper, Katia confided in Svetlana.

'A soldier, an officer came to see me at home. He wanted to know who told me Andrei had been poisoned. I looked in his eyes and I knew at that moment they'd killed him.'

Later, Svetlana apologised to Vasiliy. The loss of her brother, also a conscript at the time, had never been properly explained, as a result of which frustration and longing had been her constant companions since adolescence. Her mother and father's attempts to find answers had been rebuffed and she'd been too young to do anything about it. Now, she'd snapped at her young colleague when all he'd done in breaking into her recollections was to ask if she'd like a cup of coffee. Vasiliy combined a smile with an effortless shrug of his shoulders to show the apology was accepted and all was well between them, before turning for the vending machine. She looked at her notes, her eyes drawn to the underlined sections. What was key? The whole thing was full of gaps. Where would you start? Conscripts, poison? She checked herself, placed her notebook in the top drawer of her desk and shut it firmly. She'd actually contemplated investigating this. Was she mad? Demchi would go ballistic. It was out of the question. Demchi was right. 'Stick to what you know,' she told herself, and yet, Katia's search for answers mirrored her own.

*

By the time Svetlana arrived at her apartment, Ivan was already back, his music too loud and a dull thud coming from the wall, as her next-door neighbour protested.

'Vanya, for goodness' sake turn that down!'

Ivan omitted to offer her any greeting but with a scowl reluctantly lowered the volume. She decided to change first and attempt meaningful communication later.

Looking in the mirror, the perfectly blended left side of her face contrasted with the other smudged, irregular side, where tragedy and tears had vandalised the immaculate canvas of her skin. She touched her cheek, looking for clues in the strange shapes and shades that faced her, as the superstitious might read tea leaves. She closed her eyes and descended the steps to the palm-lined beach she'd learnt to visit in her self-hypnosis classes, back when she wasn't sleeping. The soles of her feet sank into the sand, its grains tickling between her toes. Warm sun was on her back, a gentle breeze caressed her and a soothing soundtrack was provided by waves alighting on the shore. Her mind thus cleared and anxieties dispelled, she opened her eyes, beginning the first sweep of cotton wool and cream to remove her make-up. Some of the pores in the skin of her nose looked blocked and were visited by cleanser and facial scrub, until she was happy with the result. Tweezers removed a rogue lash from her eyebrow as she concluded her routine. She pulled on a pair of jeans, swapped her white blouse for a pale blue sweater and ventured out from the sanctuary of her bedroom.

'I've done some *borsch* to start, but do you want sausage or pork and onion for supper?' she asked.

'Sausage,' grunted Ivan.

Outstretched arms could almost reach across their small kitchen and a couple of paces would cover its entire length. It could have done with a fresh coat of white paint but there was always something more pressing. There was a time when Ivan would have willingly done it, out of love and respect for his mother, but that time of opportunity was now over. Svetlana had learnt an economy of movement, a method for getting the best out of this tiny enclosed space, which she put to good use as she set about her preparation.

'How was your day, Vanya?'

'Okay,' mumbled Ivan.

His elbows were on the table as he contemplated the steaming bowl of *borsch* in front of him. No serving of this delicious soup was ever the same, a basic recipe of beetroot, cabbage, beef and vegetables but a constantly variable end product made an enduringly strong antidote to the Moscow winter. In his history lessons Ivan had learnt of the imperial past of Russia and the dynasty of its tsars. He looked at the rich mix of purple and crimson in his bowl and imagined this must have been the colour of royal blood, so much more interesting than the uniform, plain colour spilt by millions of ordinary citizens in all those conflicts he had been taught about. Within minutes, he had finished his soup and made a start on his sausages.

'Did you learn anything interesting?'

'No,' said Ivan, firing a warning shot against any further attempt to draw him into conversation.

Svetlana gave up and reconciled herself to try again when conditions were more favourable. While Ivan had lost his appetite for conversation, he had not lost his appetite. His mother was a good cook who made delicious wholesome food. He ate heartily but apparently could not bring himself to say the food was appreciated as he stood up, grunted and placed his empty plate in the sink, before returning to his room, shutting the door behind him. Svetlana sighed. Music started up again.

The computer went through its usual round of clicks and whines as it booted up ready for the Orlov copy to be tightened up for her sub-editor, the following day. While waiting, she thought she'd indulge herself with a few moments on the beach and soon her practised regime had transported her there. She descended the steps and the familiar sensations welcomed her to a special place but this time there was a sailing dinghy on the beach, which she, as the sole custodian of this space, had not given permission to be there. She walked to it and there behind, kneeling on the sand, was a woman in a winter coat and scarf at the end of a ring of stones sprinkling something on the sand: breadcrumbs, thought Svetlana. She felt herself floating, hovering just above the scene unfolding before her, no longer able to sense the sand between her toes. Slowly and with difficulty, the woman unscrewed the top from a jar and poured water into the sand, which thirstily devoured it. The woman turned, studied her observer and removed her scarf. It was Katia. Svetlana sat bolt upright, her careful routine for leaving the trance instantly abandoned. She was unnerved to have her private place, her reliable refuge, compromised like this. She looked down to see her hands shaking and felt her heart beating against the walls of her chest.

Svetlana didn't drink in the week but this jolt to her equilibrium justified a departure from her regime. Within minutes she was on the internet scrolling through articles about military investigations, a glass of red wine at her side. She brought up page after page, flitting from link to link. From what she could see, the military pretty much looked after themselves. There'd been a number of attempts to bring investigations under civilian control but this had always been resisted. She would have a word with her best contact at the Prosecutor's office, Maksim Pechenkin, who fancied her and parted with perhaps more information than he should in the hope of some future romantic interest on her part. That was not going to happen, but he was harmless and useful so she was tolerant of his attention. Katia had explained that the officer who visited her house had no interest in her welfare but was pressing for information as to why she'd asked about poison and what the source of her enquiry was. If it was an accident, a fall, why would you bother questioning a grieving widow? This obvious contradiction and Katia's sincerity had taken Svetlana to her basic starting point for any investigation. Did it feel right? It most certainly did not. There was a story all right, she could smell it, but her dilemma, of course, was whether she should be looking into it at all. She had promised herself that she'd help Katia as far as she could so a bit of background investigation couldn't do any harm, could it? There was no need to keep Demchi in the loop because she wasn't writing a story, just educating herself in an area she was weak in. In reality, she knew what Demchi would say if he knew, but told herself he'd give her some latitude in recognition of their professional respect for each other.

The telephone rang. Ivan emerged from his room and answered it as Svetlana was still rising from her desk.

'Hi, Granny, how are you...? Yes, I'm coming over tomorrow after school. I'll be at yours about five-thirty... I will. See you tomorrow. I'll pass you on to Mum... Okay, bye, Granny.'

Svetlana's Garden

He handed the phone to Svetlana who wondered whether she'd have to wait until she had a grandson to receive such a spontaneous display of affection and respect.

'Hello, Mama, how are you...?'

Their news exchanged and birthday arrangements having been made, Svetlana replaced the receiver and made a mental note to pick up some lemonade to take to her mother's the next day.

Maybe it was the wine, but Svetlana did not drift off to sleep as she usually managed to do. She tried reading for a while before turning off the bedside lamp, but a welcome slumber would not come. In the near darkness, she looked at the luminous hands of her alarm clock, which showed 1 a.m. She was going to be tired and abandoned her plan to get up early to finish the Orlov text she'd neglected earlier. There was only one thing for it – she'd have to go to the beach. She shut her eyes, stretched her arms, tensed then relaxed her fingers as her routine began. Before she was able to take the first step away from consciousness, the picture of Katia offering her scraps of bread and water appeared. She opened her eyes and stared at the ceiling. Was there now to be no refuge? Why hadn't she listened to Demchi?

Chapter 4

Boy did he need a drink! It was one-fifteen in the morning as Nick helped himself to two miniatures of vodka and some orange from the minibar in his room at the Metropol. He'd been up and travelling for sixteen hours but his body clock was still behind, on Madrid time. He was tired all right, but sleep was out of the question until he'd wound down a bit.

And as for his arrival at Sheremetyevo airport, well, he didn't know whether to laugh or cry. Was it trial by ordeal or a useful crash course in Russian administration for a journalist who had been softened by sunshine and the relative efficiency of Barajas? The plane had actually made a good landing. He'd put it in the top twenty per cent in his experience. Then it started. A number of people seemed to rush past him as he left the aircraft, either briskly walking or almost jogging. Did they know something he didn't? They did and he cursed himself for not having done a bit of research or even speaking first to Kyle Hughes for some pointers. He'd found himself well back in the queue at passport control, the walkers and joggers in front of him well rewarded for their efforts. How could it take so long to check each individual passport? Over an hour had passed and while he was nearly at the front the passport officer in his queue left his post not to return for a full fifteen minutes, apparently after taking a break. He tried to talk to a security guard who shrugged before turning his back and walking away.

'How long are you staying?'

The rude passport officer facing him commenced a minute examination of the Visa and every single page of the American passport Nick presented. He could have had a Cuban passport, following in the footsteps of his father but it had never been an issue. He thought it might be now.

'I'm covering for a colleague who's had a car crash. It might be some months.'

'Oh, you speak Russian,' said the officer, disappointed that he had lost a weapon in his armoury of hostility. 'Don't forget to register with the authorities if you're staying that long.'

He sat back in his chair and returned to thumbing through the passport, page by page. He studied Nick's photo and looked at him suspiciously before eventually stamping his departure form and a spare page in the passport. Then, he tossed it across the counter, without looking up.

In the baggage hall suitcases had overflowed the carousel and were strewn about. Nick feared the worst, but no, his case was present and intact if a little grubby from lying on the floor waiting for him. Mercifully, he cleared the green channel at customs without being stopped and emerged to see rows of unfamiliar faces of friends and relatives unsure as to when their loved ones would be reunited with them. Victoria had said she'd arrange for the Moscow office to provide a driver. He scanned the pieces of cardboard and paper held forward and aloft looking for his name but to no avail.

No, c'mon. Not here, not now, he thought.

Nick was self-conscious and felt exposed with all these people facing him. He had to move and reconciled himself to taking a taxi but had not reckoned with the near stampede of drivers competing for his business as he emerged through the main exit into the open. Did he have a big sign on him that read 'Foreigner: Please Exploit'? He was pushed and jostled as each competitor tried to cajole him in the direction of his particular cab. Suddenly, a firm hand was planted on his shoulder. He turned to see a large man, unshaven, maybe six-four, wearing a black leather jacket and a leering grin. The other drivers stepped back a pace, to await the event.

'Mr Mendat?' enquired the grinning one, in English, holding up a photo of Nick and a piece of card with *Mendat* written on it.

'Yes,' replied Nick, in Russian.

The card and photo provided some reassurance that he was being met, not kidnapped. Mendat was close enough. The other drivers let out a collective sigh of resignation and turned together like a shoal of predatory fish in search of other distressed prey.

'I am Slava and am spoken eengleesh. I'm have cigarette, sorry.'

Nick was grateful for the invitation to greet his new companion informally as Slava and not by his proper first name of Svyatoslav. This was an encouraging sign.

'I'm Nick,' he reciprocated, in Russian, 'and if it's okay, Slava, can we speak Russian as I need to practise?'

'No problem,' his driver assured him, grasping his hand for the firmest handshake he could ever remember.

Slava more than filled the driver's seat of his black Volvo, man and car together creating a picture of menace.

Does he double as a getaway driver in his spare time? thought Nick.

He used to have a Lada, Slava explained, but it had been too small for him and had given him backache. He had a friend who was a 'special car dealer' who had done a great deal for him on the Volvo. Nick didn't enquire further. He'd picked up intonation in the word 'special', enough to know that in this context, it meant shady goings-on. He congratulated himself. Maybe he'd get up to speed quicker than he'd thought, but soon realised that he'd need a refresher course in Russian swearing. He'd forgotten it swaggered around as the baddest boy of bad language, wearing a bomber jacket of disdain and brandishing a switch-blade of extra crudity, compared to other tongues.

'Nick, I'm not a racist but the fucking blacks are taking over some streets in the city at night and the worst thing is you can't see them fucking coming.'

'Hmmn,' said Nick.

He wanted to be non-committal, reluctant to agree with such sentiments but anxious not to offend the hospitality Slava was showing him.

'I mean, they won't do a decent fucking day's work and what with them fucking each other up the fucking arse all the time, it's a fucking disgrace, really.'

Nick was beginning to think eengleesh might have been a better choice after all. He contemplated the seemingly endless suburbs with their rows of look-alike apartment blocks. He thought he'd change the subject.

'What's the traffic like on this road during the day?' he enquired.

'Fucking awful!'

'Well, you did ask,' Nick told himself.

The minibar fridge was obviously very efficient. The vodka was really cold, the way it should be, as was the orange. He watched as the clear and the cloudy untidily wrestled with each other in his glass, contemplated the concoction he'd made, and then drank it down in one, feeling the cold liquid traverse every centimetre of his oesophagus before impacting on his stomach. That had definitely hit the spot.

'Welcome to Moscow,' he greeted himself, as he reached for a refill.

Chapter 5

Chekhovskaya metro station was part of Svetlana's favourite route to the Public Prosecutor's Office, on Bolshaya Dmitrovka ulitsa. It gave her the chance to nod to images of Chekhov at either end of the station hall and to the statue of another of her literary heroes, Pushkin, in the square above that bore his name. Two masters of words, each able like the conductor of an orchestra to move his audience with the instruments at his disposal: words, tone, intonation, jealousy and pathos, swimming in the soup of emotion he'd made but under control of it, just. What use was an author if he became so upset at his story that he lost the ability to tell it? It made Svetlana think back to her school days. She'd been occasionally lonely, when one or other of her friends wasn't talking to her. As she'd sat alone on the bench in the corridor, Anton and Aleksandr had then become her occasional companions instead. They seemed to understand everything. When she'd been through her rebellious phase as a teenager, she'd nevertheless kept her respect for her elders, as she'd learnt through these authors that she didn't know everything, while they did, or so it appeared to her. She would imagine herself as the heroine in their stories, the victim of unrequited love, the mother of a lost child or a dying soul. When her tears flowed as the scenes overwhelmed her, she'd learnt to keep her finger poised over the last line she'd read, so the story could be taken up again when her composure returned. How could they write such things, how did they ever manage to finish a story without love or tragedy disabling them along the way? She had seen her share of real life tragedy in her work; lives ruined by scandal, corruption and sometimes naked cruelty. To her the emotion was

Svetlana's Garden

part of the story and she tried to reflect that in her own style while never bending the facts to suit. She looked up at Pushkin standing astride the giant pedestal below him, his cape flowing, hand tucked in his jacket as if checking his heart was still there and not destroyed instead by all it had been forced to bear witness to. She bowed her head momentarily, in utmost respect, as the noble author looked down kindly on his ignoble imitator.

Svetlana and Maksim had an understanding that if it was on the record, she'd make an appointment to see him in the office but if it was off the record, they'd have coffee at Coffee Bean, off Pushkinskaya ploshchad. Today, it was off the record.

'Sorry I'm late, Sveta.'

Maksim, approaching, bumped into a chair in his haste to reach her.

Today, she allowed him to greet her with a kiss on the cheek. She didn't always allow that or he'd take too much encouragement from it, so usually it was just his gentle handshake, which would linger a little longer than it should.

'No problem, Maks. I've ordered cappuccino for you. I hope that's okay.'

'Yes, that's great. Thanks.'

Maksim looked around him, as if checking to see if he was being followed. This was not likely, as administrative assistants in the narcotics department of the Moscow Municipal Prosecutor's office just didn't warrant that sort of attention. He was definitely just a cog in the machine. He sat down.

'Thanks for meeting today. I was hoping you could do me a favour, with a bit of information.'

'I'm always happy to help you if I can.'

Maksim moved his hand to touch Svetlana's. She was ready for him and seamlessly moved hers to wave at the waitress heading in their direction with their cappuccinos. A peck on the cheek from Maksim was the sum total of physical contact with him she'd planned for that day. The waitress put their drinks down with a smile as was the Coffee Bean way, unlike so many places, where a legacy of Soviet indifference to service seemed to hang around like fog which wouldn't lift.

'What do you know of investigation into military matters?'

'Sveta, that's not my area. Military stuff is dealt with by the Deputy Prosecutor General's office but I don't know how they work, day to day.'

'Could you find out for me?'

'Why, what's going on?'

'Nothing, really. I just need to understand better how things work.'

'Military stuff's not usual for you.'

'No, it's just a small sideline to a bigger story I'm working on.'

'I'm not sure I can help you with that,' said Maksim.

'Why not?'

'For one thing, it's not my business and for another it's not wise to be poking your nose into military matters if you don't work there. That much I do know.'

Svetlana could see her plan was going to have to alter. There was a tone in Maksim's voice, which indicated he really didn't want to take this favour on. He was studying the ornate ceiling with its gold features, hoping, she thought, for a change of subject.

Sveta, you'll have to, she thought.

She reached out and gently scraped the back of Maksim's hand with the nail of her middle finger. Instantly, he was attentive and eager to help. Men, and Maksim in particular, were such a pushover that this gave Svetlana no satisfaction. She'd have liked to show him more respect but her research had left her convinced that only somebody with access to inside information could offer any hope of names and installations in the district where Andrei had been stationed.

'What is it you need to know?' asked Maksim, a dewy eyed look crossing his face.

'I need an example of the structure in a military district. Let's say Chita in Trans-Baikal.'

'Why there?'

'No reason, it just seems as good an example as anywhere.'

Maksim was becoming uneasy again and took a sip of his cappuccino, leaving him with a thin moustache of chocolate. Svetlana smiled at him.

'What?'

'The moustache doesn't really suit you.'

She rubbed her top lip. Maksim wiped the chocolate away, the humorous moment making his guard drop again.

'I'll see what I can find out but I'll need to be careful so it may take a while.'

'Thanks, Maks. I really appreciate it.'

The reporter rose from her chair and he followed her to the exit. She touched his elbow and kissed his cheek. She reckoned he deserved a reward after all, and the hope of another would keep him motivated to help her. As she walked away, back towards Chekhovskaya metro, Maksim called to her.

'Sveta, you do know what you're doing, don't you? Some things are better left alone.'

She smiled, before turning for the station.

*

Later, back at her desk, Svetlana stared at the blank screen of her computer.

'It works better if you turn it on,' quipped Vasiliy.

'I'm thinking.'

'What about?'

'A boy.'

'What boy?'

'A dead one, a mystery, an accident, that wasn't.'

'What?'

'Vasiliy, how do you track down a witness who may be a hoax, with no name and no address?'

'You can't... but you could advertise like a lonely hearts column.'

'Vasiliy, have you got a moment?' called Demchi, from the doorway of his office.

'Be right with you,' answered Vasiliy.

He shrugged at Svetlana before turning on his heels for Demchi's office.

She thought about what he'd said. *Advertise? That was a long shot. Lonely hearts column?* She didn't think so. However, maybe Vasiliy had an idea, after all. She could work something into one of her columns, disguised as part of the story. It would be nothing more than hopeful but at least it had a chance of being picked up by the mystery witness, if one really existed.

Hang on a minute, she thought. *You don't mess with the facts, remember. But you're not messing with the facts... the facts are the same. You're just inserting a separate item.*

So that was settled, or was it? She pictured herself looking up at the giant figure of Pushkin and him looking back at her.

Aleksandr, this is different... but the cause is just. What should I do?

In her reverie she looked up, while he looked down. There was no noise, no crowds and no traffic, just a scene from a silent movie playing out as a grey sky drifted by overhead. A break in the clouds allowed a shaft of sunlight to bathe them both momentarily in light and warmth. She had her answer. Now, it was settled. She withdrew from her daydream and switched on her computer.

The Orlov story was running in the morning and the sub-editor was planning to place it quite prominently on page two. It had already been pre-approved and would not be looked at again. Her writing style was quite tight, not using three words when two would do, so it was going to be difficult to re-write it to accommodate the insertion. Part of the piece related to evidence going missing and it was here she reckoned she could make her point. She scrolled up and down the page, looking for words she could lose or a paragraph she could re-write to free up space for her additional sentence. It took her an hour, thinking it funny how it could be more difficult sometimes to write a small amount than a large piece. She then inserted her sentence: *This is similar to the case of Andrei Ivanovich Petrov, a conscript who died in mysterious circumstances.* She sat back and reviewed the whole piece. It was fine. The facts were as before, the piece had the same tone and feel without any noticeable format changes. The bait was attached to the hook. She would now cast out the line and see if anything would bite.

*

INN had two offices in Moscow. The main one was on Bolshaya Tatarskaya ulitsa where the production studios were, while the other was at the south end of ulitsa Pravdy. The station reckoned it was good to have an ear to the ground in a traditional news street and this argument had, for the time being, won out over the economic one to trim rental costs in such a fiercely expensive city as Moscow. Nick was struck by how traditional it was compared to the production office, bordering on quaint. There was even an old American-made Underwood typewriter, with Russian Cyrillic alphabet, in a glass case in the corner of the office, which overlooked the street. It reminded him of his days as a cub reporter at *The Boston Phoenix*, where there was also an old Underwood.

'Do you want to go for a drink after we've finished up here?' asked researcher Konstantin 'Kostya' Bereznity, who had offered to show Nick around and make the introductions.

'Tomorrow, Kostya, if that's okay 'cause I want to finish moving in at Kyle's apartment.'

'No problem,' replied Konstantin.

'What's the best metro station to use?'

'Belorusskaya. Turn left as you leave the office, then left again when you reach Leningradsky prospekt.'

'Thanks. See you tomorrow,' said Nick, as he made for the door.

Outside, fresh snow began to fall, while the wind rose and fell between the buildings with an eerie groan. Some things he was learning quickly, but picking the correct clothes was not one of them. His expensive, soft leather shoes from Madrid were wet through in no time. He told himself he'd have to dry them out slowly or they'd be ruined. His woollen hat was better than nothing but, tomorrow, he would buy a proper fur *chapka ushanka*, if this was what the coming months had in store for him. Did people walking by always keep their eyes on the pavement? he asked himself. He could not remember a single soul making eye contact with him. Maybe it was just the weather. Despite leaving early, by the time he reached the entrance to Belorusskaya metro, there were plenty of commuters making their way. A beggar was partially blocking the stairway holding out a battered Starbucks cup, a small ragged child clinging to her skirt. Was she real, or a professional? It was hard to say. If she was genuine then it was a sad sight indeed but if she was acting, she was very good at it. The commuters ignored her, anxious to escape the cold and reach the shelter below. Nick went with the flow, but as he neared her she looked so pathetic that he decided to give her a few rubles and stopped abruptly, his hand foraging in his coat pocket for some change. Behind him, a woman, forced to stop without warning, slipped and let out a yelp of alarm. From the corner of his eye, Nick saw the beginning of her fall. He moved to catch her but his hand was caught in his pocket and by the time he'd freed it his attempt to hold her and break her fall was doomed. He watched, horrified, as she escaped his grasp and continued her descent, discarding her handbag as first her elbow and then her head met the concrete of the sidewalk.

She seemed stunned and for a few seconds unable to take in what had happened. Slush mixed by the feet of so many pedestrians began to seep into her clothing.

'I'm so sorry...' said Nick, bending down and extending his hand to help her up '...are you okay?'

He took in her cold and hostile look. She ignored his hand and moved first onto her knees before rising unsteadily to her feet. She reached out for the wall bordering the steps, but as soon as she leant on it she screamed out loud, apparently in great pain. Nick's reaction was to hold her to try to offer comfort.

'Take your hands off me!' shouted Svetlana, with real venom in her voice.

He held his hands up, as a victim facing a loaded gun might do.

'I'm sorry. I was just trying to help.'

'I don't need your help. Go away!'

'But you're hurt. Can't I at least get you a taxi, maybe?'

'Go away!' she said, with deliberation, narrowing her eyes.

Nick dithered, unsure whether to press on with attempted chivalry or retreat, before a mumbled 'really sorry' accompanied him as he turned for the stairway into the metro. The beggar scowled at him as he passed her, leaving her empty handed.

*

'Sveta, what on earth happened to you?'

Svetlana walked through the dark, wooden doorway of her mother's apartment. Ivan was already there, eating, of course. Even he, realizing that his mother was in real difficulty, took the trouble to come over to her.

'Are you all right, Mum?'

'I had a fall by Belorusskaya station. Some idiot stopped right in front of me and I slipped.'

'Let me look at you,' urged her mother. 'Oh, Sveta, you've got a nasty bruise and a cut on your head... I'll get some ice. Sit down, sit down!'

Svetlana sat on the settee, letting the large cushions envelop her. Within moments she was feeling the soothing effect on her forehead and temple of some ice cubes wrapped in a tea towel.

'Thanks, Mama. That's much better.'

Ivan, seeing that his granny had the situation under control, returned to his food.

'You can't go to work tomorrow, Svetochka.'

'I'll see, Mama. It's just that I've got one or two things on at the moment.'

'It's out of the question. You'll need to rest. You can have my bed tonight and Vanya can sleep on the settee.'

'I'll be okay.'

'That's enough... and anyway, you're going to have a black eye in the morning. Anybody would think... You're staying, that's final.'

Svetlana knew why her mother had checked herself. It had been particularly difficult in the winter to explain why she was wearing sunglasses, but they had helped to shield her from too much scrutiny and Dima from too much loss of reputation. Everybody knew he'd hit her in another of his drunken rages, railing against the injustice of his world, drowning as he slowly and inevitably forgot how to swim in the new sea that followed the fall of communism. Inside he'd been a good man. Russian men might have lacked the sophistication of some of their western counterparts but when it came to flowers, they had them beaten every time. How often you would see a Russian man purposefully striding down the street with a bunch of flowers held out like the Olympic torch – a triumphant declaration of love. Dima had been wonderful with flowers, taking the trouble to pick out the best blooms. 'Look at the colour of these,' he would say, bending on one knee to present them to her. 'The only colour in nature better than this is the colour of your eyes!' He had the ability to induce in her a woozy feeling as if she was floating. He'd been irresistible and she'd fallen hopelessly in love with a man who was well read but wonderful with his own words, spontaneous and funny. But, maybe the highs and frequent terrible lows of Russian literature led him to believe that they were scripts to be lived, not stories to behold. When the facility he worked at was privatised he'd lost his job. It turned out that the existing manager had appropriated most of the valuable assets and set up a rival factory run by his brother and other family members. Such manoeuvres, where fortunes were made by the crafty and ambitious, became commonplace in the commercial chaos unleashed by Boris Yeltsin, who became less and less able to control the genie he'd let out of the bottle. Svetlana, incensed by the trick perpetrated on her husband, took her first steps as an investigative journalist, determined to expose such frauds upon ordinary citizens. Meanwhile, Dima, unable to find work, had taken solace in vodka, which more and more replaced his beautiful wife as his companion in life. Inevitably, she'd had to end it. They'd divorced many years ago to protect what was left of their family from further harm. Ivan, she reckoned, remembered more than was good for him but what could she do other than demonstrate her love for him at every opportunity he would allow?

'Okay, Mama, we'll stay,' said Svetlana.

Looking up at the few cards set out on the sideboard, she reached into her handbag, took out her own card and a small gilded frame with a picture of her grandfather in it. The frame had survived her fall, unlike the bag of fresh *pirozhki* she'd picked up from Olga's deli, which were crushed but probably still edible.

'Happy birthday, Mama,' said Svetlana, handing the picture over.

Her mother looked at it before pressing the faded black and white image to her lips, a tear forming in her eye, which she gently wiped away.

'Thank you, Svetochka. He was a good man. I wish you could find a good man.'

'Mama, stop it. That's the last thing on my mind right now.'

The doorbell rang.

'Oh, that'll be Polina.'

'No, I don't want her to see me like this!' exclaimed Svetlana.

'Don't be silly, dear. She'll understand. She knows all about clumsy men,' said her mother, heading for the door.

*

Nick could tell Kyle's car crash had come as a shock. His place was apparently just as he'd left it – a mess. He'd not be returning for a good while, as the block was definitely not wheelchair friendly. The apartment itself was okay, but Nick could see he was going to be cleaning up for the next couple of hours as he put down his enormous suitcase, which they'd held for him at the Metropol. The bedroom was large and painted a warm, pale orange with a good sized bed. He sat on it to test the firmness of the mattress: *not bad*, he thought. The living room was typically male, with a large TV, leather settee and armchair, a drinks cabinet and little in the way of detail. There wasn't a scented candle or cushion in sight. No girlfriend, Nick figured. In the kitchen there was a lingering smell of coffee, which was encouraging. Madrid just didn't do instant coffee. It had spoiled Nick with the vast range of tastes and aromas available, the perfect complement to city interaction. He inspected the cupboards. Bingo! A large jar of ground coffee and a back-up sachet of Columbian beans graced the shelf, alongside some packet meals.

'Shit food but great coffee,' said Nick.

The food he could sort out, as he'd passed a good supermarket only a hundred metres down the road. He'd go later but right now it was time to clean up.

Three hours later, the place was looking good with the floors swept, fresh bedding and the smell of furniture polish circulating on the breeze from the window he'd briefly opened, despite the cold outside. Certainly, washing Kyle's second-hand underpants and socks had not been the highlight, nor for that matter had cleaning layers of burnt-on grease in the grill but, overall, he carried a certain feeling of smug satisfaction as he sat back and surveyed his work.

It was late, so on reflection, he thought he'd postpone shopping and pop out for a pizza, maybe picking up some bread and milk for the morning, on his way back. While cleaning, he'd noticed that Kyle had a couple of proper fur hats including an *ushanka* with ear flaps. He was sure he wouldn't mind his new colleague taking advantage of a little weather protection. Apart from decent food, Kyle seemed to have most things a guy could need.

Nick decided on a small pizza restaurant, just off ulitsa Pokrovka, the type that serves in and out. The waiter ignored him as he entered, so he took a corner table anyway in the red and white painted salon before scanning the menu. He decided on a quatro stagioni and a beer. Eventually, his order was taken, with Moscow indifference and no hint of Italian brio. This place was making an early bid to cross itself off his list of possible regular haunts. He sipped his beer and inspected the lifeline on his left palm to give himself something to do as he waited for his food. It was a long line, so he figured he'd many years ahead of him but that fork along the way was a bit troubling. The pizza was actually not bad. Maybe the chef should do front of house as well.

He was half way through when a guy and what looked like his girlfriend entered, he in a jacket and tie and she in a knitted dress and boots. They could have been anybody. Nick supposed they were coming in for a takeaway but was surprised to watch them walk calmly past the servery to the back of the restaurant, followed by the waiter, bearing a look of resignation. Within two minutes they'd left, with as little fuss as when they'd arrived. The waiter, it turned out, was the owner and Nick picked up some of the similarly colourful language Slava had regaled him with, on the journey from Sheremetyevo.

'Trouble?' asked Nick.

'Bastards!' said the previously indifferent restaurateur. 'It's hardly worth trying to run a business in this shithole of a city!'

Nick had to admit the whole experience was coming from the alternative school of customer service but at least the guy had feelings, after all.

'What's the problem?' he asked.

'Where are you from?' came the question to a question.

'Boston, USA but Madrid for the past few years.'

'Read about it,' said the owner, picking up a discarded newspaper from a vacant chair and tossing it over.

Nick looked down at a slightly crumpled copy of *Search for Truth*, thumbing through the various exposés of backhanders and protection rackets, interspersed with advertisements. The copy was serious but the layout reminded him more of *The National Enquirer*. His eyes were drawn to a story about money changing hands for permission to demolish an historic suburban church, to make way for an extension to a shopping development. This was good stuff. He liked the punchy but emotive style. His eyes rose to the top of the column to check out the author.

'Svetlana Dorenko,' he muttered.

Then there was a double take at the accompanying photo. It was her! The lady at the metro station. He sat back and considered his situation. Was this good or was it bad? A grin crossed his face. He had a name to a face, the key starting point for any journalist. Things were looking up.

Chapter 6

Kyle Hughes was being treated at the American Hospital on Grokhol'sky pereulok. By the time Nick got there, it was already past eleven and he'd promised to be at the production studio for half-twelve, for a meeting with the rest of the news team. This was going to be a short visit.

'Kyle, long time, no see,' said Nick, as he entered the private room.

'Nick Mendez, in the flesh. They told me you were coming to Moscow but I didn't expect to see you so soon.'

'You look like shit, but that's better than I thought you'd look.'

'I feel like shit,' said Kyle, gesturing to Nick to take the seat at the side of his bed. 'How've you been?'

'Good... but I'm missing the sunshine already.'

'Yeah, it's a bummer at this time of year.'

'Really appreciate you letting me use the apartment.'

'Hey, no problem.'

'I cleaned it up a bit for you.'

'Huh... sorry about that but I wasn't exactly expecting visitors, if you know what I mean.'

Kyle did look like shit. He was plastered and bandaged over most of his body, with only one arm free. On the flesh that could be seen, blue and black bruises testified to the violence of his accident. Nick looked him up and down.

'You sure it was a car crash and you didn't just piss off some gangster?'

'Hey, I wasn't driving.'

'Only I was reading a paper called *Search for Truth* last night and if half of what was in there is true, it's a bit scary.'

'I read it occasionally, but it's mostly moderate level city stuff and not really our kind of material.'

'I bumped into one of their reporters – literally bumped into her.'

'Oh yeah?'

'Svetlana Dorenko. Do you know her?'

'I know of her, but I don't know her.'

'What do you know?'

'The people on the street like her. They think she speaks up for them but that won't count a flying fuck with the people she's writing about. Anyway, I thought you'd want to ask me about the presidents getting together. You know, what we do... big stories!'

'Kyle, you know how it is. It's news, yeah, but it's all packaged up for us, a done deal weeks before these guys show up to take the glory.'

'Nick, packaged news or not, it pays the bills – and the medical insurance,' said Kyle, pointing to his plaster cast.

'I guess.'

'Who's showing you round?'

'Konstantin'.

'Oh... okay. He's a good guy. In fact, they're all good apart maybe from Valentina – okay to your face but can be a bitch behind your back.'

'Yeah? So this girl...?'

'Valentina?'

'No, Svetlana Dorenko. Is she a good source for us?'

'Unless she takes tea with the president, I don't think so but she's still a bit of a looker, if you're after some company.'

'That's not what I meant.'

Kyle tilted his head and raised his eyebrows.

*

Svetlana's Garden

In a small over-lit meeting room, the production team had begun its discussions. It was twelve-forty as Nick opened the door and silence descended, as if a stranger had entered a cosy locals' bar.

'Sorry I'm late,' said Nick, as sincerely as he could.

After a moment of judgement, it was Valentina who rose first, holding out her hand.

'Hello, Nick... Valya. I think you met everybody else, yesterday.'

'Er... yeah.'

'We were just saying that Kyle will be a hard act to follow, but I'm sure you'll manage.'

Nick released her hand. This half praise and Kyle's warning put him on guard. He resolved to stay there as far as Valentina was concerned.

The meeting dragged on longer than Nick thought it should. He was used to JF's 'that's a wrap' style, in Madrid. Here, they seemed to need three takes at everything. Nevertheless, he tried to play his part but found his mind wandering to the fierce look he had been dispatched with by the feisty, injured journalist. His mother had always been strict about good manners towards women: you held a door open and you stood up on a bus to offer a seat. To leave a woman, injured, alone and fending for herself, was something that would never sit easily with him. Even if she had refused his attempt to retrieve the situation at the scene, he would have to try again or his mother would never forgive him.

'Is that okay, with you, Nick?' asked Konstantin.

'What?' replied Nick.

'Final briefing at six, live broadcast at six-thirty and a recorded brief for the networks at seven?'

'No problem.'

*

Roman Dubnikov, unshaven but suited, opened his desk drawer and took out a bottle of Saproshin vodka and two shot glasses. He filled them both, before pushing one across the desk. Maikov preferred to use his surname only, as he thought it gave him an edge. He scrolled down a series of images of, mostly, teenage girls on his lap-top as Dubnikov observed.

'How many?' asked Dubnikov, when Maikov had finished.

'Thirty-three.'

'I don't need that many. There's some use left in the last lot and the Chechens will pay shit for them anyway.'

'It's thirty-three, a package deal. If you don't want them, Novokoff will have them.'

'That rabid dog...'

'His money isn't mad, even if he is.'

'How much?'

'Sixty thousand... dollars,' said Maikov, before downing his vodka.

'Sixty thousand!'

'It's a fair price. You know I deliver quality.'

'Fifty-five thousand,' said Dubnikov beginning a period of silence, while the two men examined each other's eyes for hints of weakness. Maikov was an experienced middle man. He liked to see himself as a commodities broker. He sourced product, drugs, guns, women, whatever the main gangs needed. He had a reputation for delivering and was careful not to double-cross any of them as he realised, whatever the temptation, his brokerage would end with a bullet in the back of his head. He also knew his clients' particular foibles. Dubnikov could be unpredictable and liked the last word. He tried to read him but Dubnikov did not flinch, returning his stare without blinking.

'Fifty-five thousand,' confirmed Maikov extending his hand, which his client shook firmly.

'Good, we'll have a drink,' said Dubnikov.

He re-filled their glasses. Maikov removed a pen-drive from his laptop and gave it to Dubnikov.

'They'll be ready on Friday. Do you want them delivering to the usual place?'

'Yeah, Vadik will deal with it. Are any of them going to give him trouble?'

'There's a Tajik who's fiery, otherwise no problems.'

'Vadik will break her in.'

'He'll enjoy that.'

'He will.'

Dubnikov showed his visitor out before returning to his desk. He knew Maikov's claims about quality were usually accurate, which made fifty-five thousand a decent price. There'd be no hundred-dollars-a-night dogs in there. With Maikov's girls he could put them at the best *tochkiy* and get five to seven hundred dollars a night out of them, so even with the exchange rate he'd make his money back and soon be into profit. As for the girls, they would do as they were told. Oh, of course there were always the ones who thought they were going to a regular job or who decided to give you some grief. Vadik soon had them in line. In fact he looked forward to the feisty ones. After he'd raped them, slapped them around and told them to remember what the point of a blade on their eyelids felt like, he tended not to have any more trouble. Anyway, they were fed, housed and given medical attention when they needed it; that was enough. Dubnikov saw them as an investment, which is why he bought quality not the diseased bargain-basement junkie crap the Chechens put out on the streets. God, he hated those fucking Chechens. If turf wars weren't bad for business, he'd blow them all away.

A 'ping' came from his computer and he turned to face the screen. He reached for his mobile phone and dialled a number from the memory.

'Sveta, it's Roman. Time for a chat.'

*

Svetlana put her mobile down and sighed deeply. She'd really wanted to tell Dubnikov to go to hell but never could. His business disgusted her: pushing drugs to kids and putting teenage girls on the streets to sell themselves. He was everything she despised and yet, also one of the reasons she stayed alive. 'Sveta, if it wasn't me it would be somebody else,' he would say and at least on that they agreed. Frankly, she couldn't see the point of their chats but

Dubnikov insisted on it just to 'keep in touch'. Maybe he was worried she'd turn on him one day and saw this as a way to reinforce the message that they needed each other. At least he'd agreed to postpone it for a few days, after she'd explained about her fall. They were candid with each other and she knew he'd believe her story was true.

Her mother was right about the black eye. The ice had helped but there it was, a real beauty. The jokes would be coming from her colleagues and the irony was that this time her story of an accident would be true. She gently pushed the tip of her finger into the top of her cheekbone recalling the old scale of damage she'd created for herself, all those years ago. It could have been worse, a seven, she reckoned as she judged the underlying damage from the pain she felt at her own touch. It would take maybe a week to disappear and it could be hidden with make-up, after perhaps four days. As she lowered her hand, she noticed a broken nail. How had she missed it last night, this aberration compared to its perfect siblings? She took her treasured Mont Bleu crystal nail file from her bag and gently stroked it in one direction only across the fractured nail, gradually shaping it so the jagged became smooth once again.

*

It started as soon as she got to the office.

'Looks like you better get a new roof – the old one's leaking!'

'Stick to journalism – you're boxing's crap!'

The jokes kept coming at her, but not from Vasiliy.

'Demchi's mad with you, wants to see you as soon as you get in,' he said.

Of course, she knew what it was. Just because she'd been off for a day, she didn't think Demchi would have missed it, did she?

In fact, Demchi wasn't angry or maybe that had already passed. It was worse: he was hurt. He tossed the latest edition at her, opened on page two, a red ring circling the article.

'What's that?'

'What's what?' she replied.

'Don't even go there, Sveta. What is that doing in this story?'

'It's part of the story.'

'Bullshit! Don't you get it?'

She did get it, but thought it better to let him get it off his chest. Then it got worse. Demchi handed her a fax from *Rossvyazokhrankultura*, the media watchdog agency. She scanned the words on the page: *...believes that the publication of this material may fall under the purview of Article 161 of the Russian Criminal Code (The Impermissibility of Disclosing Information from Preliminary Investigations)...*

'That's rubbish. There is no preliminary investigation.'

'Of course it's rubbish but it's a warning. Most of them have been shut! I don't want us shut down! I have a responsibility to everybody here. You have responsibility!' His voice was rising in volume, so maybe the anger hadn't quite passed, after all.

'How could you do this? We don't do military! D'ya hear me? We don't do military! What the fuck is that doing in there anyway?'

An accusing finger pointed to her article. He paused, giving her tacit permission to answer.

'It's a real story.'

'Yeah, but a military story!'

'It's corruption.'

'It's military! We don't do military! Why have you done this? I back you – trust you – and then this shit!'

The word trust wounded her badly. He was right, of course. What she should have done was trusted him, gone to him with the story, instead of indulging herself. He'd probably have said no but at least he'd still trust her and right now he didn't. She felt as if a spell had been broken.

'Demchi, I'm sorry.'

'You're sorry! I want you to be sorry for everybody who works here because you're putting their jobs on the line!'

He stared at her, his fists clenched tight. God, how she'd hurt him. She knew he loved her, loved her work, loved working with her and she'd betrayed him. Pain was etched in his face.

She lowered her eyes, not worthy at this moment to look at him.

'Forgive me,' she pleaded softly.

It was heartfelt. She was wretched and his forgiveness was needed, not just wanted. Of course, Demchi's forgiveness would not come cheaply or quickly. This breach of trust would take a long time to repair. She stared at her hands, one crossed above the other and waited.

'You're going to need a new roof – looks like the old one's leaking,' said Demchi, his voice now quiet in the calm after the storm.

Of course, she'd already heard the joke but smiled nevertheless, grateful for this break in the ice as she wiped a tear from her eye.

'I'm sorry, Demchi.'

'That's not enough.'

'I know.' She swapped hands, still looking down.

'What is the story?'

When she'd finished, Demchi sat back, tilted his head at the ceiling and shut his eyes, deep in contemplation. He was so long like that Svetlana wondered if he'd actually dropped off to sleep.

'Demchi?' she whispered.

'I'm thinking.'

His eyes remained shut. He thought a while longer.

'When I was a young reporter, younger than you, I was great friends with Dmitriy Kholodov. He was investigating the military, like you want to. They got him in his office with a bomb. There was a trial. Of course, they were acquitted and compensation was even paid! Officially, unsolved.'

He opened his eyes, sat forward and clasped his hands together pointing two trigger fingers at Svetlana, as if taking aim.

'The story is good. There's probably evil to expose, but we're not going to run with it.'

She'd heard that tone before. It was final.

'If you say so,' she conceded.

'Because we'll put our people in danger – their jobs, maybe their lives – so that's it. Okay?'

'Yes.'

'If you want to run with this personally, I can't stop you but keep the paper out of it... understood?'

'Yes, understood.'

'I think you should forget the whole thing. If you want the GRU and the FSB on your tail, you're going the right way about it.'

She finally looked up, her face a picture of contrition. Demchi hadn't finished.

'And if you do confide in anybody, confide in me. That's it.'

The audience was now terminated but at least Demchi had thrown her a scrap of comfort food at the end. She was relieved he still cared for her, but was deeply troubled that she'd hurt him so and resolved, as she returned to her desk, never to let it happen again.

'He was like a bear with a sore head yesterday. Nobody dared to go near his office,' said Vasiliy.

'I'm sorry. I let you all down.'

'No, you didn't. We all admire you. You and Demchi are the heartbeat of this place... I love working here, with you.'

In an instant, she was on her feet, her arms around Vasiliy and hugging him as hard as she could. This kid refused to kick her when she was down.

'Thank you, Vasya... thank you!'

Vasiliy blushed. He was not used to a woman holding him physically and froze until she relaxed her grip on him to sink back into her chair. His face flushed red, as she looked up at him and smiled at this precious moment, which had started the recovery of her spirit. Vasiliy fidgeted uneasily, until a recollection put him back on track.

'I almost forgot. This came for you,' he said.

He handed her a small envelope.

'Who sent it?'

'No idea. It was hand delivered to the mailbox, downstairs.'

She turned the envelope over and then sat, stock still, staring at her name in child's handwriting, writing she'd seen before.

'Sveta, what is it... what's wrong?' asked Vasiliy.

'It's him.'

'Who?'

She opened the envelope and unfolded the single piece of paper inside to see the same childlike scrawl spell out the words *The answer's in the cards.*

'Sveta... who?' asked Vasiliy.

'The witness, Vasiliy... the witness. He's not a hoax, he's real!'

Excitement overtook her. She wanted to tell Demchi but that situation was just too raw. She knew to leave the old wounded bear to return to his cave, to lick his wounds. In a day or so, they could start the painful process of reconstructing their relationship.

'The answer's in the cards!' she blurted out. 'The answer's in the cards. What does that mean, Vasya?'

'I don't know and anyway, why the charade? Why doesn't he – or she – just talk to you?'

Svetlana stared at the note, silent but with her mind racing through the possibilities. She thought of the note Katia had received, secretly and with stealth. There was so much she didn't know.

'Think... think. What do you know?' she asked herself. *You know he's not a child. He reads newspapers – and he's probably in Moscow – and he's real – but he doesn't want to be found – or can't risk being found!* 'He's in danger Vasiliy.'

'What?'

'He's in danger. He has to stay anonymous.'

'I don't get it.'

'Trust me, Vasya.'

'I always do. You know that.'

She looked again at the note. On one level, she was further ahead as she had confirmation, but on another, she was not. Where did she start with a lead like this?

'Cards...? What kind of cards?' she asked. 'Small cards, big cards, place cards...?'

She took a deep breath and calmed herself, reaching for the notebook she always kept next to the telephone. Opening a fresh page, she wrote down each of the key words as she saw them, circling them as she did: Military; Poison; Questions; Witness;

Afraid; Cards; Warning; Answers; Andrei. She stared at the small collection of planets on the page, each seemingly orbiting the other but could find no obvious next step. In situations like this, she'd normally call everybody together to kick the problem around, often with an idea emerging. This time, however, she was on her own. Demchi had made that more than clear. 'Vasiliy!' she exclaimed to herself, turning to him.

'Vasya, I'm sorry, I shouldn't have mentioned this again. It's not fair to get you involved. The paper can't run this and Demchi's right to keep everybody out of it. Just forget it, will you?'

Vasiliy paused and considered the request before giving her a knowing wink.

'I'm here if you need me.'

'Thank you, Vasya.'

'Sveta, visitor for you!' called out Larisa, the office junior, from the doorway.

'Who is it?' asked Svetlana.

'Don't know, wouldn't give his name.'

Svetlana and Vasiliy looked at each other, their thoughts on exactly the same track: *it was him, the witness. He'd decided to come in, after all.* She dropped her notepad on the desk, unconsciously brushed her hair back with her hands and set off for the stairs down to reception.

She almost jumped off the last step. There he was, her witness, his back to her in a long overcoat, dark hair tousled from removing his hat.

'Good morning,' she said warmly.

Nick turned to face her.

'Good morning. I wasn't expecting such a friendly welcome.'

Chapter 7

First on site was Vasiliy, who'd taken the call before phoning news through to Svetlana. He'd managed to take some quick shots with his digital camera, before the *politsiya* had put their cordon up. By the time she arrived, Vasiliy had already managed to talk to a few bystanders.

'Sveta, it's not Kerimov, it's his son!'

Kerimov had had a run-in with the Moscow Education Department, after he'd been screwed over on the business necessary to land a public contract for the construction of eight new primary schools. He'd agreed to pay the bribe to have his tender accepted, but he'd totally lost it when, after parting with the money, he was informed that he'd have several relatives of the procurement officer on his payroll. He'd given them an ultimatum that he either got his money back or he was going to *Search for Truth* with the story. This was his answer.

Apparently, a lone gunman on a motor bike had pulled up beside the silver Porsche at traffic lights and fired four or five shots through the driver's window, before speeding off. Il'ya Kerimov had stood no chance, his body lying half in and half out of the open driver's door while blood from his shattered jaw soaked his shirt and dripped from his cufflink onto the cobbled surface below. Svetlana looked on, horrified.

'Bastards!' Now, it's the children who pay,' she said to Vasiliy.

They'd write something but it would now be detached commentary, not close to the heart, which she preferred. They had probably reckoned Kerimov was good for some more money somewhere down the line, so why get rid of him when the death of his son sent out the same warning. For sure, he'd now be thinking about the future of his remaining child, Lidiya. His wife would leave him if anything happened to her. So, his silence was assured. Svetlana thought she'd better stay away from the funeral to protect him. There would be another opportunity to pass on her condolences. Would there be any prosecution? Unlikely, and certainly not of the corrupt officials who had added insult to injury with their employment demands.

'What now?' asked Vasiliy.

'Now? Nothing. Go home. There will be other stories, tomorrow.'

'You sure?'

'I'm sure, go on.'

'See you tomorrow,' said Vasiliy, as he put his camera away, turned up his collar and set off for the metro.

Svetlana, hands in her pockets, the fur of her hat dancing in the breeze, stood and watched as two officers casually leant on the young Kerimov's car, each smoking while they awaited the ambulance announcing its imminent arrival with a wailing siren. She had seen this sort of thing played out a number of times, hoping her efforts and those of a brave minority like her might galvanise some resistance to this corrosive corruption. It was almost dark as she watched the body's removal, the flashing lights from the ambulance creating the appearance of slow motion. She shivered as the cold finally penetrated her excellent clothing; it was time to go. There was nothing she could add and nothing more she needed to know. The system had prevailed, again.

*

Sanduny, as Muscovites knew the Sandunovskie Banya was one of her favourite places. She adored its mixture of Russian, Greek and Turkish styles of architecture, its rich blue, green and gold colours and its history. Many writers had sought sanctuary here, where rest and recuperation replaced their tension and drama. She had already returned twice to the wooden steam room, from the pool, to bask in the heat and humidity produced by the large furnace at the end of the room. When the sweat ran and when she could stand the heat no more, the impact at her own hand of the birch *venik* on every centimetre of her skin worked its magic, leaving her glowing and cleansed. She was weary of Kerimov, of blood and unjust tragedy. Here in Sanduny was where she needed to be, free of clothes, her anxiety surrendering to the irresistible lure of the warmth and water that enveloped her. Later, as she lay face-down on a marble massage table, she was even able to smile at the encounter in reception with the foreigner, which didn't seem so bad now, after all.

What a shock she'd received when he'd turned to face her, this clumsy fool, not the witness she was expecting.

'Oh, it's you,' she'd said unable to think of something more inhospitable. She'd watched him looking at her bruised eye, longer than he should. She figured he'd come, hoping to get closer and to start over, but for her he was a nuisance she didn't need.

'I came to apologise.'

'You said sorry yesterday. It doesn't get stronger with repetition.'

She watched him try a smile, but didn't flinch. A telephone rang somewhere in the background. Svetlana glanced at the concierge behind his desk, a clear plastic sign with gold letters grandly announcing him as 'Concierge Pyotr Shulgin', chairman and managing director of his four-metre-square empire, but who simply returned to studying his newspaper.

'I really am terribly sorry. I'd like to make it up to you. I'm a reporter, like you – Nick – Nick Mendez.'

She held her pose and expression.

'Never heard of you.'

'I'm at INN... posted here to cover for Kyle Hughes.'

Now she had heard of Kyle and that he was a good operator, unlike this imbecile.

'You should have spoken to him; he'd have told you to bring flowers.'

'What?'

'I'm not your teacher. Ask him.'

'He's in hospital. Can't get about.'

She said nothing.

'Could we get a cup of coffee or something?'

She listened to the sound of her own breathing as she just stood there, dismissive of his efforts.

'Okay, maybe another time. Look, I really would like to make it up to you.'

He reached for his wallet and took out a business card, proffering it to Svetlana. She stood, unmoved. He stepped to his right and placed the card on the corner of Pyotr's desk. The reception chief executive shot him a menacing glance, as Nick turned for the door to make a trudging retreat.

'If there's anything, just call.'

She'd taken Nick's card from the concierge's desk and put it in her pocket, meaning to bin it when she was back upstairs.

Maybe she'd been a bit hard on him, she reflected, as the scent of massage oil mingled with the pressure that skilled hands were applying to the muscles of her back and neck. She enjoyed the different touch of a woman. She had no leanings in that way but in this place she was able to be naked and relaxed next to a woman, without any stigma. For the masseuses it was work of course, but some would enjoy the opportunity to chat if that's what their clients wanted. Today, it was Yelena who put her hands gently round Svetlana's neck before moving with more strength to push and pull with the tips of her fingers along the ridges of her shoulders. Svetlana slowly closed her eyes, feeling the lids come gently together as she shut down one of her senses to allow the enhancement of another. Yelena's hands, given willing licence by Svetlana, roamed the length and breadth of her elegant back, busy fingers sometimes nestling in the gaps between her ribs before moving on. The touch was sensitive and sensual, contrasting with the hard marble below her but not, for Svetlana, erotic. She'd need a man for that. However, were she that way inclined she could see that for those *lesbiankiy* lucky enough to find a partner like Yelena, there would be special moments of sensitivity, as a falling rose petal might land, something a man would find difficult to replicate. Her eyes stayed closed as she and her other senses surrendered to the pleasure dispensed by the roving fingertips.

Afterwards, she decided to treat herself in the restaurant, ordering smoked salmon and *bliny* with salad. She reached in her pocket for a tissue and felt the card she'd meant to throw away, placing it on the crisp linen tablecloth where it was framed by her knife, fork and spoon.

Maybe this foreigner can help after all, she thought.

She tapped the card with her fingernail, leaving a crescent-shaped imprint. Resources at *Search for Truth* weren't going to be available, that was certain but this guy, this 'Nick Mendez', he'd have resources and he owed her all right.

*

Svetlana didn't cry any more when she went to help out her evangelical Christian friend, Richard, at Kursky railway station, which she did most Wednesdays. Richard had come to preach many years before, but when he saw the street children he'd decided to feed them instead. She'd considered herself streetwise and experienced, an effective gatherer of news, but she'd realised there was another level to go to. Those children had done her a favour, of course. Sasha had been nine when she'd first met him, one of thousands of homeless children living a feral existence in Moscow, preferring that to abuse at home or harsh conditions in state orphanages. The reporter had been following a lead about funds for a shelter being diverted to officials in the mayor's office, when she'd first set eyes on this little boy and his eleven-year-old sister, Marina. They'd been effectively orphaned by their feckless heroin-addicted parents who didn't know or care where they were. That first meeting had shocked her. They lived in a little den they had constructed from a cardboard box and some plastic sheeting in a dark corner of the vast Kursky railway station. During the day they roamed around begging, checking the vending machines for any loose change and occasionally receiving left-overs from a sympathetic waiter or waitress. On a good day, they'd make quite a few rubles, which they used to spend on food, pop and gaming machines. At night, they huddled together for warmth aided by an old blanket they'd stolen from the basket of a platform guard's dog. They were dirty and in danger of beatings during periodic *politsiya* raids paid for by shopkeepers' bribes but nevertheless preferred this to the tiny damp squat and loveless anarchy they'd come from.

'What's your name?' she'd enquired of Sasha, his wide eyes suspiciously scanning her from his smudged and lightly bruised face.

'Sasha,' he mumbled.

'Where's your mum, Sasha?' The little boy looked to the ground, silent. 'Sasha...?'

'She doesn't care about us,' said his sister, as she emerged from behind the Coke machine where she'd been keeping watch. The tone was emphatic. This was a non-subject.

'Hello, who are you?' asked Svetlana.

She looked at the pale, pretty face of a skinny little girl in old jeans and a torn brown cardigan, clearly the boy's sister.

'Who are you?'

'I'm Svetlana. What's your name?'

'Marina.'

'How long have you been here, the two of you?'

Marina just shrugged. They were interested, as they had to be to get by, but cautious from bitter experience as a stray animal might be, not knowing if it would receive a treat or a kicking.

'Would you like a drink in the café?'

She'd watched as they each hungrily devoured their chosen *pirozhki*, followed by chocolate. For them, they had almost but not yet completely lost the ability to absorb affection. It was the beginning of a bond, a necessarily loose attachment, but one that would endure, nevertheless. On her Wednesday visits she would sometimes see them, sometimes not. Once, she'd persuaded them to try a shelter but that had only lasted two days before a strict regime and discipline made them flee, leaving them, at least, net beneficiaries of a shower each. As time went by, Svetlana had reconciled the initial urge to sweep them up and take them home with the realisation that they were foot soldiers in an army of street children that would not be tamed. She could do only what she could do. With Richard, she would occasionally feed those that wanted to be fed, and use the pen to urge social policy which would help to counter the purges and beatings temporarily 'clearing up' the problem. As for Sasha and Marina, well, they no longer hesitated when they saw her, mutual respect having been established.

These days, aged eleven and thirteen, the faces were still angelic but now with the ability to harden at will. Sasha was regularly to be seen sniffing glue from a paper bag, his bright eyes glazed over, his movements erratic. There was little point talking to him at times like this but when his head was clear he was a willing informant, somehow picking up news before even the street knew about it. Marina had a pimp who sold her young body for her or allowed her to do it herself, as long as the pathetically low proceeds were handed over promptly. She had no idea if she was HIV positive and dismissed all Svetlana's suggestions that she should take a test.

'There's no point,' she said, with sincerity.
'Where's Sasha?'
'He's hurt.'
'Where?'

Marina nodded in the direction of their little retreat. Svetlana found Sasha, badly beaten. He'd been high on fumes the evening before and hadn't reacted as fast as some of the others who'd scattered as the *politsiya* swept through. He had a bad cut to his skull where a baton had struck him, bruises on his face and fingers broken on his left hand after he'd instinctively put it up to deflect a blow. She lifted the corner of the filthy blanket he was huddled in to inspect his injuries more closely. He managed a weak smile.

'Can you walk?'
He nodded bravely that he could.
'Come on,' she said, helping him gingerly to his feet.

Later, in the clinic, he looked better after being cleaned up, eight stitches inserted in his head wound and his fingers set in a splint.

'You better pay more attention, next time.'

'I guess,' said Sasha, before drinking the liquid paracetamol the nurse handed to him.

On the metro back, Sasha was in better spirits.

'Are there any new strangers at Kursky?' asked Svetlana.

'All the time.'

'But, older, maybe?'

'A few.'

'A secretive one?'

'What?'

'Low profile, doesn't want to be found.'

'There was one, for a while. I called him the Artist but he's gone now.'

'The Artist?'

'Yeah, he painted, on walls and stuff; thought I wasn't looking but I was.'

When they arrived back at Kursky station, Svetlana's mobile rang. It was Maksim, from the Prosecutor's office. She considered leaving it but thought he might lose his nerve, and if he had information she wanted to hear it.

'Hi Maks, how are you...?

'Fine, Sveta. Look, can you meet me in thirty minutes?'

'Yes, if I'm quick. See you then. Bye.'

She turned to Sasha.

'You going to be okay?'

He nodded, giving her a thumbs-up as he turned for the station concourse.

'Oh, Sasha, does "the answer's in the cards" mean anything to you?'

The young boy looked back and shook his head.

*

There was no time for reverence today as she hurried past Pushkin's statue, nodding briefly. Maksim was fitting this little newsflash into his break. Bless him. He'd bought her a cappuccino, which was still almost warm.

'Here,' said Maksim, as he passed her a plain envelope across the table, glancing over his shoulder. 'It's a list of who does what and where but it doesn't exist and you didn't get it from me, okay?'

'Of course, Maks, you know how it is.'

'There's another name... not on the list...'

She tilted her head and widened her eyes.

'Chernekov – he's ex-Kamera.'

'Kamera?' she asked, surprised to even hear public mention of the FSB's secret poisons centre, dating right back to the days of the NKVD. It was a non-department these days. 'How do you know?'

'Pure coincidence. Three years ago, he was arrested in a drugs raid on the Grachev team's warehouse.'

'What was he doing there?'

'No idea. We'd barely opened a file and taken his picture when the order came through that he was Kamera. We dropped him, straight away.'

'And you're mentioning him now because...?'

'I saw him the other day...'

She looked at him quizzically.

'In the building... with GRU identification!'

She sat back and studied the contours of the top of her cappuccino while she tried to make sense of Maksim's information. The stuff in the envelope she reckoned would be useful routine postings but why would an FSB poisons expert who hangs around with a mafia gang now be working for military intelligence?

'I gotta go,' said Maksim, pointing to his watch.

'Sure, Maks... look, thanks. I know you've probably gone a bit too far with this.'

In fact, she knew he had. Yes, of course, he hoped one day to get in her knickers but he was clearly genuinely fond of her too. He'd done this for her, as though down on one knee to present his information, knowing it would be more valuable and better received than flowers or chocolates. She placed her hand on his bicep and squeezed it gently while she kissed his cheek. He began to blush but then was gone.

*

The list Maksim had given her helped her to understand the military prosecution structure and who was who in the Trans-Baikal Military District, but nothing leapt out as particularly important. She was mildly disappointed, but, on reflection, why should she be? Good reporting was mostly just methodical application and lucky breaks were few and far between, once there was a lead to follow. The evening before, while making supper for Ivan and herself, she'd kept visiting her desk to glance at the list to see if a line of enquiry presented itself but it hadn't. Later she'd searched the names on the net but had come up with nothing of any apparent significance. So, here she was, sitting facing the foreigner and in need of his help but with a full tank of redress due to her.

'Milk?' enquired Nick.

He held a small white jug at an angle above her steaming cup of coffee.

'No, thank you.'

A long pause followed. She didn't feel angry with him any more; that had passed but neither should he get the wrong idea that somehow he was forgiven.

'How can I help?'

'There was a boy, nineteen, Andrei, the son of Katia...'

She related the story to him while he sat, silent and attentive, occasionally risking eye contact. When she finished, she reached for her cup and sipped at the strong black coffee.

'I have a question,' said Nick,

He leant forward, placing his forearms on the table edge and locking his fingers together. She raised her eyebrows to signal her attention.

'Do you trust your editor?'

'Completely,' she replied.
'And he's told you to drop this?'
'Yes.'
'Have you ever gone against him before?'
'No, we debate and then agree. I don't need to go against him... usually.'

She felt herself on the end of his silent question, a common reporter's technique. She could feel herself failing to hold shut the door to the secret cellar, which had for so long remained hidden in the deepest recesses of her mind. Who was this foreigner? How had he managed to take her to this place of dread in so short a time?

'I had a brother, Pavel, older than me. Our childhood was... difficult.'

She paused to gather strength.

'When I was ten and he was fourteen, I was bullied by a group of older boys on the way home from school. Pasha saw them and came to rescue me. He fought like a tiger but they beat him badly as I stood screaming at them to leave him alone. He was in hospital for many weeks. He was my hero. I loved him.'

The silence would give her no respite. She shivered as the painful memories made good their escape.

'We were inseparable. He was a good student, despite our difficulties. He wanted to be a doctor.'

Nick sat back but said nothing.

'He was just eighteen when he was conscripted. I walked with him to the station and we waited for the train. We laughed at our reflections in the puddle on the platform. Then the train was there. I stood and watched it disappear into the distance... He waved from the doorway the whole time. I looked at my reflection in the puddle for a long time and wondered what would happen to me now. Something told me I'd never see him again.'

'What happened?'

'My mother tried to get answers. They wouldn't speak to her; just said it was an accident. Now I'm sure it wasn't.'

'Investigating Andrei won't bring Pavel back.'

'Did I ask for your advice?' said Svetlana, her control returning.

'Sorry, it's just that...'

She ignored him, reaching into her bag to pull out a copy of Maksim's list, to which she had added 'Chernekov – Kamera – GRU'.

'Can you help me with these?'

He scanned the list and then looked at her with a shrug of the shoulders. She carried on.

'They're the people in the Trans-Baikal Military District where the boy died, but Chernekov...? I don't know what his connection is although he's been in Moscow.'

'Should I speak to my editor about him?'

'It's up to you.'

'He'll probably tell me to drop it.'

'I don't care.'

It was her turn to move the chess piece of silence across the board. She'd been in check but had escaped to move from defence to attack. She waited.

They walked from the café in Sokol'niki Park, hands in pockets, the birch and maple trees garnished with first winter snow. Most of the trees had shed their leaves but the maples were hanging on here and there to some golden remnants, and unsung heroes of lilac, heather and red berries made the most of the white backdrop the snow provided. They walked in silence, save for the gentle crunching of fresh snow beneath their feet. Turning a corner in the path, they came into a birch grove where sweethearts had left carved messages, one to another, in the bark. 'Lev loves Mariya', proclaimed one 'Valya and Anya', another. Svetlana stood still, her eyes fixed on a message clearly carved some time ago: 'Lara will always love you, wherever you are'. Nick had moved on a few paces but returned to her.

'Larisa is my mother's name,' he said.

She was taken by surprise.

'Your mother is Russian?'

'From Samara, but she studied here in Moscow for two years, before going to Cuba with my father.'

She studied the words. Who was 'you'? Was this some love so forbidden that the object of it must remain hidden or was Lara just driven to proclaim to the world the feelings in her heart but judged that the world did not need to know more?

'Perhaps your mother wrote this.'

'I don't think so.'

'What's your father's name?'

'Juan – Ivan, I suppose, in Russian but he uses John in the States mostly.'

'So, Nikolai Ivanovich, you have Russian blood... and a strange accent.'

She turned and regained the path.

*

It was too late to cook. He was still trying to work out whether it had gone well with Svetlana, or not. They were speaking and he had a list of names to go back to her about so that was progress, wasn't it? Of course it was, he concluded, as the microwave pinged to announce the end of its four-minute journey to heat his ready-made chicken and potato. He poured a glass of red wine for himself. Yes, it was chicken, and white wine went with chicken but he enjoyed the warmth of red. He'd picked up a case of Georgian red on offer at his local Perekrestok supermarket and it was time to make a start on it. He'd missed the beginning, but as a long-term fan of the Boston Bruins he knew the game well and Dynamo Moscow v SKA St Petersburg was a killing ice hockey contest to watch on Kyle's giant TV. This was quality guy time, no question.

Later, when he woke, he was disorientated, thinking himself in Madrid. His eyes moved to the screen to see some sort of soap opera in progress. His brain, processing thoughts in Spanish, took some time to recognise the language as Russian. It was two forty-five in the morning and he'd drunk too much. He didn't remember opening the second bottle, but there it was, almost empty, as evidence. He downed a large glass of water to try and stave off the worst effects of his forthcoming hangover. He saw the envelope

Svetlana had given him, thought about opening it but decided to wait. Maybe it was the booze talking but inside that envelope was trouble. He knew it and tonight he wasn't ready for it. Outside, the vast city awaited him.

*

'Sveta, great to see you,' said Dubnikov, as he kissed her on both cheeks.

It was ten in the morning but he still smelt of alcohol, his unshaven whiskers pressing against her face like coarse sandpaper.

'Have a seat,' he half offered, half commanded. 'Drink...? Of course not.'

He picked up the receiver from his desk phone.

'Borya, can you fix some coffee... for two.'

He faced her, putting the receiver down. She didn't want to be there but tried not to make it look too obvious.

'How have things been?' she enquired, not caring in reality but anxious to move things along so she could get away.

'Things...? Things have been okay, Sveta. The Chechens are a pain in the arse, as usual, but nothing we can't handle.'

'Il'ya Kerimov...?'

'Was that us...?'

'Yes.'

'No. We'd have done it, of course, but we weren't asked, so you can write about it, no problem.'

'Who was it?'

'Grachev.'

Her eyes widened involuntarily and she cursed herself that she'd displayed overt interest but Dubnikov was sharp and missed nothing.

'What...?'

'Do Grachev and Chernekov mean anything?' she asked.

'Should it?'

He was interrupted by the door opening and a young man entered with the coffee. Svetlana was perversely amused at the sight of this thug, an assassin, carrying coffee and biscuits on a tray. It had a certain surreal quality, she thought. Dubnikov waved him away as he inspected the colour and consistency of the steaming drink.

'Should it?' he resumed. 'Who's Chernekov?'

'Ex-Kamera.'

'Is he? You sure you want to know?'

'It may be nothing.'

'Then leave it as nothing.'

'I can't.'

Dubnikov poured their coffee and passed her a cup. She took the drink but held her palm up to decline the plate of biscuits he proffered.

'I'll make some enquiries,' he said.

Svetlana accepted he'd made a mental note of another favour to be redeemed, at some point in the future. He stirred his coffee, before going through his little ritual of clinking the spoon twice on the deep blue china cup, as if patting it for good luck. He sat back and smiled.

'And how is Mr Mendez?'

Now that did surprise her. Of course, Dubnikov would come to know but she just didn't think for a moment it would be so fast. She wasn't prepared and she hated being caught out like this.

'Fine... I guess.'

Dubnikov folded his arms, smiled... and waited. She knew she wasn't going to get away with a brief platitude but she hadn't worked out the situation with Nick Mendez herself yet.

'He's a TV reporter.'

'I know... we have him on the TV at the villa in Marbella,' he said, pausing. 'You fucking him?'

Dubnikov had overstepped the mark, his pseudo chivalry towards her exposed for what it was, the front of a character founded on crudity and ignorance.

'No!' she replied, her tone of voice hard with indignation. 'And if I was, it's none of your fucking business!'

He sat back and grinned. She was cross with herself that she'd not handled it with a bit more cool. This oaf was enjoying himself and she should never have played his game.

'Whoah... calm down! I'm only interested in your welfare.'

The lying toad! The only thing Dubnikov was interested in was Dubnikov. She wanted to punch him but he'd probably enjoy that too, the sick bastard.

'His mother's Russian, from Samara.'

She'd blurted this out as if it would put Dubnikov in his place and make him more respectful. She instantly regretted handing over information that he had no right or need to know. She just wanted to be out of there. His grin disappeared. He'd had his fun and now it was time to get down to business. He leant forward and looked her straight in the eye.

'You were followed... in Sokol'niki. The FSB know the two of you are talking.'

The tone had changed as quickly as turning on a lamp. This conversation she could handle. The FSB was bad news. She should have known better. They'd generally leave her alone but, of course, they'd have a look at the foreigner and now they'd be looking at her. She drew breath and sighed.

'I'll be more careful.'

'You'll need to be. We can only watch your back so far.'

'I know.'

Dubnikov pushed his chair back and stood. The meeting was over and she was released.

*

When Svetlana turned her mobile back on there was a text waiting for her, from Richard.

Sasha has news about artist – wants to see you.

She acknowledged his text and descended the steps at the nearby metro on her way to Kursky station. Within twenty minutes she was there.

There was no sign of Sasha or Marina. She went to their den and put her hand on the blanket. It was cold. She stood on the main concourse, slowly turning, scanning the travellers moving this way and that. Fifteen minutes passed and it was now becoming difficult to distinguish one face from another. There was a tug at her coat sleeve. She looked down to see Sasha, today wearing his impish face and a wide grin. He beckoned to her to follow him and set off ahead. He had a well practised way of moving through people, seeming to glide as he did so. She had trouble keeping up with him. They went by several platforms, before reaching the stairs to one of the underpasses.

'Sasha, wait!' she implored.

The boy scampered down the steps ahead of her, looking back to beckon her on again. They were in an old part of the station, less frequented these days since some of the route changes. Here, graffiti meandered around the advertising posters, snaking mementos of stealthy visitors. Sasha disappeared from view round a corner.

'Sasha!'

'Come on!' came the reply, repeated by an echo from the subterranean space.

She turned the corner to see Sasha standing still, his almost white bandage covering the splint on his hand contrasted against the gloom.

'Look!' he commanded, his face triumphant.

She reached him and looked at the wall where he was pointing. Facing her was a mural painting: part of a face, some hair swept over a forehead and an open eye, staring and framed as a playing card – the ace of hearts. In the bottom corner was a signature. The artist's name perhaps? She strained to make it out in the poor light, but with concentration she was able to distinguish the letters AIP.

'AIP... who's AIP?' she asked herself.

She didn't know if it was her heart pumping or her head rushing first.

'Andrei Ivanovich Petrov!'

Chapter 8

Svetlana reached for the receiver and let her hand hover over it, as if giving final contemplation to a chess move, before picking it up and dialling Nick's mobile.

'The FSB are watching you – us.'

'How exciting! I've only been here a short while and already I'm marked out as a spy.'

'It's not funny. This is not Madrid or Boston. We'll have to be more careful.'

'Careful about what? We haven't done anything.'

'Have you still got the list?'

'Yes, it's right here.'

'Hide it. Don't leave it at your apartment. It's better if we don't meet for a few days... to calm suspicion.'

'But –'

She replaced the receiver, cutting him off before turning towards the kitchen. Ivan put his head round the door.

'What's for supper?' he asked.

'*Golubtzy.*'

'When's it going to be ready?'

'You hungry?'

'Starving.'

'Okay... about twenty minutes.'

Ivan withdrew to his bedroom, leaving Svetlana to finish preparing the meal. She tried to cook in batches, making enough for three or four nights as the hours she worked could be unpredictable and she liked to leave nutritious food Ivan could heat up or, otherwise, he'd just eat junk. She reached into the fridge before taking out the dish of minced pork and rice wrapped in cabbage leaves. As she busied herself about the kitchen, her mind kept returning to the mural in the station.

Where are the others? she thought. *The answer's in the cards... There are more cards – but where?*

She turned on the oven, put some foil over the dish and put it in to heat up, before sitting down to contemplate the enormity of her task, which had now been made more difficult.

'Idiot foreigner,' she mumbled, in a feeble attempt to deflect the blame she felt for avoidably drawing FSB attention to herself. Actually, she felt pretty stupid.

'Of course they'd check him out. It's your own fault.'

Ivan ate his supper as usual, quickly and without speaking. Svetlana didn't bother trying to make conversation; he wouldn't respond anyway.

*

For a few days she kept a low profile, working normally and making no contact with Nick. In any event, he'd had his hands full reporting on the presidential summit, which she thought a good thing. This had given her an opportunity to re-tune her senses of feel-right and feel-wrong, which usually served her well. She reflected that maybe she'd let the whole situation gather a momentum it didn't deserve, resolving to be calmer and more calculating in her approach.

'Thought you might like this,' said Vasiliy, as he sneaked a pastry into the gap between her keyboard and screen.

'You're naughty.'

'Yeah, but you're going to eat it anyway,' he replied, a conspiratorial grin on his face.

She shook her head at him as he evidently enjoyed the gentle rebuke. Having reminded her that he was very much a fan of hers, he leant forward, his voice dropping.

'Where are you up to with it?'

'Vasya, not here. Things are awkward enough with Demchi already.'

'Let's go out then.'

There was something in his voice, a faint trembling but with a hint of excitement too. It was a weak scent but Svetlana nevertheless knew this was a trail to follow. She rose from her chair, scooped up her pastry and made for the stairs.

'Vasya, where are we going?'

'You'll see,' said Vasiliy.

He marched determinedly across ulitsa Pravdy, before cutting down the alley opposite their office. Svetlana struggled to keep up, her footing not as secure as his in the slush that filled the shaded passage. A flash from Vasiliy's camera, beyond a metal fire escape, temporarily lit up the scene for various rubbish bins standing at sentry duty by grey padlocked shutters.

'I should have known,' she said, as she looked at a playing card painted on the brickwork.

'How could you?'

'He knows where I work. Of course he'd put one nearby; you just would.'

She took in the detail: a boot, some grass and concrete. At the top was the ten of hearts and in the bottom corner, AIP. Vasiliy took another photo, just as fresh flakes of snow began to dance in the biting wind that whipped through the alley.

'Let's go, Vasya.'

They sat in the window seat at Olga's deli, two steaming mugs of hot chocolate in front of them. Vasiliy flicked between the images he'd just taken and the ones he'd brought from Kursky station after Svetlana had told him of Sasha's find.

'It's not much use, the screen's too small,' he said.

'We need more anyway...'

She checked herself, conscious that in her language she'd just included Vasiliy as one of the investigators.

'I'm in this, Sveta.'

'But Demchi –'

'Sveta, I'm in.'

They sat in silence, occasionally sipping at their sweet dark drinks.

'When I first started, I disobeyed an instruction to keep my nose out of a case.'

'From Demchi?'

'No, before I came here,' said Svetlana.

'And...?'

'It doesn't matter. If I told you to keep your nose out of this one, would you?'

'No, Sveta, I want to be a reporter, a good one.'

She sipped again at her drink, a silence returning between them.

'Are you going to do any work today?' asked Olga, as she wiped the adjoining table.

'We are working,' said Vasiliy.

'Really? Well, if that's work, I'll have your job and you can come behind the counter and have mine.'

Svetlana put her hand over her mouth to hide her grin.

'Come on, Vasiliy, you're out of your depth here,' she said, as she put on her hat.

'I remember what it was like to do a proper –'

The door shut cutting short Olga's reminiscence. It was hard to know which was sharper, Olga in full flow about the shortcomings of the young or the wind, which blew straight in their faces as Svetlana and Vasiliy made their way back to the office. Once there, Vasiliy linked his camera to his computer and displayed the images of the two murals, side by side. She studied them carefully, her eyes passing from one to the other and then back again. After five minutes, she was none the wiser, before there was a click and the screen went blank. Vasiliy had seen Demchi leave his office and head in their direction. It was good he was paying attention.

'Sveta, that piece on Kerimov wasn't your best,' said Demchi, as he walked past.

She looked at Vasiliy who shrugged. This situation was difficult for her. She'd been so used to breezing into Demchi's office to kick a story around. Now, it was different; it was formal, polite. It was obvious to her that he was still very hurt, although privately she wondered if maybe he wasn't making a bit of an example of her too, which disappointed her. She shrugged back at Vasiliy. It would have to take its time. He brought the images back up.

'There's more of them out there... I know it. Where, though? Where?' asked Svetlana.

'The kids can help,' said Vasiliy. 'Offer them a reward. The one who finds it gets something, as does the one who told him to look.'

'Simple as that?'

'Yeah, simple as that.'

Svetlana closed her eyes, picturing in her mind the thousands of homeless Moscow youngsters scurrying here and there in search of the hidden street art, hoping for a few rubles for their trouble. After a minute or so, she rejoined the conversation.

'It's a good idea – but it's a bad idea.'

'How's that?'

'The artist is staying hidden for a reason.'

'So?'

'If he's in danger, the children could be in danger.'

'Why?'

'It just doesn't feel right.'

'Think about it. A kid sees a painting and gets a message to you. Where's the danger in that? It's just a bit of social networking. This kid Sasha you keep going on about, he could sort it for you.'

'I'll think about it.'

'Up to you,' said Vasiliy, pretending indifference. 'Anyway, how's your international TV reporter friend?'

'He's not my friend,' she snapped back at him.

'Just asking,' said Vasiliy, holding up his hands.

'Sorry, it's my fault. I should have known the FSB would be watching him.'

'And now they're watching you?'

'Probably.'

'Have you seen him?'

'Not for a few days.'

'You should be okay. He's been doing his job and you've been doing yours. Just keep your head down. They only have so many people to go round, you know.'

*

'Registration?'

'What?' asked Nick, looking up to see a burly member of the *politsiya* and his shorter, skinny comrade.

'OVIR Registration.'

Nick cursed himself. He'd forgotten to go to the OVIR to register his visa. In reality he'd not quite forgotten, it was that he'd have needed a letter from the owner of the apartment, then a letter from Kyle as the real tenant, not to mention probably having to return several times because they couldn't process it that day, for one reason or another. With more pressing things on his mind, like the presidential summit, he'd calculated that it would wait and that a twenty dollar bribe would extricate him from any *politsiya* check. Indeed, it probably would have done had he not left his small roll of notes in his other coat. That would teach him not to nip out for a newspaper, with only a hundred rubles and no identification.

'I've forgotten,' mumbled Nick.

His inquisitor waited, anticipating the appearance of a passport with some money – dollars or a thousand ruble note folded into an inside page.

'Passport!' he demanded of Nick.

'In my apartment...'

The politsiyonaire was not only surprised but insulted that this foreigner should be so contemptuous of the well known alternative rules: either have the correct documents and stand your ground or be armed with an appropriate amount of acceptable currency. He deserved to be arrested. Perhaps that's why he pushed Nick so hard, when putting him into the back of the Ford patrol car.

On the way to the *politsiya* station, Nick was able to reflect that he'd not driven much in the streets since he'd arrived but had instead seen plenty of the metro. The aging car clattered down ulitsa Chaplygina, ignoring two red lights on its way.

'You must be fucking stupid... I hope you have some friends,' said the driver.

'I do. Good friends.'

The car began to slow and pulled into the car park of an office block.

'What's your name?' said the officer as he drove to a stop, his skinny colleague keeping a look out.

'Nicholas – Nikolai'

'Well, Nikolai, I'm Lev and we have a problem.'

'We do?'

'Yes,' said Lev, taking a printed sheet from the glove compartment. 'You see this?'

'Yes.'

'This is a tariff of the official fines you're looking at...'

Nick pretended to study the sheet. The lull in conversation indicated to him that he was expected to speak again.

'Is it possible to talk about this?'

'We always try to help, don't we, Pasha?'

'Always,' confirmed his thin companion.

'The thing is...' said Lev '...it looks like you're going to need a friend to help you.'

'Is it okay if I make a call?'

'Of course.'

Nick reached for his mobile, then hesitated.

'Should my friend be able to help, what sort of help are we talking about?'

'It depends on whether it's Russian friends or American friends and, of course, how long they take to get here, these friends of yours,' said Lev, stroking his chin.

'American friends?'

'How many have you got?'

'About twenty...?'

'I think you'll need a few more than that.'

'Thirty?'

Lev drew a deep breath and turned to Pasha.

'I see why it is so difficult to negotiate with Americans and why it is necessary to have a lot of patience before the real talks start.'

'I might be able to arrange for a hundred friends to come round?'

'That would be excellent. We'd be delighted to see them,' confirmed Lev, patting Nick on the shoulder.

Nick dialled Konstantin's mobile only to reach his voicemail. He looked at Lev, who was already sensing an unwelcome change of plan.

'I think it might have to be Russian friends instead.'

'I see. That's a shame but if four thousand of them arrived...'

'Can I speak in private, for a moment?' said Nick, pointing to his mobile.

'Of course...' said Lev, opening his door 'Pasha and I will have a cigarette.'

With a little trepidation he scrolled through his address book and dialled Svetlana's number.

'Svetlana Dorenko.'

'Svetlana, it's Nick. I've got a problem...'

*

Frankly, she'd felt like telling the careless fool to rot in a cell, but the last thing she needed at the moment was official *politsiya* records being created about him.

She wore a scarf around her face, apparently to protect her from the weather but, in reality, to hide her identity as she handed the envelope to Nick through the window of the patrol car. He moved to hand it to Lev who pulled back.

'Put it in the seat pocket!' she told him.

Nick slipped the envelope in the vinyl pocket behind the front passenger seat and looked at Lev for permission to leave. A nod of the head gave him that permission.

They walked away and didn't look back.

'I'm sorry,' he said.

'Leave it!'

She didn't so much as glance sideways at him as they moved along. The silence between them filled a full five minutes, before he tried again.

'I have some information about your list... back at the office.'

She stopped and turned to face him, the scarf slipping below her nose to show the steam from her breathing. He waited.

'Here...' she said, handing him fifty rubles '...to get you back home. Meet me at the entrance to Poxoronka Cemetery at three this afternoon.'

With that, she turned and left him.

*

Oh good, not high on something, she thought, as she caught sight of Sasha, at Kursky station.

'Where's Marina?' she asked, as she reached him.

Sasha rolled his eyes skywards and shrugged, his code to say she was with a punter somewhere.

'Are you hungry, Sasha?'

He nodded enthusiastically.

'Okay, but first I want to have a look at your head.'

'It's fine. Leave me alone.'

'Stand still and let me look... Stand still! Not bad. It's healed quite well. Okay, take off that bandage. I've brought you another one.'

Sasha would know that Svetlana meant it and that his treat was dependent upon his co-operation. In any event, he appeared to be quite enjoying the attention, no doubt the first he'd had from anybody since she'd taken him to the hospital.

Later, she had tea while he enjoyed Coca Cola and cake. She leaned forward to indicate his full attention was needed.

'The artist, have you seen him?'

Sasha shook his head.

'Seen any more cards?'

He shook his head again before taking a swig of his drink from the bottle.

'I need your help. Can you get the others to look for the cards?'

She observed Sasha's expectant look. On the streets, all services had a price.

'It pays two hundred rubles for the one who finds each card and two hundred rubles to you for organising it.'

'Three hundred...?'

'Don't get clever, Sasha. Two hundred.'

A broad grin crossed his face as he took her hand and shook it theatrically to signal they had a deal. He raised his cola bottle and she her glass of tea as they both toasted their arrangement.

'How will you do this, Sasha?'

'It's easy. We'll use the metro. They'll know to look.'

Silently, as if a ghostly apparition, Marina was there, the pale skin on her neck lightly bruised by fingers placed round it by an over-enthusiastic client, or perhaps her pimp as punishment for some perceived misdemeanour.

'Are you okay?' asked Svetlana.

Marina ignored her, but lunged forward and grabbed the remains of Sasha's cake from his plate, turning her back in the face of his protests to stuff the sweet crumbs into her mouth.

'That was my fucking cake,' sulked Sasha.

Marina stuck out her tongue at him. He stepped up and tried to slap her.

'Stop it! We'll get some more,' said Svetlana, standing between them.

With chocolate cake for Marina and fresh drinks for both of them, order was restored, at least until a troop of baton carrying *politsiya* arrived on the main concourse. By the time Svetlana turned back to look at them, Sasha and Marina were on their way swerving with practised precision through the travellers until they merged with them and were gone.

She now had time on her hands and decided to re-visit the artist's first work. She bought a small torch and set off across the station in search of the underground area Sasha had taken her to. It had seemed a lot easier the last time, her only problem then being to keep up with her young guide. She made a number of false moves and was on the point of giving up when a chill came upon her, a sense of foreboding she could not explain. She shivered and involuntarily tightened the belt on her coat, as if to help keep out the cold. Looking up, she recognised the grinning blackened teeth of the graffiti caricature of a politsiyonaire, which had briefly amused her previously. She was near. Round the corner Sasha had shown her, there it was – the ace of hearts. She moved the narrow beam of the torch across the surface of the picture, the hair flaxen in the artificial light, the skin sallow and the eye both terrified and pleading. Her sense of foreboding increased. The rustle of a blown piece of paper startled her. Suddenly, she had an overwhelming feeling she was being watched but could see and hear nobody. Was there somebody lurking in the shadows at the end of this subway? She swivelled around and shone the puny torch into the darkness. There was nothing.

'We will find them...' said Sasha, resuming their interrupted conversation as Svetlana made for the metro station '...you better bring plenty of money.'

'I'll be back in a couple of days. Send word through Richard if you hear anything sooner.'

Sasha winked at her as the escalator took her down.

*

'Bring plenty of money!' Svetlana muttered to herself, chuckling. *The boy's not short of cheek.*

She held the steel pole tightly to steady herself as the train rocked to and fro on its journey to Alekseevskaya.

'Would you like to sit?'

'What...?'

'Would you like to sit?'

She looked down to see a boy, maybe sixteen, half out of his seat balancing himself and his large rucksack, gesturing to her.

'Thank you, that's kind.'

They somewhat awkwardly changed places in the busy carriage and she settled onto the warm surface of the just vacated seat.

It was common to offer up your seat to a *babushka* on trains but for younger women it would usually be a reflection of their attractiveness. For a moment, she worried she was perceived in the former category but his shy glances reassured her that her relative youthfulness was not yet in question. She smiled inwardly.

Her mind returned to Sasha and the search parties he would organise. 'Plenty of money,' she repeated in her head. Of course, she had no idea how many cards would be found. Judging by the scant detail in the two she'd seen so far, it would take quite a lot to make a meaningful picture, if that's what the artist had in mind.

Shit, you can't use the paper's fund, she thought, *and I certainly can't afford it. The foreigner will have to help; he owes me that, at least.*

It was quite a distance from Alekseevskaya metro to the cemetery but she was on time as she approached the entrance, only to feel a hand on her shoulder. She turned to see Nick and stepped back a pace, saying nothing. He did not have permission to touch her. Nick lowered his head and hands, in submission.

'Sorry,' he said.

'Again, Nikolai Ivanovich. You're sorry, again. Come on.'

She turned for the entrance and he followed, keeping half a metre behind.

Once inside, her pace slackened and he moved to walk shoulder to shoulder with her.

'Here's the money I owe you, it's some in rubles and some in dollars. I hope that's okay.'

'That's fine.'

She took the cash from him and stuffed it in the bottom of her bag, while continuing to walk.

'I won't forget my passport and some cash next time.'

'Better to register with the OVIR as well.'

'Yeah... I've a bit to learn.'

'Today's understatement.'

'I thought it would be easier here, speaking Russian... with a Russian mother.'

'Then you were wrong and... complacent.'

They walked a long path between tall trees towering over monuments to long lost citizens, some of them with legacies of greatness, some of infamy as informants able to watch from the grave but no longer to report to their state masters. Svetlana smiled at the irony, as she recognised the name of a former KGB great but said nothing. The late afternoon sunlight bathed the path ahead of them, the wind for once at peace. As they reached a crossroads, where four benches overlooked a carefully tended flowerbed, Svetlana gestured to him to sit.

'What have you to tell me?'

'Well, I checked out the list. Some of the names came up but nothing unusual, just past postings, promotions, decorations... the usual stuff.'

'Any pattern in the postings?'

'I'm looking at that but need more time.'

'Is that it?'

'About the list, yes but there's something else.'

'What?'

'We have a source at the network. Let's just say he's well placed. We help each other out, from time to time.'

She did not interrupt again and gave him her full attention.

'You're not the only one interested in Chernekov. He's being tracked. In the last six months, he's travelled a lot but particularly to Vysokogornyy and Chita. He's been to Chita six times.'

'Do you know what for?'

'No.'

'Can you find out more?'

'Maybe, but my source wants to know your source.'

'No chance. You know that.'

She rose from her seat and waited for him to stand, before strolling once more towards the setting sun. As the temperature dropped, the snow became firmer underfoot with patches of ice where other feet had previously trodden.

'Two of the cards have been found, one at Kursky station and the other near my office.'

'What do they show?'

'Not much. There's part of a face on one, just a boot and some grass on the other.'

'Have you photographs?'

'Yes.'

'Can I have them?'

'Not yet.'

'Are there more?'

'I don't know, but I guess so. The street children are looking. I need some money to reward them. I can't go to my editor for it.'

'It's fine.'

'He wouldn't sanction it.'

'It's fine. I'll take care of it.'

'It won't be much. I mean –'

'I'll take care of it.'

A squirrel scurried across the path, picked up a berry which had fallen, and climbed a nearby tree. Nick pointed to it as it climbed.

'He's taking dinner home to his girl.'

She nodded slightly, but did not speak.

'Can I get dinner for you?'

'I'm not your girl.'

'I know but –'

'I'm not your girl.'

They walked on approaching a group of *babushkiy* surrounding a freshly filled grave. Their generally old clothing and woollen gloves testified to the humble circumstances of the deceased, his widow and her grieving friends. There was no headstone. Perhaps one would follow, but for now a simple wooden cross kept company with a tired-looking bunch of flowers, still in its brown paper wrapping. As Svetlana and Nick approached, out of the respectful silence came the sound of gentle but anguished weeping of the widow, her friend urging a tissue upon her to wipe her tearful eyes and running nose. As they drew level, the anxious woman looked up and gestured to them to stop. She pressed the tissue into the hand of her bereaved friend, wrapping her fingers around it before taking three careful steps towards them. She ignored Svetlana, speaking directly to Nick.

'Please, sir, what is your name?'

'It's Nikolai,' intervened Svetlana.

'Does he not speak himself? We need a man to say a few words of respect for Valentin Sergeiovich.'

'Where are your men?' asked Nick.

'All gone... Valentin was the last, a soldier, a worker.'

Nick took a pace forward and bowed his head.

'I'm not from Moscow – from far away.'

'You are a man. We need some words from a man for a comrade – Oksana needs some words.'

'I wouldn't know what to say... I mean...' He looked up to meet her stare. 'Really, I don't think I could.'

'Idiot,' she muttered as she turned back to the grave, her plea sidestepped by this weakling, in his expensive coat. She returned to the widow, putting a comforting arm around her shoulder as the remnants of the sun dipped below the horizon and dusk was upon them all.

Svetlana gently tugged at Nick's sleeve, encouraging him to leave before the situation became any more awkward. He stood his ground and then stepped forward, breaking her grip. He placed himself at the end of the grave and despite the cold, removed his hat.

'Russia remembers you, comrade Valentin Sergeiovich...'

The whimpering widow became silent as she turned to look at the tall stranger.

'As a boy you learned to appreciate the value of friendship. As a man you learned to appreciate the value of comradeship. This great country owes you and all like you a debt of gratitude, for it is soldiers and workers, like you, who have protected and built a land fit for its children to live in. When there was danger you stood firm, when there was hunger you provided and when there was laughter, you led the celebration. While you have passed on from this life, those who have known you and especially your beloved Oksana will treasure your memory, for ever. Your body is free from pain, all your debts have been paid, whatever needed to be forgiven is forgiven and your soul is cleansed. Take with you the special love of your wife and take with you also the special love of this great nation, this Russia.'

Nick stood, his eyes closed and his hands crossed in front of him, having delivered his show of respect due to this simple citizen. Svetlana, who had moved quietly to him as he spoke, glanced sideways at him but with his eyes still shut he missed the way she looked at him. When he did open his eyes, Oksana was standing in front of him, her arms outstretched. Before he could react she had him in a bear hug and planted firm kisses on each of his cheeks.

As they sombrely made their way to the exit, Svetlana reached out an elegant gloved hand and touched him on his elbow.

'Your accent is improving,' she said.

Chapter 9

The GRU maintained a sense of history and a sense of humour. Oleg Chernekov couldn't resist a little grin every time he walked past the marble inlay of the Batman-like GRU symbol, at the entrance to its headquarters, adjacent to Khodynka Airfield in Moscow. Many didn't see it but he knew his superheroes and the irony was not lost on him. One of his real heroes, however, was Grigori Mayranovski who as Stalin's biological weapons chief had tested his concoctions on prisoners of war, delighted that Russian doctors put their deaths down to natural causes. As far as he was concerned, Mayranovski and people like him were true patriots. They got things done that needed to be done.

'Coffee, Colonel?' asked his assistant, as Chernekov lowered his heavily built frame into the high-backed leather chair behind his desk.

'Tea today, please, Yegor.'

He switched on his computer and opened a couple of letters, while he waited for it to boot up.

'Here you are, sir.'

Chernekov's favourite glass was placed in front of him, a thin slice of lemon dancing round the teaspoon, left upright, as was the Russian way. Chernekov's deep-set eyes were drawn to an encrypted email in his inbox. His assistant withdrew discretely. The message was decoded and marked 'Top Secret'.

Regret to advise latest results are again inconclusive. Please advise if further live test with phase eight molecular manipulation is authorised.

He drew a deep breath and then let out a long, heavy sigh. While disappointed, he had a philosophical side when it came to the development of poison. If it took time, then it took time. He clicked the reply button, before painstakingly typing out his message with the trigger fingers of each hand.

Negative. Will attend personally in the next 56 hours. Prepare facility but not pre-test procedures.

Within seconds, the message was in transit. He picked up his tea, squeezed the lemon with the spoon and took a sip to check he had the mix as he liked it. There was a knock at the door.

'Come!' shouted Chernekov, before taking another sip of his tea.

'Captain Malenkov is here to see you, Colonel.'

'Thank you, Yegor. Show him in.'

Gennadiy Malenkov, a KGB veteran and now a captain in the FSB with special responsibility for counterterrorism entered the room. His pointed nose, greased-back hair and frameless glasses gave him a rodent-like look. Chernekov didn't really care for him but tolerated their enforced relationship. Orders were orders, after all. Malenkov put his hat down on the corner of Chernekov's desk.

'Good morning, Oleg. How was your last trip?'

'Long... and cold,' replied Chernekov.

'Are you travelling again?'

'Yes. Unfortunately, it's necessary.'

'I take it there are still problems with the new product?'

'Nothing that can't be resolved.'

'They are becoming impatient, perhaps wondering about your commitment...'

Chernekov, furrowing his brow, looked straight at Malenkov.

'Do they want it quickly or do they want it right?'

'You have had eighteen months, already.'

'I am not making bricks from clay, you know.'

'Some people are beginning to think maybe you are.'

'My commitment is beyond question.'

'You don't really like me, do you, Colonel?'

'My feelings are irrelevant. It's my work that matters.'

'How much longer?'

'I don't know. There are problems... with the tests.'

'Oh yes, the tests... You've been careless, I hear.'

'Careless...?'

'Our army appears to be a few conscripts short.'

'Some casualties were almost inevitable. I wanted to use prisoners.'

'It's too sensitive. Not enough discipline in prisoners. Now, how long, Colonel?'

'Maybe six months. I don't know.'

'Our counterterrorism strategy is being compromised.'

'Terrorists?'

'I don't think it's the army's place to question who the Kremlin classifies as terrorists, do you?'

'I was not always in the army.'

'Well, you are now. I'll report the continuing delay and hope for better news when we meet next.'

Malenkov picked up his hat and left, closing the door firmly behind him.

'Rat-faced little shit!' said Chernekov, addressing the back of the door.

*

Nick answered a call.

'Is that Nick?' asked a voice, in English.

'Yes.'

'It's Peter – Peter Hubbard. We met at Madrid airport.'

'*Shit!* He'd forgotten about this guy and he'd hoped he'd forgotten about him.

'Oh... Peter. Yes, hi. How are you?'

'Fine, just fine. The station gave me your number. I hope it's a convenient time to call?'

'Well, I was just –'

'Only I was wondering if we could catch up for that drink. I've got a couple of things that might be of interest to you.'

'Okay, but my schedule's a bit tight.'

'How would this afternoon be, say six p.m., at the Metropol?'

'I think that should be okay.'

'Great, see you then.'

Before he could think, Hubbard had rung off. Nick placed the receiver down and recalled their brief meeting at Barajas. There was something a little unnerving about Hubbard, but he just couldn't quite fathom it out. He shrugged, poured himself a glass of orange juice and switched on the kettle to make himself a coffee.

It was still bugging him later, as he stood in the queue to present his visa for OVIR registration. The wait seemed endless but he figured he'd have to go through with it, nevertheless. Maybe he'd been a bit unlucky to be stopped for a document check, but he wasn't going to take any chances again. He'd called in to see Kyle at the hospital so he could sign a letter to confirm Nick was renting from him and the apartment owner had been happy to put the necessary detail in writing, particularly as Nick had brought vodka for him and chocolates for his wife.

'Next!' called out the official to Nick as his patience eventually paid off. He stepped forward.

Afterwards, he checked his watch as he descended the steps, folded his stamped registration and placed it inside his passport. It was three-thirty p.m. He grimaced at the time he'd lost queuing and then offering explanations to the irksome OVIR official. It was too late to go to the office but too early to meet Hubbard.

'C'mon, Nicky, let's have a look at this picture she was going on about,' said Nick to himself, as he tucked his passport in his inside jacket pocket.

By the time he reached Kursky railway station, it was more or less dark. Svetlana had described where in the station to look but it turned out to be more difficult than he thought. After half an hour of searching, he'd still not found the place and was becoming disoriented, re-visiting the same areas.

'You lost?' asked a voice from the shadows.

'Not really... I was just looking for something,' replied Nick, straining to see who was talking to him.

'Looking for a girl?' asked Marina, stepping forward into the artificial light. 'Four hundred for sex, two for a blow job.'

'That wasn't what I was looking for,' said Nick, looking the skinny, tired child up and down.

'You sure, mister?'

'I'm sure... but I could do with some directions.'

'She's not a tour guide. Fuck off and let her get on with her work!' ordered a voice from the stairs above.

Nick stepped back to see a short stocky man in jeans and a bomber jacket, part of his right ear missing.

'Excuse me?'

'You heard. If you don't want to fuck her, then just fuck off!'

Nick took a moment to consider the situation.

'Okay, how much?'

'She told you... four hundred.'

Nick took out his wallet and selected four hundred ruble notes, moving towards the pimp on the stairs.

'Not me, idiot. Give the money to her.'

Nick stepped back. Marina walked to him and snatched the notes from him, quickly concealing them in her clenched hand.

'Follow me,' she said.

Marina set off down the adjoining set of stairs, with Nick close behind. When she reached the bottom she went into the stairwell, where it was almost dark. Nick couldn't see properly but suddenly felt a hand on his belt starting to undo the buckle.

'Stop it! I don't want to have sex with you.'

'You must.'

'No.'

'You must. He'll hit me.'

'No! Tell him what you want but I don't want sex with you.'

'Am I not attractive?'

'Of course you are.'

'Okay,' she said, as she reached again for his belt.

'No...' said Nick, stepping back. 'I don't want sex.'

'What do you want?'

'You shouldn't be here.'

'This is my home. What do you want?'

'I came to look for a picture, a painting on a wall, a playing card. Do you know where it is?'

'No,' lied Marina.

A lengthy silence followed. Nick realised neither information nor salvation was on offer and turned for the stairs, his interest in finding the playing card now lost. He reached the top of the long flight of stairs and looked around for the entrance to Kurskaya metro.

'That was quick. I hope she was good to you,' hissed the pimp from behind him.

'Great,' said Nick, as he strode away without looking back.

*

Nick checked his watch as he walked into the elegant Shalyapin bar on the ground floor of the Metropol, with its leather armchairs, grand marble columns and chandeliers. He was a few minutes early. There was no sign of Hubbard, so he went over to the bar and ordered a beer. As he watched the bubbles rise to join the white head on his drink he heard Hubbard announce himself.

'Nick! Good afternoon, dear boy; right on time.'

Nick turned to see an outstretched hand and shook it firmly.

'What can I get you, Peter?'

'That's very kind. I'll have one of those, if that's all right,' said Hubbard, pointing to Nick's beer.

Nick glanced at the barman who merely nodded as he reached for another glass.

They took a corner of the bar, settling into deep red leather chairs.

'Good health!' said Hubbard, raising his glass.

'Cheers!'

'How are you finding things here, Nick?'

'It's a bit of a contrast but I'm settling in okay, I think.'

'Good, good... I must say I enjoyed your piece on the summit communiqué. I thought you caught the mood really well.'

'Thanks.'

'Always did like this place... just something about it. Communism never seemed to change its character, unlike so many of the others.'

'You mentioned you had some things of interest for me...?'

'Interest – yes – things of interest. Have you been to the ballet yet?'

'No, not yet.'

'You should go. Actually, you could do worse than fix it up through the concierge here. He'll sort you out some good seats, for a decent tip.'

'Peter, you asked to see me...'

'Yes... Do you know about the Levitsky matter?'

'The dissident killed in London?'

'Yes.'

'Of course, you couldn't miss it.'

'Messy...'

'When is murder not?'

'Left a lot of bad feeling – coming to London to murder people.'

'I'll bet,' said Nick, sipping his beer.

'The thing is, it looks set to continue and my people are worried.'

'Your people?'

'The people I represent –'

'British Secret Service?'

'The people I represent... are worried. The Russians made a bit of a hash of it really. They almost got away with it, but once we knew what we were looking for then of course there was a trail leading straight back to Moscow.'

'Which is a dead end?'

'Without co-operation, that's exactly what it is.'

'All very interesting but what's it got to do with me?'

'Well, my people have been speaking to your people.'

'INN?'

'Not exactly.'

'Peter, I'm a reporter. I'm not a politician or a spy or whatever you are... I just get news and report it.'

'Exactly my point.'

'Your point? You don't seem to have a point. D'ya know, I think I'm just going to finish my beer and leave.'

'Please hear me out,' said Hubbard, holding Nick's sleeve.

'Well let's cut to it, shall we?' said Nick, putting his drink back down.

'There are more Russian dissidents in danger, in London, New York... in Boston. Only next time there won't be any trails left behind. They won't be that stupid.'

'I'm listening.'

'What do you know about Kamera?'

'Nothing. I mean, I've seen the name but don't really understand.'

'Poisons, powder, liquid, paste, gas... poisons designed to kill.'

'Like James Bond?'

'Not really. Real poisons killing real people. Your people think you might help to save some lives, not to mention keeping some diplomatic channels from closing down.'

'Why isn't an American talking to me about this. Why you?'

'We're already having a row with the Russians about assassinating dissidents. No need to start another one.

'And I can help by...?'

'Being a reporter.'

'I don't get it.'

'Just report the news.'

'The news you give me? No way! I only report the truth.'

'We wouldn't have it any other way.'

'I follow my own stories...'

'Of course.'

'My way...'

'Naturally, dear boy.'

Nick sat back, interrupting the momentum of the conversation. He realised he was being drawn in, implicitly agreeing to work for these guys, whoever they were. He kept quiet, sifting the information, considering his options.

'What's the story?'

'A new poison.'

'From these Kamera guys?'

'We don't know. Probably, but our source doesn't know.'

'That's not much of a story.'

'It will be if men and women start dying in your country and mine, with no apparent cause.'

'What makes you think anybody will give me information?'

'You're a respected reporter who's never revealed a source. You have credibility.'

'Huh... not everybody here thinks so.'

'I'm sorry?'

'Nothing, just a private joke.'

'I see.'

'You got anything else?'

'No, I'm afraid not, just what I've told you.'

'And your people are working on it, right?'

'Yes.'

'It sounds a dangerous story?'

'You'll be okay. You're too high profile.'

'For what?'

'To get in any serious trouble.'

'Coming here, the flight attendant told me not to make enemies in Moscow.'

'You have new friends.'

'Your people?'

'Of course.'

'Forget it. I'll choose my own friends. If there's a story – if – and my station wants to run it, then we'll look at it.'

'You'd be saving lives. They'll be much more cautious if it's being reported publicly.'

Nick rose to his feet.

'Well, if there's nothing else, I guess we're all done here.'

Hubbard downed the remains of his beer, stood and held out his hand to Nick who took it, in return.

'We never did meet at the British Embassy about Picassos did we?'

'I must have been mistaken,' said Hubbard, a faint grin crossing his face before he turned and walked briskly from the bar.

*

It was after nine when Svetlana rang, pouring a glass of wine while she waited for Nick to pick up.

'You okay?' asked Svetlana.

'Yeah. You?'

A silence befell them, as she listened carefully, just able to make out his breathing. She spoke first.

'That was a good thing you did... in the cemetery.'

'It seemed the right thing to do.'

'It was.'

'What's all that noise?'

'It's Ivan. He has a friend round so they're playing their latest tracks. Hold on...'

She closed the door to Ivan's room and settled herself back into the still-warm armchair, her senses compensating as she heard the music less in her ears but now felt the bass beat reach her through the soles of her shoes.

'You sound a little strange. Is everything all right?' he enquired.

'Not really. I saw Katia today.'

'The dead boy's mother?'

'She's so upset. I think she's on the edge of a breakdown. I told her about the cards.'

'Was that wise?'

'She's come this far, fought her way here. She has a right to know.'

'But what about the FSB?'

'She has a right to know.'

She reached for her glass of wine.

'Do you have wine, Nikolai?'

'Do you?'

'Yes.'

'*Za zdarov'ye!*' said Nick, as he took a sip from his glass.

'*Za zdarov'ye!*' she replied.

The background beat of Ivan's music faded out, leaving them temporarily unaccompanied.

'Why did you ring, Sveta?'

'D'you know, I'm not sure. Maybe it was what you said at the graveside.'

'Huh...?'

'Perhaps I felt I owed you an apology. You spoke like a Russian... It sounded like it came from the heart.'

'I have Russian blood.'

'I didn't think so, but now I think... maybe.'

'I forgot flowers.'

'Flowers?'

'At the grave.'

'Words were the right gift. Flowers are for lovers.'

'I've a lot to learn...'

'Yes, you have.'

'But, I am learning?'

'Yes, Nikolai, it appears so.'

She let her elegant finger circumnavigate the rim of her wine glass as the receiver nestled between her ear and shoulder, enveloped in her rich dark hair. She realised she had his attention. It was one of those moments she knew well, when a man was open, stripped of defences and able to be manipulated in any way she wanted. It crossed her mind to have some amusement at his expense, but something made her decline. She was not sure what it was.

'Do you still want to take me for dinner, Nikolai?'

'I was afraid to ask.'

'I know... but now you are not afraid.'

She waited.

'Are you free for dinner... tomorrow?'

'That would be nice... but don't bring flowers.'

Chapter 10

Chernekov looked down at the lights of Chita, as the Ilyushin IL-76 descended towards Domna air base, south-west of the city. He was becoming an old hand at this journey and took it in his stride like the professional he was. There were however two things he didn't like: the Eastern Siberian weather in winter and that odious clown of a base commander at the training centre, Rebikov.

Moscow could be cold, but here at night it was something else. As he descended the steps, the gusting wind rocked him from side to side and the exposed skin around his eyes struggled to deal with the shock of a temperature of minus thirty-two degrees, with further to fall before the night was through. Waiting for him was his usual driver, who saluted Chernekov as he approached, before holding the door of the 4x4 open for him.

'How was your flight, Colonel?' asked the corporal, starting the still-warm engine.

'Fine, thank you, Corporal.'

'Will you be staying long this time?'

'I don't know... it depends.'

They drove on as a flurry of snow danced around them, the heater struggling to clear condensation and the windscreen wipers frantically scrabbling to retain some visibility.

'Major Rebikov invites you for a late supper, if you feel up to it, sir.'

'Does he now? That man seems to do nothing but eat, drink and fart.'

'I couldn't comment, sir.'

'Of course you can't... but at the risk of bringing Russian military discipline to its knees, I can. The major is a total arsehole.'

'Yes, sir.'

'Yes, sir, you agree or yes, sir, you're noting my comment?'

'I'm noting your comment, sir.'

'It's okay, you know where you stand with me.'

'Yes, sir,' said the corporal, grinning broadly.

*

Rebikov was already half cut by the time Chernekov was shown in to see him.

'Oleg! Come in, come in, let's have a drink,' said Rebikov, filling two shot glasses with vodka.

'I'll eat first, Victor...'

'No problem... of course. Shurik, some *plov* for the colonel.'

Rebikov's *ordinaret* nodded, clicked his heels and left the room.

The door to the wood-burning stove was open and the two men sat next to it. An orange glow mixed with Rebikov's red blotchy complexion, as the flames danced upon the logs. Chernekov looked at him with barely disguised disdain.

'How are the men?' he enquired, searching for something to make conversation about.

'Cowards and bastards, to a man!' replied Rebikov.

'I'm sure not all of them are.'

'Cowards and bastards! I'd shoot the whole lot of them and start again if I could.'

'We are supposed to be training them here, not killing them.'

'I don't think you're in a position to lecture me. After all, some of the problems we've had are down to you,' sneered Rebikov.

'I don't think I like your tone, Major. I do what I have to do to defend our country.'

'Well, that makes two of us.'

A knock at the door interrupted the conversation, as the *ordinaret* swept in with a bowl of steaming *plov*, and made for the wooden table in the centre of the room.

'Over here, please,' said Chernekov with deliberate courtesy as he reached for the bowl.

He contemplated the mix of rice and lamb with its strong aroma of garlic, before taking the first delicious mouthful. He'd thought himself not particularly hungry but this had changed his mind and he tucked in heartily.

'Anything else, sir?' asked the *ordinaret*.

'No, that's all. You can go,' snapped Rebikov.

The momentum of his conversation had been interrupted by the food's arrival. He stood up, retrieved the half-full bottle of vodka, filled up his glass and handed Chernekov his still-full glass.

Half an hour later, the vodka and the warming effect of the food within, assisted by the stove without, had improved the atmosphere considerably between the two men.

'We have to be more careful... say less,' said Chernekov.

'Less about what?'

'The conscript losses.'

'Why? Who's asking questions?'

'Well, it's just that...'

He paused. Rebikov was on the edge of serious drunkenness and the issue was too sensitive for him in that state.

'It's better kept low key. We'll pick it up tomorrow. I'm going to get some sleep,' said Chernekov, pushing his chair back and rising to his feet.

*

After an hour and a half reviewing the data, Chernekov and his assistant had settled on the formulaic changes for the next round of tests. As a good team, they had been through this process many times before over the years, but this was proving a tough assignment. Their problem was that they had managed to produce a gas that was untraceable in post mortem examinations, but which could not be kept reliably at bay by the available gas masks. When they had found a formula the masks would keep out, their temporary triumph had been cut short once the pathological tests had been carried out and traces were found. Their masters had demanded and expected a weapon of true stealth, for what they had in mind. So important was the project considered that they had been provided with a new facility on the edge of the base, where access was strictly regulated and security was tight.

'Is Rebikov a problem, Stepan?' asked Chernekov of his assistant.

'I think so. He's becoming worse. I think he'd benefit from a transfer to a new base.'

'Can he be trusted?'

'He's not a traitor...'

'That's not what I meant. He's a fool, not a traitor.'

'His drinking is noticeably worse these past few months.'

'How has he handled the men? They must be asking questions by now.'

'He ignores them, or beats them.'

'An indiscretion could undermine the whole project.'

'I know.'

'We must hurry with our work.'

'Because of Rebikov?'

'Yes, of course, but there's political pressure.'

'Pressure?'

'I had a visit before I flew out this time.'

'Do we need to worry?'

'Not yet, but I think it would be a good time for a breakthrough. Can we test tomorrow?'

'Yes.'

*

Rebikov seemed subdued as he met Chernekov outside the training chamber. The summer grass had long since disappeared under a blanket of snow and the trees looking on seemed pre-occupied supporting the weight of their pristine, white, winter companion. Newly painted wood testified to a repair of the door frame and contrasting patches of cement covered cracks in the concrete. At least Rebikov had been able to organise that. Sergeant Leontev joined them.

'Are we satisfied that it's airtight now, Sergeant?' asked Chernekov.

'Yes, sir, it is.'

'Good. We've scheduled another exercise for tomorrow. Can you have the men ready for zero-eight-hundred hours?'

'Yes, sir.'

'Thank you, Sergeant. That will be all.'

Leontev saluted and turned to leave as fresh snow began to fall. Chernekov pulled open the door and stepped inside, beckoning to Rebikov to follow him. They stood for a moment and heard the gentle whistle of the wind at the still-ajar door. Rebikov was sober now, so Chernekov thought it a good moment to see how much information had leaked out.

'Who knows about the tests?'

'Only Leontev.'

'You sure?'

'Of course.'

'And Leontev...?'

'Completely reliable; he's been with me six years. He's said nothing.'

'And the men... what do they think?'

'They don't think anything.'

'How do you know that?'

'They follow orders.'

'You cannot order them not to think.'

'They follow orders. They know nothing. It's just a routine exercise to them.'

'The reason I ask is that a mother from Gorokhovets was told her son, one of your men, was poisoned.'

'Why wasn't I told?'

'GRU has dealt with it.'

'I should have been told.'

'Perhaps... perhaps the informant was holding a grudge against you?'

'I should have been told.'

'Petrov.'

'Who?'

'Andrei Ivanovich Petrov – the dead private. Who was he close to?'

'I don't remember him. Leontev will know.'

'The mother has been dealt with but we'd be interested to know who contacted her, just in case he's real and can think for himself.'

'I'll tell Leontev to report to you.'

'Good... and perhaps it would be advisable for you to be a bit less memorable, in future. So, I'd start by catching up on some paperwork while tomorrow's exercise is in progress.'

'Progress, will there be progress?' said Rebikov, sarcastically.

'Who knows, Major? Don't forget to speak to Leontev.'

Chapter 11

It was not often, these days, that Demchi had a smile on his face, what with his son's recent illness and the general increase in pressure from *Rossvyazokhrankultura*, but today he was upbeat.

'You two, come in here!'

Svetlana and Vasiliy looked at each other before they rose to make for his office. The young assistant automatically picked up his notebook. When he and Svetlana were together, he took the notes.

'Sounds promising,' said Vasiliy.

'Hmmn,' she murmured.

'Come in and sit down, both of you,' urged Demchi, evidently excited about something.

'What is it, Demchi?' asked Svetlana.

He shot her a glance, which she took as a reminder that there was a wound still in the process of healing, before pushing a photograph and an invitation card across his desk. She recognised the photo immediately: it was Kerimov and the invitation was to the mayor's reception for journalists.

'That piece on Kerimov wasn't your best but it looks like it struck lucky,' said Demchi.

'I don't follow. I didn't write much, to keep the heat off him.'

'It's not Kerimov that's had the heat. Turns out the guy in the education department who screwed him over had also screwed the local chief prosecutor's daughter.'

'And...?' asked Vasiliy.

'The Kerimov case is perfect for them. The prosecutor gets his own back, the mayor's office cosy's up to the prosecutor and we get the credit, taking some of the pressure off us.'

'But they were suing *Kommersant* recently.'

'Yeah, yeah... The people at *Kommersant* can look after themselves. It's *Search for Truth* I'm worried about.'

'Should we be seen accepting invitations like this?' asked Svetlana.

Demchi locked his fingers together and drew a deep breath.

'Yes, we should. In fact, Vasiliy, they said if we needed another place to just ask. Go and give them a call, will you.'

'Now...?' he asked, rising to his feet hesitantly.

'Now, Vasiliy.'

When the door closed, Demchi turned to Svetlana.

'Sveta, I've been running the show here for years. Credit me with some sense, will you?'

'But, they're just creeps.'

'I think the lot of them are on the take and I despise their attitude but sometimes we need to deal with the real, not the ideal.'

'I'm sorry, Demchi, it's just that I thought you –'

'Thought what? Thought that I was taking leave of my senses?'

'No.'

'I've hardly slept in a week.'

'Because of Misha?'

'No, he's okay now, much better than he was. They were going to close us. I've been working on it behind the scenes.'

'Why didn't you say?'

'There was no point... would have just worried everybody.'

'You should have spoken to me.'

'What could you have done?'

She hesitated, looked down momentarily and then raised her head to look him straight in the eye.

'I could have supported you.'

She reached over to place her hand on the back of his. He allowed it to linger there.

'Maybe I should have,' said Demchi.

Eventually, he leaned back in his chair, his hand sliding from under hers.

'Yes, you should have, and next time –'

'I know, Sveta.'

She let the moment drift, before continuing.

'What will happen now?'

'We'll play along. The Kerimov thing was a bonus, but I'd already agreed to tone things down.'

'Tone things down?'

'Sveta, we have to stay open. The political climate changes like the seasons. It will become easier for us again but if we get closed down we won't come back from it.'

She knew he was right, of course... once again.

'Are there some people we can't touch?'

'A few, for now... And I read everything before it's printed,' replied Demchi.

'Okay, if that's the way it has to be.'

'It does.'

'Do I have to be nice to the mayor's press officer at the reception?' asked Svetlana, chuckling.

'Definitely! We have to celebrate this new era of understanding... until the season changes.'

*

The front door opened, as Svetlana carefully applied her eye liner.

'Is that you, Vanya?'

'Yeah,' grunted Ivan.

She heard him open the fridge door, hungry as always.

'Don't take anything out of the fridge. There's *grudka* in the oven for you.'

'Okay. Is there any *borsch*?'

'Yes, but you'll have to heat it up.'

He merely grunted in response.

'Vanya, I'm going to be out for dinner tonight but I won't be late back.'

Ivan ignored her.

'Did you hear me?'

'Yeah.'

She shook her head, closed her eyes for a second and then opened them to continue her make-up. She gently traced over the line she'd already drawn near to the roots of her lashes before finishing with a small upward curve at the outer edge, sat back and looked in the mirror, checking her work. If she said so herself, her dark eyes were one of her best features and she was blessed with thick lashes that curled naturally upwards.

'Where's the salt?' shouted Ivan.

'In the spice rack, where it usually is.'

She twisted the brush to load it with mascara before applying it gently and precisely to each set of lashes. Her hand hovered over the oval tray of eye shadow, before settling on a gently shimmering pale blue, which she applied under her eyes and a slightly darker blend for her eyelids and above. As her head rose, she opened her eyes to view her reflection in the mirror, a faint grin turning up the corners of her mouth as she satisfied herself that the necessary eye drama was in place, should she feel inclined to use it. Her foundation and blusher were, as always, immaculate and needed no more thought but she found herself unusually hesitant when it came to lipstick. Perhaps she was still feeling a little guilty that she had almost unconsciously changed her perfectly presentable underwear for the delicious Cavalli black lace thong and bra she'd treated herself to at New Year. Why had she done that? Should she change back? After all, it was just dinner with a man she had no intention of sleeping with, that night. No, leave it. She felt good about herself but perhaps the scarlet lipstick was a step too far. She stroked a short line across the back of her left hand and repeated the process with a less flamboyant shade of mid pink. She spread out her fingers then closed them together, her attention drawn to the elegant varnish on her beautifully manicured nails. The decision was made – mid pink it would be to accompany her nails and add an extra touch of class.

When she'd finished, she looked in the mirror and mischievously blew herself a kiss before opening the wardrobe to take out her dress. There was no indecision now, as she'd made up her mind that afternoon that she'd wear her sapphire blue cocktail dress. She didn't have many clothes for evening wear but this one had her full confidence. After stepping into it, she slowly pulled up the zip allowing it to slide gently over the bumps in her spine, enjoying the sensation. Her fingers gently joined as she finished with the hook and eye.

Not bad, not bad at all, for an old girl, she judged, as she gave herself a final check in the wardrobe mirror.

*

Svetlana had been impressed to hear they were going to Café Pushkin on Tverskoy bulvar, where booking a table at short notice showed significant initiative. She was less impressed to find herself standing alone, looking down the considerable length of the ornate cherry wood bar, on the ground floor. There was no sign of him, as she scanned the seething animated throng in front of her, until suddenly there was a parting of the ways and somebody made his way, shoulder by shoulder, through the crowd to emerge in front of her.

'I saw you from the stairs,' blurted out Nick.

She stood, tall and elegant, a wry smile crossing her face as she forgave him for not being at the door to meet her.

'Hello, Nikolai.' He stood, silent, his lower jaw slightly separated from the upper. Eventually, he spoke.

'Hello, Sveta. You look wonderful.'

'Thank you. How did you get a table here, at such short notice?'

'INN has an arrangement. I didn't know, but apparently it does.'

'Ah yes, of course, an arrangement.'

'We're eating upstairs, in the Library.'

'That's nice. It's many years since I've been here, a bit out of my price range.'

'Shall we?' she said, stepping forward.

Nick shepherded her through the crowd that barred their way to the stairs, with his left arm bent ahead of him and his right arm protectively around her shoulders, but separate from them. As she ascended the stairs she was conscious of him following half a step behind, perhaps anxious to avoid the impression he was inspecting her slim toned bottom. She stifled a smile at his predicament, already enjoying herself.

Their table was by a tall window that looked out over the boulevard, its broad central reservation rich in snow-covered trees mischievously deflecting the lights from traffic. White flakes caressed the window panes, before falling to nestle on the sill below. The chill outside contrasted with the warmth inside, amplified by the series of high wooden bookcases near to them, filled with the works of Russian and foreign literary masters. Soft lighting spread itself over the dark green tablecloth that set the stage for the immaculately arranged glasses and cutlery.

They had champagne as an aperitif while studying the large newspaper-like menus, liberally sprinkled with letters of the old Russian alphabet, which had fallen out of use. She watched him study the wine list and returned his momentary look but gave no outward reaction to the stirring within.

'Let's drink a toast,' said Nick, raising his glass.

'To what?'

'To happiness... *Za schast'ye!*'

'*Za schast'ye!*' she responded, sipping at her pale, gold champagne.

The sensation of its bubbles playfully tickled her nose before she lowered her glass and placed a finger across its rim, pointing in his direction.

'What makes you happy, Nikolai Ivanovich?'

'I... er... I don't really know. A number of things. I don't really know.'

'Well, don't you think you'd better decide? Will the caviar make you happy, do you think?' she said, nodding at his menu and releasing him from his awkward corner.

'Perhaps, although I had my eye on the *ukha*. I love soup, always have.'

Their immaculate waiter, dressed in nineteenth century attire, approached.

'Sir, madam... are you ready to order?'

She chose black caviar with *bliny*, followed by stuffed pike while he ordered his *ukha* and a beef stroganoff, both of which he'd have found difficult to source with any authenticity, in his previous posting.

'Tell me about Madrid, what's it like?'

She'd thrown him an easy ball with which to play himself into the game, his shoulders dropping as he visibly relaxed.

'It's a great city. I enjoyed it very much. It's not so intense as Moscow and although it snows occasionally, it's not like this,' he said, thumbing in the direction of the window.

'What are the people like?'

'*Madrileños?*'

'Yes.'

'That's a difficult one. There's so many foreigners. Most families seem to have somebody from another part of Spain, but I guess they're pretty friendly and love to socialise, night and day.'

'They party here, the youngsters.'

'I believe so.'

'They'll be here for breakfast. This place is open twenty-four seven.'

'Yeah...?'

The waiter brought their first courses, laying them down with a flourish before pouring them each some of the Chablis Nick had ordered. He bowed slightly and took his leave.

'What's your editor like, in Madrid?'

'Huh. JF – Jack Freeman. He's good, pretty much lets you get on with it. He trusts you, if you know what I mean?'

'I think so.'

'Mind you, you have to be on time. If you say you'll deliver, you have to deliver.'

'Could you say anything?'

'I don't follow.'

'Can you report the way you want?'

'You mean can I speak my mind?'

'Yes.'

'Sure, of course. Look, in the States it's part of the reporting culture and in Europe generally it's okay to say what you want – if it's true.'

'Are reporters or editors ever killed?'
'Excuse me?'
'Killed, for what they say?'
'No way – well, apart from the odd wacko.'
'Wacko?'
'Lunatic. Crazy person.'
'Oh, okay.'

She placed some caviar on the side of one of her *bliny*, lifted it to her mouth and took a bite, gently chewing as the flavours merged deliciously, her shaded lips lightly massaging each other. She realised he was staring again, perhaps fearful that she could so easily cast a spell on him, when she was not even trying. She sniggered as he stirred his soup and a fish head bobbed up, mouth open as if laughing at him. He pushed it back under with his spoon and took a sip of his wine. Her smile disappeared.

'Demchi – Mr Demochev, my editor – he's in danger.'
'Now?'
'Always, to some extent. It varies.'
'On what?'
'Who has power, who is losing power, who has powerful friends. They were going to close us down but he's done some sort of deal.'
'So, he's okay?'
'Maybe – maybe not. But it's more important than ever to keep him out of this matter about Andrei Petrov.'
'I went to the station, to see the picture. I couldn't find it.'
'I'll show you, when the time is right.'
'And you, are you in danger, like Demochev?'
'The same – but not the same. I have a roof to give me some protection.'
'You mean a mafia gang?'
'It's necessary. I don't like it, but it's necessary. If I want to work, I have to stay alive – and I have a son.'
'Does Ivan know what he wants to do?'
'No, it's too early. He has time yet to decide.'
'Would you let him be a journalist?'

'Of course. It's his life, but I would not want him to be... not here.'

'Why don't you leave?'

She laughed, putting down the wine glass she was about to drink from.

'Nikolai Ivanovich, this is my home. It's all I know.'

'You could... you speak some English.'

'This is my country, Nikolai. I have spent many years, in my own way, trying to make it better. I cannot leave.'

'But –'

'I cannot.'

The waiter arrived to fill their glasses. She took more caviar, while he finished his soup.

'Is everything satisfactory, sir... madam?' enquired the waiter.

'Fine, thank you,' replied Nick, as the man glided on to his next table.

'Tell me... about your women,' she commanded, ambushing him and offering him no chance of easy platitudes for answers.

'There's not much to tell.'

'Liar.'

She waited.

'I mean... can't we do this later, when I've had a bit more to drink?'

She lowered her head, allowing her dark locks to fall forward partially obscuring her face before sweeping her hair back with her right hand and fixing him with her deep, dark, perfectly made up eyes. His defence was broken, before it really began.

'There was a girl, many years ago.'

'You loved her?'

'Yes.'

She gave him no respite.

'Your wife?'

'No.'

'Ah, somebody else's wife...? You like complication?'

'Yes and no, in that order.'

'And she returned to him?'

'Yes.'

Svetlana thought she could detect the beginnings of a tear in the corner of his eye. Good, he was telling the truth. She could not abide the waste of time created by liars. She decided to throw him a lifeline.

'And now, a girlfriend, in Madrid?'

'No, nobody.'

'No?'

'No.'

'So you are alone. If you disappeared, no one would miss you. You would make a good Russian.'

'I am Russian,' he stated, with unexpected certainty.

She looked at him as he straightened his shoulders and pushed his jaw forward. The bookcase behind framed him, with a backdrop of works by Dostoyevsky, Chekov, Derzhavin, Fet and Tolstoy. The waiter approached, without the insolent swagger unnoticed by foreigners but reserved for them nonetheless. Nick delivered his main course wine order confidently, almost without accent. Of course, she knew of his mixed parentage but for the first time he looked like he fitted in.

'Sometimes I wish I wasn't,' she said.

'Wasn't what?'

'Russian... When I was a girl I used to dream about living somewhere warm – somewhere with an orange garden and blue skies.'

'I can perhaps...'

'What?'

'No... It's nothing.'

She looked at him and wondered what it was he'd stopped himself from saying. It would wait.

Their food arrived and they both ate heartily. Nick avoided French wine and accompanied his stroganoff with a Russian red from Krasnodarsky region.

'What will you do when your colleague recovers?'

'Return to Madrid, I guess.'

'Huh, now your Russian blood flows, we will see.'

'What do you mean by that?'

'We will see.'

This enigmatic response was all she was going to allow, the gentle closing of her eyelids signalling that the curtain had come down on this particular act in their dialogue. She took a sip of wine and smiled at him.

'Somebody else is looking for poison,' he whispered, leaning forward.

'Who?'

'I don't know exactly – British Secret Service, I think, and the CIA. He wouldn't say.'

'Who wouldn't say?'

'Hubbard, Peter Hubbard – or that's what he said his name was. He spoke to me at the airport in Madrid, said we'd met previously.'

She moved to interrupt him but he held his palm up to silence her.

'Anyway, I met him at the Metropol. He – they want me to look into a story about a new poison.'

'Our poison?'

'I don't know, but a poison you can't detect. They're worried it will be used to silence dissidents and avoid embarrassments like Levitsky.'

'And if you find out something?'

'To report it. They think if it's publicised, they'll hesitate to use it.'

'They won't.'

'Won't what?'

'Hesitate to use it. Nikolai Ivanovich, listen to me. If my life is in danger for the stuff I report then you would be in great danger to do this.'

'He said I'd be safe, too high profile...'

She smiled and raised her eyebrows.

'I see your American blood still flows, too.'

Her smile disappeared.

'Nikolai, I'm not joking. This is not Boston, not Madrid...'

'What if it's the same story, Andrei's story?'

'I don't know. Some days I wonder what we've got into here. Should've listened to Demchi.'

'I wouldn't be anywhere else...'

'What?'

'Than here.'

He touched her hand with the tips of his fingers. She allowed it.

'Sveta, what you do is real reporting. I was cruising in Madrid, stories on a plate for me. This is what we do – Katia, the cards, Hubbard. You know there's a story, an important story.'

'I was looking for an answer, not a story.'

'The story is the answer.'

She wanted to tell him there was a choice but she'd known for a long time now that she would not let Andrei's death lie. Her brother's unsolved mystery had haunted her all these years. She'd met up with him in her dreams and made a promise to find out what had happened to his comrade in arms, a promise she would keep.

Svetlana tipped Nick's fingers from the back of her hand.

'I'll show you the cards... tomorrow.'

'Tomorrow?'

'Kursky station, by the ticket office, at noon.'

*

They'd said nothing, made no pact but when they'd moved downstairs for coffee and brandy, death and poison had been left behind, subjects for another day.

Svetlana held her glass with both hands, warming the delicious spirit, which was completely obscured by her long fingers.

'Tell me, Nikolai –'

'I like it when you call me Nikolai.'

She ignored him.

'What do you do when you want to completely switch off?' she asked.

'Sport. I watch sport. American football and ice hockey – I love ice hockey. And you?'

'The *banya*, or if I really want to lose myself, ballet.'

Svetlana's Garden

'To dance?'

'To watch. My dancing days are over.'

'But you used to dance?'

'Yes, but I had to study and anyway I grew too tall.'

'There's something about the way you move. I couldn't figure it out – but now I see.'

She put down her glass and gathered her hair, holding it behind her head in an impromptu pony tail, before releasing it to cascade over her shoulders, an act of rebellion against the restricted, tightly tied styles she'd endured while dancing. He held the glass at his mouth but did not drink from it. Only when she reached for her glass again did he allow the waiting spirit to pass his lips.

*

She surmised the pleasant blush of alcohol might give him thoughts of taking her hand as they travelled in the taxi to her apartment, but he made no such attempt. She had those gloved hands, one on top of another, resting in her lap, her face, barely exposed by her fur hat, looked resolutely forward.

When they arrived he was first out and hurried round to open her door.

'Wait here,' he said to the driver, as she stepped out.

The sky had cleared allowing the moonlight to cast giant shadows from the rows of identical apartment blocks around them. There was no wind and just the subdued background thrum of traffic on Eniseyskaya ulitsa to accompany them.

'I just wanted to say something.'

'It's late, Nikolai... and a little cold for speeches.'

'But can I see you again... like this, I mean?'

'Of course. Perhaps the ballet, or hockey. I like hockey very much.'

'Which would you prefer?'

She leant forward, kissed him on each cheek and then whispered in his ear.

'Remember, you are Russian now. What would you decide?'

Chapter 12

Deputy Energy Minister Leonid Kutaisov opened the lid of an engraved silver box and offered cigarettes to his counterpart at the Russian Security Council, Yevgeniy Shkadov, and to Vadim Zheronkin, head of strategic development at Gaztec. Each politely declined. Facing them was Malenkov, fidgeting a little, given the company he was keeping, but with a smug smile on his face nevertheless, which exaggerated the narrowness of his nose.

'Do you have some good news for me, Captain Malenkov?' asked Kutaisov, not offering him the courtesy of a cigarette.

'Deputy Minister, I'm pleased to report that Colonel Chernekov's latest round of tests has been successful, and subject to a confirmatory second test tomorrow, we appear to have overcome our recent difficulties.'

'At last! This is indeed good news.'

Kutaisov beckoned to Shkadov and to Zheronkin, who each leant forward to form a huddle with their host. Kutaisov glanced up at Malenkov and then threw a perfunctory wave in his direction.

'That will be all, thank you, Captain.'

'Yes, Deputy Minister,' said Malenkov.

He rose to his feet and collected his coat from the chair next to him, before making his way across the rich, red and gold carpet of Kutaisov's office and into the long corridor outside.

That Kutaisov's a pompous arse, thought Malenkov, reminding himself that all three of the superiors he had just left behind had started their careers in the KGB, like him. He'd hoped for a little more comradeship but comforted himself that perhaps his years of service, and particularly his work on this case, might lead him too into political office.

He pulled on his black leather gloves as he walked down the first floor corridor, being careful not to step on the joins between the light oak blocks that made up the surface below his feet.

*

By eleven-thirty, Svetlana had already arrived at Kursky station, hoping to meet Sasha to see how he and his street team were getting on. She scanned the concourse, expecting to distinguish his animal-like movement from the more conventional progress of passengers going about their business, but there was no sign of him. She went to their den, where she found Marina huddled up in the grubby fraying blanket they shared. The girl barely acknowledged Svetlana, her face blank and eyes staring. Svetlana put her hand down to steady herself, only to feel the damp corner of the blanket. The child had wet herself but lain there, nevertheless.

'*Zaikin*, what is it? What's happened?'

Marina seemed suddenly to realise Svetlana was present, weakly extended an arm and made brief eye contact. Svetlana took her right hand and rolled up the sleeve of her thin jumper to see fresh bruises on her upper arm. She pushed up the other sleeve to see the same thing, and puncture marks on her forearm. She could not tell if Marina's state was down to the beating she'd had or the drugs she'd injected.

'I'll be back. Wait here,' said Svetlana, retreating from the den.

She walked to the station exit and out into the cold grey of the early afternoon. Fortunately, Richard was there with his van and a small queue of children waiting for soup.

'Richard, do you have a blanket?'

'Hi, Sveta. Yeah, just a moment.'

'And some of those hand-wipes?'

Richard emerged from the back of his van, with a blue woollen blanket and a packet of wipes.

'Thanks, Richard, I won't be long.'

'Go on. See you later.'

Svetlana hurried across the main concourse, the blanket under one arm and her handbag under the other. Suddenly, Nick was in front of her, blocking her path.

'Sveta, it's me.'

'Not now, Nikolai. Wait for me here. I've something to deal with first.'

She left him standing in his expensive coat, *ushanka* sitting on his head like a fur crown, tilted slightly to one side. She hurried on, not looking back until she reached the den where Marina had not moved in the time Svetlana had been gone.

'Marina, sit up, sit up!'

She helped the child up and eased the old damp blanket from under her before opening the packet of wipes. She'd learnt to give bed baths while looking after Dima's mother, in the months before her death. Gently she cleaned up the poor kid, trying not to hurt her where she was bruised on her thighs and buttocks from the kicks her pimp had administered, probably because Marina had been high and unable to work. When she'd finished, Svetlana wrapped the skinny girl in the clean blanket, held her in her arms and gently rocked her to and fro until she slept.

*

Nick looked cold, despite his thick woollen coat. He stepped from foot to foot and hugged his arms around himself. Then, she was near him.

'Are you okay?' he asked.

'Yes,' she said coolly, before walking past him, her hand beckoning him to follow.

As they reached the stairwell, she took a torch from her handbag, switched it on and led him round the corner to the playing card. She shone the light on the picture, moving it from the blood red heart, across the streaks of blond hair to the pale blue eye, frightened and chilling. Nick looked on silently.

'Is it the Petrov boy?' he asked.

'Maybe.'
'And the other one?'
'The other card?'
'Yes. Does it match?'
'No. It's the same, the same artist, but another part of a picture.'

She reached into her bag and took out a slightly creased photo, before handing it to him. He took the torch from her, a shadow falling across her face as reflected light fell on his. She watched his eyes move between the two images, while from the gloom behind them the breeze whispered eerily.

'Let's go. It's creepy here,' said Svetlana.

He continued to look at the images as if he'd not heard her.

'Nikolai, let's go!'

'Just a moment.'

'Why, what is it?'

'Something, something. I just can't place it.'

'It'll come to you. Let's go. I don't like it here.'

They climbed the stairs to the concourse above, as she tucked the torch in her bag and put her gloves back on. The station was enjoying its early afternoon calm, before the city disgorged its workers, many of whom would make their way there. They moved effortlessly towards the exit until, suddenly, she spun Nick round by grabbing his coat sleeve.

'Stand still!' she commanded. 'Don't move!'

She stood close, facing him, the fabric of their coats temporarily meeting as she put her hand on his chest and sneaked a view over his right shoulder.

'Sveta, what is it?'

'Be quiet and stand still.'

The station's distinctive smell was pushed to the background as her perfume filled the air. Perhaps surprised by the sudden closeness of her, she could feel his quickened heartbeat. They stood like this for only a few seconds, before she peeled away in the direction of the exit.

'Come on,' she said.

'What was it?'

'FSB.'

'Watching us?'

'No, just duty officers but we don't need the attention.'

He looked back, but all seemed normal, just a couple moving slowly away from them, apparently consulting a map.

'How do you know?'

'You just know.'

As they passed through the main exit, Richard was closing the hatch on the side of his van. She went to him and Nick followed.

'Thanks for the help, Richard.'

'Don't mention it.'

Richard glanced past her at Nick.

'This is –'

'Mr Mendez,' said Richard, interrupting her. 'I enjoy watching INN when I'm in Europe; it's sometimes difficult to get here.

'Nick, this is Richard.'

'Hi, Richard, good to meet you,' said Nick, stepping forward to offer a handshake.

'You too,' said Richard, taking his hand before turning to close the bolt on the hatch.

'You back tomorrow?' Svetlana enquired.

'Yeah, late afternoon, gotta pick up a batch of old trainers. Some of them will be fine for the kids.'

Richard opened the door to his van and put a foot inside before turning back to Svetlana.

'Oh, by the way Sveta, Sasha was here earlier – says he's got news for you.'

'What news?' she asked.

'Dunno, but he said he'd be back soon.'

They waved, as Richard started the engine and slowly pulled away, his ageing van ill equipped to do battle with Moscow's seething traffic.

'You got any cash on you?' she asked Nick.

'Dollars and rubles.'

'How many rubles?'

'About six thousand, I think.'

'That's fine. We won't need that much.'
'For what?'
'For Sasha, if his news is what I think it is. Fancy a coffee?'

*

She traced a heart shape with her spoon in the chocolate on the top of her cappuccino.

'Is that your heart?'

'It's Pavel's, my brother.'

Svetlana stirred her drink, the shape fading away into the milky blend. She put the upturned spoon in her mouth, the milk chocolate and warmth providing a delicious little treat for her. She saw him watching as she slowly and deliberately pulled the spoon from her closed lips, flicking it with the end of her tongue as it left her mouth. He averted his gaze as a shy boy might. A grin crossed her face and left again before he looked back.

'Has your broken heart mended, Nikolai?'

'Well, a lot of time has passed.'

'That's not what I asked you.'

'That was a different life, one I thought I was going to lead. I have another life now.'

'As good?'

'Different.'

'Yes, that's why you have no girl: attractive man, but full of fear.'

'That's not –'

'Not what? Not fair? Who said any life was fair?'

'I'm too busy for a relationship.'

'That's rubbish – too scared.'

'And you, you're afraid too.'

'Ah, cornered he attacks to defend!' she said, pointing her spoon at him.

He stood up.

'I'm hungry. You want something?' he asked.

'Yes.'

'What d'you want?'

'You choose. I trust you.'

Her phone bleeped, as a message arrived. It was from Ivan to say he'd be late back from school. She texted a reply and pushed the send button, before looking up to see Sasha, a broad grin on his face.

'Sasha, you startled me.' she said, as she put her mobile back in her bag. 'Well, you look very pleased with yourself. What is it?'

'Cards!'

'Cards? More than one?'

'Three!' he announced triumphantly.

Sasha stepped back, as Nick approached.

'It's okay, Sasha, it's okay. He's a friend.'

'You must be Sasha. I'm Nick,' said Nick, holding out his hand.

Sasha did not take it, but instead looked at Svetlana.

'That's a funny name.'

'Nick comes from America. There, it's short for Nikolai, like Kolya is here.'

'What does he want?'

'He's a reporter, like me. He's going to help us with the cards... and pay you your money!'

Sasha visibly relaxed. Anyone who would pay him money was a friend in his eyes. A silence followed.

'Have I missed something?' asked Nick.

'Sasha and his friends have found three more cards,' she said.

'Three?' asked Nick.

The young boy nodded and held up three fingers.

*

'Come on, come on,' beckoned Sasha.

He led them through a dark archway into a courtyard, overlooked by six stories of ageing apartments, with peeling beige paint and rusted railings. Icicles hung from a broken and neglected metal downspout that had long since ceased to perform any function. Corroded bars covered the ground floor windows, not that there could be much worth stealing here. An abandoned Moskvitch, formerly somebody's pride and joy, sat forlornly on deflated tyres, a blanket of snow not entirely hiding its accumulated sadness.

Two young lads, with unkempt hair and grubby, weary faces emerged from a doorway to greet their young companion. Sasha turned to Nick.

'Six hundred,' he said, putting out his hand.

'Four hundred,' said Svetlana. 'We agreed two hundred for you, and two hundred for the one who found it.'

Sasha pointed to himself and to his two friends, counting as he did.

'One, two, three. Two find it, plus me.'

He crossed his arms, his street craft ahead of hers. They had not discussed the consequences of a joint discovery, but her momentary indignation dissolved into a smile as she realised she'd been outsmarted, on this occasion.

'Six hundred please, Nikolai.'

Nick counted out the money, which he handed to Sasha, who then divided the cash between himself and his friends, each inspecting its authenticity before secreting it into their pockets. The business concluded, the three boys crossed the courtyard to a large communal waste bin and put their shoulders to it, moving it a couple of metres to one side. And there it was, the eight of hearts, unmistakably painted by the same artist.

Svetlana and Nick looked on silently, taking in the shoulders and back of the head of a crouched and vomiting young soldier, his invisible hand buried in long grass. There was a blemish on his forearm, where some brick had flaked away under attack from the winter's fierce frost. Eventually, Nick reached into his pocket and took out his camera before taking three shots of the card, checking the LCD screen each time to make sure of a good image.

'He's army,' said Svetlana.

'Yes,' replied Nick.

Sasha interrupted the moment, his friends having slipped away silently and un-noticed.

'Do you want to see the others?'

Svetlana and Nick looked at each other and said nothing but turned as one to follow the boy, who was already halfway across the courtyard. They had trouble keeping up with him as he seemed to skip across the snow and ice underfoot, while they slithered after him, arms outstretched as if balancing on a tightrope.

'He was vomiting. Poison?'

'Who knows?' replied Nick, as they followed Sasha down steps and into Trubnaya metro.

'Sasha, wait! Where are we going?' called Svetlana.

'Kievskaya,' called back the scurrying street child, before finally coming to a halt near a ticket office. It was clear to Svetlana that he had no intention of buying his own ticket with his recent earnings, not that he'd bother with tickets if he could get away with it.

They made their way down the escalator and took the train north, changing at the first stop for their journey west on Koltsevaya circle line 5. The dark-grey train hissed its way to a halt and Sasha pushed his way on, extending no courtesy to the passengers trying to alight.

They sped along, the carriage rocking rhythmically. Regular announcements in a female voice meant travel on the circle line was anti-clockwise, while a male counterpart indicated when travel was in the opposite direction.

Svetlana sat, watching Nick and Sasha standing side by side, the boy's natural agility and balance allowing him to ignore the movement that had other passengers hanging on to the nearest point of support. At the end of the carriage, a tramp had fallen asleep on the floor in a drunken stupor, the space available to him dictated by how close travellers could brave to go before his smell became unbearable. Svetlana looked at him through a sea of legs, before sadness descended on her as she looked back at Sasha, realising this could be what the future had waiting for him, if he stayed on the street. One day his agility and charm would desert him and he would be at the city's mercy, his journey in life perhaps to ride round in a circular train, hiding from the bitter cold outside. She shivered inwardly at his potential fate.

Soon, they pulled into Kievskaya and then made their way up to the street through great marble halls whose walls and ceilings were graced by murals depicting the wondrous efforts of happy communist peasants in Ukraine, the heroism of Russian forces and, of course, the uplifting work of comrade Lenin.

Sasha led them into the huge Dorogomilovsky market, a seething mass of people and colour. The smells of almost every kind of edible produce filled the air, competing with each other but allied with the calls of their stallholder, promoting the benefits of his particular wares. As they moved through the busy corridors, the warm aroma of cooked chickens was overwhelmed by the next-door display of herbs and spices. An irate marketeer ran in front of them to gesticulate at a sneak thief running off into the distance, while Sasha seamlessly took advantage of this brief distraction to help himself to a juicy red apple, nonchalant and unseen. Svetlana watched the young boy move through the crowd with practised ease. Barely stooping, and with a magician's sleight of hand, he picked up two five ruble coins, dropped by their fussing *babushka* owner. Even before she had time to turn and look for her tumbling change, he had moved on, undiscovered.

Five minutes later, when they had reached the edge of the market, Sasha led them through a gateway to a small car park, where some of the stallholders kept their vans.

'Wait there!' he ordered, turning to face them.

Svetlana and Nick stood side by side, her boots and his shoes sinking slightly into the slush-covered grass. Sasha bit into the apple.

'Where did you get that from?' asked Svetlana.

Sasha just smiled and took a second bite.

'Eight hundred,' he mumbled, as he continued to chew, withdrawing his other hand from his pocket and holding it out.

'Sasha, it's four hundred: two for you and two for the finder.'

'Two cards,' interrupted Sasha.

'What?'

'Two cards – eight hundred.'

He stepped towards Nick, who glanced at Svetlana for clearance to give him the money. She shrugged. Nick counted out eight hundred rubles and placed them in Sasha's palm. Within an instant they were deposited at the bottom of his trouser pocket. He raised his right arm, his trigger finger pointing straight at the pair of reporters. Svetlana met his eyes with hers.

'What is it, Sasha?'

'There!' he said, continuing to point.

Svetlana and Nick both turned inwards to look over their shoulders, their eyes momentarily blinking with recognition as they crossed each other's gaze. On the concrete-panelled fence, not five metres behind them were two more cards, the two and six of hearts. She finished her turn while Nick, his lace loose, nearly lost his left shoe as a frozen rut in the ground tried to hang on to it. Sasha handed over money to a tall, skinny youth who'd been sitting on the footplate of a nearby van, casually watching events unfold. Nick joined Svetlana and reached for his camera to take photos in the fading light. He took an extra one of her, when she was not expecting it.

'Don't do that! I don't like having my picture taken.'

He smiled. She didn't.

'That's not much help,' said Nick.

He pointed to the two of hearts, showing no more than some grass and a sliver of concrete.

'Yes, it is. These are pieces in a jigsaw. Every piece will have its place. I know they will.'

'Mind you, the six looks interesting.'

The other card showed the military-clad, face-down torso and legs of a young man, an open door pressed against his waist. Svetlana knelt down and removed the glove from her slightly trembling hand, before placing her fingertips on the painted body of the soldier. The concrete was rough and unforgiving, not much of a resting place for this poor soul. She closed her eyes and spoke in a whisper, to herself.

'Darling, Pavel, my protector. I wish I could have protected you... and this young man.'

Her head filled with the image of her brother as he waved to her for the last time, from his train. She could still smell the diesel from the locomotive and see his brave smile in the puddle on the platform.

'They can't hear you, you know,' said Nick.

'What?'

'The dead can't hear you.'

'What do you know of the dead?' she snapped, turning her back to him.

'I'm sorry, I was just trying to help.'

She shook as she quietly sobbed. She felt Nick's hands on her shoulders.

'Sveta, I'm sorry.'

'Nikolai, just leave me. Take the boy to that café, over there.'

She felt him gently press on her shoulders, before withdrawing to leave her with her reminiscence.

'Sasha, you hungry?'

Sasha nodded enthusiastically.

'Come on then,' said Nick.

*

When she joined them, only the slightest smudge to her mascara gave any clue that her normal composure had been disturbed.

Sasha's paper plate held the crumbs remaining from the *pirozhki* he'd hastily eaten, while he was now concentrating on a large chocolate ice cream cone, apparently so delicious that even Svetlana's arrival at the table didn't divert his attention. She surveyed the grubby, grey-painted café, channels worn into its bare floorboards by the to-ings and fro-ings of many thousands of Muscovites who'd chosen here to take refuge from the throng outside. Spindly stainless steel legs supported old, green Formica table tops at varying angles, while they awaited customers from the impatient and muttering self-service queue. Around the room, ice cream was prevalent, Russians eating it, whatever the weather.

'I got a cappuccino for you,' said Nick, as Svetlana took her seat.

'Thanks.'

She put her fingers to the now tepid plastic cup. Sasha finished his ice cream and wiped the remaining chocolate from his face with his sleeve, adding another streak of colour to the already chaotic garment.

'Gotta go,' he said, rising from his seat.

'Why?' asked Svetlana.

'I have work to do...' said Sasha, winking mischievously '...some of us can't afford to sit around in cafés.'

He was gone in a moment and before the smiles had left their faces.

'He's quite a character,' said Nick.

'Yes, he is.'

'Could really make something of himself.'

'You think so?'

'Sure, why not?'

'You have to own a rope if you want to climb a mountain.'

'What do you mean?'

Her phone rang and she put up her hand to interrupt Nick as she answered it.

'Hello... Vasiliy, hello. How's it going? Oh, and happy birthday...'

She chatted for a short while, before putting the phone back in her bag.

'You're invited to a party,' she said to Nick.

'A party?'

'Yes. Vasiliy is twenty-two today and his mum is cooking.'

'Great, I've never been to a Russian birthday party. What do I bring?'

'Vodka... and flowers.'

'I thought flowers were for lovers.'

'And for mothers, Nikolai, and for mothers.'

Chapter 13

Malenkov sat down without being asked as Chernekov signed some papers his assistant had brought him.

'Thank you, Colonel. Will you require a car to take you to General Gurov's reception?'

'Please, Yegor – can you organise it?'

'Yes, sir, of course. Will there be anything else?'

'No, thank you,' said Chernekov, as his *ordinaret* turned to leave.

'Congratulations, Colonel,' said Malenkov.

'Congratulations?'

'On your successful tests.'

'I don't need congratulations, I'm just doing my duty. It was only a matter of time.'

'Nevertheless, our political masters are very happy. I thought you'd like to know.'

'I'm not bothered about their happiness.'

'Oh, come now, Colonel, we know that happy politicians make both our lives easier.'

'I'm still not bothered about them, but I can I'll tell you something that is bothering me.'

'What?'

'Somebody told Petrov's mother.'

'Petrov, the dead conscript?'

'Yes. Somebody told his mother he'd been poisoned.'

'I thought the mother had been sidelined?'

'She has, but the informant –'

'Is out there somewhere?'

'Somewhere.'

'And powerless, so not important.'
'I don't like loose ends.'
'Who does?'
'I'd prefer to tidy it up. This work has been too important.'
Malenkov sat back and looked at Chernekov, weighing up his stern face.
'And how can the FSB help?'
'What?' asked Chernekov.
'That is what you want, isn't it?'
Chernekov separated his hands and placed them palms down on the desk in front of him.
'When I was last down in Chita, I made a few enquiries.'
'And?'
'It turns out the boy had only two close friends. One's still there and thinks it was an accident.'
'And the other?'
'Was discharged on medical grounds: breathing difficulties.'
'So pick him up from home and get rid of the problem, if he is the problem.'
'He never went home. Turns out he and his stepfather couldn't stand each other, or that's what the stepfather says.'
'Where's home?'
'Kazan.'
'Stepfather any idea where he might be?'
'No, but he did run away to Moscow for a year, when he was fifteen.'
'So he's a civilian now... and missing. Looks like more carelessness.'
Chernekov shot him a look of instant menace, causing Malenkov to wipe the developing smirk from his face.
'Got a name for him, Colonel?'
'Katenin – Yakov Katenin,' replied Chernekov.
'Height?'
'One-metre-eighty.'
'Hair?'
'Light-brown.'

'Weight?'
'About seventy kilos.'
'Anything else?'
'Like what?'
'Anything unusual?'
'He paints.'
'Does he now? Any good?'
'Leontev, down at Chita, showed me a few of his pieces, landscapes mostly, but not bad, not bad at all.'
'Pity then he couldn't fight as well as he could paint.'
'Just see what you can do to tie it off. We don't want him talking to reporters like Obukov or Svetlana Dorenko.'
Malenkov chuckled.
'Don't concern yourself with Obukov. He's stepped out of line once too often and won't be reporting anything after his accident next Friday. As for Dorenko, don't worry, it's not her style. Although, she has been seen talking to an American TV reporter, so we may keep a loose eye on him, but that's another story.'

*

As he entered Starbucks, on Leningradsky prospekt, Chernekov checked his watch. He was running a little late, but still had time to get back and change out of his civilian clothes before the general's reception. Grachev, sitting right at the back, was waiting for him.
'What's the news, Oleg?' he asked, as Chernekov took his seat.
'Success.'
'Excellent. When?'
'You can't have the lethal version. We agreed.'
'I know, Oleg, relax. I'm a man of my word. Now when?'
'We've done the tests but we have no stock. I have a small team, answering to me. I could get you a useable amount in about a month, but I have to be careful.'
'Of course, of course. Oleg, I trust you. You've always delivered, so what's one more delay?' said Grachev, leaning across the table to give the moonlighting colonel a playful push.

'And the money?'

'Half will be in your Swiss account tomorrow and the rest, on delivery.'

'Good.'

'Shall we have a drink, and I don't mean this shit?' enquired Grachev, holding up his empty mug.

'Next time. I have to change and be out again in an hour.'

'Pity. Okay, next time, Oleg.'

Chernekov pushed back his chair, shook Grachev's hand and made for the exit. As he walked down Leningradsky prospekt, he wondered what to spend the money on. He quite fancied a place by one of the Italian lakes. He was due some leave soon so perhaps he'd go and have a look. In matters strategic, the interests of his country were paramount but his minor business on the side with Grachev would have no effect on Russian strategy or operations so, in his mind, he remained in the forefront of patriotism.

He walked a little faster, not wanting to be late for the reception.

*

It was nearly eight p.m. when Svetlana and Nick reached Vasiliy's parents' apartment on the fifteenth floor, bearing vodka, rolled herring and a large bunch of red carnations.

They could hear several bolts being withdrawn from behind the steel-plated front door. Nick thanked fortune that he was not a pizza boy tasked with negotiating deliveries to this landing full of similarly fortified apartments. Eventually, the door swung open and Vasiliy greeted them.

'Sveta! Come in, come in.'

Nick followed Svetlana and watched, isolated for a short while as she was submerged under the kisses of Vasiliy's mother, father, grandmother and siblings. When she emerged, she slipped off her long woollen coat, while Nick involuntarily checked out her tall slim figure as she stood there in dark blue jeans and a lavender sweater. She turned to beckon him forward.

'Everybody, this is Nikolai Ivanovich, a reporter, like me. He lives in Pokrovka.'

A collective 'oooh' went up at the revelation that Nick lived in such a high-flying area of Moscow.

'It's not my apartment. I'm just borrowing it,' rushed Nick, correcting the possible impression that he had ideas above his station.

'Welcome, Nikolai Ivanovich. I am Nikita,' said Vasiliy's father stepping forward to shake Nick's hand, '...and this is my wife Viktoriya.'

Nick held up the flowers he'd been holding, half-hidden behind him and offered them to Viktoriya, a spontaneous smile crossing her face.

Five minutes later, after all the introductions, they sat around a table burdened with the weight of generous amounts of food and drink. Nick surveyed the dishes in front of him, each seeming to elbow the other for position. The herring they'd brought had been given pride of place in the centre but looked pale compared to the colour-splashed salad and grated beetroot, which were its near neighbours. Viktoriya reached over with a large slice of salted pork and placed it on Nick's plate.

'Help yourself, Nikolai. Come on, don't be shy,' she urged.

'What do you report, Nikolai?' asked Nikita.

'Well, interesting stories.'

'Is it thieves and liars, like Sveta?'

'No, politics and politicians mostly,' said Nick.

'There you go, thieves and liars,' retorted Nikita, re-filling Nick's glass with vodka.

Nikita began the construction of an invisible wall, intended to divide male conversation from female.

'How old are you, Nikolai?' asked Viktoriya.

'I'm thirty-nine.'

'That's a good age. Are you married?'

'No, haven't found the right person, yet.'

'It's time you were.'

'What?'

Svetlana's Garden

'Married. A man needs a good woman – like Sveta,'

'Be quiet, woman. Let the man have his dinner!' interrupted Nikita.

Nick met Svetlana's glance and felt himself blushing. She came to his rescue, changing the subject.

'Nikolai is a TV reporter, for INN,' she said.

'INN? What's INN?' asked Nikita.

'*International News Network*. You can get it on cable and satellite,' added Vasiliy.

'So you read the news?' enquired Nikita.

'No, he –' began Svetlana.

Nikita signalled for her silence. She did not have his permission to scale the invisible wall.

'Well, I don't read the news. I'm one of those guys the newsreader cuts to when they say "here's our Madrid correspondent".'

'Madrid? Were you in Madrid?' asked Vasiliy's fourteen-year-old sister.

'For five years,' replied Nick.

'I want to go to Madrid,' she added.

'You do?'

'When I'm eighteen.'

'You have to study first,' said Viktoriya.

Nikita pulled his shoulders back and drew a deep breath. Insufficient respect was being shown with these uninvited contributions to his conversation. Order restored, he continued.

'Tell me, Nikolai, what do you make of the direction our president is taking the country in?'

This was a question he'd rather not have had to deal with, on first meeting. He sensed from Nikita's suddenly earnest stare that a fudged answer was not going to be acceptable. He had one chance in two of getting it right. Svetlana paused, a helping of green leaves and peppers hovering over her plate. Like everybody around the table, she waited for his answer.

'It's unfortunate –'

'Unfortunate? It's disgraceful, that's what it is!'

Svetlana tipped the salad onto her plate and let go the breath she had been keeping. Nick's answer had been as diplomatic as he could make it, but it was the correct answer, nevertheless. Emboldened by Nikita's powerful endorsement, he thought he'd better expand his response.

'Russia needs, in my view, to embrace the outside and not retreat from it.'

'Absolutely!' responded Nikita. 'We are humans, not robots. We need laws but not dictators.'

'Darling, it's Vasya's birthday,' Viktoriya reminded him, putting a hand on his shoulder.

He paused.

'We'll talk some more,' he said to Nick, as he filled his glass again before rising to propose a toast.

Over the next hour, they feasted with hands criss-crossing the table reaching for *pirozhki*, pork, fish, and all manner of their delicious companions. Dishes and plates assumed odd angles, while Viktoriya proceeded to bring in Vasiliy's birthday cake, accompanied by his younger sisters.

'Make a wish, Vasya!' said Svetlana.

Vasiliy closed his eyes, the others suddenly quiet and respectful of his private moment.

'What did you wish for?' she asked.

Vasiliy just smiled.

Later, Svetlana gave Viktoriya and Vasiliy's two giggling siblings a hand to clear the dishes before they all returned to the living room where Nikita broke into song. He was soon joined on the chorus by the others, except for the uncertain Nick. His newfound confidence had deserted him on this one, but as he listened, childhood lyrics taught to him by his mother but long since forgotten, started to return. He hesitantly joined in the choruses until recollection and vodka combined to make him a full participant, under Svetlana's watchful eye.

*

They heard the door bolts slide shut as they made their way to the elevator. It was after midnight and there was quite a journey ahead of them. The silver doors eased open and they stepped in, fifteen floors separating them from the ground below. She watched him as his finger hovered over the buttons, waiting to make his selection. The whiskers he'd grown slightly softened his strong jaw and his broad shoulders seemed to fill the width of the capsule. A firm push on the ground floor button had them enclosed with just a dim light and some vulgar graffiti for company. His turn was interrupted by the back of her hand, stroking his cheek and then turning so her fingers could trace his jaw-line, her nails moving through the dark stubble. Her palm moved to the back of his neck as she allowed him to finish his turn, before drawing him to her. With her high-heeled boots, she was almost as tall as him and needed only to rock forward slightly on her toes to place her mouth level with his. Her boldness met no resistance in the split-second it took for her to press her lips on his. She felt the roughness of his skin on hers as it contrasted with the softness of his mouth. Her tongue followed the line of his teeth, tasting the lingering traces of brandy Nikita had offered him, before pushing its way through to meet his. She raised her hand to the back of his head, her fingers splaying out through his thick dark hair as he wrapped his arms around her waist and held her to him, engaging in her lustful ambush. They held each other vice-like as the lift descended, their tongues wrestling passionately before the moment was broken by the almost violent halt of the elevator as it reached its destination. She stepped back and watched him, silent, standing with her back pressed against the steel cage, arms stretched out sideways along the railing. She tipped her head forward slightly and narrowed her dark eyes, focusing on her prey, electricity flowing between them.

The doors opened with a low groan but Svetlana and Nick didn't move. Only as the two metal sentries began to close did Nick reach out, his forearm momentarily trapped, before the doors retreated once again. She passed him, without breaking eye contact, as she slipped on her gloves, her breath turning to steam as it met the cold of the open-air lobby. She came to a halt and he moved to her side.

'He followed us,' she said.

There, facing them, was the freshly painted seven of hearts with its now familiar dimensions, a loose streak of paint halted in its tracks when it had frozen, as if shot while running for the border.

She ran to each concrete pillar around them, peering out into the semi-darkness examining the shadows for any sign of movement that might reveal the whereabouts of the recently departed artist. There was none. She returned to his side.

'He's gone, hasn't he?' said Nick.

'Of course,' she replied.

Svetlana recognised the door frame as the continuation of the one she'd seen at Dorogomilovsky market as she'd mourned again her dear, departed brother. There was no face, no staring eye or flaxen hair but there was a hand, pointing and disdainful. Dima had always said that artists with real talent painted good hands. He'd joked that impressionists couldn't do hands, so they weren't real artists.

'Do you see it?'

'What?' he replied.

'Contempt.'

'Where?'

'In the hand. Our artist does good hands.'

'He can paint, all right. Will he speak to us, do you think?'

'He is speaking to us,' she said, pointing at the mural.

Nick was wearing the same coat he'd had on at the market and still had his camera, which he took from his inside pocket. The flash cut through the darkness as he recorded the picture of this apparent crime scene.

'We'll put them all together,' he said.

'Tomorrow. Come for supper, after work. It's not safe to have them in the office.'

'Okay. What time?'

'I'll call you. It's cold, and I want to go home.'

A hundred metres away, the artist, rucksack over his shoulder, had watched the darkness being broken and silently observed as they faded from view. He put a second woollen hat over the other one he wore, turned and walked into the arms of the night.

*

Nick couldn't sleep. *Had that really happened? Had he really surrendered all the initiative to her?* He'd had ideas for her. He was going to woo her for as long as it took, but without warning she'd just turned round and taken him, there and then.

'One of a kind,' he said, as he studied the image of her he'd sneaked for himself.

He reached out and rested the tip of his finger gently on the screen, stroking her hair, wishing she was with him now. He looked at his watch to see it was three-fifteen, as he rolled in his glass the last teaspoon of the extra vodka he'd poured but shouldn't have. Madrid, with its sunshine and brio seemed a long way off. Now, here he was in this cold and sometimes forbidding city, where smiles were in short supply. Right now, there was no other place he wanted to be.

*

'Vanya, we have a guest for dinner: Mr Mendez, a TV reporter,' said Svetlana.

'Who for?'

'INN.'

'What's that?'

'It's an international news station. One day, when you go travelling, you'll see it.'

'Huh, travelling, fat chance!'

'You'll go travelling, if you study hard and learn English.'

'I am, you are, he is,' said Ivan, in English.

'There you are, you can if you try.'

'It's too difficult.'

'No more difficult than Russian to an English speaker. Mr Mendez speaks Russian. He had to learn.'

'What does he want?'

'He's helping me with a project.'

'What kind of project?'

She was in two minds about telling Ivan anything concerning the Petrov case, but this was as talkative as he'd been in ages and she feared an early return to the usual communication by grunts and monosyllabic 'yes' or 'no'. She decided to grasp the opportunity as she made some cereal and pastry for his breakfast.

'A soldier was killed.'

She saw Ivan's look of sarcasm and incredulity.

'I mean strangely, not fighting,' she went on.

'So?'

'So, I'm looking into it and Mr Mendez is helping me.'

'What does Demchi say?'

'I'm not doing it through the paper.'

Ivan raised his eyebrows and looked at her for an explanation. None was offered. The phone rang and Ivan answered it.

'Hi, Misha...'

He turned for his room and shut the door behind him – end of conversation. Svetlana sighed, frustrated that a rare opportunity to talk was lost but, upon reflection, perhaps grateful Ivan did not know more.

She made herself a coffee and then sat at her computer to check her email. Her mind drifted to the night before. She smiled when she recalled the look on Nick's face but sat up with the sudden realisation she'd not just been toying with him. She'd meant it and she wanted to be close to him again.

So, Nikolai Ivanovich, what now? What shall I do with you, an American? My father would not approve.

There was mail from Demchi asking her what time she'd be at the mayor's press reception.

'Shit... shit, shit, shit!'

She'd forgotten to put it in her electronic diary. Her system was usually foolproof. She'd put the entry in for the correct day with a reminder for the day before. This time, no reminder box had popped up and now she was double-booked. The reception was from four to seven-thirty and she'd been planning to cook for Nick at eight. He'd just have to come over later. She called him on her mobile.

'Sveta, do you know what time it is?'

'Yes.'

'I didn't get in until two.'

'What do you want me to do about it?'

'Did you have to call so early?'

'Yes, I'm working. Anyway, look, I'd forgotten about the mayor's press reception. It's at four and won't finish until seven-thirty, so you better come round at eight-thirty. I should be back by then.'

'Okay.'

'Right, see you then.'

'Aren't you forgetting something?'

'Pardon?'

If he was fishing for romantic comments, he was to be disappointed. That was one moment and this was quite another.

'Address?'

'Address, yeah, right. It's Lenskaya ulitsa, twenty-eight, on the fourteenth floor. See you later.'

'You will.'

She put her phone down and made for the kitchen. She'd planned to be back for six and to cook something fresh but that was no longer feasible. It was at times like this that her childhood and adolescent experiences in Yaroslavl served her well. Back then, access to ingredients was sporadic, but still her mother had managed to produce wholesome, tasty meals for the family, a skill Svetlana had inherited. She examined the contents of her tiny freezer, some smoked salmon coming to the fore as being on the menu. She took it out to defrost before slipping on an apron over her jeans and white T-shirt. There was maybe an hour, but no more, if she was going to reach the office at a reasonable time, so she set to work with the ingredients at hand.

*

Demchi seemed nervous and Svetlana was somewhat withdrawn. Containing her cynicism about events like the mayor's reception took some doing. Vasiliy, on the other hand, appeared buoyant at the prospect of mixing with such famous company or, in some cases, infamous.

When they reached the top of a flight of stairs leading to the reception at City Hall, they joined a small queue waiting to have their invitations inspected by a broad, be-suited assistant who looked and acted more like a nightclub doorman than a civil servant.

'Next time, wear a tie,' said Demchi to Vasiliy.

'Sorry, I didn't realise it was going to be so formal,' he replied.

'Okay, second door on the right,' said the assistant, handing them their passes without grace and ogling Svetlana in her black trousers and cream blouse.

Her heels click-clacked on the black and white marble floor as they made their way along the wide corridor.

'He's just a thug, like the rest of them in here,' she said.

'Shush. Now, behave yourself. Remember that things will change. So, today, act like they're our friends,' commanded Demchi.

They entered the vast reception room, which was already busy. A rich, red carpet covered the floor and faced a cream ceiling with gold detailing, from which hung magnificent crystal chandeliers. On the oak-panelled walls were pictures of former mayors from Soviet times, their expressions cold and unsmiling. The three journalists each picked up a glass of champagne, before making their way in.

'Gregoriy Maksimovich, how good of you to come,' said the mayor's press officer, Evgeniy Bakunin, offering a bony hand.

'It's a pleasure. Thanks for inviting us,' said Demchi, as he received Bakunin's weak handshake.

'This is –'

'Ah yes, Svetlana Yuriyevna... I'm a great admirer of your work.'

'Thank you,' said Svetlana, easily able to deal with his stinking lie, but recoiling from the slightly wet kiss he landed on the back of her hand.

'And you must be Vasiliy Telyanin. Welcome,' said Bakunin, reaching for his hand.

Well, at least he'd done his homework, which was more than could be said for many of his predecessors from a time when the press was merely an adjunct of the Soviet state.

'We're really very grateful for all your hard work on the Kerimov matter. The Mayor is determined to confront corruption, wherever it appears,' said Bakunin.

'I'm sure,' replied Demchi,

Svetlana recalled it was more or less common knowledge that this mayor had a palatial villa in Marbella, in his daughter's name, not to mention the yacht moored at Puerto Banus.

'Yes, we've been meaning to extend some hospitality to our friends in the press for some time now. The Mayor will touch on it in his speech, later.'

'That's nice,' said Demchi, tossing into the conversation one of the many platitudes Svetlana suspected he'd prepared.

'We see members of a vibrant, free press as very important to our city's wellbeing,' added Bakunin.

'Important enough to protect them?' asked Svetlana, ignoring Demchi's scolding look.

'I'm sorry?'

'Protect them from assassination?'

'It's very unfortunate that there have been a number of unexplained incidents, but as you know, this is a complex city and I'm confident the *politsiya* and the FSB will bring the perpetrators to justice.'

She could feel a whirlpool of anger swirling inside her as she pictured the bloodied faces of former journalists, mutilated by the exit wounds of bullets to the back of the head. She wanted him out of her sight.

'I look forward to that. Excuse me, there's somebody I must speak to.'

She crossed the room and spotted Konstantin Golovnin from *Izvestia*. He was okay; nothing too far outside the line, but at least you could speak to him, in confidence. A smile crossed his face as he saw her approach.

'Sveta, long time no see. How is Moscow's premier investigative journalist?'

'I'm fine, but right now I'm looking for a friend to talk to.'

'So, Bakunin is not your friend?'

'You could say that.'

A waiter walked by with champagne on a silver tray. Golovnin reached out, took Svetlana's nearly empty glass and exchanged it for a full one.

'A toast to friendship then, Sveta,' he said, clinking his glass against hers.

'*Za zdarov'ye*,' she replied.

'I hear Demchi's in a bit of a spot.'

'Who told you that?'

'Oh, you just hear things.'

'He's no fool.'

'You're right, of course, but there are still some clever people who've gone missing. Keep your eye on him. You know how he is, too protective of his people.'

'Maybe he needs his own roof,' she joked.

'Maybe,' said Golovnin, not laughing. 'He could organise that while he's here.'

'How do you mean?'

'Grachev.'

'What?'

'Over there, behind you.'

She looked round and, sure enough, there he was, one of Moscow's premier mafia gang leaders but, today, in his assumed role of legitimate businessman.

'How did he get invited?'

'You're not seriously asking me that, are you? You of all people know how these things work.'

'Yes, I suppose so.'

She was interrupted by a gentle tap on the shoulder and turned to see the angular features and beady eyes of Malenkov. She clocked him instantly as FSB.

'Svetlana Yuriyevna, I wonder if I might introduce myself, with your permission?' he said, nodding to Golovnin.

'Of course,' the latter replied. 'I was just going to have a word with Stepan over there, anyway.'

He took his leave.

'I didn't know the FSB were in the business of journalism, Mr...?'

'Malenkov, Captain Gennadiy Malenkov... and is it that obvious?'

Svetlana shrugged.

'What can I do for you, Captain Malenkov?'

'I understand you've made the acquaintance of a television reporter, Nick Mendez, an American.'

'So? I wasn't aware that breached national security or any of the Criminal Codes.'

'No, no, of course not. I was just naturally curious, that's all.'

'Don't you have bigger matters to attend to... like over a hundred journalists murdered and not one crime solved?'

'It's not my field but I have many colleagues working on those cases.'

'And Nick Mendez is your field? What is he, a terrorist?'

'Who knows? Russia still has many enemies and it's necessary to keep up our guard.'

'I'm sure the FSB has satellite television and is well aware he's an established news correspondent.'

'Many such correspondents have turned out to be foreign agents.'

'Really?'

'Yes, really, and we wouldn't want to think that an important Moscow citizen like you could be compromising herself.'

'Thanks for the concern, but I think I'll be fine.'

'You didn't actually say what the nature of your relationship was with him?'

She stifled the reflex that had her on the point of telling him it was none of his fucking business. Instead, she reminded herself that FSB attention would be very unwelcome. He was just fishing and she decided not to take the bait.

'As you mentioned, he's just an acquaintance. Good afternoon, Captain Malenkov.'

She turned in the direction of Demchi and Vasiliy.
'Oh, just one more thing, Svetlana Yuriyevna...'
She half turned.
'Yes?'
'Does the name Yakov Katenin mean anything to you?'
It didn't, but journalist's instinct told her it should and she mentally filed it, for later.
'No, should it?' she replied.
'No, not really. Just naturally curious.'
She turned her back to him and took a step forward.
'What about Andrei Petrov?'
For a split second she froze, before moving on.
'No,' she said, without looking back.

*

It was eight-fifty p.m. when she opened the front door to her apartment. Moving through to the living room, she saw Nick facing Ivan, as if challenged by a guard dog, and unsure whether to run or confront. If there had been any conversation between them, it was not evident.

'Oh, I see you've met Mr Mendez, Ivan. Sorry I'm late but the mayor spoke longer than he was supposed to.'
'I told Ivan to call me Nick. I hope that's okay.'
'Of course, no need to be over-formal. Are you hungry?'
'Starving.'
'What about you, Vanya, did you eat the *pelmeny* I left for you?'
'Yeah... and I had a burger with Misha 'cause Granny gave me some money.'
'You know what I think about burgers.'
'Oh, once in a while can't hurt.'

She interrupted Nick's defence of Ivan with a glance. It was a mild rebuke, but after thirty minutes in her apartment, he was not qualified to be contributing advice about her son's nutrition. Nick lowered his eyes.

Ivan stood up and made for his room.

'I've got some homework to finish. Nice to meet you,' he said to Nick, as he sauntered away, shutting his door behind him.

'How did I do?' enquired Nick.

'Too early to tell, but he spoke to you, that's something, I suppose,' replied Svetlana.

She disappeared into the kitchen and emerged with a glass of red wine for him.

'Thanks.'

'You're welcome.'

'Sveta, I've brought some prints of the cards. Have you some sort of board I can fix them to?'

She went back into the kitchen and came out with a pin board, the calendar and various flyers relegated to a shelf, to free up space for this more important task.

While she finished preparing their supper, he sipped his wine and assembled the cards in what seemed like their best positions.

They dined on smoked salmon, *pelmeny* and underlying sexual tension. That Ivan might appear from his room at any time ensured the tension would remain unresolved for this evening, allowing them both to give attention to the cards.

'I've set them out as I think they should be. It's too little to make a lot of, but it's a start.'

She let him help to clear the dishes from the table before they moved to the settee and looked down at the images. He reached for her hand but she withdrew it, at the same time pointing to Ivan's room.

'So, let's see what we've got,' she said, resting her chin in her hands and her elbows on her knees.

She silently contemplated the images, eyes scanning backwards and forwards across them, trying to imagine what might fill in the blanks in between.

'You were right about the hand. He can paint,' said Nick, eventually.

'He can. His name, by the way, is Yakov Katenin.'

'Who?'

'The artist.'

'How do you know?'

'From the FSB.'

'The FSB told you his name?'

'They might as well have. That's his name. Malenkov asked me if it meant anything to me.'

'Malenkov?'

'FSB... at the mayor's reception: Captain Gennadiy Malenkov. Demchi knows him, but didn't say much. Mind you, he didn't have to. I already knew.'

Nick gave her a questioning look.

'Malenkov's a sadist. He enjoys it. I saw it in his eyes.'

'Why didn't you tell me over supper?'

'I didn't want to put you off your food,' she said, sniggering slightly.

'Am I supposed to be frightened?'

'You should be.'

Ivan's door opened and he strolled through to the kitchen, returning with a glass of orange juice. He saw the pictures on the board and made a detour to the front of the settee.

'Is this the soldier who died?'

'Maybe,' said Svetlana.

Nick looked at her, apparently apprehensive that she'd told Ivan.

'Should've worn his gas mask, shouldn't he?'

'What?' she asked.

'Like the other guy. He's sick, but he's alive.'

'Gas mask?'

'Yeah.' said Ivan.

They looked at him blankly.

'Gas mask!' he said, pointing at the image of the young man vomiting.

'Where?' asked Nick, looking the image up and down.

'In his hand!' said Ivan, his voice rising with apparent impatience.

They looked again.

'Sveta, in his hand. Here,' said Nick.

He placed a fingertip just above the apparently hidden hand of the vomiting young conscript. She focused on the few square centimetres he was pointing to. There it was. The hand she thought buried in a clutch of long grass was in fact obscured by the dark green camouflage of part of a gas mask. Realisation crossed her face. Ivan, his work done, regained the course he'd set for his room, gently shaking his head as he went.

'It was gas... and that's a gas chamber!' exclaimed Nick.

When he looked up she was staring straight at him, unblinking and earnest.

'What? What is it?' asked Nick.

'Malenkov knows. He asked me something else. He asked me if Andrei Petrov meant anything to me.'

'You told him no, right?'

'Of course. I had my back to him.'

'Even better.'

'He knows, Nikolai. He'll come for us. This is not your problem to solve. You should leave Moscow, leave tomorrow.'

'You really want me to leave?'

'Yes, I don't want to be responsible for this.'

'That's no longer possible.'

'Of course it's possible. Nikolai, don't you fear danger, real danger?'

'Sure... but then you kissed me like that, and now I fear losing you more than danger from Malenkov.'

He held out his hand.

Svetlana closed her eyes, recalling the chill that had descended upon her, as with her brief hesitation she'd given herself away to Malenkov's enquiry, sensing the eyes following her as she'd walked back to Demchi and Vasiliy. Her prophecy of danger was now certain. She opened her eyes and searched deep into his. There was fear all right, and recognition by him of the gravity of their situation. He was not kidding himself, which she thought good. She looked further, wanting to see if his words were the product of mere bravado or, instead, of a true heart. She took her time in reaching her conclusion. After so long fending for herself, here was a man offering to support her in the face of peril. Her romantic feelings were confused and far from resolved. That would have to wait. Right now, she was simply struggling to come to terms with the fact that this man, with much to lose and a ready escape route, wished instead to stand by her side and fight. Ivan, if he appeared, would just have to live with her decision, as she eventually reached for Nick's hand, encasing it in both of hers before pressing it gently to her cheek, where it halted the downward progress of a solitary tear.

Chapter 14

Katia looked pale and tired as she put the kettle on the stove to make them some tea. Svetlana gave her a reassuring pat on the shoulder as they moved to sit at the simple wooden table in her kitchen. A branch, swaying in the cold Gorokhovets wind outside, tapped pleadingly against the window as if begging admittance and respite from the winter's cruelty.

'Have you been eating?' asked Svetlana.

'I don't feel like eating.'

'You must try.'

'Why, Sveta, why must I try any more?'

'For Andryusha – for Andryusha.'

'I miss him so. My heart aches for him.'

Svetlana reached out and took hold of Katia's piteous, trembling hand.

'He was poisoned... by gas, in what looked like an exercise.'

Katia raised her head, indicating to Svetlana she was listening.

'The cards, the paintings I told you about, there have been more – clues, we believe. The picture is not complete but there's soldiers, a gas mask, and a gas chamber.'

'And Andrei?'

'We believe so.'

The kettle started to boil and Svetlana made to stand, before Katia gestured to her to remain seated.

'Go on,' said Katia, as she prepared their tea.

'Do you know Yakov Katenin?'

'No, I can't – just a minute – yes. Yakov... Andrei spoke of him in one or two of his letters. Wait a minute and I'll get them.'

Katia abandoned the brewing tea and left for her bedroom. Svetlana turned to the window, able now to give the distressed branch some attention. She watched its erratic dance for a few seconds, resolving to put it out of its misery and cut it off before she left. Katia returned.

'They're gone!'

'What?'

'The letters, they're gone!'

'Are you sure?'

'In the case under my bed. That's where I keep them, where I always keep them. They're gone!'

*

Svetlana had been loath to leave Katia, such was her distress.

'Fucking bastards!' she screamed at the misting windscreen of her ageing Lada as she drove from the village to join the M7 highway back to Moscow.

'Fucking bastards!'

Not content to rip out the poor woman's heart, now they were stealing her memories, as well.

'Fucking bastards!'

Her anger was in danger of making the car leave the road and she allowed herself to drive faster than she should on the ice and snow beneath. Her expletives began to help and, as her rage subsided, she had the presence of mind to stop and collect herself. She stepped from the car, making sure to leave the engine running. This was not a place and time to be stranded. A weak sun retreated below the horizon as darkness marched over the land, while Svetlana looked back at the now twinkling lights of Gorokhovets. She wasn't sure how long she'd stood there in contemplation, but the distinctive screech of an owl cutting through the uneven thrum of the car's engine, startled her. She looked up to see a grey silhouette, atop a telegraph pole. It watched her, motionless and silent as she stared back. Her body began to shiver through cold or fright, she knew not which. With night falling, this was the owl's time, not hers. She moved on.

Svetlana drove through the darkness, the feeble headlights of her car overpowered by those of oncoming trucks, which seemed at any moment likely to cross the icy road and crush her but which, despite the frequent potholes, somehow held their course. She wished she'd set off earlier: a sign indicated she still had a hundred and sixty kilometres to go before she'd reach Moscow. This was not an enjoyable journey and images of Katia, her spirit so feeble this time, kept filling Svetlana's head, along with those of the cards. Her resolve, however, was only strengthened by the day's ordeal.

'I'll find you. I'll fucking well find you!' she said out loud, with steely determination.

A series of late nights and early starts had begun to take its toll. She could feel her heavy eyelids in danger of closing. A couple of kilometres further on, she came to a truck-stop with a small, garishly lit café. It was definitely not her kind of place, but she needed some food and coffee to revive her for the rest of the journey.

Opening the door, she stepped into the low-ceilinged, cream-painted room, its atmosphere heavy with smoke and smelling of diesel. Faces turned to look at her, winks and nudges passing on the news of her arrival. She wondered when a woman had last stepped in here, unconsciously tightening the belt on her coat, as fifty pairs of eyes looked her up and down.

'You lost, luv?' sneered a fat driver, his blue overalls stained with grease.

Years ago she would have turned on her heels and retreated but the situations she'd dealt with for the paper, in the intervening time, had hardened her and this idiot was but an amateur. She stopped and turned to look right at him, unflinching in her demeanour.

'Do I look lost?'

She waited for an answer, but none came, as the bravado of her enquirer and his table full of friends deflated. She resumed her path to the counter where the owner stood in a dirty apron, hands on hips, a cigarette drooping from the side of his mouth.

'Do you have soup?' asked Svetlana.

'*Solyanka*; today's special.'

'Fine, and coffee, please.'

She took a seat next to a window and watched the lights dance through the trees lining the road outside. She ignored the glances of the men. The stares were more difficult but, with some modest effort, she ignored those too. Her soup arrived, the proprietor spilling some on the red plastic tablecloth as he put it down, but making no effort to wipe it up. Coffee followed, together with a bread roll, wrapped in a paper napkin.

'Ninety rubles,' came the gruff accompaniment to the questionable service.

She handed over a hundred ruble note, taking her chances as to whether there'd be any change. She thought it unlikely. The thick *solyanka* with its bacon and sausage was warming and surprisingly tasty. She dipped her bread in it as she took a sip of the strong, black coffee and contemplated the difficult road ahead.

*

By the time Svetlana arrived at the outskirts of the city, the traffic has subsided from its rush hour worst and she was able to reach her apartment block without too much difficulty.

Ivan was sprawled out on the settee, watching television.

'Nick called. Said it wasn't urgent and he'd call back.'

'What time did he call?'

'Dunno.'

'What time, Ivan?'

'Maybe about two hours ago.'

She reached for the phone and dialled.

'Hi, it's me... Sorry, I left Katia late and the road was awful.'

'I'm glad you're back, anyway. Can we meet up?' asked Nick.

'When, tomorrow? Okay, but I have to meet Demchi at three, so let's call it five-thirty.'

'That's fine.'
'Okay, see you then, Nikolai.'
She replaced the receiver.
'A man called.' said Ivan
'Did he leave a number?'
'No, he called round; here, at the door.'
'What did he want?'
'Didn't say. Just asked if you were in.'
'What did you say?'
'Told him I didn't know when you'd be back.'
'What did he look like?'
'Small, pointy face... bit of a creep.'
'Next time, don't open the door, okay? Okay?'
'Don't go on about it.'

Malenkov. It was Malenkov. How dare he come to her home, with her son there! She resolved to confront him, the next morning, down at Lubyanka, her outrage genuine. Beyond her indignation, however, lurking in the shadows of her mind, fear began to plant its tiny seeds of doubt. Visiting Malenkov at the FSB's headquarters to say what she thought of him was easy, but the rest of it she had no clear plan for. At times like this, she fell back on a trusted remedy. She made for the bathroom and turned on the taps, before going to her bedroom to change.

Svetlana tied her hair up, let her robe fall and slowly immersed herself in the warm, welcoming water. It had been a long, difficult day and a bath would make it all right.

*

'Where did you get this?' asked Malenkov, standing in his cramped room at Lubyanka.

He turned and looked expectantly at Valentina.

'It was on his laptop, in the office. He'd just gone to the toilet, so I took a quick copy.'

'Interesting. I think he likes Mrs Dorenko. It's a weakness, don't you think... sentimentality?'

'No, I don't. It's perfectly possible to be sentimental and still do your duty.'

Malenkov shrugged, as he put down the print of the photo Nick had snapped of Svetlana, at Dorogomilovsky.

'Any idea where this is?' he asked.

'No.'

'Can you copy the hard drive?'

'Maybe. I'll see, but he's only been careless once, so far.'

'Twice.'

'What?'

'Leaving his computer on, and taking this picture – that's twice.'

Malenkov looked at the photo closely, squinting. He took off his glasses, reached in his pocket for a cloth and, following a practised routine, gently cleaned the lenses. He put the spectacles back on and looked again.

'What do you make of these?'

'What?'

'In the background,' he said pointing for emphasis.

'Nothing. Just graffiti.'

'Come now, lieutenant, and you a journalist. Look again.'

Valentina reviewed the image, before turning to Malenkov.

'A soldier?' she enquired, tentatively.

'A dead soldier, painted by a live artist: Katenin.'

'Katenin?'

'A conscript, now discharged. A talented artist, apparently... and a traitor. He's leaving them clues, the little shit!'

Malenkov picked up the print and then tossed it disdainfully back down.

'We need to find this guy. Do you have Mendez's schedule?'

'The formal schedule, yes, but his free time schedule, no. They're left to their own devices.'

'Does he trust you?'

'I guess so.'

'Hang around a bit more. Look for any contacts with Dorenko and any mention of paintings.'

'I'll see what I can do.'

'We must all see what we can do. This must not be allowed to develop.'

Valentina picked up her coat and made for the door where she gave Malenkov a perfunctory wave. He nodded an acknowledgement as she left.

He looked at the photo again, rubbing his chin as he realised the issues of Petrov and Katenin would have to receive higher priority.

Chapter 15

Nick was anxious to see her and took the last three steps in one as he emerged from Chekhovskaya metro. Pushkinskaya ploshchad was busy, but there she was, standing out from the crowd, distinctive as ever and gazing up at her hero, Pushkin. When he was near to her, he reached out and placed a hand on her shoulder.

'Nikolai! Sorry, you startled me.'
'Deep in thought, eh?'
'I often come here for inspiration, for answers.'
'And did you find them?'
'Not yet.'
'Because I interrupted you?'
'No, because it's complex. Malenkov came to my apartment. That bloody FSB bastard came to my home!'
'I'm sorry.'
'You have no reason to be sorry. It's not your fault.'
'But, if I'd –'
'If you'd what?'
'If I'd left you alone, at the beginning, when you asked me to.'
'He'd have come for me anyway. I was foolish – should have listened to Demchi.'
'Then you'd have been beating yourself up about the boy's mother, wouldn't you?'
'Maybe. My home – came to my home – spoke to my son! Bastard!'
Nick clasped his hand to her elbow.
'Come on. Let's have coffee... out of the cold.'

Svetlana's Garden

They walked, side by side, across the square in the direction of Coffee Bean, as fresh snow began to fall. He watched the flakes alight on the fur of her coat, their gentle approaches in stark contrast to her indignant mood. The surface had not thawed all day and their feet crunched in unison on the ice beneath.

Nick held the door for her as she removed her hat and gloves, before moving straight to a table in the corner.

Within minutes, they were contemplating two steaming cups of black coffee.

'I don't take sugar,' she said.

'Today, you do,' said Nick, as he finished pouring the contents of a sachet into her cup. 'It will improve your mood.'

'My mood is fine.'

He tilted his head, raised his eyebrows and smiled at her benignly. She tried to maintain her stern expression but slowly it cracked under his gaze.

'Stop it,' she said, giving him a gentle push.

'What?'

'That – that look.'

'What look?'

'That one.'

'The one that's making you smile, you mean?'

'Yes. I don't feel like smiling.'

'Ah, but you are, so things can't be all that bad and you have an ally. You're not alone with this.'

Their fingertips rested on the table, millimetres apart. He returned the look that was seeking reassurance the alliance was steadfast. Keeping her in sight, his fingers advanced across the brief no man's land between them and rested atop her outstretched hand. His smile remained, but the slight mocking element it carried faded away.

'Thank you, Nikolai.'

'For what?'

'It's been so many years, fighting on my own... to have somebody.'

'That's enough. Anyway, it's time for a Russian and American to fight on the same side.'

'But you are Russian now, remember?'

'I remember we're on the same side,' said Nick, turning his hand over to entwine his fingers with hers.

In the next moment, there was a knocking sound coming from somewhere. Svetlana looked over to see someone at the window, beckoning to her.

'It's Maksim, my contact at the Prosecutor's office.'

'Get him to come in.'

'I don't think so. You're a complication he doesn't need.'

She pushed back her chair and made for the door, scooping up her gloves as she went but leaving her hat.

Nick watched as she shook Maksim's hand and hesitated before accepting his kisses on both cheeks. Their conversation was brief but animated. Nick saw the Prosecutor's assistant turn and quickly disappear into the flurries of snow that had become heavier since he and Svetlana had arrived.

She sat back down, her cheeks reddened from the sudden cold, drops of water falling from the ends of her dark hair as flakes of snow melted. He indulged himself with a moment to take in her unkempt beauty.

'What was it? What did he want?'

'He's scared... been moved. Told me not to call him again, until things have died down.'

'Until what's died down?'

'He didn't say... but you can guess if he can't be seen with me.'

In the great scheme of things, this was a minor reverse, but a reverse nevertheless. They each contemplated its significance, in silence. He spoke first.

'Assuming we put all this together: the cards, the Petrov boy, Katenin, Chernekov... Assuming we do, what were you going to do with it? I mean, Demchi won't print it, and I guess no prosecutor will?'

'I – I thought...'

He waited.

'D'ya know, Nikolai, I'm not sure. It depends how high it goes.'
'Who will know? Malenkov?'
'Maybe.'
'Why don't you speak to him?'
'Oh, I'm going to speak to him all right. Coming to my home, asking Ivan about me.'
'I mean, there you are. You can tell him you're pissed off about that, but while you're there, you can see if you can pick up any information about how far up the chain this all is.'
'He's not a fool.'
'No, he's not a fool, but he's not a genius either if he's been in the service a long time and he's still only a captain.'
'He has weaknesses.'
'Exactly, like chess. Play the game and look for weaknesses.'
'Like chess?'
'Yes.'
'Remind me about chess sometime, Nikolai.'
'Excuse me?'
'Nothing.'
She stirred her coffee and took a sip.
'It's sweet. You're starting to develop a knack of doing the right thing. It's a little unnerving.'
Nick gently drummed his fingers on the table top, trying unsuccessfully to stifle a self-satisfied grin.

*

'Hi, Nick, it's me!'
Reception on his mobile was a bit hit and miss that afternoon, in Pokrovka.
'Who? Who's calling?' he asked, in Russian.
'It's me, Victoria.'
'Vicki, how are you? Where are you?' asked Nick, unconsciously slipping into Spanish.
'I'm at Barajas.'
'Where are you going?'

'Moscow.'

'Moscow?'

'I have leave due: so, I thought why not? Never been to Moscow.'

'Are you alone?'

'No, I'm with Pilar, my old school friend. We're hoping you can show us the sights.'

'Yeah, sure, but you should have given me a bit more notice.'

'Thought I'd surprise you.'

'Well, you have all right. When do you arrive?'

'Eleven tonight, your time.'

'At Sheremetyevo?'

'Is that how you pronounce it?'

'How are you getting to the city?'

'Thought we'd catch a cab.'

Nick recalled his own chaotic arrival at the airport. Resourceful girl as she was, he quickly formed the view that although he didn't fancy a late night trip to Sheremetyevo, even she'd be out of her depth there.

'It's okay, I'll meet you.'

'You will?'

'Yeah, at eleven. I'll be there.'

'You're a prince. See you then.'

'Okay. And Vicki–'

He'd wanted to remind her that Moscow weather was not like Madrid, but she'd already hung up. He'd text her.

Nick looked at his watch.

'Shit!' he said, in Spanish. 'I mean fuck!' he corrected himself, in Russian.

He was late for his briefing with the production crew. INN wanted the energy squeeze on Ukraine broadcast to be put together carefully, given its sensitivity.

On the metro, Nick began to regret offering to be Victoria's taxi service. He had the use of a pool car, but in the time he'd been in Moscow, he'd only done a couple of short journeys and the airport at night was far from ideal. *Too late now though*, he thought. The train made good progress and he was only ten minutes late at the studio.

Nick walked in as the others were still helping themselves to tea and coffee.

'Okay, ladies and gentlemen, let's get started,' said production head, Jeff Prentice.

The meeting covered that day's news items. The Ukraine energy story was going out second. Nick had squirmed slightly, when it was suggested his report might be filmed outside Lubyanka. While the FSB were keeping tabs on him, there was no need for provocation and his suggestion of Gaztec headquarters as a venue did rather trump Lubyanka. It was going to be cold, but at least these days they'd make maybe fifteen to twenty hours' use of the feed, and as long as he didn't mess it up, they'd need only one take.

'Thanks, guys,' said Nick, as he left the room.

He made his way down the corridor to his office and pushed the door open.

'Valentina. Can I help you?'

'Oh hi, Nick,' said Valentina, a blush rising up her face. 'I was just checking to see if I'd left my mobile here.'

'And did you?'

'What?'

'Leave it here?'

'Seems not.'

'Then you're finished, right? Only I have to go over my piece, for later.'

'Sure. Sorry, I'll keep looking. Try Stepan's room, maybe.'

'Right.'

Nick watched her go. It felt a bit strange, but he dismissed it and sat to run through his notes.

*

The receptionist knew who she was, of course, but at FSB headquarters this stuck-up, bitch-reporter would have to follow procedures like everybody else.

'Is he expecting you?'

'No.'

'Then, you can't see him.'

'Well, I know he wants to see me, so he might be disappointed if you don't tell him.'

'How do you know he wants to see you?'

'He came to my apartment, looking for me.'

The receptionist, hair pulled back and tied in a bun, her face devoid of make-up save for some badly applied eye shadow, did not flinch as she looked Svetlana up and down.

'I'll ask. Name?'

'I'm sorry?'

'Your name?'

'Dorenko, Svetlana Dorenko.'

'Huh.'

A delay followed as the enquiry made its way to Malenkov's assistant. Svetlana watched as the gatekeeper kept her eyes fixed on her while she awaited a response.

'I have a Svetlana Dorenko in reception, asking for Captain Malenkov... No, she doesn't... I've already told her, but she says he wants to see her... Very well.'

She replaced the receiver and folded her arms. Svetlana thought this vaguely ridiculous, and anyway, wasn't the FSB supposed to be on a charm offensive or something?

The phone rang and the receptionist picked it up.

'He'll be right down. Take a seat,' she said, her face assuming an expression of mild disappointment.

While waiting, Svetlana checked her mobile to see if she had any messages but there was nothing. She replaced the phone in her handbag and looked up, just in time to see Malenkov striding towards her, hand outstretched.

'Svetlana Yuriyevna, what a pleasant surprise. It's not often people volunteer to come here.'

She ignored his weak joke but shook his hand as she stood to look down at him.

'Is there somewhere private we can talk?' she asked.

'Of course, of course. Follow me, please.'

Malenkov turned and set off down a long corridor, looking back only once to check she was following him. She watched his short strides and thought it time he applied some fresh polish to the scuffed heels of his black leather shoes.

'Would you like tea, or coffee?' he asked, as he went.

'No, thank you,' she said casually.

He could have shown her courtesy previously, by not coming round to her apartment, but it was too late now for superficial niceties. He held the door for her as he ushered her into a modest room, furnished surprisingly with what looked more like a dining table and chairs than office furniture. A bookcase was mounted on one wall, packed with leather-bound volumes. Black and white pictures of former KGB officers adorned the others.

'Sit, please,' he said, pulling back a chair.

She looked at the reflection of her varnished fingernails in the polished cherry wood of the table, before folding her hands together.

'Why did you come to my apartment?'

'I don't remember leaving any name.'

'Why did you come to my apartment?'

'Just naturally curious.'

'Don't ever come to my apartment again! If you want to speak to me, you can contact me at the paper. I'm sure you have the number.'

'I'm sure we have. Forgive me, I intended no discourtesy and if I may say so, you have a fine-looking son.'

'Leave my son out of it.'

'Of course – of course. I just wanted to compliment you.'

'What is it you really want, Captain Malenkov?'

He drew a long breath and then let out a sigh, removing his glasses as he did.

'My job is to try to keep our country and its citizens safe.'

'The only thing making me feel unsafe, at the moment, is the FSB. What is it you want?'

'Believe it or not, Svetlana Yuriyevna, I do respect your professionalism. I believe you are dedicated and sincere about your work, but can I ask you to accept that I may also be dedicated and sincere about mine.'

She had the feeling he'd used such a line many times before, but it was effective nevertheless and her momentum was interrupted. He continued.

'I have to deal with all sorts of people in my line of work: plotters, terrorists, criminals and... traitors.'

'Are you suggesting I'm a traitor?'

'Absolutely not. Svetlana Yuriyevna, you and I probably don't agree on many things, but then many of our citizens don't always agree. That doesn't make them traitors.'

'But somebody is?'

'Regrettably, I believe so.'

'What's that got to do with me?'

'I came to your apartment to help you.'

'To help me?' she asked, unable to hold her sarcastic laugh.

'Yes.'

'I'm fascinated. How can the FSB help me?'

'By warning you that you are in danger of drifting into state security territory. That is my job, not yours. Right now, you and I probably have economic or political differences in our views, which are not important, but I would not like us to have a difference which was important.'

'You're warning me? Warning me off, you mean?'

'I didn't put it that way.'

'I don't care how you put it. What is it you're warning me off, Captain Malenkov?'

'Do you remember me mentioning a name when we met at the mayor's press reception?'

She looked at him blankly. She would not feed him, he would have to feed himself. He waited a moment, just in case.

'We are interested in the whereabouts of a young man called Yakov Katenin. Do you know him?'

'It's only a short while since I told you I didn't.'

'I know, yes. I just wondered if things had changed, in the meantime.'

'No.'
'Only, I think young Katenin is letting his country down.'
'A traitor, you mean?'
'I believe so.'
'And how exactly has he let his country down?'
'I'm not at liberty to go into any great detail.'
'Now, that really doesn't surprise me.'
'Svetlana Yuriyevna, I don't consider this matter to be flippant.'
'I can't consider it to be anything, if you don't explain yourself.'
'You're sure you don't know this man?'
'I told you.'
'I wish I could believe you, but I don't, you see. I believe you know more than you're saying.'
'Believe what you want.'
'I think you could put yourself in danger.'
'I'm always in danger.'
'I don't mean the kind of danger Dubnikov and his thugs protect you from.'

She allowed her eyebrows to rise.

'Of course we know about your roof.'
'Of course you do,' she said, regaining her deadpan expression.
'I'd like to know what you know about Katenin.'
'I know it doesn't get stronger with repetition.'

She was interrupted by the photograph that Malenkov slid across the table, and which came to a halt against her folded hands. She looked at it, this time lowering her head so he could not see her eyes inevitably widening at what she saw. She looked silently at a copy of the picture Nick had taken of her, at Dorogomilovsky market. Her heart beat faster, but she kept her composure, despite this damning intervention.

'That is you, Svetlana Yuriyevna, and I believe the pictures in the background were painted by Yakov Katenin. I also think you are a very good reporter, which makes me believe you know Katenin painted those pictures.'

She said nothing. Actually, right then, she didn't know what to say.

'I'll ask you again: what do you know of Yakov Katenin?'

'I know he paints, because you've just told me, and you think he's a traitor.'

'I was hoping for a little more co-operation. How can I put it? A little more realism.'

'Can I go now?'

'Of course. You're not under arrest. You volunteered, remember?'

She rose to her feet. Malenkov had the good grace not to seek to shake her hand.

'I'll show you to the exit,' he said.

'It's all right, I remember the way. I'll show myself out.'

She turned back to face him as she reached the door.

'Don't come to my home again. Don't speak to my son.'

'If you stay away from Katenin, I won't need to,' he said, replacing his spectacles on his nose.

Chapter 16

Dubnikov reclined in his chair, his feet resting on the desk as he took a brief nap. The ring of his phone interrupted his slumber and he wearily reached for the receiver.

'Yes...?'

'The girls are here. Can you inspect them?' said his assistant.

'Is it necessary?'

'It's your investment.'

'My investment... Yes, I suppose I should inspect my investment. Okay, I'll be down shortly.'

He swung his feet from the desk, stood and stretched, before making for the door of his office and out onto the wooden staircase, which creaked with each foot-fall. His mobile rang.

'Svetlana.'

'I need to see you about something. If I came over in twenty minutes would that be all right?'

'Well, I am popular all of a sudden. Of course, I'm always happy to see you...'

He looked at the screen of his phone but it added nothing to what she'd said. He carried on descending. When he reached the ground floor, he walked across the grey, ice-covered courtyard behind the building and slid back the heavy steel door of the warehouse. In the cold, the steam from his breath entered first. A gaggle of young women were standing in the corner, some shivering. He walked over to them past steel girders supporting the high, whitewashed ceiling, a home to numerous spiders' webs.

'Stand up!' barked Vadik, as Dubnikov drew near, an officer ready to inspect the guard.

The girls stood involuntarily to attention. Dubnikov walked along the line of them, stopping from time to time to stroke hair or feel the firmness of a thigh or breast. A girl who looked about fifteen, but was probably younger, showed tracks of tears across her pretty, slightly grubby face. He looked at her but said nothing. *Fine*, he thought, her tears marked her out as one that would not make trouble and she would be a good earner. Next to her, with tinted hair and dark eyes, was this group's apparent troublemaker, slouched, insolent and chewing gum.

'What's your name?' he asked.

'Zolushka,' she smirked, announcing the character westerners know as Cinderella.

'Well, welcome, Zolushka. I have plenty of charming princes waiting to meet you.'

'Fuck you!' she snarled, spitting her gum into his face.

Dubnikov moved on. He heard but didn't actually see the blow from Vadik that dropped her to the filthy concrete floor, where she landed with a dull thud. It was a pity she'd be out of action for a few days, but setting the example was worth it. None of the other girls dared move to help her. They would now help him, instead.

'I want you all to think of this as a hotel. I am the manager and you will be looking after the guests. Like all good hotels, we look after our guests well. I don't like to hear reports of poor service. If, however, I do, I will tell him and he will tell you, so you are clear what's expected of you.'

Vadik grinned at the girls, making sure, with the exception of the unconscious heap on the floor, that they knew how much he was looking forward to receiving bad news.

Occasionally, when a new group arrived, if Dubnikov liked the look of one of them, he'd take her into the corner to give him a blow job. He thought it a bit like sampling the wine of a newly opened case. He was giving serious consideration to the youngster with the tears, when his mobile rang.

'Yes...? Okay, tell her I'm on my way.'

He nodded a passing goodbye at Vadik, who acknowledged him with a wave.

*

'Sveta, welcome!' said Dubnikov, as he took his seat behind the desk. 'To what do I owe this visit?'

'I might need a bit of extra help.'

'What kind of help?'

'Malenkov, at Lubyanka.'

'Wait a minute, Sveta. You know we don't do FSB.'

'And Dolgonosov?'

'Is purely a business arrangement, but if you've come here to ask for the sort of help I think you want, then this is going to be a short conversation.'

'The bastard went to my home, questioned Ivan.'

'I'm sorry... but I did try to warn you, in my own way.'

'I know.'

'What did he want?'

'He's after a source?'

'And the American, is Malenkov after him too?'

'I don't know.'

'What does your source say?'

'I've not spoken to him.'

'Huh, not much of a source. Let Malenkov have him.'

'No, I can't. I made a promise to somebody very special.'

He sat forward, putting his hands on the front edge of the desk.

'Sveta, I have to say I admire you, but you can be stubborn. I have to co-exist with the FSB. I may do some business with them, here and there, which is one thing but go up against them...? That's not possible, even for you.'

'Can you at least watch out for Ivan – and Nick – Mr Mendez?'

Dubnikov smiled.

'I'll see what I can do.'

'Thanks,' said Svetlana, rising to leave.

'Come again soon, Sveta.'

*

They actually saw it coming, but when the puck hit the perspex in front of their seats, the loud thwack still made them jump. Dynamo were taking on Moscow rivals, Spartak, and there was a capacity crowd in high spirits. She hadn't been joking when she said she enjoyed hockey. Dima had been a big fan of Dynamo for many years, so Svetlana had taken up supporting them, too. The irony that they were the ex-KGB team was not lost on her, although the merger, while strengthening resources, had diluted the team's receding security service history. Right now, clothed in tight black jeans, blue jumper and a Dynamo scarf, she was swept up in the game as it ebbed and flowed.

'Come on – come on – pass!' she shouted, her words rising to mingle with the cacophony created by those of thousands of others.

Nick watched her revel in the moment, as a Dynamo player violently body checked his opponent right in front of their seats, leading to a flurry of punches and counterpunches that the frantic whistling of the referee struggled to break up. Two departures to the sin-bin followed, at which she was on her feet, pointing an accusing finger.

'It's a bloody disgrace! Referee, you should be ashamed!'

She turned to Nick.

'Did you see that? Did you see that?'

He nodded and smiled.

'No way – no way should he have been sent off! The other guy was behaving like a girl!' she exclaimed.

Nick smiled again and held out his palms to indicate his bafflement that this piece of out-and-out thuggery had resulted in such a penalty.

At the end of the second period, the scores were tied on 3 – 3 and Nick indicated they should take a break for a quick coffee. They made their way along the row where a couple of apparent helping hands took the opportunity to have a feel of Svetlana's lovely bottom as she passed by. She'd long given up protesting as it just appeared to be part of the ice hockey scene.

He ordered milky coffee for both of them and passed hers to her.

'Thanks,' she said, her voice having acquired a slightly husky tone from all the shouting she'd been doing.

'It's quite a game. They sure don't hold back here in Moscow!'

He took in her piercing look.

'Why hold back?'

He didn't know what to respond with. Too late, he'd lost the moment as she smiled and let out a little snort.

'What time are you leaving for the airport?'

'I need to be on the road by about ten-fifteen.'

'Okay, no problem. I'll catch the metro.'

'I'll take you.'

'You'll be late.'

'No, I'd prefer to take you.'

She sipped her coffee and looked at him over the rim of her cup.

'Is she pretty?'

His nervous grin answered first.

'Who?'

'Victoria, your PA.'

'She's not my PA now, and yes, she's pretty. Does that bother you?'

'Should it?'

'No.'

'Then it doesn't. Come on, let's get back.'

They went in to see the scores still tied. Nick took his seat and Svetlana, having skilfully negotiated fifteen metres of grope run, regained hers. As the minutes ticked down, the match became pulsating. Nick had to admit it: the atmosphere was every bit as good as a night at the Bruins. A counter-attack down the right drew a collective breath of anticipation as Dynamo players swept by, exchanging short passes. A sharp clack heralded the cross from which they scored low down to the Spartak goalkeeper's left. As one, the Dynamo fans rose letting out a gigantic roar of approval. Svetlana punched the air and turned to Nick, hugging him in a celebratory embrace. He held her in return, enjoying the sporting thrill of the moment but also the feeling of her breasts, for once not covered by a fur coat, pressed against his chest. He released her and sat, before his now growing erection became too obvious. He calmed himself before the final whistle went, which was met with thunderous applause.

They made their way out of the stadium and down to the car park. Nick held the door for Svetlana as, wrapped once again in her coat and gloves, she slipped into the front passenger seat. She smiled as he closed the door.

He glanced at his watch.

'I can catch the metro, you know. It's no problem.'

'No, we're fine.'

Svetlana briefly smiled. He saw it from the corner of his eye.

'Nikolai, Malenkov has a copy of the picture you took of me at Dorogomilovsky.'

'What?'

'The picture, is it still on your camera?' she asked.

'No, on my laptop... but how did he get that?'

'I don't know. He already knew about Katenin, but it just draws you in more. You need to be more careful... And, don't take any more pictures of me!'

'I'm sorry. I never thought there'd be a problem.'

'That's just it, Nikolai Ivanovich, you didn't think, and from now on you're going to have to.'

He felt chastised, but wasn't sure she was angry. As they drove on, he felt her reassuring hand on his shoulder.

Later, she stepped from the car outside her apartment and shut the door while he lowered the passenger window to bid her a final goodbye. She put her head through the window.

'Thanks, I had a great time.'

'Me too.'

'By the way, did you like my tits?'

'Yes...' he spluttered.

'I noticed. Drive safely, Nikolai.'

*

'Nicky, you're going to have to practise a bit more,' said Nick, as the lights of oncoming traffic danced unpredictably in front of him.

He was still fifteen kilometres from Sheremetyevo and it was already twenty-two-fifty, but he reckoned he'd be fine, given the passport and visa delays he'd had himself. *The journey back to the centre should be okay*, he thought, as the BMW he was driving had sat-nav and he'd be able to program their hotel straight in, as long as the girls hadn't chosen something really obscure.

His mind drifted back to Madrid, where he recalled himself immersed in the bustle of his favourite tapas bar, felt the caress of the warm sun as he strolled through Parque del Retiro and watched smiles, lots of smiles. His attention was swiftly returned to the M10 motorway as a huge truck sounded its horn, when Nick's car drifted into its path. He accelerated away from the angry beast, resolving to keep his mind on the road from then on.

By eleven-fifteen, he was parking up in Terminal D's car park, where he selected a luggage trolley, unsure as to whether there'd be any free in the terminal itself. This one shared the wayward genes of every trolley he'd ever selected, or maybe he was just unlucky with trolleys. He and his recalcitrant companion made their way across to the terminal building, the grey night sky not doing justice to its vast spans of glass.

Of course, he'd been right about passport delays. By half-past midnight, there was still no sign of them, despite their plane having arrived only five minutes late.

'Have you got a light?' asked a *dedushka*, shuffling past.

Nick raised his eyebrows and pointed to the nearby no smoking sign.

'Shithead,' came the response, as the old man moved on.

'Nick – Nick!'

He looked up and there coming towards him was Victoria, with her equally attractive friend. Within seconds, she'd crossed the fifteen metres separating them and was hugging Nick, planting kisses on each of his cheeks.

'Wow! Vicki, that's quite a welcome. It hasn't been that long.'

'It's so good to see you. I missed you. It's just not the same in Madrid, without you.'

He stepped back to look at her.

'You look great!' I brought you a trolley.'

'I'd have preferred flowers,' she joked, grinning cheekily. 'Anyway, we have a trolley.'

She turned to indicate Pilar, five-six tall, early twenties, with silky, olive skin and a ready smile.

'This is Pilar. She's attractive, no?'

'Very. Hi, Pilar, I'm Nick.'

'Hi, Nick. It's good to meet at last. Vicki has told me lots about you.'

'Good stuff, I hope.'

The two girls giggled. Nick suddenly felt the age gap between him and them.

'Come on, the car's across the road. Here, let me push that,' he said, stepping forward.

They made their way to the car park, Nick pushing the trolley, with Victoria and Pilar just behind him.

'He's cuter than on the TV, Vicki,' whispered Pilar.

Nick just wanted to be back at his apartment. He was beginning to feel like a father picking his daughter and her friend up from a party.

In the car he switched on the sat-nav, while Victoria sat next to him up front and Pilar settled in the back seat.

'Where are you staying, Vicki?'

She shuffled through her papers, looking for the hotel voucher.

'It's the Belgrad. Do you know it?'

'Heard of it, but don't know where it is, exactly.'

'It says here, Calle Smolensk.'

'Oh, Smolenskaya ulitsa. Yeah, I know that.'

He put the details in the sat-nav, nevertheless, thinking he needed all the help he could get until he'd driven a bit more in Moscow.

'How long are you staying?'

'Three weeks.'

'Three weeks! I hope you've brought plenty of money. This place is more expensive than Madrid, you know.'

'Pilar runs the money. She's brilliant at finding bargains.'

'I hope so.'

'And anyway, you'll be able to show us a few places, won't you?'

'I'll see what I can do, but I'm pretty busy at the moment.'

They drove down the motorway towards the city, mostly in silence, as the two girls took in the sights and began to come to terms with the contrast in climate. Nick was about to reach for the radio, when Victoria spoke.

'Do you have a girlfriend here?'

His reply was much too quick.

'No.'

'What's she like?'

'I have a friend, not a girlfriend.'

Victoria drew her legs up on the seat and turned towards him. This appeared much more interesting than the apartment blocks standing sentry along the route.

'Well, what's your friend like?'

'She's nice.'

'And...?'

'There's not much to say.'

'Ahh, you like her, don't you?'

Nick shrugged. He was just an amateur at relationship interrogation and, young as she was, Victoria was out of his league on this one.

'What's her name?'

'Svetlana.'

'Is she a spy?'

'No,' said Nick, laughing nervously. 'She's a journalist.'

'I'm looking forward to meeting her,' said Victoria, reaching out a finger and touching him on the arm.

She turned to Pilar and the two of them sniggered conspiratorially.

*

When he arrived back at the apartment, Nick switched on his laptop to check his email. While he'd only done it a couple of weeks ago, something made him change his password again. He thought he'd do it weekly, from now on.

There was mail from Svetlana, inviting him over for supper, the next night. He replied, confirming he'd be there. There was another email he didn't recognise. He opened it.

'How the fuck did you get my private email?' he enquired out loud, before realising his naivety.

He read on. Was this some sort of code? If so, it was working as he had no idea what it all meant. The author was 'Peter'. *Peter – Peter – Peter who?*

'Hubbard! It's you, isn't it?' he said. 'What is it you want now? What's this all about? I tell you, Hubbard, or whatever your name is, all this spy-type shit just makes you look stupid.'

He looked again, his mind dulled from the lateness of the hour. He recalled the mantra of his favourite lecturer as a student, 'Look for the keys and the door will open', by which he'd meant: find the key points of a story, and the detail would follow. The words on the screen made no sense collectively, so Nick started to try to pick out key phrases, scribbling them down on a piece of paper and hoping for inspiration. Twenty minutes later, he was no further on, until he tried reversing the words. That was it! The text was mostly an extract from a weather forecast, but in the middle, there was a sentence that did make sense. *I've left two tickets for you at the Bolshoi box office. I hope she enjoys it.*

'You're a jerk, Hubbard, a stuck-up, British jerk... but thanks for the tickets,' he said, as he shut down his computer.

'So, that's the hockey and the ballet. What next?'

He switched off the light and made for a well-earned rest, hoping to dream.

Chapter 17

For Yakov Katenin, painting in the pale light of dawn was far from ideal but the chances of being caught then were lessened, and anyway he was confident in his technique, familiar with the colours of the cards. He'd slept with the spray cans next to his skin, inside his old but thick clothes. In this way, he could keep the paint useable, when otherwise it would have frozen. When he'd first arrived, it was more difficult. He'd slept rough at Kursky station, watching and learning from the street children, but now he'd found a spot in the roof space of an old apartment building, next to the head of the elevator shaft. Of course, the motors were a pain but with time he'd grown used to it as those living next to railway tracks ceased to really notice trains passing by. An old mattress he'd recovered from a roadside skip and installed in his hiding place gave him the chance to sleep, provided he wrapped up well against the cold, which given the damage to his lungs he was careful to do.

He'd done lots of landscapes as a kid, but later had become proficient at portraits after drawing and painting innumerable images of his own wiry frame, deep-set eyes and brown hair, reflected in his bedroom mirror.

In the foreground, he completed the balance of Andrei's face, with a second staring, frightened eye to match the one on the card at Kursky. When he'd finished the head and shoulders, which would complete the anonymous torso at Dorogomilovsky, he stepped back to check his work. It was Andrei all right, and a good likeness, not of his usual self, but at the moment of his terrified death.

'I miss you, Andryusha... my friend.'

Katenin bowed his head and thought well of his departed comrade. He stayed like that for some seconds, until a scampering alley cat ran across his foot and startled him.

He shook the spray cans once again and bent the stiffened bristles of his brush. With deliberate but flowing sweeps, the form of an army officer began to take shape, missing a hand but arm outstretched and his shoulders broad, beneath the uniform of a major. The face acquired features and fury in equal measure, as the ranting, flushed image of Rebikov became clear for waiting witnesses. He finished the border of the card with practised ease, before adding the flourish of a heart in one corner and a joker in another. His work was done. Now, it was the turn of others.

*

When Svetlana reached the office, Vasiliy was waiting for her at her desk.

'Have you heard?' he asked.

'Heard? Heard what?'

'Eduard Lyakhov's been shot!'

'No. When?'

'Just this morning, on the way to his office.'

She slumped into her chair and then sat forward, with head in hands. Vasiliy fidgeted uneasily.

Lyakhov was an eloquent lawyer. His style was to use few words to reduce arguments to their simplest and most understandable form. In his career, he'd taken a similar approach. Something was either right or it was wrong and he'd chosen to follow right, as he saw it. He'd represented a good number of journalists who had faced political pressure, designed to silence them.

'I told him – I told him,' said Svetlana, almost whispering.

Vasiliy mumbled.

'Why? Why?' she asked, volume returning to her voice.

'Because he did what was right... like you,' said Demchi, who'd arrived, unseen.

She lifted her head from her hands and looked at him, struggling to hold back the tears of sadness.

'I don't always do right, but he did. Why, Demchi?'

'Come with me.'

Without protest, she rose from her seat and followed her editor to his office.

When he put his arms round her to console her, she began to cry, this moment without hope leaving her drained and directionless. He held her as a father would a daughter.

Later, they sat together with tea in the corner of his room. There was not really much to say. They knew the territory, they'd been there before and knew they would be again. Lyakhov had been one of those individuals who'd had no choice. He'd have hated to live in any other way than the path he'd chosen.

'When's the funeral? Do you know?'

'Not yet,' replied Demchi softly.

She closed her eyes.

'Do you ever go to sleep wishing you could wake up in another place – another time?' she asked.

'Yes.'

'Demchi, sometimes I feel so feeble. I used to be strong – every day – but not now.'

'You're human, not a machine.'

'Sometimes I think it would be easier to be a machine in this city.'

She opened her eyes to see Demchi's benign smile. He took a cigarette from the packet on the coffee table next to him and then put it back down.

'Have you spoken to Mariya?' she asked.

'I called. Spoke to their son. He said she was with the funeral director.'

'I'll go to see her, poor woman.'

'No, I'll go. Edik and I went back a long way. I can speak for all of us.'

'But –'

'Sveta, I'll go.'

Demchi lit his cigarette and took a long drag on it, before smoke streamed from his nostrils. She watched the paper burn down and looked at the yellow stains on the skin of his fingers, the legacy of thirty a day for more years than she cared to remember.

'Where are you at with the Petrov boy?'

'But, I thought you didn't want to talk about it.'

'We can't run it, but it doesn't mean I'm not interested... or don't care.'

She looked at him as he put the cigarette to his mouth again.

'We think he was poisoned, in a military test.'

'We?'

'Nick, the INN reporter.'

'I thought you meant Vasiliy... but you wouldn't, would you?'

Demchi stared straight at her.

'He wanted to.'

'He's out of his depth – not developed his senses yet.'

'I'm keeping him out of it.'

'How's that? He works with you. How do you keep him out of it?'

She felt his steady look upon her. Demchi had a point. Lately, she had tried to keep Vasiliy away from the boy's case, but of course Demchi was right and her assistant just worked too closely with her to be free of potential trouble. She stayed silent.

'Do you know who did it?' asked Demchi.

'No, but there's clues?'

'What kind of clues?'

'Pictures – street paintings.'

'Any good?'

She looked at him, unsure.

'The paintings, are they any good?'

'They're a series of playing cards. They scare me.'

Demchi pulled a face, as he struggled to find room in his overpopulated glass ash-tray to stub out his cigarette.

'What does the American say?'

'He's going to help.'

'Oh yeah? Is he going to send the FSB on leave for you?'

'Malenkov's already warned me off.'

'Of course he has. Sveta, leave it while you still can. You have a son.'

'That's what he said.'

'Then leave it. Back off. I'm already going to be saying a few words at Edik's funeral, but I don't want to be speaking at yours.'

*

Whenever she was feeling a little sorry for herself, as she was now, Svetlana thought of Marina and Sasha, fending for themselves and living rough at Kursky station. She'd not seen them for a while and decided to visit. Of course, Nick was coming round for supper and she still needed to shop but her local Perekrestok would be open until late, so she could pick up the fresh ingredients she needed from there.

While Savelovskaya was actually a bit closer to the office, she preferred Belorusskaya as a station and usually walked there, instead.

The station offered relief from the chill outside as she walked to her platform. While a flexible neck was advisable to see them at their best, she always enjoyed looking at the octagonal, brightly coloured mosaics in the elegantly sculpted white ceiling above. Of course, the scenes of idealistic, Belarusian peasant life were not how it was, but it always gave Svetlana a moment of escape for her imagination, when she could feel sun on her skin and the smell of hay in her nostrils. It was strange, in all this time she'd only been once to Belarus when visiting Minsk with Dima, before Ivan was born. Maybe that was why she liked this station so much, because it reminded her of a happy time when her heart could fly high with hope and expectation.

As the train made its way, she scanned through a copy of *Novaya Gazeta* she'd picked up on the way to Belorusskaya. She read a variety of other papers whenever she could, reckoning that studying different journalists' styles would give her own an edge. She could see no mention of Lyakhov. Maybe the story had broken too late, or perhaps another dead human rights lawyer just wasn't news any more.

Approaching the escalator, Svetlana took careful, deliberate steps as the heels on the particular boots she was wearing were a bit narrow and last week she'd had to hang on to the handrail as one of them had slipped from under her. Reaching the summit, just as a nearby tannoy broadcast an announcement, Svetlana covered her ears and made her way across the concourse in the direction of her favourite café. She recognised one of Marina's friends and asked after her, but the young girl shook her head and shrugged. There was no sign of Marina or Sasha.

Svetlana ordered tea and waited. It struck her, following the discussion with Demchi, that she'd better speak to Vasiliy.

'Vasya, hi, it's Sveta. Look, you need to know Demchi spoke to me about Petrov, about you...'

'Is he worried?' asked Vasiliy.

'Of course he's worried. Look, we'll have coffee in the morning and talk about it...'

'Fine, with me.'

'Okay, bye, Vasya.'

She stirred her tea and pressed the lemon slice with her spoon. She thought about Nick and as she did the near and far noises of the station receded. Snapshots of him appeared in her mind, one after another: the fool who'd tripped her up, naive in the back of a patrol car, confident in a broadcast and kissing her in a lift. She smiled. *Better wear the Cavalli*, she thought. She ran the tip of her finger across her palm, wondering if his touch would be so sensitive.

'Who knows?' she whispered.

Her thoughts drifted to Ivan. For so many years, he'd been the man in her life, offering her companionship and in his own way loyalty as she'd watched him grow. Her personal romantic hopes had been put on hold as she'd led him away from the ruins of her marriage to Dima and tried to mend him, as well as she could. He was making good progress at school according to his teachers, and was becoming a star of the ice hockey team. Her mother thought Svetlana over-protective and counselled her to allow Ivan a bit more freedom to develop.

'He'll find his own way,' she'd say. 'There comes a time, Sveta, when you realise you can only guide them.'

If that was so, then what about this American? If she let him into her life, would he have wisdom and be a good guide for Ivan?

The end of her spoon had become hot from standing in the tea. She held it between her thumb and forefinger, closed her eyes and imagined the warmth making its way up her arm and into her body. A tap on the shoulder brought her out of her daydream.

'Guess who.'

'Hello, Sasha. How's it going?'

He sat next to her, his stale odour indicating that it had been some time since he'd had a wash. She wrinkled her nose and then decided just to deal with it.

'How's Marina?'

'Not seen her for two days.'

'Is she in trouble?'

'Don't think so. She's missing sometimes; always comes back.'

Svetlana felt better for Sasha's casual reassurance.

'Do you want a drink?'

'Yes – and four hundred. Have you money?'

'Another one? You've found another one?'

Sasha grinned and nodded, tapping his finger on his chest.

'Myself, I found it.'

'Where? Just a minute, if you found it yourself, how come it's four hundred?'

'Two for me and two for the one who found it. That's me!'

She broke into laughter at his cheek and ingenuity. She wondered what he might achieve if he could ever get himself out of there.

'What do you want to drink?' she asked, as she rose, still chuckling.

*

Sasha led her to the most northerly exit from Kurskaya metro, where they emerged on Nizhniy Susal'nyy pereulok. Snow was now falling. The young boy had no hat but seemed oblivious as he strode into the stiff breeze. *I'll buy him one*, she thought. He took her to an alley between two brick built office buildings and there, just a few metres in and visible from the street, was the playing card Svetlana had been looking for. She studied it, while Sasha turned his back to the wind and wiped snowflakes from his eyebrows.

'Thank you, Sasha. You've earned four hundred... and a new hat.'

Sasha grinned, but then wrapped his arms around himself. Svetlana resolved to get him back to Kursky, where a hot chocolate would revive him but needed to quickly take a photograph. She had only her mobile with her but its camera was good and if she could just stop the snow for a moment, there'd be a decent enough image. Loath as she was, she slipped off her long fur coat and immediately felt the cold penetrate through to her skin.

'Sasha, hold this up a moment to block the snow.'

The boy stepped forward and held the coat as if a curtain, allowing Svetlana just enough time to take a couple of shots, before she put it back on and set off for the station.

*

She left Sasha with his hot drink, while she tracked down a hat for him. She selected a thick woollen one that he could pull down over his ears. She hoped he'd keep it, at least for a while.

As she walked through the main entrance at Kursky on her way back, her trained eye clocked two FSB agents looking at passengers entering and exiting. One held a photograph in his hand, glancing at it repeatedly. Her journalist's curiosity kicked in, and having walked past them, she doubled back to try to catch a glimpse of the image that was so occupying them. Just a couple of paces away, she stopped, as if adjusting her boot, before rising slowly to look over the elbow of the nearest officer. Her glimpse took a second, maybe two, before she moved on, anxious not to arouse suspicion. *So, Yakov, that's what you look like*, she thought. There was no reason why the likeness she'd just seen was Katenin. It could have been any young soldier but her instinct told her it was him.

'I hope you have somewhere to hide. Run there, now,' she whispered.

She tried to put a voice to the face she was having her imaginary conversation with. Its tone would be one with courage and sensitivity, as befits an artist, and somewhere in there would be note of vengeance. Normally, her informers were people she'd see over and over again. They'd slip her snippets of news for a small reward, safe in the knowledge she'd always keep their anonymity. This informer? No, not this one. His news was far too big, too dangerous. They would work together just this one time and might never meet. For him, the net had now been cast upon the water and if he didn't swim away to a safer place, he would be caught. He'd been lucky, so far, she figured or maybe cunning but would either of those qualities now step in to save him? Suddenly, she longed to see him, to thank him for his bravery but also to tell him to flee. Merit often had nothing to do with who lived and who died in Moscow but Katenin, she figured, deserved to see what he could make of the rest of his young life.

'But, Yakov, if they saw you... with me?'

She didn't need an answer to her own question.

As she walked back into the café, she could see that Sasha had stopped shivering but his still pale hands were wrapped around the last vestiges of warmth from his mug of chocolate. She presented him with his hat, which he enthusiastically pulled on. He gave her a thumbs-up sign and a beaming smile. She ached for him when he smiled like that, in response to someone caring for him. It was a rare sight. Suddenly, he appeared guarded, perhaps wondering if some discount might be sought for the gift.

'I've earned my money, haven't I?'

'Yes, Sasha, I think you have.'

She reached into her bag, took out her purse and discretely counted out four hundred rubles, while the young boy's eyes followed the fall of every note.

'Shall I keep some for you? Some savings?'

He sniggered at her apparent joke, grasped the money and stuffed it in his pocket, while shooting quick glances around him for anybody else who might know of his financial windfall. Seemingly safe in the knowledge that only the two of them knew, he turned to Svetlana.

'These pictures, who is it? What's happening?'

'It's best you don't know,' replied Svetlana.

He fell silent, his eyes falling in the direction of his ragged brown shoes.

'Sasha: what?'

'My mum used to say that.'

She could have kicked herself. Whatever he was thinking in his silence, it was bad, she figured.

'Sasha, I'm sorry... Sasha.'

She took his hand but it made no difference. He stood stock-still. They were like this for maybe a full minute before her pressing palm broke through his trance. He looked at her, his cheeky grin returning as quickly as it had left.

'Are there any more?'

'More?'

'You know, pictures.'

'I don't think so.'

'Shame... Okay, I gotta go.'

With that, he turned on his heels and was gone, no doubt, she thought, for an urgent engagement with the nearby gaming machines that he would more readily feed than himself.

Svetlana took her mobile from her bag and brought up the photo she'd just taken. She'd forward it to Nick.

You owe me 400. See you about 7, she wrote in her text, before pushing the send button.

She stood, her chair scraping noisily across the café floor as she did. She made a mental note to try not to do that again.

*

By the time Svetlana arrived home with the shopping, Nick was waiting for her.

'Sorry I'm late. Has Ivan not let you in?'

'I knocked, but there was no answer.'

She opened the door, to find a note from Ivan saying he was going to stay at his grandmother's and not to worry.

'What's wrong with a little communication?' said Svetlana, pointing to the note.

Nick picked up the lined piece of paper, before smiling.

'He is communicating.'

'What's wrong with speech? Do all teenage boys forget to speak?'

'Mostly.'

She looked skywards, before moving to the kitchen with the two bags of food she'd brought from the supermarket.

'Is *baranina* okay?'

'Yeah, great.'

'I've got *morskaya* for starters; they're not homemade,' she said, as she unpacked the bags.

'Is this your mum?' asked Nick.

She put her head round the door of the kitchen to see Nick holding a silver frame containing a black and white picture of her mother.

'Yes. She was beautiful, wasn't she?'

'Still is, no doubt.'

'Pretty good, for her age.'

'You have her eyes.'

'Sure, of course. Help yourself to a glass of wine. I'm going to change, while the oven heats up.

She moved with long elegant strides across the living room and reached for the handle of her bedroom door.

Soon, seated at the dressing table, her favourite brush slowly stroked her thick, dark hair, which gently stretched and then recoiled with each sweep of her hand. She smelled her wrist, concluding that the Chanel Allure that was one of her favourites was in need of revival. She sprayed a refresher, fascinated by the apparently weightless mist illuminated by the lights surrounding her mirror. In the reflection, she saw her underwear draw and turned to look at it, before seeking reassurance from her twin in the mirror. They showed each other the same conspiratorial grin for a second or two, before she reached across and opened it, taking out her treasured Cavalli bra and thong.

She closed her eyes to maximise the sensation as she slowly drew the delicate black lace over her feet and along the creamy skin of her toned legs. When the gorgeous fabric had nestled into place, she stroked herself momentarily to celebrate the partnership of two such feminine companions, before tugging slightly on the thong to feel it tighten between the cheeks of her still taught bottom. Standing now, her delicious breasts disappeared into the cups of the matching bra as she seamlessly linked the hook and eye behind her.

Nick was flicking through CDs when Svetlana emerged, wearing drawstring black linen trousers lightly hugging her hips and her favourite lilac sweater that just revealed the first couple of centimetres of her cleavage.

'Put one on... anything you like,' she said, as she passed him en route to the kitchen.

'What do you like?' he asked.

'You choose.'

'She slipped a plain apron over her head to protect her clothes as she prepared their meal, but within she felt sexy. She cooked as if a mistress anticipating the arrival of her forbidden married lover, secretly longing to capture permanently his affection. That was not her, of course, but she was enjoying the mischief of the moment.

The sound of Fernando Perez, singing in English, drifted into the kitchen. She called out to Nick.

'Missing Spain, are you?'

'No, just like his stuff,' he shouted back, above the music.

Protecting her hand with an oven glove, she pushed a white dish across the bars of the first shelf of the oven and shut the door. There were forty-five minutes to wait. She poured herself a glass of wine and joined him.

Nick turned down the music, before picking up an alabaster piece from the chess set, next to the television.

'It's a nice set.'

'It's Ivan's. His grandmother bought it for his tenth birthday, when he won the junior championship at school.

'He must be good, then.'
'Yes, but he doesn't play enough now.'
'Computers and stuff?'
'You know how it is,' replied Svetlana.
'Do you play?'
'Of course.'
'Do you fancy a game?'
'You play?'
'I have Russian blood, remember,' said Nick.

She bent over to pick up the board, setting it down on the coffee table. He reached forward and arranged the pieces, while she manoeuvred an armchair into position to sit opposite him.

He started boldly, a little recklessly, she thought, while her early moves were designed to protect the key participants for later battle. Within twenty minutes, he'd already lost a rook and a knight for the meagre exchange from her of a single pawn.

'Perhaps you need to be more careful.'
'I like to attack.'
'You do, don't you? I'm going to check on the food – no cheating.'
'Nothing's worth winning by cheating.'
'Always?'
'Always.'

She drew a deep breath and leant forward a little, allowing him to catch a glimpse of more of her cleavage, before she stood.

Svetlana returned from the kitchen bearing cutlery and quickly set two places on the simple white tablecloth, atop the small dining table.

'You do move like a ballet dancer.'
'Really?'
'I have two tickets, for the Bolshoi.'
'Lucky you,' she sniggered.
'Don't make fun. They're tickets for us.'

She simply smiled at him, reassuring him that she was pleased with his indirect invitation.

'Come and sit at the table. We can eat now.'

She brought in their *morskaya*.

'Can I have some more wine, please?'

'Sure,' replied Svetlana.

She reached for the bottle and re-filled his glass, before filling her own.

Within minutes, he'd finished his first course.

'You're hungry, Nikolai.'

'Had to skip lunch to work with my editor.'

Svetlana lit a small candle, placed it between them, and then rose to fetch more food.

Nick seemed to take more time with his main course. Svetlana watched him through her wine glass. She thought him more handsome than she'd originally supposed. He must have shaved early, for tonight, there was a distinct shadow on his chin and his slightly crumpled blue shirt showed he'd come straight from work.

'This is great.'

'Glad you like it. How's your PA, what's her name?'

'Victoria.'

'Yes, Victoria.'

'Fine, I guess; not spoken to her today.'

'Oh.'

She sipped some wine and let it roll around her tongue. He looked puzzled at her question. She was puzzled she'd asked.

As the candle flickered, it projected an orange glow onto his face, which danced, seemingly in time with the music. She tried to guess where it would move next, until he picked up his glass to drink.

'Are we going to finish the game?' asked Nick.

'Of course. It's important for you to try and win,' said Svetlana, looking him straight in the eye.

She met his quizzical look.

'For your prize, Nikolai.'

'Prize?'

'Me, Nikolai, I'm the prize. If you can beat me, you can have me... tonight.'

She looked at him as he struggled not to choke on the mouthful of wine he'd just taken, his initial look of shock giving way to a widening grin that she returned fearlessly.

'Are your mother and father going to visit, do you think?' she asked coolly.

'Probably not.'

'What about your boss, from Madrid?'

'No.'

'Would you like coffee?'

'No, thanks.'

'Well, the dishes can wait... Shall we...?'

Svetlana pushed her chair back without taking her eyes off him. She was cheating, of course. The poor man's senses were scrambled just when he needed to be in control of them. She was half way to victory already and enjoying every moment. Her extended palm indicated the waiting chess board and its expectant characters.

Nick sat back down on the settee, apparently contemplating his next move. Svetlana covered her mouth to hide a developing grin as she realised the hand reaching out for his remaining knight was now trembling slightly, when previously it had been steady. The hand withdrew to repeatedly stroke his stubbly chin. She waited, moving silence to the fore in her parallel game that he seemed not to be aware he was playing. Svetlana had already analysed the moves he could make with the knight, all of them poor from his point of view. She was ready with a response. The hand returned to the knight, opting for a move that took it to a more advanced position but out of personal danger. She said nothing as she moved a rook through the just vacated space and took one of the bishops he could have used to sweep diagonally across the board in the later stages of the game. Within half an hour, he had lost three pawns and two more significant pieces. The queen, so valuable for her flexibility and potential, looked threatened at every moment in this game, which was slipping away from him.

She excused herself for a moment, returning with two shot glasses and a bottle of cold vodka.

'Here.'

'Is that for courage?' asked Nick.

'Nikolai, shut up and drink it. It will help you play like a Russian.'

'Huh, right.'

Little by little and subtly, she allowed him to claw his way back into the game as she left him the odd opening to exploit. Nearly an hour passed, with hardly a word spoken, as she manoeuvred him slowly into a winning position. At last, she watched, waiting for his hand to seize the moment and move his queen to take hers, leaving her king at complete mercy, in checkmate. Svetlana had to bite her lip to stifle the 'No' which she was about to exclaim, as his fingertip rested on the remaining rook he had, ready it seemed to make an alternative move. He didn't look up, but perhaps her intake of breath was an interruption enough to make him pause and reflect. Changing hands, he knocked over Svetlana's queen.

'Checkmate!' he said, rising to his feet.

She looked up at him from under her dark eyelashes to see his hand extended towards her. She took it as a knowing grin began on her face.

*

She already knew from the gentle and playful way he'd started his advance upon her as they'd entered the bedroom that he was capable of great tenderness. Later, she'd be able to reflect on his light touch as he'd caressed her stomach with the back of his hand, before it had swept up and turned to cup her breast, holding it as his mouth descended to envelop a firm, proud nipple. She'd remember too the tip of his tongue as it made its way along the ridge of her thigh, en route to its soft but insistent massage as her wetness had begun, in readiness for him. Underneath she'd felt his pent-up passion and she'd sent hers out to meet him head-on, encouraging him, willing him not to wait, urging him to be bold and set aside his manners. She'd finally released him as she interrupted the urgent rhythm of her mouth on his cock.

'I'm yours, Nikolai,' she said.

She reached down between her long slender legs to guide his eager manhood into her, momentarily, almost unconsciously assessing him for length and girth as her fingers wrapped around it. While she wanted no mercy, she was nevertheless taken aback at the force with which he entered her prepared and willing body. She gasped involuntarily as his fabulous, rampaging advance pushed aside velvet walls and impaled her to the hilt. She reached out and clasped her hands to his buttocks, extending the moment. Still she held him, her nails pressing a centimetre down into his flesh. Her hands moved to his head, fingers running through his hair as their mouths joined and he was released to feast upon his willing prey. She met his almost savage thrusts, revelling in his masculinity and her total surrender to it. He did not stop and left her no respite, her lungs struggling to catch breath between her own cries of pleasure.

'Come on, Nick, come on!'

His exertions seemed to allow him no air or energy for a spoken reply but her shameless urging finally released his pent-up seed. She felt through her fingers the spasms of his body, while agitated pulses, deep inside, announced his emerging climax.

She held no resentment that her own building orgasm had been interrupted, not far from its destination, and she was entirely reassured that her reciprocal reward would not wait long.

'I'm sorry I –'

The tip of her finger on his lips shut him up and she turned on her side to face him as he reached out and gently stroked her hips. They stayed like that, silent and watching, as the sweat dried and breath returned to them.

'Looking back, I never could have imagined this.'

'Looking back, Nikolai, neither could I. What happened to you?'

'You taught me.'

'You learned.'

They looked at each other's eyes closely, both smiling. She could not resist, purposefully and suddenly wiping the smile from her face as she turned her back on him.

'Sveta...?'

'And now, now you have had me, you will move on.'

'No, it's not like that.'

She started to shake as she giggled, leading Nick into laughter.

'Well, lover boy, how will it be?'

'Like this,' said Nick, as he turned her head back to meet his kiss and drew himself up behind her.

Chapter 18

Leonid Kutaisov looked down on the illuminated map of the Baku to Sup'sa pipeline.

'I want us distanced from this, Colonel.'

'Deputy Minister, we plan to be in and out in a day. And if there's any comeback, it'll look like a South Ossetian issue,' said Chernekov.

'No deaths on this one. Georgian relatives have long memories and ask too many questions.'

'The product is ready – non lethal.'

Chernekov leant forward and pointed to the map.

'We're going to take out the installations here, here and here.'

'How long to repair them?' asked Kutaisov.

'A year, at least, maybe more.'

'And we can repeat it?'

'Whenever you want.'

'When are your men going in?'

'We're watching the weather.'

'Keep me posted.'

'Of course, Deputy Minister,' said Chernekov.

He watched Kutaisov climb the short flight of stairs out of the grey-painted operations room, before closing the map program. Its image collapsed into the screen, leaving only his own reflection looking back at him. He saw a man, sure of his role and steadfast in it.

*

Now she'd let him into her life, Svetlana was anxious to learn more about Nick. It mattered. Vasiliy had actually picked up the story, but she'd fed it to Nick and he'd said he was going to use it in his broadcast. The network was running an organised crime themed week and this piece seemed just right.

Demchi had raided the budget to upgrade the cable TV service to the office, so she didn't have far to go to see Nick at work. She flicked through the channels on the remote until the distinctive INN logo appeared, at the top of the screen. Dave Sullivan, daytime news anchor, speaking in English, was breezing through a story about an oil find off the coast of Chile, effortlessly moving his eyes between his written notes and the teleprompter.

'And now, over to Moscow where our correspondent, Nick Mendez, has news of a bank robbery that has the authorities baffled – Nick.'

The picture flickered and then there he was. The normal pause followed, the one where the viewer is just beginning to think there's a fault, before the correspondent begins to speak. Svetlana was unable to hide an affectionate smile as she stared at the screen. There he was, standing outside a branch of Moskovsky Industrialny Bank, the late morning sleet whirling around his heavy, camel-coloured coat, with his hat unwisely removed for the broadcast. He began, in English.

'Thanks, Dave. I'm here outside the Pyatnitskaya Street branch of Moscow Industrial Bank, which was sensationally robbed, yesterday afternoon. I say sensational, because the bank was full of customers and staff but nobody saw anything! CCTV shows staff and members of the public falling to the ground, unconscious, apparently victims of some sort of gas attack – but then tests have shown no trace of anything, which is puzzling investigators. With everybody unconscious, nobody sounded the alarm and the robbers were able to just walk in and help themselves to many millions of rubles. Police captain, Artur Kikorov, told me earlier that they were looking for five masked men, believed to be members of one of Moscow's mafia gangs but that they had no firm leads. Organised crime is a big problem here in Moscow, with the authorities struggling to make headway, coupled with allegations that law enforcers are often on the payroll of the gangsters. Certainly, bank robberies have been on the increase, but this looks like being a really tough one to crack. Nick Mendez, for INN, Moscow.'

'Huh, not bad, Nikolai,' she muttered.

Vasiliy walked in.

'Oh hi, Sveta, here you are.'

'Just watching Nick's report on the Moskovsky Industrialny robbery. It's in English; didn't follow all of it. You got any more news?'

'Nothing. What about Dubnikov?'

'Did it, or knows about it?'

'Either.'

'I'll ask him.'

'How do you disable all those people and leave no trace? It's really odd.'

Svetlana just looked at him, unsure what to say or whether to speak, at all. Was he safer informed, or kept in ignorance? She made a decision.

'I am in danger, Vasya, and so are you. I want you to have a long career.'

'So do I,' responded Vasiliy.

'You respect me, don't you?'

'Always.'

'And I you, so listen carefully. I believe the bank robbery is linked to Andrei Petrov's death.'

'Linked? What link?'

'Gas, some sort of gas.'

'Petrov died. Nobody died here.'

'The artist's pictures show a gas chamber and he served with Petrov. He's been here and the FSB are asking me about him. I don't have all the pieces in this jigsaw, but I'm going to find them.'

'I'm going to help you.'

'No, Vasya, you're not!'

'But I want to.'

'Demchi's right, I can't work with you on this.'

'Demchi's ordered you to keep me out of it?'

'He's ordered nothing – just – well, he's right. Vasiliy, you could die on this – I'm not joking.'

'I want to be like you... investigating, fearless!'

'Vasiliy, I'm not fearless. I'm scared.'

She rose from her chair and stepped forward to hold him in a light embrace. She whispered to him. 'This is your time, but your time to live, Vasya. Live, and experience will make you a great investigator, but if you die now, you might as well have been morning mist that just faded away.'

'I don't know what to say, when you talk like that.'

'You don't need to say anything.'

'And you, Sveta, what about you?'

'I have come too far... I cannot turn back.'

She gave him a peck on the cheek, before letting her embrace slip. They stood face to face for a moment, silent. Vasiliy smiled.

'Sveta, I –'

'I know, Vasya.'

His smile slowly faded.

'I'm hungry. Think I'll brave Olga's deli. Moskovskaya and *bliny* for you?'

'Yes, please,' she replied.

Vasiliy left her alone as she reached for her mobile and dialled.

'Hi, it's me. You look quite handsome on the TV.'

'Thanks. Can you get out for a coffee?' asked Nick.

'No, I have to work now, but later is okay...'

'I'll cook.'

'You can cook?' asked Svetlana.

'Of course. Thought I'd try something Russian...'

'No, something Spanish. Surprise me.'

*

At Lubyanka, Malenkov sat stroking his chin as he watched a replay of Nick's broadcast.

'Mr Mendez, I think you too are meddling in areas that are not your business,' he said, before letting out a weary sigh. 'Why can't you just keep your nose out of our business?'

There was a knock at the door.

'Come in,' barked Malenkov.

His assistant entered, apparently testing the atmosphere, before advancing.

'You wanted to see me, Captain?'

'Yes, Il'ya. I'd like to know who Colonel Chernekov is associating with in his spare time. Can you arrange that for me?'

'Of course, Captain.'

'Good, thank you. That will be all... No, wait a minute. Mr Mendez has a colleague from Madrid visiting Moscow, Miss Santos. I think we'll keep a loose eye on her too.'

'Yes, sir.'

*

Chernekov had arrived first at their usual rendezvous point, at Starbucks, on Leningradsky prospekt. He was still ordering his coffee, when Grachev tapped him on the shoulder. Chernekov looked at him with barely suppressed anger.

'What do you want to drink?' he asked curtly.

'Green tea,' said Grachev, returning his stare before moving to a vacant table at the back.

Chernekov put their drinks down, spilling some of his coffee and watching a small stream of it snake to the edge of the table, from where it dripped to the floor below. He took a seat.

'What the fuck were you thinking of?' he asked of Grachev. 'You knew it couldn't be used, before the military.'

'Calm down, my friend.'

'I'm not your friend.'

'Well, I'm yours, and I've already deposited a bonus in your account.'

'I'll have the FSB and GRU on my back.'

'Can they prove anything?'

'No, not yet.'

'Well, you have nothing to worry about. Anyway, you're too important to them. I needed the element of surprise.'

'There's surprise all right. Even the foreign press are reporting it. I should never have supplied you.'

'Oleg, I would have received it sooner or later, and anyway, you might as well make some money.'

'If anybody asks, say nothing.'

'Relax, it's untraceable, remember. I might even share some with the other gangs to keep the cops guessing.'

'I can't see you, not for a while.'

'Okay, but in the future, we'll catch up.'

'We'll have to see.'

'No, we won't. We will be meeting again.'

'Are you threatening me?'

'Of course not: I'm just pointing out that there's a bond between us that can't be broken.'

The two men looked each other straight in the eye, Chernekov trembling slightly.

'Three months – at least three months.'

'Fine, Oleg, fine. We have more than enough for our immediate needs.'

'Don't use it, for now. There are – plans – and publicity would be most unwelcome.'

'If you don't talk about us, we'll have no need to talk about you and we'll all be happy.'

Chernekov stood and made for the exit, without shaking Grachev's hand.

*

'How was your granny?' asked Svetlana.

'Fine,' mumbled Ivan.

'Did the plumber arrive to fix her tap?'

'Dunno.'

'Well, didn't you see the tap?'

'No.'

It was going to be one of those evenings. In a way, she'd started to deal better and more philosophically with his reticence to speak. If she couldn't get anything good out of his mouth, she might as well get food into it. Emerging from the kitchen, with a bowl of his favourite *borsch* and some *plov*, she set them down in front of him.

'I'm having supper at Nick's this evening, but I won't be late back.'

Ivan waved in acknowledgement, a spoonful of soup already in his mouth.

Svetlana made for the bedroom to change.

'Don't forget to finish your history essay. I want to look at it tomorrow, before you hand it in.'

Ivan did not bother to answer.

A few minutes later, she was ready and walking down the grey concrete corridor towards the lift. She heard the hiss of the doors as they opened and saw a young mother emerge, with a child at her side. She picked up her pace, as the block was not well served with elevators, and to miss this one might add a good five minutes to her journey. The doors were almost shut before a large, leather-gloved hand shot forward to stop their progress.

'Thank you,' said Svetlana.

Her words unconsciously tailed off as she saw the large, blond and smiling figure of an FSB officer. He had no badge, of course, but he might as well have done, so attuned were her senses after all these years as a journalist. She hesitated briefly, before stepping in.

'Floor?' he enquired.

'Sorry?'

'Which floor?'

She thought of Ivan, suddenly not sure she should be leaving him. Was this another of Malenkov's games to unnerve her? If it was, it was working.

'Er... one.'

'Me too... Just put my little boy to bed and my wife says I can go for a drink. It's been a long day.'

She ran his words through her brain, processing them for any hint of insincerity, but there was none.

'I've not seen you before.'

'We just moved in, last month.'

'Where were you before?'

'Mytishchi, but the commute was terrible and it's much easier here.'

The lift eased to a stop and the doors softly groaned as they opened. He was telling the truth, she concluded, slightly shaken by the realisation that FSB officers could be caring fathers to young children. She thought Ivan in no danger from him, so would continue her journey.

He stepped aside to allow her out.

'Thank you.'

'Vitaliy – I am Vitaliy.'

They shook hands awkwardly.

'I'm –'

'Svetlana Dorenko, I know. My wife reads your paper, all the time.'

'Right... Enjoy your drink, Vitaliy.'

'I will.'

As she walked to Babushkinskaya metro, she looked back, just to check. There was no sign of her new FSB neighbour, nor anybody else following her. Perhaps she could look forward to her evening, after all.

*

Nick had earlier cooked them stuffed hake, one of his favourites from Madrid, it turned out. She'd been impressed by the subtlety of the flavours and the perfect texture he'd achieved for the flesh of the fish, so easy to overcook. They'd held hands across the table, silently smiling at each other, as the steam rising from their coffee drifted in front of them. Svetlana felt a stirring in her heart as she allowed the partial dismantling of the defences she'd so assiduously built to protect her from harm. This former fool was winning her over with his trust and affection.

Later, when they made love, Nick was charming and gentle as she felt his hands slide lightly and effortlessly across her skin, while she moaned softly into his ear. Her pleasure was heightened not just by the selfless attention he was giving her, but by her realisation that he was taking his own enjoyment from hers. His fingers ran across her body like those of a maestro pianist, a masterpiece of pace and pressure, seeking out the perfect performance. Her breathing quickened with his as, step by step, he took her higher, towards her approaching orgasm.

'Oh Nikolai!' she cried out as she surrendered totally to the breaking wave sweeping her along in its path, while Nick joined her in his own climax, repayment for the emotion he'd invested in Svetlana.

Afterwards, she lay face down on his back, slowly twisting his hair around her fingers. The sweat was drying from her own exposed skin but remained between them as she gently rocked him. Straying light from passing cars slipped through the blind and danced across the ceiling.

'What are you thinking?' she asked.

She heard his broken whisper, in reply.

'This city... and you are really getting to me. Where have you been, before now?'

'Waiting, Nikolai.'

Nick turned and took her in his arms as her head rested upon his gently rising chest. He was her new protector.

'What will become of us, Nikolai?'

He hugged her and planted a kiss upon her forehead, before they drifted off into a brief slumber.

It was nearly eleven when she woke. She rocked Nick until he roused.

'It's late and I have to go.'

'I'll take you.'

'No, it's fine, I'll get the metro.'

'It's not fine with me. I'll take you. I want to be with you.'

She smiled, reached out her hand to turn his head and kissed him on the lips.

*

Malenkov watched them through his windscreen as they made their way across the underground car park to the waiting BMW. He smiled knowingly as Nick held the door open for Svetlana.

'What a handsome couple,' he sneered, as Nick started the engine and pulled away.

*

'Traffic's not bad,' said Nick, to Svetlana.
'There's an FSB officer living in my block.'
'What?'
'Met him before, on the way here. Says he moved in recently, with his wife and young son.'
'You believe him?'
'Strangely, yes.'
'Just what we need, the FSB, right on your doorstep.'
'Probably nothing to do with Malenkov's department; seemed an okay guy.'
'Anything more from Malenkov?'
'No – but he'll be watching me – and you.'
'Haven't noticed anything.'
'You will. Your broadcast won't have gone without mention.'
'It's generated a lot of feedback to the network.'
'I'm not surprised.'
'If it was gas, is it our gas?'
'Who really knows? But, it seems logical.'
'If it's military, what's it doing in a bank raid?'
'Careful, Nikolai... I can see your foolish side again.'
Nick looked across at her.
'Military stuff gets sold all the time. Why should gas be any different?'

'Right.'

'My guess – and it's only a guess – is that it's Grachev. Remember, he was seen with Chernekov.'

'So, it's good for bank robberies but what do the military want it for?'

'Who knows, but we're not interesting Malenkov because of bank jobs.'

'Maybe I can raise the temperature a bit.'

'Yeah?'

'I could do a piece speculating that it was gas and that it was sold by the military.'

'I'd buy a bulletproof vest first.'

'No, seriously, you can't print anything but I can shake things up.'

'I don't think so.'

'Well, think about it.'

'Tomorrow, Nikolai, tomorrow.'

She leant across, put her arm round his shoulder and kissed his cheek.

*

She waved to Nick and watched the tail lights of his car fade into the distance, before turning and walking into the lobby of her apartment block.

To her surprise, she was met by Vitaliy, her new FSB acquaintance. He was drunk and sobbing profusely.

'What is it?' asked Svetlana.

'My son – my son. He's sick but there's no doctor arrived. Bastard!'

He stumbled, falling to one knee and hitting his head on the wall.

'What number?'

'What?'

'What number is your apartment?'

'It's not right. Bastard – bastard!'

Svetlana took hold of his shoulders and shook him strongly.

'Vitaliy, what number is your apartment?' she shouted.

'Thirteen-eleven,' he slurred back.

She pushed the button to call the lift and waited what seemed an age for it to descend from the eighth floor.

When she arrived, the front door was open and she walked straight in.

'Hello!' she shouted out.

'In here,' came a tearful reply.

She made straight for the bedroom from where the voice had come, to see a slim, brown-haired woman, perhaps in her late twenties, cradling a listless toddler in her arms.

'I'm Svetlana. How long has he been like this?'

'For just a few hours. He has a fever.'

Svetlana felt the child's brow, which was hot and clammy. She brought a lamp close to his face and he flinched, groaning at the same time. A blotchy rash covered his legs. She looked around.

'Where's the kitchen?'

'Through there,' said the young woman, pointing.

Within moments, Svetlana returned with a glass, before holding it firmly against the child's skin. The rash remained as she looked down. While she could not be sure, she suspected meningitis and remembered the terror she'd felt at the loss of her school friend, Klara, all those years ago.

'What is your name?'

'Vera.'

'Okay, Vera, we have to get him to hospital, right now. Get your coat.'

They descended together, straight to the basement car park, bypassing Vitaliy somewhere on the way. Fortunately, Svetlana had the keys to her Lada in her bag and she opened the back door to allow Vera, cradling the child, to sit.

She drove faster than the old car was really built for but suspected every spare minute would count. The children's hospital was on the other side of the city, but would add maybe forty-five minutes to their journey, so she decided to make for Botkin hospital, which was nearer.

'Will he be all right?' asked Vera.

'The hospital will help him. Just keep him as still as you can.'

The frightened mother clung to her only child, repeating over and over again, 'It'll be all right, Tolya.'

It seemed that every traffic light was against them, but eventually Svetlana drove into the hospital grounds and headed for the emergency department of the white, angular-shaped complex. She parked as near as she could to the entrance, before shepherding Vera and the helpless little Anatoliy through to reception.

A few minutes later, she watched as swing doors closed behind the trolley carrying the tiny patient, with his mother in pursuit. She was unsure what to do next. There was nothing she could physically add to the situation but having been drawn into the whole emergency, she was anxious to see if the child was all right. She checked her mobile, to see a missed call, but had no signal. Outside, the air was freezing but three bars of signal strength showed on the miniature screen as she looked down at it. Ivan had called a few minutes before. She dialled and waited only a moment for him to answer.

'Vanya, it's me...'

'Are you okay, Mum? Where are you?'

'Yes, I'm fine, but I'm at Botkin hospital. The neighbours' child is very sick and I drove here with his mum.'

'Shall I wait for you?'

'No, get some sleep now. It's late. I'll be fine... Bye, love you.'

She returned to the waiting area and took a seat, under the watchful eye of the night receptionist. Over two hours passed, during which she watched an assortment of ill or injured patients pass through, each face etched with some level of distress. Her feet were sore and eyes heavy. As the time approached three-thirty, somebody stood in front of her. She looked up to see a handsome junior doctor with a benign smile, a stethoscope around his neck.

'Svetlana Dorenko?' he enquired.

'Yes,' she muttered in reply, her head now clearing.

'I'm Doctor Gerasimov. I'm treating the little boy you brought in.'

'Will he be all right?'

'It's hard to say. He's very ill, but your quick action has given him a chance.'

'Is there anything I can do?'

'Yes, go home and sleep. Waiting here will make no difference.'

'And Vera?'

'We've reassured her, as much as we can, but she wonders if you can get a message to her husband.'

'I'll try, but he was drunk.'

'Thank you. Now, if you'll excuse me, I must return.'

'Of course. Thank you, Doctor.'

*

The door to the Kanatov's apartment was ajar when Svetlana arrived. She quietly pushed it open and stepped inside. Before she reached the living room, she heard Vitaliy's laboured snoring. She found him sprawled, half-on and half-off their green velour settee, an empty vodka bottle on the floor next to him. She was too tired to be angry, merely shaking her head in resignation at his fecklessness. She left him a note and closed the front door behind her as she headed for her own apartment.

All was quiet. Ivan slept peacefully, while she brushed her teeth, and then slipped into her favourite cotton pyjamas. Exhausted, she climbed into bed and pulled the duvet over her. Sleep would shortly overwhelm her but just before it did, a grin crossed her face as she remembered – a strong man was by her side.

Chapter 19

It was against his better judgement, but he'd been two days without food and hunger dictated that Yakov Katenin put his fear to one side and earn some money.

He could knock out a pencil sketch in less than ten minutes, earning maybe fifty rubles or if it was a tourist, ten dollars. With that, he could keep himself with food in his belly and some stolen café warmth for company as he moved from place to place. The summer would give him benevolent light and the opportunity to work outdoors, on the edges of Moscow's parks and gardens. The harsh winter in this city condemned him to occasional skulking around secondary tourist haunts, grabbing a few minutes to balance his pad on his knee, while his practised eyes flitted between page and subject. He would nod enthusiastically at anything the usually English speaking travellers said, even though he'd no idea what they were saying. 'Picture, ten dollars, yes' and 'thank you', was all the vocabulary he needed. His sample work and temporary charm usually landed a client within a short time.

He made his way along the alleyway between one of the former industrial buildings at the Winzavod Gallery, not far from Kursky station and waited by the exit, holding the door open for emerging patrons before sneaking in himself. His necessarily acquired cunning helped him dodge capture on CCTV cameras and to adopt the demeanour of a genuine visitor, until an appropriate moment.

'Picture, ten dollars?' he asked a passing couple, brandishing an image remarkably similar to the initially defensive wife who faced him.

'I don't think so, thank you,' came the reply.

Svetlana's Garden

'Picture, ten dollars' repeated Katenin, this time sweeping his hand, as if casting a spell, across the eyes of this would-be client and then across those of his previous muse.

'Ten dollars?' she enquired.

'Ten dollars – picture – thank you.'

He did not wait for a final confirmation, but launched instead into a blur of movement as his right hand traced an emerging likeness of the woman, while his left theatrically framed her face. Within minutes, he was finished, turning to present the portrait for approval.

'Very nice. Very good likeness,' came the evidently pleased response.

'Picture, thank you,' said Katenin.

He tore the page from his pad and exchanged it for the proffered ten dollar bill.

'Hey, you, come here!' bellowed a voice from the far end of the corridor.

Katenin instantly turned his face from view and in seconds was out of the building, before the burly security guard could get near him. He kept moving, the money firmly held in the grasp of his clenched fist.

Later, his normal ability to blend in was temporarily lost as he ravenously devoured a large, stuffed baked potato at the first green-painted Kroshka Kartoshka stand he reached, interrupting himself only occasionally to sip the yet-to-cool hot chocolate accompanying his meal.

When he'd finished, his attention turned to the proprietor's portable television, hoping as he did when he read each day's discarded newspapers, to see some progress in Svetlana's investigation. There was nothing. He wondered what she was doing. *What more did she need?* Her writing had convinced him she would be the one and the supportive mutterings he'd heard on the streets had reinforced that. *Enough time has passed,* he thought, and resolved to contact her, dangerous as that might be.

*

The first two weeks of January brought school holidays for Ivan. Traditionally, in the first week, he'd accompany his grandmother to visit his aunt in Kaluga, and would look forward to spending time with his cousins.

'Do you want a flask of soup?' asked Svetlana.

'I'll get some on the train,' replied Ivan, zipping up his rucksack.

'Let's save some money.'

'I'll get some on the train.'

She thought about taking him on in the argument but relented. Partings and train journeys were still sensitive for her.

The doorbell went and Svetlana moved to look through the spy-hole. It was Nick. She let him in and kissed him. Ivan scowled.

'Are you on a journey, Ivan?' asked Nick.

'To my cousins,' replied Ivan, as he gave his mother a hug and made for the door.

'He goes with his granny at this time, each year,' said Svetlana.

'Do you want a lift over there?'

'I'm getting the bus,' replied Ivan curtly, as he brushed past Nick and shut the door behind him.

Svetlana and Nick looked at each other. Nick shrugged.

'There's some way to go.'

'Give it time.'

'It's just that I was hoping to make a bit more progress.'

'He'll come round. Do you want coffee?'

'Yeah, that would be good.'

She boiled the kettle, while he leant on the doorframe of the tiny kitchen.

'I've been thinking.'

'About?' she enquired.

'Well, I thought if I'm going to up the pressure, shouldn't we look for some proof?'

'Of...?'

'The pictures show a gas chamber, right?'

'Yes.'

'And the boy was posted to Chita?'

'That's what Katia said.'
'So, chances are the gas chamber's in Chita.'
'We don't know that.'
'I'm betting it is. We can go.'
'Do you know how far away Chita is?'
'We have a week free, don't we?'
'Actually, eight days, because Ivan's staying a bit longer this time.'
'Okay, that's it, we're going!'
'Flying's too obvious. Malenkov will be on to us.'
'So?'
'Have you been on the Trans-Siberian train, Nikolai?'
'No, but I've heard lots about it.'
'It will be easier to slip out of Moscow.'
'Okay, that's it then.'
'I think you're forgetting something.'
'Which is?'
'Even if this gas thing is in Chita, it will be on a military base. You can't just turn up at the gate and ask for a guided tour.'
'Let's just get there. I've pre-recorded tomorrow's piece and I'm due some leave.'
'I can't tell Demchi. I'll have to ask for leave.'
'Well, do it. Ask him today and then book the tickets!'
Svetlana looked at Nick as he stood to fill the frame of the door. His assurance impressed her. The ping of the kettle as it switched itself off broke the moment.
'Okay,' she said.
She carried their coffee through and sat down. They looked at each other across the table, Nick wearing a slightly self-satisfied grin.
'Nikolai, you won't...?'
'Won't what?'
'Pick me up and then let me fall?'
'I've already let you fall once. I won't do that again.'
She linked her fingers with his and squeezed, while she looked deep into his eyes.
'It's just that –'
'Sveta, shut up and take me in there, instead!'

His self-assurance today was irresistible. She liked it and now she'd be late for work.

*

Nick waited for Victoria and her friend in the lobby of the Hotel Belgrad. They'd already been here over a week and he'd not caught up with them. The cream and brown marble floor and the decor weren't too bad, certainly better than the bleak, twenty-storey, Soviet era exterior suggested.

'Hi, Nick,' said Pilar, in Spanish.

'Hi...'

In that moment he'd forgotten her name, but she skilfully sidestepped his embarrassment for him.

'Vicki's still getting ready, so she said "Hey, Pilar, can you go down to meet Nick"... and, here I am.'

She looked great, standing there in a dark-pink cashmere sweater and maroon trousers, which hugged every curve. Nick reminded himself not to stare.

'Thanks, Pilar. How long's she going to be?'

'Who can tell? You know Vicki. Shall we have a drink?'

'Er, sure.'

They made their way to the bar, where Pilar slipped into an armchair as Nick signalled to the waiter for service.

'What will you have?'

'Wine, please – red.'

'And, Vicki?'

'Normally, wine, but here she's been ordering Admiralskaya and Red Bull. I think she's getting a taste for it.'

'Let's go with wine.'

Nick finished the order and returned to sit next to her. She crossed her leg in his direction and smiled at him.

'So, Pilar, what have you seen of Moscow?'

'More night than day. We've been clubbing quite a bit. They have some really good ones, don't you think?'

'Not really been to any.'

'You should. Why don't you come with us?'
'We'll see. I think I'm a bit old for that sort of thing.'
'No, you're not. There's lots of older guys.'

In the background, he heard the click of heels on marble and raised his eyes to see Victoria coming towards him, in boots, a short, close-fitting red dress and a long fur coat. His eyes widened as the vision approached him and Pilar's words faded away. He'd seen her casually dressed many times, of course, but this time there was something different and edgy about her. Her hair was radiant, eyes flashing and a slight swagger had attached itself to her walk.

'Put your eyes back in,' scolded Pilar playfully.

Nick put his hand under his chin and pressed upwards to close his half-open mouth, before standing to meet her.

'Hi, Nick. Sorry I'm late.'

He leant forward and put his arm round her waist as they kissed on both cheeks. She felt young to his touch and smelt fabulous.

'I got you wine.'

'Great, thanks. We thought you'd forgotten us.'

'No, not at all. I was just really busy with work.'

'And your girlfriend?'

He didn't respond. The two girls looked at each other and sniggered.

'Are we going to eat?' continued Victoria.

'Sure, of course. There's lots: Russian, Chinese or European?'

'Russian, of course – we're in Moscow,' said Victoria, pushing him on the shoulder.

'Okay, just a minute,' said Nick, tapping numbers into his mobile.

The waiter sidled by, pretending to be busy, while he gave the girls a good look-over. If he'd had film star looks, they might have acknowledged him but his merely pleasant features gained him no more than practised indifference as he was ignored, while their host chatted to the restaurant.

'Okay, we can go to Godunov. They can fit us in and the food's good there.'

Wisely, Nick had decided not to drive. He'd figured they'd be having a few drinks and with his impending train journey, the last thing he needed was to be spending the night in a police cell. They left the warmth of the lobby and emerged into the cold evening air, where three trails of steam from their breath accompanied them to the waiting Volga taxi. Nick held the door open for his young companions to sit in the back, before walking round to the passenger side and taking the seat next to the driver. He issued a destination in Russian, now with only the faintest accent, before half turning to continue his conversation, in Spanish.

'How's JF been while I've been away?'

Victoria chuckled.

'Oh you know, good mood one day, bad the next. Probably depends how Sofia's treating him,' she said, referring to Freeman's long-term, on-off mistress.

'Right. And the office move?'

'It's been put back. Money, I think. Don't know if it's going to happen.'

'That's where we were,' interrupted Pilar, pointing out Propaganda club as they passed by. 'Can we go back later?'

'Let's eat first,' said Nick, hedging his position.

A short while later, they arrived at the restaurant on Teatralnaya ploshchad. Nick paid off the taxi, while the girls made final adjustments to their clothes and hair before entering. They stepped inside, where Victoria and Pilar looked slightly taken aback at the sight of so many paintings on the walls and the elegant ceilings.

'Well, you wanted Russian,' said Nick.

They were shown to their table by a smiling waitress with waist-length, shimmering blonde hair, who turned out to be from Latvia. Nick watched Victoria eye her suspiciously.

He translated for them, describing the varied dishes set out in the menu.

'Your voice has changed,' said Victoria.

'How do you mean?'

'It's deeper. I mean, I like it.'

Nick smiled at her and then returned his attention to the menu.

'Tell you what, why don't you just order for us? We trust you, don't we, Pilar?'

'I do, sure. Go on, Nick, you do it.'

Have these girls been practising their double act since they were born, he wondered. They seemed to have a way of making him feel he was on a small stage somewhere, under a spotlight, with an audience of two. Nevertheless, he assumed the responsibility and spoke their order to the still smiling waitress. As she left them, Nick caught Victoria's slight frown.

'Don't you like her?'

'She's fine... And, anyway, I could grow my hair that long if I wanted to – and probably without the split ends.'

Soon they were enjoying *boyarsky*, a salad with sturgeon and caviar.

'Good?' asked Nick.

'Fantastic,' answered Pilar, as Victoria, her mouth full, nodded in agreement.

After their main course and half-way through their second bottle of wine, a Russian ensemble in traditional dress took to the floor and started to sing. Victoria and Pilar soon joined more enthusiastic sections of the room, clapping along in time with the music. Nick observed them with a smile, glad for this brief time that he'd managed to hold back the city and give them a glimpse of something more authentic.

Over a break in the music, they had coffee.

'I'm going to be away, for a week or so.'

'Nick! We'll almost be going back by then,' said Victoria. 'When will we see you again?'

'As soon as I get back, I promise. We'll have another night out.'

'You promise?'

'I promise. Why don't you get the train to St Petersburg and have a couple of nights there?'

'Is it like Moscow?'

'No, quite different.'

'We'll think about it.'

Nick could see disappointment in her face and felt obliged to agree when she reined in her apparent upset to make an announcement.

'Right, if you're going to leave us, we'd better party tonight. Let's all go to Propaganda!'

On another night he might not have been allowed in, deemed just not sufficiently cool to get past the face control operated at the door by burly bouncers. Tonight, with an attractive foreign girl on each arm he sailed in. Victoria and Pilar were by now in high spirits. The thumping music seemed to grab them and pull them towards the dance floor, where they merged with the heaving, gyrating mass as predominantly blue and purple lights alternated to make even the air look alive. Nick took sanctuary at the bar. He was heavily outnumbered by those younger than him, but was reassured to see a few of his contempories milling about looking quite relaxed.

'Red wine – two – and Admiralskaya and Red Bull,' shouted Nick above the music to the spiky-haired barman, who nodded back at him.

He somehow found a vacant table in the corner and thought he'd better stay there to await the girls. A short while later they found him.

'Come and dance,' shouted Pilar, holding out her hand.

'In a minute... Let's have a drink first,' replied Nick, above the noise. They sat with him. Pilar sipped her wine as Victoria poured the mixer into her vodka.

'How did you know?' she asked, holding up her glass.

'A little bird told me,' he replied, pointing at Pilar.

Reluctantly, he danced, unable to hold them off any longer. Actually, he danced well, the alcohol he'd consumed having relieved him of some inhibitions. A handsome young man, though superficially not bothered, had been edging closer to Pilar for some time and eventually gestured to her to dance with him. She glanced at Victoria, seeking permission, it seemed. Nick missed it, but a signal must have been given and Pilar turned to face her new dance floor partner as strobe lights reduced the room to apparent slow motion.

A little later, over another drink, Nick and Victoria sat on the small settee at their table. The volume of the music was now even louder and they had to converse nearly cheek to cheek to make themselves heard.

'Really sorry to be away... I'll make it up to you, when I get back.'

She sat back, far enough away that he missed her reply.

'What?' he asked.

She leaned forward again.

'I said: make it up to me now.'

He'd not processed the words before her mouth was on his and her hand behind his neck. The camera flash went entirely unnoticed, amidst the frantic strobe lighting and the beating sound. Her kiss did not desist and while she was temptation itself, he gently separated them and gave her a benign smile to show that he was flattered but couldn't continue. She smiled back, her expression indicating she'd gone too far but sure he'd forgive the alcohol and the moment.

*

Demchi had been surprisingly relaxed about Svetlana having some time off. He'd thought it would be good, in any event, to let Vasiliy have a bit more responsibility to bring him on.

She'd tried to book a two berth *kupe* for them, but that would have to wait until Irkutsk. At this short notice, they would have to travel in *platskartny*, in reality third class, where each carriage was separated into a number of open compartments. She sniggered as she approached the twin towered Yaroslavsky station, where she'd wait for him, amused that his current amorous affection was likely to be frustrated on the train by their near neighbours and travelling companions.

Inside, she went to the information area with its rich blue walls, ornate, gold-featured ceilings and leaded windows. Later, she passed time in the less glamorous, beige-painted waiting area as she read the *Moscow Times*, anxious as always to have the perspective of others, but also, on this occasion, to practise her English. She glanced repeatedly at the departure board.

Nick was a little late, but it was unmistakeably him striding down the platform and pulling a smart Samsonite suitcase behind him that could mark him out as a foreigner in the modest carriage they'd be occupying. For a moment, she pictured him as a screen hero, marching towards her to sweep her up and take her away to an unknown but promising future. All that was missing was for him to emerge from the swirling steam of a bygone era. Her brief reverie was soon interrupted as he drew near.

'Fucking thief!'

'Nice to see you, too,' she replied, just stopping short of a sneer.

'Sorry... It's just the taxi driver took me around the houses to screw a few rubles out of me. I hate that.'

'You finished?'

Her poised beauty and presence contrasted with his naive irritation. She held his look. This was Moscow and a taxi driver had conned him, just a little. She didn't need to say anything else as the tightened muscles of his face relaxed to reveal the warm smile he must have intended. His free hand emerged from behind his back and offered her a single scarlet rose.

She smiled and shook her head.

'What?' he enquired.

She took a step towards him and accepted the vibrantly coloured flower.

'Come on,' she said, nodding towards the open carriage door.

A stout *provodnitsa* stood to attention and looked sternly at Svetlana as she approached, before recognising her. In a passing moment, a welcome replaced indifference.

'Svetlana Yuriyevna, welcome. I am Liliya.'

Svetlana extended her hand. The attendant, not used to such courtesy, hesitated and then reached out her own hand.

'This is Nikolai Ivanovich.'

Liliya looked him up and down, frowning as her eyes reached his expensive suitcase.

'He's travelling with you?'

'Yes,' replied Svetlana.

'Huh – come with me,' said Liliya, after a brief inspection of their tickets.

They followed her down the narrow aisle of the carriage until they reached the penultimate compartment, where their two travelling companions awaited them.

'I'll bring you bed linen,' said Liliya, turning to leave.

Nick held out his hand.

'I'm Nikolai, and this is Svetlana.'

His handshake was accepted by Kirill, a stocky factory foreman, with wiry, silver hair and then by Yevgeniy, a tobacco sales representative, clearly wedded to his work as his stained teeth and fingers testified. They moved to make room for the two journalists to stow their bags and to sit. The compartment was cramped, with the detachable table between them serving as an elbow rest. Fold down PVC beds above would provide sleeping space for Svetlana and Nick, the implication already there that the two new companions would be taking the favoured lower births.

Liliya returned, with linen. Svetlana proffered the fifty rubles each for herself and Nick. The *provodnitsa* accepted one note, but closed Svetlana's fingers around the other.

'Just get that Grishkuv. Don't let him get away with it.'

'I'll see what I can do,' said Svetlana.

She hoped that Vasiliy would remember to do the follow-up work on that story while she was away.

'Let me know if you need anything,' said Liliya, as she turned in the direction of her own cabin.

New passengers, some struggling with bulging bags, moved backwards and forwards, bumping into each other in the narrow passage while they sought their own small territory to begin the journey east.

In the next compartment, a hacking cough sounded out and the four passengers exchanged anxious looks. *It could have been worse,* thought Svetlana, *a screaming baby perhaps,* as the distant sound of a distressed infant reached her from the next carriage.

'You look sleepy,' said Svetlana to Nick.

'I was out late. I'd promised to take the girls for dinner.'

'Your friend, Victoria, you mean?'

'Yes, Victoria and Pilar.'

'You didn't tell me.'

'It was a last minute thing – with us going away and them only being here for a short while.'

'Was it just dinner, Nikolai?'

She noted his momentary hesitation.

'Yes, just dinner.'

Svetlana watched his apparent discomfort and held his look with hers.

'Don't let me down, Nikolai.'

Later, they were under way as the great train gently trundled towards the darkening eastern sky. Outside a confusion of electric cables slipped by overhead to be replaced by the grim concrete walls of nearby tenements, while Svetlana took the opportunity to make up their beds. Kirill took out a pack of cards and a bottle of Moscovskaya vodka, seemingly to make his own preparations for the evening ahead.

*

Malenkov had allowed his tea to go cold. There was a microwave in the small kitchen just down from his office, but the metal holder attached to his favourite glass made that method of warming it up out of the question. He sipped at it, before swigging most of it in one, accompanied by a tight-lipped grimace.

His assistant knocked and then entered.

'Yes, Il'ya, where are we up to?'

'I thought you might like to go over yesterday's surveillance reports.'

'I suppose so. What have you got for me? Anything on Katenin?'

'I'm afraid not.'

'Hmmn.'

'But there's a report back on Mizirov's dealings with the Germans and a report on Miss Santos. It appears she's quite friendly with Mr Mendez, the reporter.'

'Really? Okay, let's start with that one.'

His assistant reached into a plastic folder and brought out a chronological log that Malenkov took his time reading. Some could accuse him of lacking flair but not of lacking an eye for detail.

'Has she seen him, today?'

'No, yesterday evening was the last time.'

'Where is he now?'

'We don't know. It was assumed Valentina was picking things up, but she said he'd taken leave at short notice and didn't come in today.'

'And Dorenko?'

'Not been to her office.'

'I'm beginning to lose my patience with Mr Mendez. He's up to no good. I can sense trouble – I can just sense it, Il'ya.'

'Do you want him to receive a reminder to keep his nose out,' asked Il'ya, handing him two photos.

'Sir, do you want to do that?' continued Il'ya, until Malenkov held up his hand to silence him.

The trained FSB eyes looked intently at the photographs, Malenkov pushing his spectacles a little further up the bridge of his nose to obtain the perfect view. After a minute or so, his focus settled on the smile. The smile was genuine and all the more useful for it. The kiss was excellent, but the smile, now that was really a bonus.

'I don't think so,' came Malenkov's, long-contemplated reply. 'I have a better idea.'

Chapter 20

The night had an extraordinary blackness about it, as Captain Viktor Kovalyov led his Vega Special Forces men silently across fields, south of Kutaisi. Each man trusted the other implicitly and they were all veterans of previous sabotage operations. Planning had been meticulous, right down to the Czech plastic explosive they carried to confuse any subsequent forensic investigation. Damaging a section of the pipeline would have been easy, but it would also have been quickly repaired. Their mission was to take out a strategically positioned pumping station that would halt oil transit using this route through Georgia, for a considerable time.

Kovalyov signalled to his men to wait while he checked GPS co-ordinates, before waving them on again. Some time later, he moved forward to look over a ridge, removed his night vision goggles and reached instead for his binoculars. There, in the distance, was their target. He surveyed the giant station, the size of two football pitches. Kovalyov had been through the approach many times on the simulator, but even a hardened veteran like him felt the extra heart beats when it came to the real thing. He signalled to his comrades to remove their own goggles and to fan out for the attack, their first task being to avoid the Georgian Special Forces troops guarding the perimeter, whose skills had been raised considerably in recent years by their CIA-funded training.

They covered the last kilometre swiftly and silently, camouflage uniforms adding to their practised stealth as the fence arose in front of them. Each man knew exactly what was required of him and at precisely zero-one-fifteen, in an upwind position, they cut three sections of the fence and crawled through across crisp, frozen straw, before donning their gas masks. By zero-one-seventeen, an invisible layer of gas was making its ghostly way across the great compound in league with the gentle breeze. The comrades advanced behind it to find prostrate bodies of the station's unsuspecting personnel. Kovalyov was the first to reach the operations centre, where he let in their communications specialist to hack into the local network and introduce the specially written virus, which would spread its malicious intent, starting with the disablement of the alarm systems. While he did this, a re-filled gas grenade of Chinese origin disabled two engineers watching over the air conditioning unit that within minutes would distribute the vile toxin far and wide.

They moved, building by building, across the vast humming site, professional and silent but secretly elated that they were not encountering resistance. *It won't be so easy next time*, thought Kovalyov. They deliberately left the giant, grey storage tanks alone, but after removing the comatose occupants, placed their explosive charges at each of the strategically selected locations, where, in ninety minutes, they would do their vindictive worst to the vital installation. An unconscious driver was pushed across the bench seat of his pickup truck, before it was driven around the site to collect the dozen or so personnel who'd been outside when they'd struck.

Kovalyov couldn't resist a laugh as he and some of his comrades surveyed the canteen at the corner of the site, busy with its unconscious occupants who were now out of the explosive's reach and safe from freezing to death.

'*Bon appétit*,' he sniggered, the first words spoken there by any of the troops.

Thirty minutes after they'd arrived, they slipped away and dissolved into the darkness as the station hummed its monotonous tune to its unconscious audience.

*

Most of the carriage was asleep, although Svetlana was not. She was drowsy after her long day, but would not surrender just yet. Below her, Yevgeniy slept silently while across from him Kirill snored gently. When she shut her eyes, the rocking of the train reminded her of the safety she'd felt while held as a child in her mother's arms. She looked at Nick, turned to face her but slumbering, his face dark with the stubble he'd grown throughout the day. She felt even safer with him there.

Her eyelids were closing as she snuggled under red blankets, when the metronomic background noise from wheels on rails was interrupted by the sound of her near neighbour clearing his throat for another bout of raucous coughing. She screwed her eyes tight shut and pulled the blanket over her ears to defend herself from the awful, grating noise, but it was too late. She was now awake and peeked out from under the covers to see Nick looking across at her, smiling. She cringed as a cackling sound preceded the next forced exhalation from nearby.

'I love you,' mouthed Nick, reaching out his hand.

Her heart began to race. It was so soon and they had much to learn about each other – but it was true.

'I love you, too,' she responded, locking her fingers around his.

A little later, she watched him drift back to sleep and blocked out the neighbouring noise by concentrating on her memories of Nick. She was able to smile now, when she recalled his first, faltering efforts, so obviously a foreigner trying to fit in. Snapshots of memories went through her mind as her smile rose and fell with them.

Svetlana didn't know what time she'd eventually fallen asleep but the first morning sound to reach her was the squeak of trolley wheels, accompanied by shouts of *'chai'* and *'kofje'*. Nick was sitting on his bed, with his feet dangling over the side as he checked his email. The signal was intermittent but they'd obviously passed through somewhere with a decent connection. He scrolled through his messages, until a frown crossed his face. She looked at him.

'What?' asked Svetlana.

Nick was about to reply, but glanced down at the still dozing Yevgeniy and stopped himself, before handing her the phone. She looked down, her face too acquiring a look of concern as she read the words on the screen.

Baku–Sup'sa pipeline attacked. Pumping station destroyed. All personnel alive but unconscious! Attackers unknown at present. Thought you'd like to know that one. Best, Kostya.

She handed the phone back to him, anxious to talk but constrained by their travelling companions below, both of whom were now stirring. She signalled to Nick to follow her as she pushed back the blankets and started her descent.

'Morning,' she said to Kirill and Yevgeniy as her feet touched the floor. They each grunted in reply, the last vestiges of sleep still clinging to them.

The two reporters huddled next to the hissing *samovar*, always available with boiling water for travellers to fix themselves a drink.

'Is it what I think it is?' asked Svetlana.

'Who knows, but it's the same as the attack on the bank. You know, unconscious victims. What's the betting analysis will show no trace of anything?'

'Do you want to go back?' she asked.

'Back? What for?'

'To report it.'

'No, I don't want to go back. We're reporting right now – doing our job. We need our proof and I reckon that's in Chita. We're not going back,' said Nick.

She looked at him, certainty written all over his face. There was no more need to question. He was right and she knew it. His strength in the face of her caution made her shiver slightly. She put her arms round his neck and kissed his cheek. Liliya walked by, pretending to be preoccupied but Svetlana caught the movement of her eye and released Nick. They giggled, like children.

After they'd breakfasted on bread, cheese and coffee, Nick took up a position by the door at the end of the carriage to take in the landscape passing by. It was a journey she'd made several times, so she preferred to watch him instead of the endless kilometres of snow-covered forest on the section between Nizhniy Novgorod and Kirov. She wondered what he was thinking as he looked impassively through the window, his shadowed face in need of a shave. Maybe this quiet time out here in the wilderness was what he needed, a finishing school for his re-education as a Russian.

Liliya appeared at Svetlana's side and the two women silently observed him, until the doughty *provodnitsa* took up conversation.

'Svetlana Yuriyevna, is he a good man?'

'He's a good man.'

'With a strong heart?'

'Unbreakable.'

'I hope you're right.'

Svetlana turned her head quickly to find the eyes behind this voice of circumspection.

'Why do you say that?' she asked.

'I have travelled this railway for eleven years and in that time I have seen many men accompanied by fear. This is such a man, your friend, your lover. It is like a ghost by his side. I have learnt to see these ghosts.'

Svetlana considered the reference to lover was impertinent and thought to scold her, but the insight of her other words kept her focused.

'He will deal with his fear.'

'Then you have chosen the right man,' said Liliya, turning in the direction of her own compartment. 'I'm having a break. Do you want tea?'

*

At Botkin hospital, in Moscow, Vera Kanatova cradled her son in her arms as she walked down the corridor to the car park, her still contrite husband at her side. The little boy had made a good recovery following Svetlana's swift intervention, much to the relief of the young couple.

When they arrived home, Vitaliy took the drowsy toddler in his arms.

'Come on, young man, it's time for bed,' he said.

Vera made them tea, squeezing extra lemon into Vitaliy's glass, the way he liked it. She carried it through to Anatoliy's room to see him sleeping, his father sitting by his side, with head in hands. Vera looked at him and for the first time in days felt love for him. When they had not been by their son's side, she had vented her fury at him as only a mother can when she protects her young. Vitaliy had been unable to put up any defence as the verbal blows crashed down upon him, and here he sat, contrition personified. Her anger was exhausted and at last she was able to allow the thought of caring for the man she loved. Vitaliy took his head from his hands and looked up, his eyes red and cheeks wet with tears.

'Vera.'

She stepped forward, took his hand and squeezed it, reassuring him that the path to redemption was open to him. He made to speak, but she put her finger to her lips to signal he should be silent and beckoned to him to follow her to the living room.

'I'm so sorry. Vera, forgive me.'

'I will try – just need some time.'

'I will make it up to you.'

'There is somebody else we owe – you owe. You must find a way to repay Svetlana Yuriyevna.'

'I will... I will find a way.'

Chapter 21

Deputy Energy Minister Kutaisov put down the receiver, clasped his hands together, drew a deep breath, and closed his eyes. When he opened them, Chernekov was looking back at him.

'Congratulations, Colonel. That was Prime Minister Tretyakov. He's very pleased and sends his best wishes to you and your team.'

'I'm just doing my duty, Deputy Minister.'

'I know, Colonel, but congratulations, anyway.'

'And the publicity?'

'There is plenty breaking but it's all confused and speculative. We will manage it.'

'It will be more difficult in the future.'

'Come now, Oleg, be proud. Enjoy your moment.'

'Thank you, Deputy Minister. If that is all, I'll pass on your kind words to my team.'

Chernekov made to stand, but Kutaisov gestured to him to remain seated.

'Deputy Minister?'

'I'm sure it's nothing, but Captain Malenkov of the FSB... Do you know Captain Malenkov?'

'Yes,' said Chernekov, nodding.

'Well, apparently he's a little worried about the Moskovsky Industrialny robbery the other day. He thinks some kind of gas could have been used, but the tests show nothing. You wouldn't happen to know anything, would you, Oleg?'

'No, Deputy Minister, I'm afraid not.'

'No, I thought not. I'm sure there's a perfectly reasonable explanation and fortunately for me, bank robbery is outside the remit of my department, eh?'

'Yes, Deputy Minister.'

For a few silent seconds, Kutaisov's eyes returned Chernekov's steady gaze.

'Thank you, Colonel. That will be all.'

Chernekov rose to his feet and saluted, before turning for the large panelled door that separated the minister's palatial room from the sombre corridor outside. He thought he'd remained impassive but was unsure what Kutaisov had actually read from his face. One thing Chernekov did know was that contact with Grachev was out of the question, for the time being.

Within five minutes, he was carefully making his way down the steps of the ministry, made treacherous by a fresh fall of snow the concierge had yet to clear. His driver opened the rear door of the Volga saloon and closed it behind Chernekov as he settled into the back seat, feeling gentle waves of warm air from the car's heater caress the stinging skin of his cheeks. He promised himself a large glass of his favourite single malt whiskey when he was back at his quarters, a taste acquired courtesy of his NATO opposite number on an exchange visit, some years before.

*

It was after midnight when the train approached Perm. Despite the late hour, Svetlana could see small groups of vendors manning their stands of various shapes and sizes as they waited for custom from passengers.

Liliya assured her that the stop here would be for at least half an hour, Svetlana mindful of the episode some years before, when she had all but been left behind at Omsk in the freezing dead of night. She stepped down from the carriage, tying the straps of her *ushanka* under her chin to put in place a final layer of protection against the bitter Ural night. Nick followed her closely.

A husband and wife both stamped alternate feet as they managed their rusting soup stand, its rising steam quickly overwhelmed by the freezing night air.

'What have you got?' asked Svetlana.

'*Solyanka* or *borsch* – which one?' came the reply and presumptuous question from the wife, her clothes sufficiently thick for protection but a strange mix of cast-off colours.

'*Solyanka*,' replied Svetlana.

'And you?' The sharp follow-up question was accompanied by a pointing finger.

'The same,' replied Nick.

They watched as the thick soup filled two takeaway cups, into which plastic spoons were placed to allow them to salvage the pieces of bacon and sausage that would otherwise stick to the sides.

'Four hundred,' growled the stocky, unshaven husband, his hands remaining firmly planted in his coat pockets.

Nick reached for his wallet, removing a glove and exposing his flesh to the bitter cold. He held out a five thousand ruble note in the husband's direction, fluttering in the stiff breeze. In exchange, he received a withering look and silence.

'I've got it,' said Svetlana.

She proffered four hundred rubles and helped him pass through another gate in his ongoing education.

They regained the warmth of the train, where Kirill and Yevgeniy had wisely stayed to play cards. However, as Svetlana and Nick sat down next to them the delicious smell of the homemade soup brought envious glances their way.

A short ring tone from her phone announced the arrival of a text message. She checked it and saw it was from Ivan, telling her that he and his cousins had been skating on the lake at the park, in Kaluga. She looked at her watch, mindful of the late hour, until she remembered that he was two hours behind her in one of the many time zones of Russia's vastness. She showed the message to Nick who smiled and shrugged, before she sent Ivan a reply. Nick reached for his phone and began to text a message of his own as the heavy train, with an initial lurch, began to pick up speed. When he'd finished, he didn't press the send button but instead passed the phone to Svetlana for her to read his message. Somehow she managed to keep a straight face.

Soup has revived me. Hungry for you now. Toilet in 5 min?

She pressed delete, before handing the phone back to him.

'That's good. I'm sure the answer will be yes,' she said.

After sixty seconds or so, Nick stood.

'I'm just going to stretch my legs,' he said.

He squeezed past Svetlana, leaving her to fight an unsuccessful battle against the urge to grin as she looked at the oblivious card players opposite her.

'Who's winning?' she asked.

'Nobody, really. Just passing the time,' answered Kirill, without looking up.

'What time do you guys want to sleep? Have I got time to wash and clean my teeth?'

'I'm okay, for a while,' said Yevgeniy.

'Yeah, me too,' added Kirill.

She reached up for her bag to take out a pink hand towel and soap, before sliding out and setting off down the corridor.

Nick had taken a chance leaving the door open but it was Svetlana who stepped into the cream plastic and stainless steel chamber, grinning at Nick as she turned the lock behind her. For a while they just stood and looked at each other. She cared not that they were in the most unromantic of surroundings, the air heavy with a bleach-like smell, for she now loved this man and longed to be with him. Their proximity but unavailability to each other since they'd left Moscow had left her with a simmering sense of lust that he'd allowed to come to the boil with his mischievous message. She put down her towel and advanced across the space between them, flinging her arms round his neck and pressing her pelvis into his as she backed him up against the plastic wall, which creaked under their combined weight. He reached out and put his hand on the edge of the basin as she ran the tip of her tongue around the inside of his upper teeth, holding his head firmly with her left hand, pain awaiting him if he tried to break free, with her perfect nails sunk a mere fraction into the skin of his scalp. She had set the tone, intending to leave him in no doubt that she was ready to engage him on any terms. He had teased this tigress and let her free from her cage. Without words, she released her grip, made him look into her blazing eyes and challenged him to try to tame her. Nick put his hands under her thighs and lifted her to him. She wrapped her legs round him as he lowered her to the small sink top and in one movement swept her sweater over her head, the shade of her lace bra a perfect match for her black trousers. She felt the advance of his tongue in her mouth and rose to meet him while her hands shamelessly clawed at his belt buckle until it was undone and his trousers fell to the level of his knees. Reaching into his underpants she felt his hardness with her right hand while holding him round the neck with her left. With a shift of balance she spun him round so their positions were reversed. She pushed his head back, until it hit the polished steel barrier behind him that purported to be a mirror. Her hand under his jaw held him firmly in position, while she leant forward and took him deep into her mouth, his gasp of breath at this pleasure assault delivering an instant hit to her already aroused senses. She continued to hold him, alternating her rhythm, tasting and smelling him, her lustful passion now irreversible. Eventually, she rose, Nick's eyes opening as hers reached the same level as his. She released his jaw and placed her hand behind his neck, pulling him towards her so that their mouths might join and he could share the taste of himself. Nick slipped to his feet, expertly unzipped her trousers and helped her to step out of them before turning her and placing her hands either side of the steel mirror. It was her turn to gasp as he entered her and began his irresistible rhythmic thrusts. With each one she saw her own reflection fall into and out of focus as he moved her backwards and forwards, edging step by step towards her building climax. He was not rough, just relentless and she was loath to interrupt the train of pleasure carrying her along, but something made her determined to demonstrate to him that toying with her passion carried consequences. She would not be tamed, this time. She turned to face him and kicked down the toilet seat cover, before pushing him to sit on it. Svetlana looked down at him, before sitting astride him and placing her hands on his shoulders. They both realised they would finish this on her terms.

*

By the following afternoon, they'd reached Omsk and with Liliya's help they were able to move to a *kupe* that had become free and where they were the only occupants, at least for the stretch down to Irkutsk. While they had started to become adept at communicating by looks alone, the privacy they now enjoyed gave them an opportunity to say some things they'd both been carrying.

'Malenkov will know we're not in Moscow.'

'I know,' said Nick.

'He'll be looking for us.'

'I'm sure.'

'What if he's waiting for us?'

'Where?'

'In Chita,' said Svetlana, her brow furrowing.

'We just have to get on with it.'

'But we need to be smarter, at least make ourselves harder to find.'

'By...?'

'Let's break the journey – buy new tickets. I shouldn't have bought tickets to Chita, anyway.'

'We can do that. We can buy through to Vladivostok.'

'I'm becoming scared, Nikolai.'

'Don't be.'

'Aren't you?'

'No point.'

'Liliya said you were... said you carried fear, like a ghost by your side.'

'What does she know?'

'Those who spend their lives watching humans understand human nature.'

'We all watch humans. I'm fine. Forget about that. Let's just find the bastards who killed the boy.'

The tone was resolute, determined. Right now, it helped her but Svetlana sometimes wondered if she'd be personally stronger without him. His protection allowed her to occasionally drop her guard, when before she'd just had to fend for herself. She looked at him.

'You're right, let's find them.'

She reached out and stroked his chin, holding it with her palm.

'You need a shave.'

'I quite like it.'

'Yeah, okay, Mister Rugged, but it's rubbing the skin from my face, so sort it out.'

'If you make me a coffee.'

'Don't bargain with me, Nikolai Ivanovich.'

'That's how it's done here, isn't it?'

'Yes, Nikolai, that's how it's done... but not with me. From now on, you can just ask. Now go and shave while I sort us out that coffee.'

Svetlana followed him down the corridor and saw him close the washroom door behind him, before she turned towards the grumbling *samovar* with their mugs and two sachets of instant, part of the rations she'd packed for them. She pulled the tap towards her and watched the granules disappear into the boiling water as it swirled, leaving bubbles dancing in formation on the surface.

Liliya walked by, apparently on her break.

'You want something stronger in those?'

'No, thanks, Liliya, it's a bit early.'

'Suit yourself. How's the *kupe*?'

'Great.'

Svetlana looked Liliya in the eye and thought to ask her to keep a confidence but in the end said nothing.

'You have something to ask me, Svetlana Yuriyevna?'

'No, it's nothing.'

'Well, if it's nothing, then if anybody asks me I've no need to tell them I've seen you, have I?' said Liliya.

Svetlana smiled and gently took hold of the *providnitsa's* wrist.

'Thank you, Liliya,' she whispered, before releasing her grip.

They shared five seconds of silent respect, before the slightly smirking Liliya turned in the direction of her own carriage.

The coffee was still steaming when Nick returned to the compartment, his face damp but his skin now smooth and glistening. She kissed him.

'That's better. You look like a reporter again.'

'What did you say?'

'You look like a reporter again.'

'That's just it though. I shouldn't look like a reporter. I need to look like anything but a reporter.'

He had a point. Why hadn't she thought that one through?

'Sorry, you're right. Okay, don't shave again until we get back to Moscow... and you'll have to lose that fancy case.'

Neither of them said it, but it was moments like this, and the realisation that this was not some sort of spy game, that chipped away at their equilibrium. Their jaunty mood declined as both struggled to keep back unspoken thoughts of danger ahead. For almost an hour, Nick read the copy of the *Moscow Times* that Svetlana had kept, while she sketched him with pencil and incongruous blue biro. As she watched him, she realised Liliya had been right. There was a ghost sitting right next to him and looking back at her.

'Let's eat. Do you want to try the restaurant car?'

Nick looked up and folded the newspaper, drawing breath.

'Okay, if they have anything worth eating.'

'Let's look. I want to get out of here for a while.'

They made their way easily through the carriages, their movements by now practised at dealing with the rocking of the train as it inexorably made its way south and east, but they had to brave icy blasts as they crossed the open metal walkways between the cars.

A surly waitress grunted at them by way of greeting, as they moved to a table in the almost empty carriage, its windows partly covered with grubby, tied-back net curtains. The menu was creased and stained by a variety of substances that would now be difficult to identify, but at least there appeared to be a fairly good selection of dishes on offer.

'Drink?' enquired the waitress curtly.

'Do you have Bochkaryov?' enquired Nick.

'No.'

'Neskoye?'

'No.'

'What have you got?'

'Zhigulevskoye.'

'Fine, I'll have one of those,' said Nick.

'Me, too,' added Svetlana, smirking under her hand as the waitress turned away.

'What...?' asked Nick.

'You've almost lost your accent. I'm really impressed.'

'I've had plenty of practice.'

'Yeah, and it shows.'

She pulled back the curtain with her hooked finger to see that they were now free from forest, with a vast expanse of snow-covered plain stretching out beside them.

'You hungry?' she asked.

'Starving. What are you having?'

'I think it might be a case of what have they got. I just have that feeling.'

Her suspicions were confirmed as most of the items on the menu were 'off'. They each settled for *dvorianskaya*, chicken with breadcrumbs and some herbs, which in the event wasn't too bad and certainly a better standard than the service that accompanied it.

Later, as she encouraged the twirling slice of lemon in her tea with her spoon, she spoke to him, without lifting her eyes.

'Do you know Lake Baikal?'

'I know of it,' replied Nick.

'What do you know?'

'It's big.'

'Is that it?'

'My mum said it was beautiful.'

'It is. For many Russians, it is a special place, a place of holiness, certainly for the locals. If we are breaking our journey, it's a good choice.'

'How far from Irkutsk?'

'Depends – depends where we go. Listvyanka is good, a village near the lake. The old bit's okay – traditional. The new bit – well, it's not exactly Madrid – Soviet architecture and all that, but it is near the water and they're used to strangers. It will take an hour, maybe an hour and a half.'

'Where will we stay?'

'We'll find something. It's not exactly tourist season.'

Svetlana reached in her bag for money to pay the bill, but Nick stretched over and put his hand on hers.

'I'll get this. I think I need some change anyway.'

She smiled at him, turned her hand and gently squeezed his to indicate her gratitude.

*

The road from Irkutsk to Listvyanka was mostly clear of snow, straight and pretty much deserted as the bus trundled along. They gazed out at telegraph poles, snow-covered hills and plucky pine trees that looked forward to spring. Svetlana checked her mobile for any message from Ivan but had no signal, while Nick continued to take in all around him.

'It's just snow,' she said.

'It's Russia – Russia I've not seen,' he replied.

She left him to his reflection, the rocking of the bus and its overwarm atmosphere making her drowsy. She rested her head back and closed her eyes, wondering if she could sleep a little in the fifty minutes or so they had left of the journey.

'Listvyanka!' called out the driver as the bus passed the first buildings alongside the road.

Nick nudged Svetlana with his elbow and she stirred.

'We're here,' he said.

They alighted in the old village, next to the shore and at the base of the Krestovka Valley, holding in its arms a collection of simple wooden houses, some brightly painted and many with corrugated roofs. Nick stood, transfixed, looking out across the vast frozen lake, with its pale, blue-tinted ice. He didn't move, even as the sound of the growling bus faded into silence amongst the vastness of the place. From a pace behind and to his side, she watched him, respectful of the interlude that had befallen him. She reminded herself that his roots were by blood and not by familiarity. What was routine for her was a new experience for him and he was still coming to terms with Mother Russia and all she had to show him. To her surprise, she watched a tear form and fall from the corner of his eye onto his cheek. She stepped forward to hold him.

'Nikolai, what is it?'

He held her in return, shaking his head. She wiped the remains of the tear from his face and kissed his cheek.

'I love you, Nikolai.'

'And I love you, Sveta... Sorry, I feel like a baby.'

'It's okay, big boy. Come on, let's find something to eat and then somewhere to stay.'

They didn't have to look long for food. Two hundred metres away, a small group stood round four-legged braziers and as the couple drew closer, the smell of smoked fish reached them. It was *omul*, the native fish of Baikal, a staple for villagers and visitors alike.

'Fresh today... smoked the way my grandfather used to,' said a small stallholder with a big voice, apparently the sales director of this micro-enterprise.

Laid out before them was an array of fish, in various states of preparedness but all complemented by an enticing aroma. Svetlana was suddenly hungry.

'We'll have these two,' she said, pointing to two substantial fish that looked properly cooked.

'No problem,' responded the stallholder.

He expertly swept up the fish and deposited each one on a piece of greaseproof paper.

'There you are, my dear.'

Svetlana, slightly surprised at the friendly service, accepted the fish from him and smelt it, feeling its warmth near to the exposed skin of her face.

'And for you, sir – does she always make the decisions?' he added, winking at Nick.

Svetlana's Garden

'No,' Nick hurriedly insisted.

Svetlana managed to smirk, while still chewing her first mouthful.

'My wife makes the decisions,' responded the little guy.

He pointed to a large woman in a thick, long, grey anorak, at least twenty centimetres taller than him, arriving with a bag of logs.

'It's fine. I like a quiet life,' he said, shrugging his shoulders.

Svetlana and Nick glanced at each other and smiled, just before the fuel-bearing wife was close enough to be in on the private joke.

'We need to stay over tonight. Do you know anywhere?' asked Nick.

'Sure –'

'My sister runs a guest house, up near the church,' said the wife, interrupting her husband who from behind her shrugged and opened his palms mockingly. 'It's got two buildings. You can have a room in the house or an apartment in the second block, if she's got any vacancies. You can't miss it – on the left, before the church – with a blue sign over a green door. Tell her Olesya sent you – and she owes me.'

'Thanks, we'll tell her,' said Svetlana.'

Fading afternoon light went with them as they walked through the village, occasionally accompanied by the sound of barking dogs protecting their territory. Eventually, they came towards a wooden church, its contrasting dark and pale pink colours difficult to discern in the approaching darkness. There, as Olesya had said, was a house, with a green door and a blue sign over it.

'This must be it. Come on,' said Nick.

'Wait a moment,' replied Svetlana.

She walked on and stopped at the steps leading to the church grounds. Nick joined her.

'What?' he asked.

'This church is your namesake. This is the church of St Nikolai. Did you know that?'

'No. And I'm not a saint.'

'No, Kolya, you're not – but you are a good man.'

She put her hand to his face and held him for a long moment.

*

Olesya's recommendation had been a good one. They'd been able to warm up by spending an hour in the *banya*, housed in a not very inviting tin-roofed shed attached to the guest house, but where the warmth and steam had revived them. Later, they'd slept well in the simple but comfortable room, after a delicious dinner of Buryat style pork *shashlik* prepared by their hosts, Dariya and her husband Semyon.

Outside, the morning sun was bright, sparkling off the snow-covered trees higher up the side of the valley. Svetlana opened the curtains and for a while watched the golden light play its tricks with the pure white snow above.

'We have to get the bus at six tonight to be in good time for the train,' she said to Nick, who was propped up in bed with two large pillows folded behind him.

'No problem. So, we can be tourists for a day. What shall we do?'
'Ski.'
'Or, a snowmobile.'
'Don't be lazy, Nikolai. We'll ski... and have a picnic. I'm sure Dariya can fix it for us.'

*

An hour after breakfast, Semyon dropped them off five kilometres further up the valley, properly prepared with the equipment supplied by his brother. It seemed that no business round there needed to advertise, as all goods and services were supplied by somebody's relative.

They climbed for an hour, carrying their skis over their shoulders, the air filling their lungs as fresh and clean as the world had to offer. Occasionally, Svetlana struggled where the snow was deepest and Nick helped her. The sun was now higher in the sky and illuminated the glorious, untouched array of what nature had laid out for them, while down below, the huge lake, looking more like an inland sea, stretched out majestically towards the horizon.

'Enough. Let's go from here,' said Nick, rolling the skis from his shoulder.

They both stood and contemplated their route down, the danger of what lay ahead in Chita temporarily banished to the back of their minds by the sensory feast before them.

'You ready?' asked Svetlana, as she pulled her goggles over her eyes.

'Ready,' he replied.

She'd not actually asked him if he could ski well, she'd just assumed it. Anxious for a moment, she looked back. His confident smile reassured her that he could.

They set off, both able to slalom through the trees, the elongated swish of ski on untouched snow the only sound to accompany them.

Including their stop for a brief picnic of omul, cheese and bread, they took nearly two hours to reach the lakeside, by which time the sun was beginning the final stage of its day's journey. The ice had acquired a pale purple hue, as Svetlana and Nick removed their skis and sat on a fallen tree at the edge of the lake, about a kilometre from the village. She hugged him and then sat back to see him once again staring out, trance-like, across the frozen wilderness.

'You're not going to cry again, are you?' she asked.

Nick didn't answer.

On the horizon, burnt orange met fading blue as the last minutes of daylight ticked away. He stood and then sank to one knee, taking her hand, her face lit by a pale golden glow that would soon disappear as the sun's fingertips slipped from the edge of the sky.

'Sveta...'

'Nikolai...?'

'I want you to marry me.'

She raised her eyebrows. He had her full attention, but she had contemplated no such early proposal and was taken by surprise.

'Mother Russia has seduced you, Nikolai, and the spirits of the lake must have cast a spell upon you.'

'No, they haven't – but you have. It's a spell I never want broken.'

'Nikolai, what has come over you?'

'You are the one – I know you are the one. It's not Russia that makes me feel alive, it's you. You have become the reason my heart beats. Marry me, Sveta, marry me?'

At that moment, the pale light finally surrendered her face to the approaching night as, heart pounding, she contemplated the enormity of the situation – and, her answer.

Chapter 22

The lunchtime broadcast had news of a meteor shower, due that night, but as Yakov Katenin watched the entrance to *Search for Truth's* offices, from an alleyway across ulitsa Pravdy, the swirling dark clouds above signalled that he and the rest of Moscow were unlikely to see it.

Vasiliy made his way down the stairs, keeping faith with his resolution to walk whenever possible and avoid elevators. His mood was upbeat. Demchi had praised his piece on Grishkuv and had even joked that Svetlana had better up her game, with Vasiliy making such progress. He left the building, still grateful to be allowed to go early to join the celebration for his sister's birthday.

By the time he reached the entrance to his block, it was dark. Two lights flanked the main doorway and Vasiliy stood under the working one to select his door key, a practised routine. He heard a rustle from behind him and turned to look. He saw nothing but a dark shadow from the adjoining apartment block.

'They followed you yesterday,' said Katenin, stepping forward, his outline now visible but not his features.

'You're the artist.'

'They don't always follow you – they don't always follow her.'

'You're the artist, aren't you?' said Vasiliy, unnerved but at the same time elated.

'Where is she?'

'Sveta?'

'Where is she?'

'On a few days' leave.'

'With him?'

'I guess so... I don't really know.'
'When's she back?'

Vasiliy hesitated, unsure if he should be giving any more information.

'Why haven't you printed it?' asked Katenin.
'We're still working on it.'
'So, you're going to print it?'
'I don't know. It's not up to me.'
'What's your name?'
'Vasiliy.'
'Do you know mine?'
'Yakov – Yakov Katenin.'
'Does the FSB know my name?'
'I don't know. She's kept me away from you; thinks it's too dangerous.'
'Then, they do.'
'Do you want to come in and get a drink or something?'
'Who's in charge of the case?'
'At the FSB?'
'Yes.'
'Malenkov – Captain Malenkov.'
'Do you know him?'
'No, I've just seen him, that's all.'
'So have I: short, glasses?'
'Yes,' confirmed Vasiliy.
'Tell her I need to see her.'
'When? How?'
'Dating ad – in your paper.'
'Saying what?'
'I'll recognise it. I know her style.'
'When?'

Katenin was gone, slipping back into the shadows as quietly as he'd arrived.

Vasiliy looked at his hand holding the keys. It was trembling.

*

Svetlana wore a more or less permanent grin on the bus back to Irkutsk. They were to be married as soon as they could.

'I thought you were going to say no, you waited so long,' said Nick.

'I was just shocked. I was never going to say no, Kolya.'

She took his hand and held it, closed her eyes and indulged herself with a daydream of them watching a beach sunset together, somewhere warm.

'What will your mum say?' he asked.

'What?'

'What will your mum say?'

'What do you think? An American – and probably a spy.'

'That's old Cold War stuff.'

'Relax, Nikolai, I'm just joking. She was brought up that way, but she doesn't think like that. I'm a product of her, remember. If you love me, then she will love you.'

'I do.'

'Then you can stop worrying about your mother-in-law, can't you?'

'And Ivan?'

'He'll be okay. I'll talk to him.'

'I hope so.'

'He'll be okay,' she said, squeezing his hand.

*

There was no sign of any FSB officers looking for them at Irkutsk, not that Nick had yet learned to spot them. Svetlana, however, had scanned the entrances and the waiting areas, her head bowed and hat pulled down, until she was as sure as she could be. They bought provisions for the journey and near to the station Nick found a shop selling a long, padded, dark jacket to replace his over-smart coat, which they took in exchange. Wisely, he swapped his suitcase for a rucksack.

Neither of them thought to ask the other to turn back. Both now knew their journey to Chita was inevitable.

Their *provodnitsa* this time was matter-of-fact in her manner, holding out little prospect of a Liliya-like bond. Nevertheless, Svetlana urged Nick to give her three thousand rubles as insurance. She showed them to their compartment in *spalny* class, a distinct contrast to *platskartny*, where they'd started their journey. The first class cabin was clean and tidy, with red curtains which would shut properly and linen already set out for them. No sooner had they sat down than there was a knock at the door. It was the *provodnitsa* with tea and some biscuits, if not a smile. The insurance was working.

They sat opposite each other, as two genies of steam rising from the glasses constantly changed shape before them.

'You hungry?' asked Nick.

'Later,' she replied.

'You're scared, aren't you?'

'Yes.'

'Of marriage?'

'No, of Chita.'

'Why don't you call your mum and tell her the good news?'

'I'll tell her in person, and anyway, it's possible they're listening in to her calls, by now.'

'We have to –'

'I know.'

'We'll be okay.'

'Sure,' she said, spreading her fingers out on the table and examining the state of her nails.

'And when we get back, we can plan the wedding,' added Nick.

He reached across and took her hands in his.

'Sveta, this is the right thing and we will be okay.'

'Yes.'

'And we'll be married.'

'Yes,' she confirmed.

'Where do you want to live?' he asked.

'Somewhere warm, maybe. We'll talk about it,' she said, lifting her eyes to look into his. 'But, first, Nikolai, we have to stay alive. If we are caught in Chita they will shoot us. You do know that, don't you?'

Nick looked at her and recalled the moment in Café Pushkin when he'd been on the point of telling her about the villa in Spain, but had stopped himself. He resolved to keep his silence until he could take her there himself as a surprise, and when he'd know from her reaction whether they'd make their home at Los Arrayanes.

'Yes, I know,' he replied.

*

'I have to say, I'm somewhat disappointed,' said Malenkov, to the contrite Valentina. 'I mean you're at the TV station, you're next to the guy, and you don't know where he is. Days he's been gone... and that bitch Dorenko!'

'I'm sorry, Gennadiy, but there was no warning. He was due in and he just didn't show up. I can't watch him twenty-four hours a day.'

'Has there been anything from Madrid?'

'Not that I know of.'

'You don't seem to know about anything at the moment. And that Santos girl, what's all that about? Why is she here? I don't like any of this. Get Il'ya and the rest of them. I want a meeting in one hour.'

'Yes, Gennadiy.'

Malenkov shot her a look.

'Yes, sir,' said Valentina turning for the door and making her escape.

'Mrs Dorenko, Mr Mendez: I don't know exactly what you're up to, but I will not be made a fool of,' said Malenkov, under his breath.

He paced the room but merely felt his frustration rising. At times like this, while others might take a pill, he resorted to music as his tried-and-tested method to restore his equilibrium. He switched on the speakers and then scrolled through folders of his computer until he came to the one named PIT, holding tracks by his musical therapist and hero, one Pyotr Ilyich Tchaikovsky. Within seconds, the plaintiff cello of *Valse Sentimentale* was soothing him, seducing him to follow the sound to a better place. He gave in, closing his eyes and gently rolling his head as tension gave way to calm, the thorny problem of the two reporters temporarily consigned to the back of his mind.

He'd no idea how many times the music had repeated itself, when a sharp knock at the door disturbed him. He clicked pause, leaving only a faint hiss from the speakers to remind him of what had gone before.

'Come in,' he called.

With some evident trepidation, the team of six shuffled in. They need not have worried, for Malenkov was now relaxed and back to his calculating best.

'Sit down, all of you. I want to review everything we've got.'

They took their seats, one by one, all seemingly anxious to please.

'Okay, we know Dorenko and Mendez are working together, and we know they know about Katenin. We need to establish and keep contact with them all, as soon as possible. Do we have any sightings of Katenin?'

There was a collective shaking of heads from the team.

'Right, get his picture out to the *politsiya* so we can have more people on the street. Tell them he's wanted for drug dealing. We'll have their attention if somebody thinks they can make some money out of it.'

'I'll sort it,' volunteered Il'ya.

'Good. Last sighting of Dorenko?'

Il'ya consulted his notes.

'Tuesday evening, seven-thirty at the Perekrestok near her apartment.'

'And Mendez?'

'Zero-one-fifty, on Wednesday, returning to his apartment.'

'Alone?'

'Yes.'

'Any unusual purchases by either of them?'

The group exchanged glances, before mumbling a collective 'No.'

'There was one thing,' said Valentina.

'Yes?'

'I could be wrong, but I think he might have had a different phone, on Tuesday.'

'We have his phone, right?'

'Yes,' said Il'ya.

'Last fix for that?'

'His apartment – at zero-two-twenty – Wednesday.'

'And since then?'

'Nothing,' said Il'ya. 'It must be turned off.'

'The bastard's switched phones! Why don't we have details? Why don't we have it? What about hers?'

Il'ya consulted his notes again.

'Switched off.'

'She's done the same,' said Malenkov. 'We have to do better than this. Any contact with her mother?'

'No,' replied Il'ya.

'We have at least got that phone covered, have we?'

'Yes, sir.'

'Credit cards?'

'Nothing, for four days.'

'Conclusions?' asked Malenkov.

The group hesitated, some looking to the floor to avoid Malenkov's gaze. Valentina eventually braved an answer.

'They're not here, in Moscow.'

'They're not here. That's right. They're not fucking here and we knew nothing about it!'

'I'll have all the flights checked,' volunteered Il'ya hurriedly.

'Does she have another passport, from Dubnikov, perhaps?'

'We don't think so.'

'And him – I'm assuming he's CIA, or connected, at least?'

'No, sir, we don't think so.'

'Think what?'

'That he's CIA. We don't know about the passport.'

'So, he's doing this for her. Interesting. What about their cars?'

'Still there,' said Il'ya.

'Okay, if we find they've not flown, they've got help – or maybe it's the train. Get images to our people at all the major stations, just in case.'

'All of them?'

'Yes, Il'ya, all of them.'

'Yes, sir.'

Malenkov drew a breath and sighed.

'Officers of the FSB, I think you'll agree we haven't exactly covered ourselves in glory these last couple of days. As far as I'm concerned, Dorenko and her American boyfriend are scum who have no interest in protecting this country. Quite the contrary, in fact. Above me, I have a commanding officer and above him he has the Kremlin. Shit comes downhill officers and if it reaches me it will, for sure, reach you. Now get out and find those fucking bastards!'

As one, they stood and moved to replace their chairs, anxious to escape before receiving another clap of thunder from the storm now raging in the room. When the last one had left, Malenkov reached out for the mouse to his computer and clicked his command for the music to start once again.

*

By the next morning, the long train had passed the junction with the Trans-Mongolian line and in another five hundred kilometres would reach Chita.

Svetlana prepared their breakfast of *bliny*, cheese and ham, while Nick went to the *samovar* to make coffee. He returned a couple of minutes later, spilling some on his shoe as he tried to hold the cups, while opening the door.

'Shit,' he said.

'Forget it. Come, sit down and have your breakfast,' said Svetlana.

He ate quickly.

'Nikolai, we'll be there later today. We must plan.'

'Like what?'

'We must assume they will be looking. Maybe not, but we must assume it.'

'Okay.'

'Have a wash now, this will be your last chance. From now on, we must be ready to move at a minute's notice. They could search the train or anything.'

'Maybe we should get off the train early.'

'Maybe, if there is a chance and transport. Without it, the weather is just as dangerous as the FSB.'

'And if we go to the station?'

'We separate. Wear your hat and a scarf over your face. We'll meet in the main square, by Lenin's statue.'

'Then what?'

'Find somewhere to stay and then we can work out how to get to the army base.'

'JF's going to help.'

'JF?'

'My boss, in Madrid.'

She wasn't following him, at all.

'Sveta, you didn't think I'd come all this way without a map, did you?'

'Wonders of technology – GPS technology,' he said, holding up his phone. 'JF's going to send me a map and satellite image. Well, a bit better than the normal image – enhanced – if you know what I mean. JF has one or two connections.'

She smiled.

'And do you have these connections, Nikolai?'

'No, I just do my job.'

'I see... but you have friends with connections, if you need them?'

'Something like that. Something like you, perhaps?'

'*Search for Truth* is not INN, Nikolai,' she said. 'Why don't you finish your coffee and then go for a wash?'

'Okay,' he replied, as he took the last swig from his cup and picked up his towel.

As the door closed behind him, Svetlana's mind drifted to thoughts of Ivan. She was missing him, even with his dark moods.

How did she find herself here, six thousand kilometres from home and in such danger?

You should have listened to Demchi, she thought, for the umpteenth time. And yet, in a strange way, she was becoming reconciled to and almost fatalistic about her predicament. If anything happened to her, Ivan would come to understand. His grandmother was wise, as for that matter was her sister, in Kaluga. They would see that her son came to know of higher concepts, like truth and principle, so that one day he might be proud. She checked her phone, but there was nothing. She presumed he was having a good time, and perhaps it was for the best to leave him be for now, given the consequences.

She looked at her hands, stretching them out as far as they would go and then imagined Nick's ring on her finger. She recalled her mother's words, "One day those hands will carry the ring given to you by the man you love." She smiled, and wished her mother was there so that she could be gently teased by her. She'd been right all along.

'Washroom's free,' said Nick, as he came back in.

'Okay, thanks,' she replied.

Walking down the corridor, she froze as two soldiers in uniform approached, but she need not have worried. They were just two young guys, returning from leave, and strolling the length of the train to relieve the monotony. She was even comforted by the low wolf-whistle that followed her when they'd passed her. They were looking at her but not for her.

When she'd washed, she applied only a little make-up, enough to mask her gathering anxiety but not so much as would make her stand out. The eyes looking back at her from the mirror carried false bravado. Behind them, she saw her own fear.

Their *provodnitsa* was coming down the corridor, as Svetlana emerged.

'Are we stopping before Chita?'

'It depends,' replied the *provodnitsa*. 'Sometimes – then sometimes not. Why, do you need something?'

'No, just wondering.'

In the compartment, Nick was finishing packing his rucksack and took the opportunity to charge his phone, one of the benefits of *spalny* class.

'We're probably not stopping,' said Svetlana, as she shut the door behind her.

'Oh yeah?'

'Yes. She said sometimes, but I got the impression we're going straight through.'

'Okay.'

'So, we'll do what we talked about.'

'Sure. I'll walk down a couple of carriages to get off. See you in the square, right?' she said.

'Right,' replied Nick.

They said little for the rest of the journey as Chita came near.

Sure enough, the train did not stop but instead entered the outskirts of the former closed city, its drab apartment blocks and offices much lower than the towering structures of Moscow. The beginnings of first light showed the hills behind, rising up and overlooking the metropolis below. The odd pair of tail lights gave away the movement of early morning deliveries, as the train snaked its way through the suburbs towards its destination. Svetlana shivered and looked at Nick, his smile in return apparently diluted by uncertainty. He rose and picked up his rucksack.

'See you in the square,' he said.

He placed a hand on her shoulder and leant down to kiss her, before reaching for the door handle.

'Nikolai... I love you.'

'I know. I love you, too.'

With a click of the latch, he was gone. Svetlana shut her eyes and let the train rock her for the last few hundred metres of the journey, before she too rose and picked up her bag.

At the door, the *provodnitsa* was waiting.

'Goodbye – and good luck,' she said.

Svetlana put her foot on the first step down to the frosted, grey tarmac below.

'Thank you, you've been great.'

'Will we see you again?'

'Do you know, I'm really not sure... but thanks, anyway.'

She didn't look back as she walked towards the exit. Light sleet began to fall, assisting her wish to be anonymous and giving her the excuse to draw her scarf tighter across her face. She hoped Nick would remember to avoid eye contact and gave thanks that he'd ditched the suitcase that would have brought instant attention to him. *Babushkiy* were already out, selling food to those commencing or breaking their journey. Svetlana mingled with their customers, before moving on. Nick had overtaken her, striding a little too purposefully while she checked out the scene in front of him.

'Oh shit!' she mouthed, under her breath.

An unmistakeable FSB officer looked on from the exit gate, hands in his pockets but eyes scanning the approaching passengers. Nick was thirty metres from him, apparently oblivious and maintaining his pace, when to Svetlana's astonishment, the officer stepped in front of another tall, male passenger and put up his hand to halt him. By the time he reached him, the passenger was handing over papers for inspection, and Nick was able to walk straight past. Svetlana let out the breath she'd been holding and, heart racing, took her opportunity to slip by with eyes firmly fixed upon the ground.

Outside, Nick was marching across the station's car park. If he was planning to walk, he'd be tired and hungry by the time he arrived, thought Svetlana. But, then again, maybe he was right to just get away and worry about his bearings later. She slipped into the rear seat of a taxi at the front of a small queue of four, its engine running.

'Where to?' asked the driver curtly.

'Main Square.'

'Lenin Square, you mean?'

'Yes,' she replied, annoyed with herself that she'd already managed to give away her lack of local knowledge to this stranger.

They drove in silence and too fast for the conditions, but within fifteen minutes she was walking across the vast snow-covered square, approaching a giant statue of Lenin, atop a heavy, square stone pedestal. The hero of the October Revolution stood, right hand in pocket, while his left held the lapel of his jacket to expose his waistcoat as he looked towards the hills and some far off future. She looked up at the imposing figure, not with reverence as she would to her statuesque friend and confidant at Pushkinskaya ploshchad in Moscow, but with contempt for the legacy of fear she considered he'd left to so many of her fellow citizens.

'You made it, then.'

She turned to see Nick approaching from her left.

'How did you get here?'

'Have you never heard the expression "follow that cab"?' replied Nick.

'Just like the movies?'

'Yeah, just like the movies.'

'Well, Nikolai, this isn't the movies. Let's get away and find somewhere for coffee to get warm.'

*

They stayed away from hotels to avoid being asked for passports and found a room in a humble guest house, a kilometre or so from the city centre. It was mostly occupied by construction workers, one of whom had agreed an informal rental of his employer's UAZ 4x4 jeep. A hundred dollars was steep, but Svetlana reckoned it was worth it and that sort of figure was also likely to guarantee discretion, as anonymity would suit both parties. Conditions would be difficult and the tough vehicle was just the sort of transport they needed, not to mention that outdoor work-suits came with the deal to offer them extra protection against the still fierce Siberian cold.

They'd reached the outskirts of the city, where Nick was still struggling to learn how to make smooth changes of the crude four-speed gearbox. He pulled over and took out his phone, then checked his watch, and waited.

'Your connections?' asked Svetlana.

'Yeah, don't want to carry this round longer than necessary but we can't risk losing the signal. I told JF eight a.m., our time, unless I called it off.'

As he finished speaking, and right on time, his phone bleeped to announce the arrival of an incoming message.

'What's he sent you?' she asked.

'A map and GPS co-ordinates.'

'Of the base?'

'No, Sveta, of the gas chamber... or what they think is the gas chamber.'

'And if it's not?'

'Then we're probably screwed. It's a big base.'

'Well, let's find out, shall we?'

They looked at each other silently for a few seconds, before Nick crunched the gearlever into first and set off, heading for Antipikha, some ten kilometres south.

As they drove down the A-166, they were passed by a number of army trucks going in the opposite direction, a reminder they were now well and truly in military territory. Cresting a hill, they saw for the first time the vast base in the valley below. While snow covered the base, it was nevertheless easy to make out the endless barrack buildings, vehicle sheds and the training grounds, all overlooked by trees stretching up the hillsides. Svetlana realised what Nick had said was true: without the GPS, they could search for days and still not find the chamber they believed was there. They had one or two clues though. She recalled pine trees in the near background of Katenin's picture, so they could discount the vehicle sheds, parade grounds and the tank training grounds. However, that still left several kilometres of base, to which trees formed a backdrop.

'Stop for a minute, Nikolai.'

'No, not here. It's not a good idea to be seen overlooking the base. Just take in what you can.'

She struggled to do that, as the jeep's heater failed to clear the side window properly. She wiped it with her sleeve, only marginally improving visibility as she peered through the smudged streaks of moisture. They descended, and as the ground levelled out, Nick handed her his phone.

'Keep it on your lap, but as near the window as you can for the signal. Shout me directions and we'll get as close as we can.'

They passed what looked like the main gate, where sentries stood menacing guard with guns at the ready.

'That's a bonus,' said Nick, tapping his thumb on the side window to indicate some contractor's vehicles next to a building having its roof renewed.

'Maybe,' she replied.

'Where next?' he enquired, as she studied the phone's screen.

'Over there,' she replied, pointing.

'No road. We need to go left but there's no road – no bloody road!' he exclaimed.

'Nick, watch out!'

A giant tank transporter was bearing down on them, its tyres the height of their jeep and its cabin towering above. Nick braked and struggled to control the vehicle as it reluctantly accepted his commands, slewing towards a marker post at the side of the road. No more than a few centimetres separated them from a sickening collision as they skidded to a halt.

'Bastard!' shouted Nick. 'Bastard!'

Svetlana bent forward to recover the phone, which had slipped from her grasp but which, fortunately, seemed none the worse.

'Stay cool, Nikolai... We're okay. Come on.'

'Bastard!' repeated Nick under his breath.

He moved off again and she put her hand on his while he held the gear lever, hoping to relieve some of the tension exposed by the near accident.

'Let's turn, where we can. This says we're maybe a couple of kilometres away.'

They passed numerous warning signs making it perfectly clear the consequences awaiting trespassers found on the base. Eventually, they came to a track, which seemed to lead along the side of the valley, through the trees above the base. Nick stopped and glanced at the screen Svetlana was holding.

'What do you think?' she asked.

'It's not exactly close, but it looks like our best bet.'

He reversed a few metres and then turned into the track. Despite its four wheel drive, the jeep initially struggled with the untouched snow. Once under the shelter of the trees, they made better progress but Nick had to concentrate while ruts and exposed tree roots tried their best to wrench the wheel from his hands. After twenty minutes, the screen showed them above and level with the red dot, indicating what they hoped was their target.

'This is as close as we can get,' he said.

Svetlana nodded in acknowledgment, silently steeling herself for the freezing hike ahead of them. Without asking, Nick commenced a series of manoeuvres to turn the jeep round to point in the direction they'd come from.

'Might need a quick getaway,' he said, as he pulled on the handbrake's noisy ratchet.

They checked their equipment. Today was calm, with little wind chill but it was still twenty-five below and they would need all the protection against the elements that they'd armed themselves with.

'Camera?' asked Svetlana.

Nick patted his chest to indicate he had the precious means to gather their evidence, tucked away under several layers to protect it from the cold.

'Ready?' he asked.

'Let's go,' she responded, opening her door and sliding down into the snow that crunched under her feet.

It was not long before they reached a barbed wire perimeter fence, and even here in the trees written warnings threatened them. With large pliers he'd taken from the jeep's toolkit, Nick cut the fence and held it back for Svetlana to crawl through before she returned the favour for him. In the distance, they heard a howl and froze as they looked at each other.

'Wolves... guard dogs?' she whispered, aware without being told that raised voices had nothing to offer them from now on.

Nick shrugged and signalled for them to press on. They made their way through the woods, thankful for the cover they offered. Distant gunfire indicated training was very much in progress, despite the penetrating cold of the Siberian late winter, but near to them they just had the grunts of the snow underfoot and the whispering of the trees for company.

After an hour, they'd covered about a kilometre when Nick checked his phone screen.

'Shit,' he said.

'What?' asked Svetlana.

He held up the screen to show her they had no signal. A hundred metres ahead, they saw clear ground but could ill afford to be wandering around directionless in the open. Svetlana looked back at their tracks in the snow to confirm the route they'd been taking, when the GPS had last helped them. Their bearings so set, they proceeded to the edge of the woods and crouched down to assess the position. On the far side of the valley, plumes of smoke rose from tanks embarking on an exercise. Moments later, the sound of their engines arrived. In front of the two reporters, perhaps fifty metres away, was a large corrugated building, pale green and festooned with icicles hanging from its roof. They made their way to it, listening all the time for the tell-tale sound of voices that would indicate whether it was empty or occupied. Svetlana peered through a panel joint to see, of all things, tractors and chainsaws. Apparently, even the army needed to carry out some husbandry of the woods from time to time. She signalled to Nick to investigate. Walking away from the direction of the main barracks and using the building for cover, they looked round its corner to see the back of another single-storey building, with snow driven a metre up its grey concrete walls. They listened again, but could only hear the far off grumbling of the tanks and the rat-tat-tat of gunfire as target practice continued. Glancing left and right, they reached the back of the concrete building, and using it for cover, worked their way to the front corner. A cleared path leading down to a small parade ground, itself connected to a track in the direction of the main entrance, indicated that this building was in at least occasional occupation. They walked across the face and gained the path, considerably easing their progress as they moved to get a better look.

Svetlana turned to face the building. Snow and icicles did their best to offer a seasonal disguise, but as she stood stock still, the shocking image Katenin had painted imposed itself on the scene in front of her. She knew exactly where Rebikov had been standing while bellowing his foul insults, where the conscripts had knelt emptying their bellies of vomit and where young Andrei had sucked in his last desperate, terrified breath. This was that place. The noise from the trees seemed to grow as if each was clamouring to unburden itself and finally confess the scenes it had been forced to witness. To her horror, she realised she'd just walked right over where the boy's body had lain. She felt the urge to be sick and began to retch as she desperately reached behind her to tug at Nick's sleeve.

'Sveta, no! No! Come here!'

Nick pulled her to him and put his mouth to her ear.

'Darling, no. We need to go. We can't do this... not now.'

She was shaking and held on to him as hard as she could, willing his soothing words to break through and calm her from the concoction of emotions that had suddenly overwhelmed her.

'Hold me, darling – hold me – you'll be fine – just hold me,' said Nick.

Slowly, her composure returned.

'I'm sorry,' she responded.

'Don't be. Just hold me.'

She looked up at him, her eyes now released from their ambush of desperation.

'I'm okay,' she said, loosening her hold on him. 'You see it, don't you? This is the place.'

The door, the frame, grey concrete and overlooking trees all told them what they needed to know.

'This is the place. Let's take our photos and then get out of here,' he said.

She released him so that he could extract the camera. Nick took a selection of shots quickly, checking each image as he did.

'That's it. Let's go,' he said.

They made their way back up the path and once again across the face of the building, Svetlana pausing to stoop and reach out a hand to stroke the air where the boy's face had been. In the distance, a number of vehicles were moving in their direction.

'Sveta, we gotta go... right now.'

Svetlana's Garden

They retraced their steps and made it back to the jeep, its windows once again frosted up. Svetlana was much more composed now and grateful that they'd managed to pull this off, so far without challenge, although she'd had a strange feeling they were being followed. After a few minutes, the warmth from the engine started to feed through and the frost receded from the windscreen in a widening arch. Suddenly, Nick turned his head, apparently having seen something. He killed the engine and stared out, putting his finger to his mouth to indicate to Svetlana that she should be quiet. Her heart began to race as she looked out intently on the scene around them.

'There!' he said, pointing.

'Where?'

'There... by that tree.'

She looked closely, to see a pair of eyes looking back at her. With ghostly movement, another pair appeared.

'It's a wolf – it's a bloody wolf!' said Nick.

Sure enough, as their eyes adjusted to the scene, they could make out the shapes of a number of wolves, their fur offering them excellent camouflage for their forest pursuits.

They both laughed, as from the safety of the enclosed cab, the sudden apprehension they'd felt slipped away.

'Looks like we were lunch. They must be hungry,' said Nick.

'I wouldn't have wanted to do this at night,' replied Svetlana.

'No way – no way. I'm not used to being hunted by wolves,' replied Nick, his voice suddenly tailing away.

They looked at each other, as his words seemed to echo in the vehicle's cabin. She took his hand.

'Oh, Nikolai, they're only just starting to hunt. What will become of us when they catch us?'

Nick started the engine and engaged first gear to begin their long journey back to Moscow.

Chapter 23

'Oh, Sveta, come here!' said her mother, reaching forward to give Svetlana a long, lingering hug. 'I knew you were seeing him, but I didn't realise it was so serious.'

'Neither did I, Mama, but when he asked me I knew it was right.'
'How did he ask you?' interrupted her mother, stepping back.
'On the shore of Baikal, in the setting sun; it was very romantic.'
'Oh... your father would have done this, too.'

For a few moments her mother's face held a whimsical smile, before changing to a look of concerned gravity.

'Is he a serious man, Sveta?'
'Is he what?'
'A serious man. Is he going to look after you... and Ivan?'

Svetlana took her mother's hand as a sign of affection and returned her earnest look as a sign of respect.

'He is a hard worker, he is brave and he does love me. I'm sure he loves me.'
'Does he drink?'
'Some wine, but does he drink like Dima? No, not like that.'
'I hope not.'
'Don't worry.'
'When are you planning it?'
'As soon as we can.'
'And Ivan?'
'I will speak to him. I'm just waiting for the right moment. You know how he can be.'
'I will speak to him too, when the time is right. His moods are normal, but he loves you. He tells me.'

'He tells you?'

'Yes.'

'Tells you he loves me?'

'Yes, Sveta, tells me he loves you.'

Svetlana put her hands to her face, as tears formed in her eyes. Sometimes Ivan's moods made her doubt his inner love and it was such a relief to hear of its ongoing commitment to her. She sniffed and wiped her nose with the back of her hand.

'Use a tissue, dear. You know I don't think that's ladylike.'

'Okay,' said Svetlana, reaching for a tissue and blowing her nose, before composing herself.

'I'll make some tea. Sit in the lounge, Sveta, and we can talk about arrangements. There'll be a lot to organise.'

There was something about how her mother laid out a tea tray, the pot, the cups and the angles somehow just so. Svetlana had tried to copy it, but never seemed to get it quite right. Their normal mugs had been replaced with two floral cups and saucers from her mother's own wedding set, of which five remained intact, silent recognition of the importance of the occasion.

'Now, how many people were you planning on?'

'I'm not sure. We haven't really got to that level of detail,' replied Svetlana.

'What on earth have you been doing with your time?'

Svetlana avoided the question and moved on.

'Well, I guess Nick will have a few colleagues, from the station here in Moscow, and maybe from Madrid. I don't know, really.'

'What about his mother and father? Are they coming? Do they speak Russian?'

'I don't know. I mean, they speak Russian but I don't know if they're coming.'

'Well, you'd better find out. You don't sound very organised, the pair of you. Who's coming from *Search for Truth*? And, what about your dress?'

An hour passed quickly, as a hand-written list was started and altered. For Svetlana, the fuss her mother made and the good natured scolding she was handing out were delicious, simply delicious.

'Right, I think we've made some progress, but there's plenty to do. Really, I think you could have done some of this while you were travelling. What were you up to, anyway?'

Svetlana didn't know about the bug the FSB had planted, but her reporter's sixth sense steered her from a truthful answer, just in case.

'Just some holiday, a few days' break. Look, Mama, I better go. I need to feed Ivan, and if I can, talk to him.'

With kisses, mother and daughter parted, and Svetlana made her way down to the street below.

*

Somehow, Victoria and Pilar had managed to sit at a table in the elegant Bosco Café with just about the best view there was over Red Square. After days exploring places away from the main tourist haunts, they'd rewarded themselves with a bit of designer shopping at GUM, the giant shopping store that occupied almost the entire length of the square. They were sipping their delivered but not yet paid for cappuccinos as Nick approached them.

Svetlana had quizzed him when he'd told her he would be meeting them again. Actually, he was flattered but not surprised to know there was an underlying jealousy in his passionate fiancée.

Victoria greeted him with a squeal and flung her arms around his neck. Pilar acknowledged his arrival with a kiss to each cheek and a more restrained hand on his shoulder. He signalled to the waiter for a cappuccino for himself.

'So, what have you seen?' he asked in Russian, before correcting himself in Spanish.

'Loads and loads. We haven't stopped,' said Victoria. 'Red Square, obviously – Babe, show him the pictures!'

Pilar scrolled through images on her camera before handing it to Nick. He laughed.

'I don't know, I'm gone for a few days and already you're in danger of creating an international incident. The soldiers aren't supposed to pose with tourists.'

'Yeah, well it was a laugh, a bit of a challenge,' said Victoria.

'I can see,' said Nick, scrolling through a few more images, chuckling as he did.

'And we saw the Kremlin, the White House and Gorky Park. I didn't know Vicki was such a good skater,' added Pilar. 'We've done lots of little back streets too – tried to find some of the real stuff you mentioned. But, today was shopping!'

'What did you get?' asked Nick.

'Not that much. Have you seen the prices in there?' asked Victoria, thumbing behind her in the direction of GUM.

'Yeah, it's steep and you can get a lot of the stuff in Madrid anyway,' he replied.

'But we got you this,' she said, rummaging in a carrier bag next to her chair and producing a brightly painted *matryoshka* doll.

'Thanks, girls,' said Nick, opening the largest doll to reveal the others inside. 'I meant to get one but just haven't got round to it yet.'

'You can take it back to Madrid,' said Pilar.

'Yes... but I'm not exactly sure when I'm coming back.'

'Isn't Kyle going to be ready to return soon?' asked Victoria.

'He is, maybe in a month, but I've got some things to do.'

'Sounds ominous, Pilar. Maybe he's become a spy.'

'No, I'm just the same. I've got a couple of issues, that's all.'

'With your girlfriend?' asked Victoria.

How does she do that? thought Nick. *With a sixth sense like that, shouldn't she be water divining in a desert or something?*

'Something like that,' he replied.

'Ahh, sounds like it's getting serious. Is there something we need to know?'

'Actually, we're going to get married.'

Victoria's face dropped and she adopted a feigned look of horror.

'But, what about me? You have to marry me.'

Nick was taken aback, not immediately sure how to respond.

'What...?' he began to splutter, before Victoria's face burst into a wide, tooth-filled grin.

'I'm only joking. Actually, Pilar and I thought you might anyway, didn't we, babe?'

Pilar nodded and smiled.

'Congratulations, Nick.' she added.

'Yes, congratulations, Nick. We're happy for you,' said Victoria, before reaching over to give him a hug and a kiss on the cheek. 'But you still have to keep your promise.'

Nick looked at her, seeking a reminder of his promise.

'You said you'd make it up to me when you got back, for going away.'

'Oh, yes.'

'Right, well Pilar's seeing Pavel tonight.'

'And Pavel is?'

'You know, the guy she met in Propaganda – speaks English.'

'Oh, yeah.'

'So, Nikolai Ivanovich – that is what I'd call you here, isn't it?'

'Yes.'

'You are taking me out to dinner. No excuses or I'll be all alone in a strange city.'

He'd been mugged and he knew it. He had promised and he did feel a bit guilty that they'd come all the way to Moscow only for him to spend hardly any time with them.

'Okay, dinner it is.'

Victoria's perfect teeth showed through her beaming smile.

'You've obviously been doing your research. Did you have anywhere in mind?'

'Here.'

'What?'

'Here. I've already booked this table for later and I've even got something to wear,' said Victoria, holding up her shopping bag.

Nick smirked and wondered why he hadn't had half this confidence at her age.

'I haven't,' said Nick.

Victoria stood.

'You're fine as you are. We can have a drink in the bar while we wait. I'm going to change.'

Victoria strode off in the direction of the ladies.

'She said you were a good guy to work for,' said Pilar.

'That's nice.'

'My boss is a woman. Total bitch!'

'Yeah?'

'Tries much too hard, you know the type.'

'I think so. Do you want another coffee?' asked Nick.

'No, thanks. I'm going to get back, when Vicki's changed.'

'Oh, okay.'

'She likes you.'

'I guess.'

'But she is very pleased for you – I mean, genuinely.'

'Thanks, I appreciate that. I'm just sorry I couldn't spend a bit more time with you guys.'

'Hey, no problem, we've had a ball.'

Victoria returned, snaking through the tables and disturbing the composure of even waiters used to the presence of beautiful young things. She'd looked great last time, but right now, in a dark orange dress with red features, she'd somehow managed to combine her Spanish roots with a modern look, perfectly complemented by her raven-black hair. She was fabulous.

'You've done it again, honey,' joked Pilar.

Victoria just smiled.

'Can you take my stuff back to the hotel?' asked Victoria, handing her bag to Pilar.

'Sure, no problem. Nick, in case I don't see you before we go, be happy and remember, a good heart breaks bad fortune.'

'Thanks, Pilar,' said Nick, a little surprised to hear an old Spanish proverb from one so young. He kissed her on both cheeks and then she was gone.

'So here we are, all alone,' said Victoria, with a coquettish smile.

'Now look, Vicki –'

'Relax. I'm just having a bit of fun with you. I'm really happy for you and you're safe... unless, of course, you don't want to be.'

'Let's go to the bar,' said Nick, rising from his chair.

*

'How was everybody in Kaluga?' asked Svetlana, testing the atmosphere.

'Good,' said Ivan, his voice enthusiastic for once.

This, figured Svetlana, was as good a moment as she was going to get.

'Vanya, I need to talk to you about something.'

Ivan sat down, without further invitation.

'You're dad was – is – in many ways – a good man – but it wasn't possible for us to go on.'

'I know,' replied Ivan.

'Relationships are funny things, as you will find out for yourself.'

Ivan waited silently. She continued.

'Most people don't want to live alone, but then they also know it needs to be the right person, not just for the sake of it. In the future, you'll meet somebody who you know is the person for you.'

'Like you did with Dad?'

'Yes, like with Dad. And he was the right person. He just found it difficult to deal with the things that happened to him later.'

'So he wasn't the right person?'

'No, Vanya, he was but nothing in life is completely certain. The thing is... the thing is... well, you know Nick and I have been seeing a lot of each other.'

'Yes.'

'Well, we get along very well, and both think that we want to be together in the future.'

'You're going to marry him, you mean?'

'We'd like to, yes.'

'It's not up to me, is it?'

'No, Vanya, but it is important. Vanya, I love you and it's important to me –'

'You do what you want. I don't care.'

'I think you do care – and I care – for you.'

Ivan looked at his mother, before lowering his eyes to the floor.

'What will happen to me?'

'We'll all live together, of course. Ivan, you're part of me and you always will be. We've looked after each other all these years and we'll continue to do so. I believe he's a good man. I believe you and he can be friends.'

'You said nothing in life is certain.'

'It isn't, Vanya, but it's not a reason to make no decisions. We make the best decisions we can. That's part of life.'

'He's American.'

'So?'

'Are we going to America?'

'We've not talked about that, at all. We'll all talk about it, if that's a possibility.'

'So we might?'

'I don't know yet. Maybe it would be good... you'd learn English. It would be easy at your age.'

'Have you told Granny?'

'I spoke to her, just before.'

'What did she say?'

'She's pleased. She loves us and just wants the best for all of us.'

A long silence followed while she watched Ivan wrestle with the prospect of his old world being changed for a new, uncertain, one. He stood and left for his room, gently closing the door behind him. Svetlana clasped her hands together and looked skywards before letting out a long, slow sigh. Then, she rose to start preparing their evening meal, unsure as to whether she'd be sharing it with her son.

Ten minutes later, the telephone rang and she picked up the receiver.

'Hi, Vasiliy, how's it going? Has Demchi been okay...?'

'Yeah, he's okay. Are you going to be in the office, in the morning?'

'Yes, I'll be in, first thing...'

She looked up, to see Ivan standing in front of her.

'Look, Vasya, can I call you back, shortly?' said Svetlana, replacing the receiver.

Ivan stepped forward and hugged her. She closed her eyes tightly, trying to hold back the tears that were already forming.

*

At Lubyanka, Malenkov's mood was tetchy. They'd kept a closer eye on Svetlana and Nick since they'd returned, picking them up at the airport, knowing they'd flown in from Irkutsk to Domodedovo, Moscow's other major airport, on the morning Ural Airlines flight. In fact, Malenkov already knew they'd been in that area from Svetlana's careless mention of Baikal at her mother's apartment, but he was anxious to fill in the gaps.

'Have the CCTV checked at Tayshet, Irkutsk, Ulan-Ude and Chita.'

'Yes, sir. Airports and train stations?' asked Il'ya.

'And bus stations. Maybe it was just a holiday to propose but, Il'ya, the new phones, disappearing like that and most of all... I just don't believe it.'

'Yes, sir. It will take a while.'

'Well, tell them to get on with it, then get back here and bring Artur with you.'

Il'ya nodded and left briskly. Malenkov sat back in his chair and gently drummed his fingers on his desk while he waited. After a short while, he leant forward, typed *Nick Mendez INN* into his computer and pressed the search button. He'd done this several times already, but experience had taught him that no matter how thorough he thought he'd been, there was always something. Images of Nick and commentary, most of it in English, started to fill the screen. Malenkov scrolled through, his limited English allowing him to pick up a superficial impression, but also frustrating him that he could not learn more about his adversary. The translation software was okay, but he knew it missed the nuances and that was where he'd find what he was looking for.

Il'ya returned, with his colleague.

'Okay, you two, sit down. I want to assess what we've got.'

'You might want to look at these first, sir,' said Il'ya, handing over some photographs.

Malenkov studied them and then started to place them on his desk, like pieces in a jigsaw. There were six, in all, including close-ups of the two from Dorogomilovsky market.

'And she thinks that little shit is not a traitor,' said Malenkov, standing back to get a better overall view. 'It's hard to tell, but this could be a gas chamber. How did the Petrov boy die?'

'A fall: hit his head on concrete,' said Il'ya, consulting his notes.

'Hmmn, something's not right about this. Keep them looking. I want the rest of these images.'

'I'll see they keep looking, sir,' replied Il'ya.

'Good. Okay, let's see where we're up to. We know they were at Baikal and we know he proposed to her. How sweet. So, they must have been at Irkutsk and we know they didn't fly there but they did fly back. Where is she now, right now?'

'At home,' said Il'ya.

'And him?'

'Out, with the Santos girl.'

'Is he fucking her?'

'No, we don't think it's like that. She and her friend really do look like they are on holiday. All their documents check out and neither was known to us. Also, she really did work for him in Madrid.'

'I see.'

'When do they go back?'

'Tomorrow night.'

'Who's watching Mendez?'

'Chubais and Petlyuk.'

'That's good. I'll speak to them. Right, that's it for now.'

Il'ya and his fellow FSB man stood, ready to leave.

'Oh, one last thing,' said Malenkov. 'Has our friend Colonel Chernekov been up to anything unusual lately?'

'No, sir, just routine.'

'Okay, but keep watching him.'

*

When Svetlana reached the office the following morning, Demchi wasn't there. Normally, he was one of the first in and last to leave.

'Where's Demchi?' she asked of Vasiliy.

'Gone for his check-up. He'll be in soon.'

'Is he ill?'

'No. Says he's fed up being nagged about it by Alina, so he's gone before you start on him too.'

'He said that?'

'Yeah.'

'I'm not his wife, but I can see why Alina gives him some grief. He's too stubborn.'

'I'm saying nothing. Leave me out of it.'

'Yeah, okay. I saw your Grishkuv piece. Not bad – not bad, at all.'

'Demchi was pretty pleased.'

'Was he now? Good, I can have a bit more time off and you can cover for me.'

Vasiliy's face changed from one carrying a slightly smug grin to one of intrigue.

'Sveta, I did cover for you, on something else.'

'Oh yeah? Come on, let's have it.'

'Not here,' said Vasiliy, thumbing in the direction of the stairs at the end of the open-plan office. 'Let's go to the interview room.'

Svetlana rose from her chair to follow him.

A minute or so later, they were both sitting at the same old, green table she'd occupied some months before, with Katia. She made a mental note to catch up with her.

'So?'

'I saw him,' said Vasiliy.

'Saw who?'

'The artist. Katenin – I saw him.'

'When?'

'While you were away. Followed me home – wanted to know where you were.'

'Did you tell him?'

'No, I didn't know where you were. I just told him you'd gone for some leave. Said he wants to speak to you – wanted to know why we hadn't published.'

'What did you say?'

'I told him it wasn't up to me. He said we're sometimes followed.'

'Following you? Me – yes – but following you?'

'That's what he said.'

'Does he still want to see me?'

'Yes. He said for you to put an ad in the dating section; said he'd know your style.'

'Was that it?'

'Yeah, that was pretty much it.'

'You haven't said anything to Demchi, have you?'

'No, of course not.'

'Okay, thanks, Vasya. Let's keep it that way.'

She rose from her chair and opened the door.

'Oh, by the way, I've got some news, too. I'm getting married.'

'You're what?'

She closed the door behind her and headed for Demchi's office to see if he was in yet. After all, she'd need somebody to give her away at the ceremony, and excited as she was about the Katenin news, she couldn't face her mother without having spoken to Demchi first.

*

Nick rolled over and looked at the alarm clock. It showed ten-thirty a.m. He'd have just enough time to shower and reach the studio for the production team meeting. He figured that after he'd had so much time off, he'd better be on time and make a good impression. He stretched, swung his legs out of bed and made for the bathroom, picking up last night's shirt he'd discarded. He sniffed it, caught the remnants of Victoria's perfume and smiled. Actually, they'd had a great night. Of course, she'd teased him but they'd enjoyed each other's company and the opportunity to catch up on developments in Madrid. He couldn't recall what time he'd got in, but remembered calling a cab for them at about midnight, intending it to drop her at the Belgrad and then take him on to Kyle's apartment. So, he assumed he'd probably been back by about half-midnight, although he couldn't actually remember coming in or putting himself to bed. He'd not had that much to drink or so he thought, but then again, he did have a slight hangover.

Nothing toast and coffee won't fix, he thought, shrugging his shoulders.

Chapter 24

With its majestic columns illuminated, the Bolshoi theatre was looking spectacular as Svetlana and Nick approached. Nick had to hand it to Hubbard, *Romeo and Juliet* was an inspired choice for the two of them the way things had developed, and the seats at the front of the dress circle overlooking the stage were excellent.

Svetlana took Nick's arm as they entered the theatre. He checked her coat for her, leaving her elegant in a knee-length black velvet dress, set off with a patterned silver necklace. He wore a tailored, dark wool suit, white shirt and striped, blue silk tie.

When he returned to her, across the marble floor, she said, 'You look pleased with yourself.'

'I've every reason to be. I'm here with my beautiful fiancée, so why wouldn't I be pleased?'

'Here we just say we've handed in the application.'

'I know. I've been doing my homework, but if it's okay with you, we'll mix the traditions a bit and fiancée is kind of a nice tradition.'

'"Fiancée" It sounds strange. I'm still getting used to it.'

'I hope this helps.'

He took her right hand in his, while with his other hand he gently slipped onto her finger a gold ring bearing a large sapphire diamond, sparkling in the light from the chandeliers above. He watched her in silence as she admired it.

'In the west, a fiancée wears a ring. We can change it if you don't like the style.'

'Oh, Nikolai, it's beautiful. I'll never change it – never.'

She threw her arms around his neck.

'Nikolai, I love you – I just love you.'

'And I love you,' he whispered.

They took their seats. Nick surveyed the magnificent auditorium, with its cream and gold features. He'd seen plenty of pictures, but they didn't do it justice without the atmosphere and expectation of something so special that he was now feeling. Svetlana took his hand, as the orchestra delivered its first notes and a tingle ran down his spine.

The performance was, of course, flawless, the dancers and musicians expecting to deliver no less, so steeped were they in the pride and artistic history of this place. All thoughts of Malenkov and his cronies were banished as emotions were swept along by the wondrous show, interrupted only briefly between acts when Nick would catch Svetlana's smiles as she looked at the ring he'd given her.

At the end, they waited for the very last of the applause to fade away, before leaving their seats. Nick stood and watched the theatre empty, until it was almost still.

'What is it?' she asked.

'I don't know. It's like performances are still going on, like echoes.'

She chuckled.

'It's your ancestors, Nikolai Ivanovich... and your Russian blood,' she said. 'Come on,' she added, pinching his bottom.

They made their way down to the foyer, where Nick left her to collect her coat. He retrieved it and turned to see Hubbard, right in front of him.

'Sorry for the intrusion, old boy, but your tail's watching Mrs Dorenko, so I thought I'd have a quick word with you here. Did you enjoy the show, by the way?'

'Yes,' stuttered Nick, taken by surprise.

'Probably best not to discuss work at your apartment, if you know what I mean.'

'It's bugged?'

'Maybe not, but let's put it this way – my people would have done – by now. Here's my number again, if you want it swept.'

He placed a small piece of paper in Nick's breast pocket, turned and walked away.

*

Her mother had wanted to talk to Ivan, so Svetlana had agreed that he could stay over with her. This gave the newly engaged couple the opportunity to spend the night together, back at Nick's.

After they'd made love, she lay next to him, her head on his gently rising and falling chest, arm across his waist. The television was an intrusion, but it guarded against the listening devices Hubbard had warned of and afforded them some privacy of conversation, if they spoke quietly.

'Nikolai,' she whispered.

'Yes?'

'I dream again.'

'What?'

'I dream again.'

'We all dream.'

'I didn't. I stopped; taught myself to stop.'

'Why?'

'Because all I saw was fear. I always seemed to be running down a corridor with somebody chasing me, but I didn't know who.'

'Nightmares. We all have them from time to time.'

'When was your last one?'

'I can't remember.'

'I can. I remember.'

'Well don't. You can dream good things now.'

'I do,' she said, drawing the back of a fingernail across his stomach.

'Are you sleepy yet?' asked Nick.

'Not really.'

'How was Ivan?'

'Okay, I think. He'll come round. It's just the uncertainty for him.'

'Yeah, I'll try my best with him.'

'Just love me and accept him into your heart, then we'll be fine.'
'I know and I will.'
'My mum thought we should have planned more by now.'
'We were busy. C'mon, we've done the registration at ZAGS, fixed a date and started a list.'
'I know. She was just... well, being a mum. She's loving it all, really.'
'I'll bet.'
'What about your mum and dad? Are they going to make it over here?'
'I spoke to them. My father's been in hospital with heart trouble, so we'll have to see but they were delighted and Mum would like to go back to visit Samara.'

For a moment, Svetlana became still and then turned to look at him.

'What is it?' he asked.

She leant over and put her mouth to his ear.

'The images... did you hide them?'

Nick put his finger to his lips, before nodding and giving her a thumbs-up signal to confirm the images were in a safe place. In fact, he'd transmitted them to JF who'd also made a back-up before Nick had deleted them from his camera.

Svetlana smiled at him and nodded back, her head returning to its resting place on his chest. She reached down to pull the duvet over them in the expectation they would soon sleep.

*

In the morning, wearing only a pair of black cotton boxer shorts, Nick busied himself in the kitchen. He made coffee and *bliny* for Svetlana while she showered.

Soon, she stood in the doorway, wearing his blue dressing gown, which draped from her shoulders and collected drops of water from her still wet hair.

'Coffee smells good.'

'Nothing but the best for you, my darling,' said Nick.

The doorbell rang.

'I'll get it,' said Svetlana.

She turned, walked the few step to the front door, and reached for the latch to open it.

Victoria wore an orange top and tight stretch jeans tucked into knee-length, studded boots. Her hair was radiant and red lipstick framed her perfect white teeth as she smiled. Svetlana knew instantly who she was.

'Good morning, you must be Svetlana. Nick's told me all about you,' said Victoria in Spanish.

Svetlana didn't comprehend the words but did understand Victoria's slightly disdainful expression as she looked the reporter up and down in her ill-fitting garment, her face devoid of make-up.

'Is Nick in?' she asked in English.

Before Svetlana could answer, Nick appeared.

Victoria reverted to Spanish.

'Hi, Nick. We're just on the way to the airport. Pilar's waiting in the taxi downstairs, so I thought I'd just come to say goodbye.'

'Right, well have a good trip, Vicki, and say hi to Pilar for me.'

'I will,' said Victoria as she stepped past Svetlana, placed her left hand on Nick's bare chest and her right behind his neck before kissing him on each cheek.

'Still in good shape, Nico,' said Victoria

Svetlana, too shocked at Victoria's brazenness to speak, took in Nick's affectionate smile as he watched his young colleague turn to leave.

'Bye, Svetlana. Sorry we didn't get time to talk but I've got to dash,' said Victoria.

Then she was gone.

Svetlana bristled.

'I can see why you didn't tell me you'd taken her out.'

'I took them both out – just for dinner.'

'Is there anything going on between you?'

'Absolutely not.'

'It doesn't look that way. How dare she!'

'It's just her way. She's like that with everybody.'

'I'll bet she is – little slut!'

'Now, stop it. You're being completely over the top.'

'Am I, Nikolai Ivanovich? Am I, really?'

'Yes, Sveta, you are. There's nothing. I love you and there's nothing going on.'

Svetlana looked at him and searched for insincerity in his face – but didn't find it. She decided to give him the benefit of the doubt, but her deliberate, frosty silence for the rest of the morning was designed to reinforce in him what she thought of Victoria and her behaviour.

*

The next week went quickly. Both Svetlana and Nick had work to catch up on and each took a share of the wedding-related tasks that needed to be done.

Demchi had been delighted to be asked to give the bride away, and this, together with the distance she'd kept between him and the Petrov case, had their relationship more or less back to where it was months before. He was even cracking jokes again, at her expense.

Of course, despite everything else, very much on her mind was the upcoming meeting with Katenin. As he'd requested, she'd put an ad in the dating section suggesting a meeting on Friday afternoon, but after dark. He was likely to need all the cover he could. She'd read and re-read the text, finally sure that no FSB observer could in any way link it to her.

You first saw me in darkness, but when the sun falls on Friday I will be able to see you there too. She'd read it a final time and then passed it through. Svetlana had thought back almost to the beginning, to the time when she'd re-visited the painting of the playing card at Kursky station, down in the shadows underneath the stairs. She'd remembered, with a shiver, the feeling she'd had that somebody was watching her. There was no proof, but all that had passed convinced her that her senses back then were correct and not playing tricks on her. There had been somebody there, and that person was Katenin. Only he would know.

Personally, she thought it unwise for them to be seeing each other at all. However, as she rode the metro to Kursky, she reflected that there was frustration building and maybe it was necessary to reassure Katenin that far from stalling, the trail leading to the culprits in Andrei's death was very much being followed. Otherwise, he might resort to something reckless. She couldn't see her tail, but assumed they followed her more or less all the time, these days. She'd need a little help, for the last thing Katenin needed was her leading the FSB straight to him.

When Svetlana reached the station, she went outside to see if Richard was there, trying to make her visit look as routine as possible. Fortunately, he was, and she was able to chat to him. While Sasha wasn't there, a couple of the other kids were and obviously word had soon reached him, for five or six minutes later, he was by her side as they walked towards the main entrance.

'How's Marina? Is she around?'

'She's okay. I saw her this morning.'

'That's good. If I don't see her today, say I was here and asking after her.'

'I will.'

'Are we having a drink in the café?' asked Sasha presumptuously.

'If you help me.'

Sasha waited.

'There is somebody following me – at least – I think there is. I need to see the picture again. Do you know a way to get me there without being seen?'

'No problem,' he said, with a tone suggesting supreme confidence. 'They'll even think you've left.'

She followed him closely, as he led her up and down stairs and along passages not accessible to the public until, five or six minutes later, they found themselves once again looking at the ace of hearts and its chilling picture, her FSB tail left far behind and chasing shadows.

'Thank you, Sasha, but I need to be alone for a while.'

'Are we still going to the café?'

'Of course.'

'Okay, I'll wait around there. See you later.'

'See you, Sasha.'

The sound of his scurrying footsteps soon faded and she was left with the picture, darkness and damp for company. She turned around and looked into the unlit blackness as the rustle of an old discarded poster disturbed by her feet echoed in the cellar-like space she occupied.

'Yakov, are you here?' she whispered.

There was no sound in reply, only that of water dripping somewhere, unseen.

She wondered if he was still on his way or, even worse, had not understood the message.

'Yakov?'

The voice was unnervingly close and startled her.

'Were you followed?' he asked.

'No – well, yes – but I lost them, with the boy's help.'

'I remember him. I was here for a while when I first came to Moscow.'

'Do you have somewhere safe now?'

'As safe as it can be.'

Katenin stepped forward from the darkness into the half-light she and the picture occupied. She could make out his features but not his eyes. The hair was short and unkempt, as though he'd cut it himself, which he probably had. Slim shoulders supported a head with high cheekbones and ears that barely seemed to protrude. He had the demeanour of hunger. A faint wheeze accompanied his breathing.

'Why haven't you printed it?'

'My editor won't allow it. The paper doesn't do military stories.'

'Then my work has been a waste of time.'

'No, Yakov, it hasn't. We have found all your pictures. We know what you were showing us: a gas chamber, in Chita.'

'Yes.'

'I've seen it.'

'Yes, of course, if you put the pictures together.'

'No, Yakov, I mean I've stood there, where you were. I've seen it.'

'Then you can imagine the nightmares I have.'

'Yakov, I know.'

'I see him, every night. He was my friend, my only friend.'

'I'm so sorry.'

'He was scared. He wanted my help and I didn't help him.'

'You were conscripts. There was nothing you could have done.'

'I could have tried. I could have been braver.'

'You are being incredibly brave now.'

'Am I?'

'Yes, Yakov, you are.'

'They'll kill me if they catch me, won't they?'

She hesitated to give him the honest answer.

'It's okay, I know the answer. This Malenkov, have you met him?'

'Yes.'

'What's he like? Is he interested in justice?'

'The FSB's justice. But truth and justice – together? No, he's not interested.'

'I want justice for my friend. I owe him that.'

'I want it too – and for his mother.'

'You've seen her?'

'Yes.'

'So, now you have a story that you can't tell. Where will justice come from? The Public Prosecutor?'

'I'm afraid not.'

'Then, from where?'

'I cannot tell the story through the paper.'

'They will kill you?'

'Probably... and my editor, too. Journalism in Moscow has boundaries. There are acceptable truths and unacceptable truths – but there is a man who can help.'

'Your husband?'

Svetlana looked at him to see the silhouette of his finger pointing at her ring that even in the dim light filtering from above projected some reflections. She laughed nervously.

'I guess artists don't miss much.'

She watched him shrug.

'He's my fiancé, what he's called where he comes from. He's a reporter, a TV reporter for an international station.'

'Is he going to report it?'

'Yes, I think so, but when we have all the evidence.'

'Then, they will kill him instead.'

Katenin's words were said in such a matter-of-fact way. It made her cringe that her life's companion could, at any time, be the recipient of a bullet in the back of the head and a brief obituary on his TV station, after which the rest of the world would move on.

'He's an American citizen. It should be different for him.'

Katenin shrugged, again.

'Evidence? What evidence?' he asked.

'We have your pictures, we have Katia and now Nick and I have pictures of the chamber.'

'That's a funny name.'

'His name is Nikolai Ivanovich. He is half Russian – and, Yakov, he understands.'

'Does he need to see me?'

'That would be too dangerous. If you are seen in a broadcast they would certainly kill you.'

'I'm dead already. If he is half Russian, he will understand that. What life is there for a citizen who cannot show his face, like me? I hide in alleys and scrounge money from tourists for portraits they don't really want. Tell him I'm ready. Tell him.'

'Your friend would be so proud of you.'

'Svetlana Yuriyevna, I miss him.'

He spoke her name for the first time, his voice rich with texture and emotion. She shivered.

'I know. We will help you get justice for your friend.'

'Tell him I'm ready.'

'I'll tell him. How will we contact you?'

'The same way.'

'Okay. Look, I'd better go but here's some money. I know how difficult it must be for you.'

She held the back of his hand, while she placed five thousand rubles in his palm and then closed his fingers around them. The touch of their hands sealed her already strong resolve.

'Thank you,' he replied, before he disappeared back into the darkness.

She retraced part of the route Sasha had shown her, before joining a public escalator and ascending to the concourse above. By now, it was rush hour and the station was rapidly filling with travellers. Even so, when she reached her usual café there were a few tables available, one of which she occupied with her steaming mug of hot chocolate.

'Is that mine?' asked Sasha cheekily.

'Didn't take you long to appear, did it? Sit down and I'll get yours.'

*

Nick had taken Hubbard up on his offer to have the apartment swept for bugs. They were doing it that evening. So, while Nick knew his tail would be following him, he'd arranged to meet Svetlana after work at Coffee Bean, on ulitsa Pokrovka.

'Hi, how's your day been?' he asked, as he kissed her.

'It's been good. I'll tell you about it.'

'Cappuccino?'

'Yes, please.'

Soon they were sitting over their coffees, their ears attuned to the need to speak quietly in places they might be overheard.

'So, did he show up?'

'Yes.'

'And...?'

'He thought we'd gone cold on the idea.'

'And now?'

'I told him we were still working on it, gathering evidence. He knows I can't print. He wants to see you.'

'Yeah, and sign his own death warrant. I thought that was the point of the cards, to keep him distanced.'

'We have the death, the cards and our pictures, but you know they'll just explain it as an accident, exploited by somebody with a grudge.'

'So, we need a witness?'

'Depends whether we want to cause trouble or seek some justice?'

'What does he want?'

'Justice.'

'Does he realise the risks?'

'Yes.'

'Say I interview him and he's good, I'll still have to see if JF will use it. Thinking about it, he's going to be more interested in the gas than a dead conscript. We're weak on that. We think it's the same gas for the kid, the bank and the pipeline but we can't prove it.'

'Why do you think the FSB are so interested in him?'

'I agree, but it doesn't prove any link. If JF's going to use it, and he may well not, we're going to need more. Even if we get more, I'll have to see him with a story like that.'

'The bank raid will be Grachev. I'll speak to Dubnikov and see if he knows anything,' said Svetlana.

'What about your friend in the Prosecutor's Office.'

'He was scared off, I think.'

'Try. What's the worst that can happen – he says no – or he really doesn't know?'

'I'll think about it.'

'So, the kid, is he really that brave or stupid?'

'He's brave.'

'Are you going to set it up?'

'Yes.'

'You'll have to do sound. I'm not bringing any of the crew in on this.'

'Sure.'

'Are we done on that, for the moment?'

'I think so.'

'Good, because I want to talk about us.'

'You've changed your mind, already?' she joked, poking his arm.

'Yeah, right. Where did you get to with the guest list?'

'It's done. Twenty-six, in all.'

'Good, I just needed to have a rough idea. I've been talking to my dad and he's okay, but the doctors have said that no way is he to travel. However, he insists on paying for the reception – with no arguments.'

'That's so kind, but I wanted to meet them.'

'You will, soon enough.'

'Have you told him about Russian receptions?'

'How do you mean?'

'Lot's of food and drink. It'll be expensive.'

'I warned him.'

'So, from your side, who've you got coming, Nikolai?'

'Konstantin.'

'Is that it?'

'No, there's Kyle Hughes, a couple of my crew and maybe Spike Ruskin.'

'Who's he?'

'He been my best friend since college days but he's in the navy and I don't know if he can get leave. So, if he can't make it, I'm going to ask Kostya to be my best man.'

'Best man? What's that?'

'You know, my wing man, the guy who takes care of everything on the day.'

'We don't have that – it's a witness. You have one and I have one. The witnesses take care of things and entertain the guests. A witness who doesn't speak Russian or know what to do? I don't think so. You'd better have Konstantin and Spike can just join in. What was the result on the restaurant?'

'They're booked up. I tried Dashkov's and they could do a party of up to forty.'

'Oh sure, if you want to give all the money to the mafia instead of just paying for the roof.'

'There you go, local knowledge. I'll try again. What about the dress?'

'My mum's on with making it.'

'What's it going to be like?'

'You'll see, a week on Friday, and not before.'

They ordered a snack and worked through the outstanding tasks for another hour or so, before exchanging kisses and going their separate ways for the evening, as Svetlana had promised Ivan she'd have a look at his school project.

*

She knew Maksim Pechenkin had been spooked by something that had happened in the Prosecutor's Office the last time they'd spoken, but she did want to close off the Grachev angle if she could. After all, Maksim had only said he couldn't speak 'until things have died down' and that was some time ago. He lived in a small apartment his father had left him, just off Prospekt Mira and near to Alekseevskaya metro, an area she knew well.

As she emerged from the station, she was conscious that she may have her FSB tail to cope with. She had developed a way to deal with this and had in her head a suitable list of sites to help her. One such place was a long narrow coffee bar, nearby, where the entrance to the washroom was concealed but offered access to a rear fire exit door. She entered and ordered her coffee before sitting near the back to read one of the newspapers provided for customers. She sipped her drink and waited. After a believable interlude, she stood and without looking back left her still steaming coffee while she made for the toilet. The three minutes that would elapse before her tail became suspicious gave her all the time she needed.

Ten minutes later, she knocked on Maksim's door, confident that she'd not been followed. He answered, peeking out, before opening the door properly. He was wearing a black polo neck jumper, jeans and slippers.

'Sveta, what are you doing here?'

'Hi, Maks, can I come in?'

'Yes, of course.'

He waved her in and then checked up and down the corridor before shutting the door behind him. They stood silently in the small living room, with its faded beige wallpaper and dark wooden furniture, an old man's décor in a young man's apartment.

'Long time no see, Maks.'

'Yes, Sveta, it is. How've you been?'

'You were scared last time we spoke. Are you still scared?'

'Maybe I over-reacted a bit.'

She looked at him, waiting for an explanation.

'I mean, they moved me and I just thought there was a problem.'

'They'd seen you and me, you mean?'

'Something like that.'

'What did you make of that Moskovsky Industrialny robbery?'

'We're looking at it.'

'You mentioned colonel Chernekov had been seen with Grachev.'

Maksim became a little tense.

'Sorry, I'm being rude, Sveta. Would you like some tea?'

She didn't really, but thought it might help him to relax if they took this a bit slower.

'That would be good.'

Maksim disappeared to the kitchen, from where she heard the running of water and the sound of clinking china.

'Are you still doing the piano lessons?' she shouted.

'Yes, when I can afford them.'

He returned with two mugs of tea and beckoned to her to sit. As she did, she took Maksim's hand until he too was sitting, looking at her.

'Did Chernekov supply the gas for the bank raid, Maksim?'

'We don't know.'

'Is it Chernekov's gas, the one he tested in Chita?'

'Sveta, the truth is I don't know.'

'But that's what the department thinks?'

'They think it's Chernekov's. I don't know anything about Chita. What's that about?'

'What about Grachev? Did he do the raid?'

'We don't know. All we know is he's an associate of Chernekov.'

'If I could help you, would you take it further?'

'Investigate it? Prosecute it? Grachev – if cleared from above – maybe, but unlikely. Chernekov? Come on, you're not serious?'

'So, nothing, in effect?'

'Sveta, you know better than almost anybody in the city how these things work. We all know the sensitive cases and unless our political masters want it, nobody's going to stick their neck on the line. Why should they?'

'Yes, Maks, I know how it works.'

*

Another ten minutes with Maksim had not taken her any further and she contemplated, with some trepidation, a meeting with Dubnikov as she made her way back to Alekseevskaya metro.

She reached for her phone and then hesitated, not confident that it hadn't been compromised yet. *Sod it*, she thought. *They already know I speak to him.* She dialled and spoke briefly with Dubnikov to arrange a meeting for the following morning.

*

Svetlana had given Nick a list of mafia owned venues, including ironically a couple of Dubnikov's, but with a request to avoid them. He'd had a look at a few other places on the internet and had a shortlist of three that had confirmed they could do the numbers and the date. He'd been amazed that she'd entrusted him with this task, but he resolved to make the reception for their guests something special as he walked over Teatral'naya metro's black and yellow granite floor, before taking the exit to Nikolskaya ulitsa. Outside, the sky was clear and the temperature had dropped to about minus twenty. He fastened the buttons of his coat and pulled on his gloves as he set off for his first inspection visit.

'Nikolai – it's okay if I call you Nikolai – I don't like to be over formal?' asked short and rotund Mark Sosunov, proprietor of Sosunov's, while firmly shaking Nick's hand.

'No, Nikolai is fine.'

'Well, you couldn't pick a better place for a reception. We make it unforgettable. You wouldn't believe the number of recommendations we get.'

'Right.'

'Let me show you around.'

Nick followed Mark as he showed off the upstairs dining room, with its Tzarist memorabilia and rich colours. Tables were already arranged in a T-shape, their crisp, cream cloths matching surprisingly well with deep blue velour chairs. An electric piano guarded the dance floor, overlooked by a modern sound system. Nick was actually quite impressed, but most of all, it just felt right.

'And who is your bride to be?' asked Mark.

'Svetlana Dorenko.'

'Svetlana Dorenko – the journalist?'

'Yes.'

'Zhenya, get out here!' shouted the animated owner.

His pretty, petite blonde-haired wife appeared from nowhere and approached.

'This is my wife, Yevgeniya Mikhailova.'

She held out her hand, which Nick took.

'Pleased to meet you. I'm Nikolai Ivanovich.'

'Zhenya, Nikolai is marrying Svetlana Dorenko! Nikolai, we are both great fans of hers.'

Yevgeniya's somewhat cool demeanour changed as a grin emerged and her eyes widened.

'Is it true? Are you really marrying Svetlana Yuriyevna?'

'Yes, on the twenty-first, a week on Friday.'

'And you are coming here for your reception?'

Nick had already decided he would not need to carry out any further inspection visits. He knew here was somewhere they were genuinely welcome – he was welcome.

'Yes.'

Mark rushed away, clasping his hands together.

'When we first came here to Moscow, we had some bad experiences. We went to a talk by Svetlana Yuriyevna and she shook our hands, although she wouldn't remember. What she said helped us a lot and we read her paper, all the time,' said Yevgeniya.

'She does have a way with words.'

'She does. She gave us courage. With courage and realism, we have built a life for ourselves.'

Mark returned bearing shot glasses and a bottle of Zarskaya vodka. Within moments, they were toasting the forthcoming wedding. The groom knew then that his bride would approve of his choice.

Nick was feeling pretty pleased with himself as he made his way back to the metro. The street was quieter now and he made good progress, but when he was about two hundred metres from the station, something made him look back, just in time to catch a figure in a dark overcoat and *ushanka* slip into a doorway across the street. Emboldened by the vodka, he turned and made straight for the doorway where he saw his shadow for the evening, impassive, nonchalant even. Nick put his shoulders back and filled his lungs, staring at the man facing him.

'Let me make it easy for you. I've just been to a restaurant and now I'm going home. So, give yourself a break. Fuck off and leave me alone!'

He received no reply, just a knowing sneer, one of contempt. Nick was learning how to spot officers of the FSB.

Chapter 25

On the way to Gorokhovets, Nick brought Svetlana up to date about Sosunov's restaurant, and she was pleased with what she heard. She'd worried that her old Lada might let her down on the journey, so Nick had offered to take her.

With some difficulty, on the frozen surface, Nick's car drew up outside Katia's modest home.

'Do you want me to wait in the car?' he asked.

'No, of course not. She'll be encouraged you're helping.'

'Better not to say too much – you know – too much detail,' added Nick.

'She's the boy's mother.'

'She's also a risk to us.'

'Okay, but try to keep things positive.'

They carefully crossed the rutted track to reach the front door, which Katia opened as Svetlana was about to knock.

'Svetlana Yuriyevna, thank you for coming. I have been anxious for news.'

Svetlana embraced her and kissed her.

'Katia, this is Nikolai Ivanovich, a reporter for television. He has been helping me and I trust him completely.'

Katia reached for his hand.

'Welcome, Nikolai Ivanovich. Come in, please.'

'Thank you,' said Nick, following Svetlana through the door.

Katia made tea for them in the midst of a slightly awkward silence, before she brought over a tray and sat herself.

'How have you been?' asked Svetlana.

'Much the same, but my sister came to stay for a week, which was nice. She's been very supportive,' replied Katia.

'That's good.'

'Did you find all the cards?'

'Yes, Katia, we did.'

'And did they confirm it? A gas chamber? Andrei?'

'Yes.'

Katia hung her head.

'And the Katenin boy, did you find him?'

Svetlana hesitated and glanced at Nick to see his apprehensive look in return.

'We need to be careful with him.'

'Is he in danger?'

'Yes.'

Katia looked at Svetlana.

'Then I will leave things to your good sense.'

'Thank you, Katia,' said Svetlana, reaching out and squeezing her hand.

'And, Nikolai Ivanovich, thank you for your help.'

'I haven't done much,' responded Nick.

'Nikolai is being modest, Katia. He has helped a great deal.'

'Then thank you, Nikolai Ivanovich. I am in your debt. I owe a debt to both of you.'

'Katia, we have been talking, Nikolai and I. We do have useful material but it has gaps and we don't think the authorities will help. Nikolai may be able to tell the world what happened but he needs help.'

'To fill in the gaps?'

'Yes.'

'And I can help?'

'It would bring danger.'

'What have I to fear? What else could they do to me? Put me in prison – kill me? I am in prison already and death would be a blessed release.'

Nick returned from his car, with camera and microphone. Within twenty minutes he had the material they wanted.

They stayed chatting with Katia for another hour, during which time she served them more tea and homemade *pirozhki*. Svetlana's admiration had grown again for this fellow mother and her original informant. She was glad they'd made the journey.

'Katia, there is something else I have to tell you,' said Svetlana. 'Nikolai and I are to be married on the twenty-first of this month. We'd like you to be our guest there.'

'Oh, that is wonderful news. I am very happy for you.'

'Will you come?'

'Svetlana, it's kind of you, kind of you both but it is difficult for me to celebrate. A wedding is not the place for grief to visit. I hope you understand.'

The two women held hands.

'We do, Katia. We understand, but if you change your mind, you'll be very welcome.'

*

'Every time I see her it fills me with rage,' said Svetlana, as Nick started the engine of his BMW.

'She's a good woman.'

'Nikolai, are we going to get her justice?'

'I don't know, depends what you mean by justice. From what you were saying, prosecutions don't sound likely.'

'They're not, so, it's up to us.'

'Run me through again what Dubnikov had to say.'

'He knew about Chernekov and Grachev, because he's got a guy inside Grachev's operation. It was Grachev who did the bank raid all right and the gas must have come from Chernekov.'

'Any chance of co-operation from Dubnikov?'

'Any more silly questions? You know he won't – he can't.'

'Okay, so once I've interviewed the Katenin kid, what else have we got?'

'You, Kolya. We've got you and your skill as a reporter. The way you dealt with Katia was fantastic, allowing her to speak, helping her along but not giving her the answers.'

'She has her own answers. Those telling the truth are easy. The liars are the difficult ones.'

'I can relate to that.'

'How did you get into journalism, anyway?' asked Nick.

'A trick.'

'What?'

'A trick, on my family and many others. Assets were stolen from the factory and many lost their jobs, including Ivan's father. I wanted answers and went looking. I've been looking ever since.'

'Did you have any training?'

'As a journalist?'

'Yes.'

'No, just picked it up as I went along. Of course, when I met Demchi, he was brilliant and encouraged me so much – you know – to develop my own style.'

'He sounds a really good guy.'

'He is. What about you? How did you get into it?'

'A bit more conventional. I studied English at university, got an internship and started at the local Boston paper. I've had a few lucky breaks since.'

'You're not lucky, Nikolai. You're good at what you do.'

Nick reached across and put his hand on her knee.

'Could you work here?' she asked.

'I am working here.'

'You're working here, but your audience is not really here, except from hotel rooms and FSB.'

Nick chuckled.

'I meant could you work here, in Moscow, for Russians?' she continued.

'Looks like I may have to. Kyle will be getting his job back soon.'

'It's different. You can't just write it and print, you have to consider all the angles.'

'How many?'

'All of them. You never know who knows who. You write about A only to find he's secretly in partnership with B, who has Kremlin connections – wrong angle.'

'Could you work in Europe or in America, Sveta?'

'These are worlds I don't know. I would be lost.'

'I'd be your guide, as you've been mine.'

'When I was a girl, I dreamt of flying away. I didn't know where – but somewhere.'

'Maybe this is your dream coming true.'

'I stopped believing in dreams a long time ago.'

'Seriously, we need to talk about it. I could work here or we could all go to Europe – or America.'

'How would Ivan be?'

'He'd be fine. Just think of the choices that would open up for him: travel, languages.'

'Tell me about Americans.'

'Americans... Hmmn. Well, each state has its own character but most people are very proud to be American.'

'Are you?'

Nick paused.

'Almost always. Sometimes, America has not had the finest moments. I mean, most don't really know much about foreign affairs but then again, there's an opportunity for you. You could tell them about Russia, real Russia, and you could write exactly as you wanted.'

'Where would we live? In Boston?'

'We could. It's a great city, educated and open minded.'

'What about Spain?'

'Huh, Spain, a passionate country. Everybody speaks with their hands. I don't know, your passion and Spain's passion, maybe it's a bit too much,' said Nick, smiling and gently pushing her on the arm.

He smiled inwardly at the surprise he'd one day show her at the villa in Los Arrayanes.

'And Russians, in Spain?'

'There are many, particularly in the south. There's a lot of black money in development down there but you often hear Russian in Madrid too, these days.'

'I don't know, Kolya. Everything's just happened so fast. Can we maybe go and visit these places – take Ivan with us?'

Svetlana reached over and put her hand on top of his, while he held the steering wheel.

A little later, they stopped for fuel at a Yukos station, its vibrant blue and green colours standing out against the snowy background. She watched him through the windscreen as he walked back across the forecourt, sure she could once again see the ghost by his side. He sat in the driver's seat and re-started the engine.

'I want to get the interview with the kid over and then I'll have to go to Madrid to see JF. We can't do anything without his approval. Will they let me back in?' asked Nick.

'It should be okay. They can't prove anything and you're still the station's Moscow correspondent. You can't guarantee it, but probably it'll be all right.'

'We'll have to risk it.'

Chapter 26

Two days later, Nick turned into an alleyway off ulitsa Mashkova at exactly eleven forty-five in the morning. He drove a hundred metres and then stopped next to a fire escape. The car was stationary for no more than four seconds but it was sufficient time for Yakov Katenin to emerge from behind a waste bin and scramble, unseen, into the back seat.

'Get on the floor and put that blanket over you,' said Nick.

He picked up speed, hoping this wouldn't be the day some traffic cop decided to stop him and supplement his income with a trumped-up allegation. He had dollars in his licence, just in case.

'Where's Svetlana Yuriyevna?' asked Katenin.

'Getting things ready,' replied Nick.

'Where are we going?'

'My apartment. It's been swept for devices, so we'll video there. I'm Nick.'

'I know, she told me.'

'Okay, we're coming back onto the main road. Better not to talk for the moment. I'll let you know when.'

Nick drove confidently but as anonymously as he could through the busy Moscow traffic. He'd long since dispensed with the sat-nav in the city centre, now knowing by heart all the main routes he needed. There was probably a tail on him but his very brief stop would not have been observed and the underground garage at the apartment gave him the opportunity to sneak the young informant in without being noticed.

As he drove down ulitsa Pokrovka, he could see his apartment with all the blinds closed, which was the signal he'd agreed with

Svetlana if all was clear. For her part, she'd checked the garage to see if any of their friends from the FSB were present, but had found none. Nick drove down the ramp and watched the electric gate draw open before he proceeded.

'Okay, we're here,' he said to Katenin, who threw back the blanket and rose to look around him.

The two men left the car and headed for the elevator.

As they approached the apartment, Svetlana was already holding the door open for them. They slipped inside.

'Hello, Yakov. Are you all right?' she asked.

'Yeah, I'm fine.'

'Do you want some tea?'

'Yes. Can I have a shower too?'

'I don't know if that's a good idea.'

'No, that's fine,' said Nick. 'If he looks clean and tidy that will confuse them when they go looking for him.'

'Okay. I'll make tea first,' said Svetlana.

She'd been busy while they'd been travelling. A green sheet held to the wall with drawing pins formed the backdrop to their impromptu studio. The video camera stood on a tripod, next to a microphone and immediately in front of two tall chairs from the breakfast bar.

Katenin emerged from the bathroom looking respectable in a pair of jeans and a casual shirt that Nick had donated. The clothes were a bit large for him, but at least he didn't smell now and his formerly tousled hair was neatly combed.

'You ready?' asked Nick.

'Yes,' replied Katenin, stepping forward to take his seat.

Nick was now dressed in a grey suit, just as he would have done for a real studio interview. Although this was going to be a low-tech affair, he was anxious to give it as much feeling of authenticity as he could. He cleared his throat and then nodded to Svetlana to start recording.

'I'm sitting with Yakov Katenin, at a location I can't reveal as he's in danger if apprehended. He's shown extraordinary bravery in agreeing to speak to me today, and thinks he can throw some light on a story that's been puzzling people all around the world. What is it that's disabled staff at a bank here in Moscow and at an oil pumping station in Georgia, but leaves absolutely no trace? Yakov, let's go back. When does your story begin?'

'I was a conscript, in the army... stationed at Chita.'

'Which is in southern Siberia?'

'Yes. They started to test gas on us – many times. Some of my friends died, including my best friend Andrei – Andrei Petrov.'

'Tell us what happened.'

'One morning, a year ago, there was another test. Andrei was afraid. We were all afraid, but we had no choice. We had masks. They were fine for most of the gases but they didn't seem to work all the time on what they were testing.'

Katenin paused and looked at Nick, who, as he often did, used only silence to prompt his interviewee.

'Andrei protested, but Major Rebikov shouted at him and forced him to join the line. It was a bad test. Most of us were ill. After we came out of the chamber, I looked back... and there was Andrei.'

'Where?'

'In the doorway, face down. I knew he was dead.'

'What happened?'

'Rebikov looked at him and then just kicked him in the head... like he was a dog. He wasn't a dog, he was my friend.'

'Did you have to take part in more tests?'

'Not me. My lungs were damaged, but others, they did. I was on the base another three weeks and then I was discharged on medical grounds.'

'Did you raise your concerns with your commanding officer?'

'That was Rebikov. What would have been the point? Andrei raised his concerns and look what happened to him.'

'Is it correct you paint?'

'Since I was a boy.'

'So did you tell your story?'

'In paintings – around Moscow. If you put them together, you can see it all: the chamber, Andrei, Rebikov, Leontev.'

'The viewers will be able to see your paintings on their screens, but I want to show you another picture. Do you know this man?'

Nick passed a print to Katenin, who looked at it closely before handing it back. Nick then held it up to the camera with a steady, confident hand and revealed the features of Chernekov.

'I don't know his name, but he visited the camp a few times – came to the chamber to watch what was going on. He filmed us – took notes – all the time.'

'Why are you giving this interview, Yakov?'

'I want justice for my friend and for all the ones who died. We were used in an experiment. Animals are used in experiments. My friend was not an animal – he was a human being.'

'Do you recognise this place?' asked Nick, showing a picture of the chamber to the camera before handing it to Katenin.

The young man put his hand over his mouth and gasped.

'That's it! That's the gas chamber, at Chita.'

Svetlana looked on with a heavy heart. Russia's history was full of the acts of brave people and here was another example, right in front of her. No, he was not running at a machine gun in defence of his mother country, he was simply speaking up for it in the full knowledge that if caught he would never have the chance to speak out again. She thought of her darling brother and of Katia's pitiful grief playing itself out in her little wooden house in Gorokhovets. As she watched, anger grew within her. These were true citizens of the country, beaten down but refusing to give in. She renewed her resolve to stand shoulder to shoulder with them.

*

Svetlana checked the departures on the internet to see that Nick's plane had left Sheremetyevo half an hour late.

'I love you, Nikolai. Come back safely.'

She picked up a coffee and a copy of *Vedomosti* on the way to the metro and en route to her mother's, where a dress fitting awaited.

A few minutes later, the train pulled in with spare seats on show, the rush hour having passed. Today, there was a particularly pushy vendor patrolling the carriages selling snacks from a backpack. The newspaper gave Svetlana the means to hide herself from eye contact, and anyway, she did just want to be left alone to read. She took in the first few pages before turning over, her eyes widening at what she saw. There was a picture of Chernekov at a ceremony, receiving the Order for Military Merit, his chest puffed up with pride.

Svetlana was surprised at the complacency that had sought fit to reward this developer of poisons. She folded the newspaper carefully to preserve the image.

When Svetlana reached her mother's apartment, the kettle was boiling.

'Tea or coffee, darling?'

'Tea, please, Mum. I had some coffee on the way over.'

'Not that takeaway stuff?'

'It's fine. It's proper coffee. It's the cups that look a bit odd.'

'It's not very nice, drinking it out of plastic.'

Svetlana turned. There was her dress, held up by a hanger and caressed by the morning sunshine coming through the window.

'Oh, Mum, it's perfect!'

'Do you like it?'

'It's wonderful, Mum. Thank you so much.'

'Try it on, dear. Come on, let's see how you look.'

Within moments, Svetlana had shed her trousers and slipped into the dress while her mother stood by, pins and tape measure at the ready.

'You look beautiful, dear. I hope that man realises how lucky he is.'

'He does. I know he does. Where's the mirror?'

'I'll fetch it. Wait a minute,' said her mother as she left for the bedroom.

Moments later, she returned with a three-quarter length, white-framed mirror. Svetlana stood in front of it, smoothing the fabric down with her hands, and then standing tall to take a look at herself. She dropped her right shoulder and then her left, before turning sideways to see her profile.

'It's fantastic, Mum, and a perfect fit.'

'Not quite, dear. I just need to take it in a fraction here,' she said, pinching the fabric and inserting two pins. 'It won't take a minute. Slip it off and put my dressing gown on while I fix it.'

Svetlana sat in the pink brushed-cotton gown and picked up a picture of her father. She held it in her palms and looked down at the image of a young man in summer, standing tall and handsome while holding the hands of his two daughters as toddlers. She'd been too young to remember the photo being taken, but it reminded her of what she could recall, a kindly man with a constant sense of humour, who was, unfortunately, too fond of the cigarettes that would eventually bring about his early death. Svetlana smiled as she cast her mind back to those days in Yaroslavl when they had little but in some ways wanted for nothing, her dreamt-of oranges excepted. Would her dad be proud of her now, a journalist in Moscow and about to marry an international news reporter? He probably would. A smile crossed her face as she recounted her mother's tale of their wedding day where her father had had to surmount a series of obstacles, placed in his path to the bride by the witnesses, as was the custom in some parts of Russia. These days, and certainly in Moscow, such rituals were not customary but she thought it might be nice if Konstantin could liaise with her sister as witnesses to arrange some suitable hurdle to test Nick's determination to claim his bride.

'Right, come on. Let's see if it's right, this time.'

Svetlana stood in front of the mirror, dropped her guard against the past and contemplated her chance of a romantic future. Her bottom lip trembled slightly as arriving hope sought to overcome former disappointments. Within seconds, her mother was beside her but slightly behind with her arm around her daughter's waist.

'You look beautiful, darling. You must accept this chance with open arms.'

Mother and daughter hugged, taking in the scent of each other's hair.

*

With Nick away, she'd bribed Ivan to accompany her with the promise of a McDonald's supper. She didn't approve, but figured that once in a while wouldn't do any harm. He was due to play basketball after school, so he'd be even hungrier than usual, especially as they'd be eating quite late. She switched off her computer, pleased that Demchi had been impressed by her draft piece on how, mysteriously, there was a problem supplying power to the new Jetta furniture warehouse on the outskirts of the city. *Why didn't these foreign companies do a bit more research?* The fact that they had cables, a substation and a contract didn't guarantee that power would be turned on – not without the switch of some dollars changing hands. She shrugged and smiled as she made for the exit.

Once on ulitsa Pravdy, she decided on a whim to look again at the painting in the alleyway. The scene was the same as she approached: gloomy and somewhat eerie as lines of light from passing headlights sprinted along the walls beside her before fading away. She passed the fire escape and looked for the painting, but there was no sign of it. As another car went by, she was able to make out the change of shade on the brickwork, evidently the work of an FSB-ordered pressure washer. Nobody else would remove graffiti from such a place. They were erasing the evidence. *But then again*, she asked herself, *what did you think they were going to do?*

'They've found two more,' said a voice from the shadows.

She recognised it instantly.

'Yakov! You shouldn't be here. It's not safe.'

'It doesn't matter any more.'

'It does. We may need you to speak.'

'I have spoken.'

'I mean, in person.'

'That won't happen. You know they won't let that happen.'

Overhead, a newly installed, concealed camera watched.

'Do you need money?'

'I always need money. You know how it is.'

'When did you last eat?'

'Yesterday.'

'Here,' said Svetlana, handing him a thousand rubles.

'Thanks.'

'You know it really is time –'

Instead of passing by, headlights had stopped at the end of the alley with what looked like a large black Mercedes blocking its exit onto ulitsa Pravdy. Three men alighted, two tall and one much shorter. They began to approach.

'Yakov, run!'

The route behind was a dead end and the fire escape offered only access to doors above with no exterior handles. Katenin slipped backwards behind one of the large waste bins and clambered in.

'Svetlana Yuriyevna,' said Malenkov, with a chilling tone as he and his FSB men drew near. 'What are you doing here?'

'I work across the street.'

'But you don't work here. Where is Katenin?'

'I don't know.'

'I thought you and I understood each other. I'll ask you again. Where is Katenin?'

'I don't know.'

A radio crackled. One of Malenkov's lieutenants put his hand to his earpiece before pointing to the waste bin.

'Wait here,' said Malenkov, as he turned back to the car.

Svetlana remained, her two guards sneering at her. Conversation with them was pointless. At the end of the alley, Malenkov and his driver were up to something at the back of the car, but she couldn't make out what it was. Moments later, she saw his silhouette turn and walk in her direction. The diminutive FSB captain drew near, one hand in his pocket and one behind his back.

'Where is Katenin?'

'I don't know,' replied Svetlana.

Malenkov's right hand emerged from his coat pocket holding a lighter, which burst into life with a bright orange flame as his left hand came from behind his back with a half-filled bottle and a rag stuffed in the top. She was still taking in the scene when she heard a deep metallic boom as the bottle smashed on the inside of the giant aluminium bin and flame erupted upwards, lighting up the surrounding brickwork. Katenin screamed and scrambled from the container, some of his clothes on fire, his hair just singed remnants. He rolled frantically on the ground, trying to extinguish the flames. Malenkov folded his arms and grinned. Svetlana rushed forward, removed her coat and sought to smother the young man.

'Yakov – Yakov – are you all right?'

Katenin, some of his skin burnt away, shook and panted for breath as shock took him over. Anger rising, she turned to Malenkov.

'Get an ambulance! You fucking bastard – get an ambulance!'

The FSB captain slowly turned to face the street and signalled to his driver, who reversed the Mercedes down the alley.

'This will be quicker. We'll see that he gets the necessary care and then tells us where the rest of these are,' said Malenkov, pointing to the newly cleaned section of wall.

'You bastard!'

'I tried to show you respect, Svetlana Yuriyevna. I don't agree with you, but I tried to respect you.'

'Fuck you, Malenkov!'

He knelt down to Svetlana's level while she cradled the wretched youngster in her arms.

'He is a traitor and you are helping a traitor. As you can see, there are consequences for those who allow themselves to get too close. I would not wish anything to befall others you may be close to. So, I expect you to return to bribes and planning permissions. I hope I make myself clear.'

After the moaning Katenin was shoved into the back of the car, they left her shivering in the snow, her beautiful coat bundled at her feet and damaged beyond repair by its mission of mercy. She sobbed uncontrollably and longed to be with Nick.

*

Nick watched as Jack Freeman stirred his coffee and then looked up.

'That's quite a story. In fact, it's great. It's just the sort of thing we should be running,' said Freeman.

'There'd be consequences,' said Nick.

'Son, look at me, will you. Do I look like I give a rat's ass about that? History's full of consequences. Big stories need to be told and this fucker is one hell of a story!'

'They'll kick me out.'

'Even better: more people will listen to you, and you might even win the fucking Nobel Prize.'

'What about INN? What about the CIA and US relations?'

'Look, son, Watergate pissed off more people than you can imagine but did that story do good or bad for the US?'

'Good.'

'Exactly. In the long run, exposing these creeps is the only thing between freedom and totalitarianism. You know – for evil to triumph it's only necessary for good men to do nothing – Churchill and all that.'

'It was Edmund Burke.'

'What?'

'It was Edmund Burke who said that.'

'Yeah, right, whatever. This is going to have the oil companies crapping themselves. But hell, they already know Russia's going to be using energy to get its own way. Where the fuck did you get this from anyway?'

'From a very brave woman and a very brave young man.'

'Oh yeah, I forgot. Congratulations!'

'Thanks. I see Vicki's filled you in.'

'Damn right. Boy, have you been busy... and all you wanted to do was go to that villa of yours. Are you two going to live there?'

'Maybe. I'm not telling her about it. I'll know when she sees it... And, don't say anything when you meet her.'

'Okay, not a word, I promise. When's the big day?'

'A week on Friday. Are you coming?'

'To Moscow?'

'Yes.'

Freeman rose from his chair and came round to Nick's side of the desk before perching himself on the end. His voice dropped in volume and an earnest look took over his face.

'Nick, this is a great story, one of the best we've ever had. As it happens, our people will approve.'

'Our people?'

'You know – our people. They're content to see this thing play out. But, there may be trouble and –'

'And if I'm in trouble, you can run it from here?'

'Something like that, son.'

'You will run it, won't you? You know... if something happens to me?'

The two men looked each other in the eye.

'I'll run it... but you're USA. We're reckoning you'll be okay.'

'And Svetlana?'

Freeman opened his palms and frowned.

'If something happens to me, can you get her out? I mean, she brought us this story,' added Nick.

'I don't know, son, can't say.'

'They'll kill her.'

'We'll see what we can do. If she does get out, we'll give her a job anyway.'

Nick offered his hand to Freeman who shook it firmly.

'Thanks, Jack,' said Nick.

'You better get married, first. I hope you'll be very happy. She seems quite a girl.'

'She is.'

'Well, get back there then. When's your flight?'

'Tomorrow morning.'

'Okay, get some sleep.'

Nick rose and went to the door before turning the handle.

'Hey, Nick,' said Freeman, as Nick looked back. 'You've done well, son. God bless you.'

'Thanks, Jack.'

Nick shut Freeman's door behind him and made his way across the office to where Victoria sat at her desk grinning widely at him.

'Couldn't bear to be without me, eh?'

'That's about it, Vicki.'

'You're not in trouble, are you?'

'Not yet,' said Nick.

'What does that mean?'

'Nah, nothing. Look, I'm not going to be able to sleep with the time difference and all. Do you want some tapas?'

'You're on. I'll show you the rest of the photos from Moscow. By the way, Pilar thinks you're cute.'

'Don't start. I'm too fragile.'

Chapter 27

The next evening, Svetlana was due to meet Nick at Sheremetyevo, but before that a full day's work awaited her. She'd not been able to sleep properly, flashbacks of the injured Katenin constantly with her, so she'd risen to leave earlier than usual. On the journey in, she thought of the young man, wondering what would become of him and feeling guilty that he'd been a victim of the danger she was bringing to those close to her. By eight a.m. she was standing in Pushkinskaya ploshchad looking up at the statue of her old friend and confidant as angry grey clouds rolled overhead. Their usual connection proved difficult to establish as she fidgeted, unnerved, for once unable to block out the petulant squawking of the Moscow traffic. She walked on across the square to the bottom of ulitsa Malaya Dmitrovskaya where her eyes were drawn to the small white Church of the Nativity of our Lady. Its five blue domes reached on long necks for the light above, which was partially blocked out by taller buildings. As a child, the Russian Orthodox Church had quietly played a significant role in her family's life, but that had later waned and finally been extinguished following her marriage to Dmitriy, a confirmed atheist. Right now, she badly wanted to escape the hustle and bustle fuelling her anxiety.

Svetlana strode forward, hoping to find some sanctuary from her distress. Unusually for her, the beggar sitting by the railings, wrapped in a grey blanket and holding out his splintered plastic cup, barely registered as she walked past and entered the church. She closed the door behind her. No sound came from within save for the clack of her own heels as she advanced across the mottled pink and grey marble floor towards the image-ringed archway ahead. Scrolled brass candle holders standing by the walls accompanied her journey forward, the orange flames flickering as her progress disturbed the otherwise sleeping air. Unlike western churches, there were no seats. She would stand or kneel as she had sometimes done as a child, the feeling of cool marble in summer heat suddenly fresh in her mind.

Through the archway facing her, iconic pictures filled the wall with gold and subservient colours as a gallery of God's representatives looked down upon her. Svetlana whimpered almost inaudibly and shivered as her solitude allowed shock to fade in the face of creeping fear and crushing sadness. She watched one of her tears as it fell seemingly in slow motion to the marble below, and then wrapped her arms around herself as tightly as she could.

'What troubles you, child?' said a soft, kindly voice from behind her.

She turned to see a *monach*, a monk to westerners, dressed in black, a cross hanging from his neck below a long, flowing grey beard and wire-framed glasses perched precariously on the end of his nose. The invitation to unburden her troubles overwhelmed her as she sank to her knees, sobbing, and held out a trembling hand, which was taken and held in return. Gradually she regained her composure as she sniffed and wiped her nose on her sleeve, anxious to speak.

'Father, why is Mother Russia so cruel to her children?'

'It is not the mother but sometimes her wayward children who forget how to behave.'

'When will it stop? When can Yakov walk tall in his own country?'

'What is your name, child?'

'Svetlana Yuriyevna.'

'And who is Yakov?'

'A young man and a patriot. He is in great danger.'

'Why is he in danger?'

'For trying to tell the truth.'

'Svetlana Yuriyevna, our Lord tried to tell the truth and was persecuted for it. Many have suffered in the name of truth, but it will win through in the end.'

'But they will kill him, Father.'

'They will not kill his spirit. Through it, he will live on to spread his truth.'

'I need to save him in this life.'

'Then you must do what you can.'

'What can I do?'

'Plead his case to whoever holds his fate and pray for God's help.'

'I have not prayed in a long time, Father.'

'Then he will look forward to hearing from you again.'

Svetlana looked up.

'Thank you, Father,' she said, slowly rising to her feet.

'Go in peace, Svetlana Yuriyevna. I will pray for our brother patriot.'

She managed a weak smile and a nod, fearful that if she spoke again tears would re-commence.

On the way out, Svetlana saw the same beggar, his cup holding a solitary five kopecks coin. She opened her handbag and gave him a generous hundred rubles in return for mumbled thanks. Now he would be able to eat or drink himself into a stupor as he wished, two more choices than he'd had moments before.

*

'Sveta, get a move on, will you, we need to push this through to subs,' said an evidently irritated Demchi.

'Sorry, I'll be finished in a few minutes,' said Svetlana, her eyes returning to the text in front of her.

So distracted had she been by Katenin's plight that it had taken her most of the day to write a piece she'd normally rattle off in an hour, before sending it through to the sub-editor. Now she just wanted to finish so she could go down to Lubyanka to plead for Katenin, and to see if prayers offered would be answered. Vasiliy brought her news that would save her the trip.

'Sveta, come here. Look at this!'

She swivelled round to see her young colleague staring at his screen. She manoeuvred her chair over to him, one of the castors squeaking as she did. Vasiliy turned on the sound as they both looked at the charred remains of a body lying next to a large waste bin. The commentator's voice faded in:

'There's a growing problem with drunken vagrants taking shelter in rubbish bins and then smoking. That's what seems to have happened to Yakov Katenin here, who apparently was so drunk he was unable to escape after he set light to paper he'd buried himself in. This is the fourth such episode in the last few months and the mayor has asked his officials to look at ways that access could be restricted, to try and cut down on this risk.'

Svetlana, her hand covering her mouth, closed her eyes and screwed them up tightly. She held her breath and fought hard to keep some measure of composure in front of Vasiliy.

'That's him.'

'Yes, Vasya, that is our artist. He didn't set himself alight. Malenkov burned him with gasoline, but not like that. He was alive and could have recovered.'

'When?'

'Yesterday, in the alleyway,' said Svetlana.

'They took him?'

'Yes, of course – for information.'

'Do you think they got it?'

'We'll see if the pictures continue to disappear.'

'Sveta, I'm really sorry.'

'I thought that maybe I could – naïve – stupid of me. And when they took him I didn't know what to think.'

'He wasn't coming back, was he?'

'No, Vasya, he wasn't coming back. Dima was right all along.'

'What about?'

'There's no God to listen to prayers.'

They sat in silence, Vasiliy remaining with her. A minute later, Demchi emerged from his office and walked over.

'Have you finished?'

'Yes,' said Svetlana.

She clicked the send button to lodge her copy with the sub-editor and then looked up at her boss.

'Have you got a drink, Demchi?'

*

As soon as he emerged into the arrivals hall, Nick knew something was wrong. In fact, he'd had a feeling of foreboding ever since he'd stepped off the plane. She threw her arms around his neck and held him, vice-like, trembling.

'Oh Nikolai Ivanovich, don't leave me again.'
'Darling, what is it? What's happened?'
'He's gone. They've killed him.'
'Yakov?'
'Yes. He's dead. Dead! I killed him.'
'No, that's not so. He knew exactly what he was doing.'
'But if only I'd been more careful.'
'He'd have found this danger by another route. It's not you.'

Nick reached behind and took her arms from his neck, stepping back to look at her. Why, despite tragedy written across her face, did she manage to look extraordinarily beautiful at times like this? He'd seen no such traits in western women.

'It's not you, Sveta. Come on, they'll be watching us. Talk to me in the car, not here.'

They made their way to the car park, Nick's suitcase rumbling along behind them on its wheels as he kept a protective arm around Svetlana's shoulders. From the balcony above, their FSB minders looked on impassively as the roar of jet engines on full boost filled the air.

He put his case in the boot before closing the lid, which was out of line and needed a good slam to shut it. A seam of brown rust edged the faded blue paintwork. Nick resolved to fix her up with a better car, wherever and whenever they ended up together. She was still trembling.

'Do you want me to drive?' he asked.

She nodded, managing a momentary smile, before walking round to the passenger side and handing him the keys.

Thankfully, the motorway was quiet as they drove south for the city. Nick stuck to the inside lane and kept a steady pace.

'What happened?'

'Yakov came to see me in the alley across from work. They'd found the picture and removed it.'

'What did he want?'

'To warn me they were looking for the other pictures.'

'We could have worked that out for ourselves.'

She glanced at him, stony-faced. He knew then was not the time for analysis and criticism of Katenin's actions. He took her hand.

'Malenkov came – knew we were there. Yakov hid, but Malenkov burned him with a bottle of gasoline. Oh, Nikolai, it was horrible. I can still see his face and his hair all burnt.'

'What did they do?'

'They took him. He was hurt, but he'd have been okay with treatment.'

'And today...?'

'On the news – left in the street. They'd tortured him and then set fire to him while he was alive!'

'You don't know that.'

She looked at him and their eyes met, then he returned his attention to the road.

'I saw it in his face – Malenkov. I know what he did.'

Nick held her hand tighter as they continued in silence for the remaining fifteen minutes of their journey.

Later, they parked up and made their way to Svetlana's apartment where there was a note from Ivan to say he'd gone round to see his friend, Misha, but wouldn't be late back. She hung up her coat before smoothing down the long jumper she wore over her jeans. Soup waited on the stove to be warmed and she finished preparing the simple *plov* she'd started before her trip to the airport.

'I spoke to his mother,' said Svetlana, adding rice to the pan of boiling water.

'Who? Katia?'

'No, Nikolai, Yakov's mother. She's Alyona Semyonova – coming tomorrow, from Kazan, to collect his body. I said I'd meet her.'

'I'll come with you.'

'No need. I'll deal with it.'

'I'll come with you,' said Nick, with determination.

'As you please.'

'I should have been here.'

'No, it was important to speak to your boss. Will he help?'

'Definitely.'

'Then he is our friend.'

'On this one, he is.'

The doorbell rang.

'Oh, Ivan Dimitriyich, why can't you remember your key?' said Svetlana, as she rinsed her hands under the tap and turned for the door. 'Really, is it that difficult?'

She opened it and standing there was not Ivan but her near neighbours, Vitaliy and Vera Kanatov. He carried their young toddler in his arms, while she held roses and a large box of chocolates.

'I'm sorry, I thought it was my son – always forgetting his key. Come in, come in!' said Svetlana.

'Thank you, Svetlana Yuriyevna, but it's past Anatoliy's bed-time. We just wanted to give you a little token. You must have thought us so rude.'

Vera reached out with her gifts, which Svetlana took from her.

'Thank you. Really, this wasn't necessary.'

'We owe you the life of our son, don't we, Vitaliy?'

'We do,' he affirmed, kissing the youngster on the top of his head.

'No, no, he probably would have been fine but it was just better to be safe.'

Nick came to join Svetlana.

'This is Nikolai Ivanovich. We are to be married next week.'

Nick stepped forward and shook the hand of each neighbour in turn.

'Pleased to meet you,' he said.

'Congratulations, we hope you'll be very happy,' said Vera.

'Thank you,' said Svetlana and Nick in unison.

'And thank you again for your presents,' added Svetlana, as Vera and Vitaliy retreated backwards and out of view.

'He's FSB,' said Nick.

'You knew that. I've already told you.'

'No, I saw it. I recognised him as FSB.'

'At last,' she replied, stroking his chin with an extended finger.

Chapter 28

The next morning, Svetlana woke slowly to see a shaft of sunlight split the room in two through a gap in the curtains. She remembered, through warmth and lifting reverie, that she was due to meet her mother to look for shoes to accompany the dress – but there was something else. Then it hit her and brought her fully awake. Yakov was dead and the tears of another grieving mother awaited her that afternoon. She rose to make breakfast and was soon busying herself in the kitchen.

'How was Misha?'

'Good. He's skating today, so can I go?' asked Ivan.

He stirred extra sugar into his bowl of steaming *kasha*. Svetlana knew he liked his porridge to be thick, so always made it that way for him.

'Have you finished your essay?'

'Handed it in, yesterday.'

'Okay, then you've earned your skating.'

'What's up, Mum?'

'I'm fine, Vanya.'

'Is it that soldier, the one who died?'

She'd tried to mask it from Ivan but had forgotten that would not work with her own flesh and blood.

'It's to do with that. It's all rather sad.'

'But you'll be okay, won't you?'

'I'll be fine,' she lied.

She saw Ivan looking at her, a spoonful of *kasha* cooling in his hand.

'I've been thinking. I don't think I'd mind living abroad for a while, just to try it, maybe,' he said.

It could have been Dima speaking. He'd had the uncanny ability, at least when sober, to floor her with a casually delivered comment. Ivan had not been taught this. It was deep inside him, a product of his father. Her mother had been right: Ivan loved her and right now his words demonstrated more than a million red roses ever could.

'Oh, Vanya,' she said, sitting down at the table and reaching across for his hand. 'Thank you.'

*

Frankly, Nick felt a bit of a fool as he looked across at his editorial team. He could see it now, but why had it taken him so long to realise that Valentina was FSB? At least the nagging puzzle of how Malenkov had come by the image of him and Svetlana at Dorogomilovsky was now solved. *What a bitch.*

'Did we ever get anything more on the Moskovsky Industrialny story?' asked Nick.

There was a general shaking of heads.

'What about you, Valentina, surely you've got some information?' said Nick, fixing her with a cold stare.

The discovered FSB officer shifted uneasily in her chair and avoided eye contact with him.

'Er, no, nothing new.'

Nick preserved her discomfort for as long as he could.

'How was JF?' asked Konstantin.

Nick released the hapless Valentina.

'He was fine. He sends his best regards and thanks for all the good work.'

That was as much as they were going to get about discussions with Madrid, particularly with Valentina present. With Katenin's death, the story had become even more compelling. However, Nick was worried that the personal angle for Andrei Petrov, so important to Svetlana, would be lost in the power of the attempt to disrupt energy supplies across Georgia. Sure enough, that's the way Jack

Freeman had seen it, chuckling and remarking that it was enough to kick off another Cold War.

'I'm gonna buy some gold because the economy's going to hit the skids for a while when all this comes out,' he'd said to Nick.

They'd even discussed the philosophical side of whether news like this was better left unsaid. Freeman had been emphatic.

'We don't make the news, son. We're just the messenger, and I'm never going to pull a story because it might upset somebody.'

Nick had returned to Moscow, emboldened by the unwavering support of his boss, and right now he felt like kicking Valentina's ass for selling out his profession so badly.

'Right, if there's nothing else, we can wrap it up there,' said Nick.

Everybody rose.

'You got a minute, Valentina?'

She stood still while the others left the room, with just the odd look back. Valentina took her seat once again and glanced at Nick, but then appeared to fix her eyes on her reflection in the glass table top.

'How long have you been a journalist?'

'Nine years,' she answered.

'And how long have you worked for the FSB?'

She looked at him.

'It's not like that.'

'I mean, what's the point? Don't you ever think to yourself you have a duty to publish the truth to people, to real people?'

'Nick, I don't think you understand.'

'Do you know, I don't care what you think because you obviously can't think for yourself if you're taking orders from the FSB.'

He was on a roll now, with disappointment-tinged indignation turning to anger. He continued.

'I try to do my job the best way I can, you know, professionally. I tell it the way it is and the day I sell out to the state is the day I retire. You should be ashamed of yourself!'

'It's different here.'

'The truth is the same. There's no right and wrong truth, there's just the truth.'

Nick stared at her.

'Now you tell your boss, Captain Malenkov, that I want to be left alone to do my job. Tell him to go and catch some real terrorists and leave us alone!'

Nick stood up quickly and left the room, slamming the door behind him. He went to his office and scooped up his laptop. He unconsciously held it to his chest as he surveyed his private space, which no longer felt safe, invaded as it had been by a malign agent of the state. With his anger barely subsiding, he decided to finish the copy he'd started in the Starbuck's down the road.

*

'What about these?' asked her mother, holding up a pair of open-toed cream shoes.

'I'm not sure. I don't really like the heel,' answered Svetlana.

They'd already done one circuit of the Okhotny Ryad shopping mall and it was looking like they were going to struggle to find what Svetlana had in mind.

'Is this all you have?' her mother asked a bored-looking shop assistant.

'There's some new stock but we haven't unpacked it yet,' came the surly reply.

'Well, can we have a look at them because there's not much here?'

With a sigh that fell just short of exasperation, the assistant turned for the back of the shop. Svetlana was unsure whether she'd gone to help or had merely walked away. She looked at her mother and shrugged.

'At this rate we're not going to have time for lunch.'

'We'll have to eat here, Mum.'

'Oh, Sveta, you know I don't like these places for food.'

'There's one on the next level. It's a franchise but the food's fine. It'll give us time.'

Without speaking, the assistant returned pushing a trolley containing half a dozen boxes. She removed the lids to display the contents, then walked behind the cash counter and folded her arms.

While her mother suspiciously prodded the leather of the shoes nearest to her, Svetlana's eyes were drawn to a pale green box containing a pair of simple elegance, with heels neither too high nor too low and contrasting stitching that looked like it had been done by hand. She reached for them, then held them up to the light to check the shade. They were just what she'd had in mind and a good omen, she thought.

'Mum, these are the ones.'

'They are lovely, dear. Try them on.'

Svetlana slipped each one on and then stood in front of a large mirror holding up the legs of her trousers to get a better view.

'What do you think?'

'Really nice. Are they comfortable? It'll be a long day and you don't want them hurting.'

'They're a great fit. Made for me.'

'Are you sure? Do you want to look at the first pair again?'

'No, Mum, these are the ones I want.'

At the till, she reached for her credit card but was interrupted by her mother who placed her hand on top Svetlana's.

'I'm going to get these for you, dear.'

'No, Mum, you don't have to do that. Nikolai and I can afford them.'

'I'm going to get them. I didn't tell you, but I knew this day would come and I have a little fund put aside. Now, I intend to use it.'

A few minutes later, they were sitting in the restaurant awaiting their food.

'Are you in some sort of danger, dear?'

'No, Mum, I'm fine.'

'It's just that Ivan telephoned me and told me that he thought you were in some trouble. It's not like him to tell me such things.'

'You know how it is with my work, there's always somebody who's not happy.'

'Sveta, is that all it is?'

'Yes, Mum, don't worry.'

'Is everything all right with Nikolai?'

'Mum, please, he's a good man. I know we're going to be very happy.'

Svetlana had been right about the restaurant. The food was pretty good – if a bit over-priced – but her mother ate well. Later, they parted company at the entrance to the metro, leaving her plenty of time to make her journey to the city's Morgue Number Seven for her rendezvous with Alyona.

She took out her phone and called Nick.

'Hi, it's me. Where are you?'

'About five minutes away,' he replied.

'Okay, that's good. See you there at four. Bye.'

Maybe it was travelling down to the depths on the particularly steep escalator, but she felt fear about to touch her. Life, at the moment, was like two sides of a coin: glorious hope on one – and tragedy on the other. She imagined tossing that coin in the air and wondering how it would fall. A propensity for superstition irritated her as she lined up her toes exactly with the edge of the ribbed steel step, afraid even a millimetre's deviation would tempt bad fate into action. *Madrid has a metro, but does Boston?* She'd have to ask Nick. *What if Malenkov found all the pictures? What difference would that make? Why is my mind racing like this?*

As she approached the morgue, Nick was waiting, as promised. He hugged her and brushed her cheek with the back of his hand.

'Is she here?'

'Don't know. I've only just arrived myself,' said Nick.

'Have you checked inside?'

'No, but we could,' said Nick, looking up. 'She's here – behind you.'

Some fifty metres away, a woman in her forties who was dressed in a simple, grey woollen coat and a dark green scarf, stepped down from the passenger seat of a black van, its flashing hazard lights scattering orange light onto the kerbside snow. Accompanying her was a girl of about thirteen who grabbed her hand and clung to it as they approached.

'Svetlana Yuriyevna?'

'Yes,' said Svetlana, extending her hand.

'I am Alyona Semyonova and this is my daughter, Mariya. It's good of you to meet us.'

'It's the least we could do. This is Nikolai Ivanovich.'

They stood awkwardly for a few seconds before Alyona stepped forward.

'Shall we go in? Mariya has school in the morning and we need to get back.'

'Of course,' said Svetlana, as she and Nick turned to follow them.

From reception, they were shown to a bare, grey anteroom by an unsmiling assistant who clearly cared nothing for whether Katenin was a patriot or not. He was just another statistic on a cold day. They sat and waited.

'Yakov was brave and cared deeply for his friend.'

'Thank you, Svetlana Yuriyevna,' replied Alyona. 'I spoke to Andrei's mother. She tells me you too are brave.'

'That's kind of her, but I just try to do my job.'

'If only we all had the courage to do your job.'

The two women looked at each other with unspoken respect, while Alyona's little girl, still clinging on, fought bravely to hold back tears and support her mother.

A door handle rattled, followed by the hiss of an airtight seal being released. A tall man, in white overalls and a green plastic apron, stood before them and pulled latex gloves from his hands.

'Alyona Katenina?' he enquired.

Alyona stood.

'Follow me. Best to leave the child.'

'Mum, I want to come with you.'

'Stay here, darling. Wait a moment, for Yasha, and we will take him with us.'

'But, Mum –'

Alyona gently prised her hand free from the child's grip.

Svetlana's Garden

'Wait a while, Masha. Svetlana Yuriyevna will look after you,' said Alyona.

'I will. Come here, Mariya,' said Svetlana, reaching for the child. 'Nikolai... would you?'

'Of course,' said Nick.

He moved to Alyona's shoulder as she followed the mortuary assistant to the still-open entrance, from where the smell of formaldehyde drifted in. They disappeared as Nick half closed the door behind him.

Svetlana, left alone with the child, put her arm around her shoulder.

'Mum will be back soon. Tell me about Kazan. Do you like it there?'

Inside, Nick stood a respectful distance behind Alyona and surveyed stainless steel cabinets, which reflected the harsh light of bare neon tubes overhead. The assistant opened a cabinet to reveal three bodies, their heads and shoulders uncovered.

'Shit!' he mumbled to himself, apparently having opened the wrong door, and unceremoniously slamming it shut.

He stepped to the next door along and opened it. There lay two bodies with a vacancy for the yet undead in the space between them. One of the bodies was naked from the chest up. The other, on the bottom row, was concealed in a black vinyl body bag, a label tied with string to its zipper bearing the solitary word "Katenin".

'Effects,' said the assistant, handing a small plastic bag to Alyona.

It contained her son's cheap watch, its strap almost burnt through and the simple silver ring she'd given him for his sixteenth birthday, and which had made it out of the morgue either because it had no great value or was the subject of orders to return it. Nick watched Alyona look down at these souvenirs of a life before she enclosed them in her hands and held them to her chest.

'I need to see him,' she said.

'Not a good idea,' said the assistant, glancing at Nick.

'Alyona, maybe it's best not to... at the moment,' opined Nick.

'He's my son. I need to see him.'

The assistant ignored Alyona and looked at the reporter instead. Nick, reinforced by the tone of her voice, took the view that she would not leave this spot without sight of her son, and nodded approval.

Back in the anteroom, Svetlana was receiving monosyllabic answers to her questions from the frightened youngster.

'And what's your favourite subject at school?'

The child drew breath for an answer, but did not have chance to deliver it before the desperate guttural cry of her mother's anguish arrived from the improperly sealed doorway. Svetlana held her and felt the little one's muscles stiffen as her jaw trembled and the tears started. She wriggled to be free, but Svetlana held her as another wretched scream forced its way out. In all the situations she'd come across in her work for the newspaper, she'd never heard such a sound. She struggled to hold her own emotions in check while seeking to protect young Mariya.

'Masha, wait – wait. Let Mum deal with this. She has to do this, but she will be here soon.'

She hugged the little girl, then kissed her on the top of her head and repeatedly whispered, 'It's all right.'

Nick watched Alyona in her desolation as she laid her hand on the blackened flesh of her only son, stripped of most of his skin, his features unrecognisable. Her tears pattered off the plain vinyl of the body bag as her knees threatened to give way. Nick stepped forward and touched her forearm.

'Alyona, come on. The funeral director will deal with things.'

'Not yet,' she sobbed, brushing his hand away.

He watched as centimetre by centimetre her lips descended to plant a kiss on the place where it was just possible to make out where the young man's mouth had been. Nick felt himself beginning to retch and turned away, holding his hand over his mouth. He took in a deep breath through his nostrils and turned back. Alyona was slowly pulling up the plastic zip with the demeanour she might once have used to tuck Yakov into his childhood bed. When she'd finished, she gently patted him on the chest before reaching for a tissue from her pocket and wiping her nose.

'Thank you, Nikolai Ivanovich. We will go now.'

Shortly afterwards, as he waved to the funeral director to come and collect the body, Nick looked back to see Alyona's daughter being held by her mother, with Svetlana's arms around both of them. He returned to them.

'Thank you, Svetlana Yuriyevna, and you, Nikolai Ivanovich. You have been very kind,' said Alyona.

'Will you not stay a little while for some refreshment?' asked Svetlana.

'No, thank you, but we must return. Mariya has school and I must work tomorrow.'

Svetlana reached into her bag and took out an envelope.

'Alyona, take this. It's not much but it is a gift from the people I work with.'

'But Katia said your paper could not become involved.'

'That is true, but my colleagues know of Yakov's bravery, and wished to show their respect.'

Alyona took the envelope and folded it in two.

'Please thank them all,' she whispered.

A few minutes later, Svetlana and Nick gave apologetic waves as the defeated, red-eyed faces of Alyona and her daughter looked back at them through the window of the undertaker's van, creeping forward to begin its sad journey back to Kazan. When it was finally out of sight, Svetlana turned into his open arms and rested her head on his shoulder.

'I despise Malenkov – him and his kind. He should be shot and left out for the crows.'

'We're going to deal with this,' Nick replied, holding her firmly to him.

Chapter 29

Nick woke first and gently shook Svetlana until she stirred. She put her hands to her eyes to block out the light and moaned.

'Oh... we shouldn't have drunk so much last night.'

'Yeah, we should. It was just what we needed after a day like that,' replied Nick.

'I guess so. Maybe you're right, maybe it did help.'

'At the right moment, alcohol is the eighth wonder.'

Svetlana didn't answer, as images of Dima stumbling and swearing at the world came to mind. She shook her head and then reached for the tumbler of water she'd had the good sense to leave on the bedside cabinet.

'Look, we have a week to go and we've paid our respects, so let's try to spend some time on ourselves, some happy time. Is it a deal?' asked Nick.

She looked at him and smiled, patting the stubble on his chin while she contemplated whether, despite Katenin, Malenkov and all that was going on, it was time to indulge themselves a little. Hell, they were going to be married!

'Deal, Nikolai. You can start by taking me dancing.'

'Tonight?'

'Yes, tonight.'

'Okay, where do you fancy?'

'Surprise me, Nikolushka, surprise me.'

'Only if you make me a surprise breakfast.'

She laughed and reached behind for her pillow, before landing it on the top of Nick's head.

'Surprise! Now, I'll get the rest of your breakfast,' she said, swinging her legs out of the bed and reaching for her dressing gown.

After they'd eaten scrambled eggs with smoked salmon and some rye bread, she felt the effects of her hangover recede.

'More coffee?'

'No, thanks, darling,' replied Nick.

'I got the shoes, yesterday. Well, Mum got them for me, if you know what I mean.'

'Oh yeah? What are they like?'

'You'll have to wait. Let's just say I'm pretty pleased with them.'

'Underwear?'

'What?'

'What's the underwear like?'

'I'm not telling. Now, that you really will have to wait to see,' she said, drawing her fingertip from his adam's apple to the bottom of his chin while grinning broadly.

'Not even if I tell you where I'm taking you on honeymoon?'

'Where, Nikolai, where?'

'Tell me some of the most romantic places in the world.'

'Most romantic places? Paris...'

'And...?'

'Venice.'

Nick's mouth curled up at the edges as he tried to stifle a grin.

'Venice? Nikolai, is it Venice? Is it really Venice?'

A wide smile broke free across Nick's face. She reached for him and flung her arms around his neck.

'Oh, Nikolai, Venice! I've always wanted to go there, ever since I was a little girl, but I never thought I would.'

'*Senza di te la mia vita non ha senso,*' said Nick, with exaggerated drama, clutching his palm to his chest.

'What? What did you say?' asked Svetlana, shaking him by the shoulders.

'Without you, my life has no meaning.'

The smile left his face.

'Are we going? Are we really going?'

'A friend of JF's owns a hotel there, a good one. We can go whenever we want.'

'Can we go on a gondola?'

'Of course – as long as the gondolier's ugly.'

'Stop teasing!'

'I mean it,' said Nick, his look earnest.

Silence took hold as she looked for corroboration in his eyes. No confirmation came before his expression cracked and he burst into laughter.

'You had me worried there for a minute. Thought you were going to be the jealous type, following me round. I've had enough of that from the FSB,' said Svetlana.

'I don't need to follow you round. You'll either love me or you won't.'

She placed her hand on the back of his.

'Then, I'll love you.'

'Well, that's okay then. I can go to work safe in the knowledge I'll be wanted when we go dancing, tonight. I'd better get ready.'

Nick stood and padded to the bathroom, half closing the door behind him.

'Oh shit,' he said, Svetlana picking up the words above the sound of the running tap.

'What is it?' she called.

The running water stopped and then he put his head round the door.

'I've forgotten a razor. I'm going straight to location and I need to shave. Have you got one?'

'Yes,' she said, grinning, 'for my legs.'

Svetlana stepped forward and manoeuvred him in the doorway so she could squeeze past. She opened the bathroom cabinet and held up a pink plastic razor.

'That?' he asked.

'Excuse me, I'm not used to having men to stay. Do you want to use it or not?'

'No choice, I guess.'

'If you blunt it, you'll have to get me another.'

She smiled, then turned for the kitchen to make herself a cup of tea. How many years had it been since she'd been able to enjoy such humble but intimate company? She stopped herself, vowing only to count forward, not backwards. While the tea was brewing, plates were cleared and a brief shopping list compiled before the click of the lock announced Nick's emergence from his grooming.

Svetlana chuckled and covered her mouth with her hand.

'I don't think it's funny,' he said, dabbing his chin with a tissue to catch the blood seeping from several nicks to his skin.

'Extra make-up for you before you go on camera,' she replied, smirking.

'I wouldn't want to be your legs if that's what they have to put up with.'

'I thought you liked my legs.'

'I do, I just wouldn't want to be them.'

'You're right, they don't complain as much as you do!'

*

Later, outside Moskovsky Industrialny Bank on Pyatnitskaya ulitsa, Nick prepared to go on camera. He'd talked strategy with JF and they'd agreed a follow-up report would be a good way to lay the ground for the twin stories of Andrei Petrov and the pipeline attack. He sat in the crew's truck as his assistant applied some make-up.

'The light's strong today, so I'm going to put quite a bit on – don't want you looking too pale. What have you done to your face?' she asked.

'It's a short story you don't want to hear.'

'Okay, up to you. Are you wearing a hat?'

'Yeah, why?'

'So I don't need to do your hair.'

'Hey, Nick, you ready?' asked his sound man.

'Yeah, coming,' replied Nick, donning the *ushanka* that would lend authenticity to a very Russian story.

He stepped down from the truck and clipped a mic to his lapel.

'Where do you want to do this?'

'Over there: less traffic echo off the buildings,' said the sound engineer.

Suddenly, Nick's steps felt heavy as he realised this was setting in train the plan he and Jack Freeman had worked out for maximum attention. Today's report would later be repeated as the opening salvo to the other stories. The authorities would see them as direct challenges to a regime where dissemination of news was always subject to unspoken lines, not to be crossed without consequences. Even as he stood on the Moscow pavement, a sister crew was revisiting the pumping station in Georgia. Trouble was just around the corner and he knew it.

'Ready?'

'Whenever you like, Nick.'

'A short while ago, I reported on the strange case of a robbery here at a branch of Moscow Industrial Bank. You may recall that police were perplexed to find all the potential witnesses unconscious but with no trace of any cause. Well, I've been following up on this story and it appears that a new type of gas is the likely explanation. Where might such a gas have come from and how did it get into the hands of organised crime? The second question is probably easier to answer as there's a long history in Russia of military hardware finding its way to those prepared to pay for it. I say military, because well financed as the mafia gangs can be, it's highly unlikely one of them has the inclination or technical resources to develop such a sophisticated weapon. Unspoken of these days, but according to some still active, is Kamera, the former KGB's secret poisons development department. It may all sound a bit like a Cold War spy story but in these days of commercial and energy politics, a truly undetectable gas would have a number of potential uses – bank robberies included, it seems. We're watching developments and will bring you more on this story as it unfolds. Nick Mendez, for INN, Moscow.'

Nick looked at his cameraman and his sound engineer.

'That okay?'

He received a thumbs-up from behind the camera.

'Got it in one,' said the sound man.

Svetlana's Garden

'Okay, great,' said Nick. 'Let's get a coffee. I'm freezing my nuts off here.'

*

'Is he in the back?' asked Svetlana.

A simple nod from Dubnikov's doorman was accompanied by a sign to move through the bar, with its patterned mirrors and red leather seats. Svetlana walked to the back of Roza's on ulitsa Arbat, one of several bars that Roman Dubnikov had opened in the city, taking the name from his mother.

His enforcer, Vadik, stood and leered at her as she approached.

'Hit any tough women lately?' she asked sarcastically.

The smirk disappeared from Vadik's face.

'It's a good thing he likes you,' he hissed, as he knocked on the office door behind him.

'Come!' bellowed Dubnikov's unmistakeable response.

Vadik turned the handle and opened the dark-stained door to reveal the mafia boss rising to his feet from a tall-backed, tan armchair.

He seemed in an exceptionally good mood as he poured coffee for both of them.

'I heard the joyous news. Congratulations!'

'Thanks. News travels fast.'

'You should know.'

'I suppose so. I've not got too much time.'

'I don't know, you're always in a hurry and never seem to have time to talk.'

'Just a busy life. Really, though, I do need to get on.'

'That's a shame because I was going to tell you about Chernekov and his meetings with Grachev, but maybe another time, eh?'

She hated it when he toyed with her. Sometimes he could be like a spoiled cat with a mouse. *Why can't he just speak without this charade?*

'Maybe just a few minutes.'

'Good, good. Milk?'

'No, thanks.'

He put milk in his own coffee and took his time to stir it in.
'We provide the roof to Chernekov's local Starbucks.'
'And?'
'Well, it appears they keep their CCTV for quite a while and our friends were foolish enough to be seen there together.'

She tried to keep her enthusiasm for this news in check, fearing it would simply encourage Dubnikov in his little game.

'When was this?'
'Before the Moskovsky Industrialny job.'
'And you have the recording?'
'Let's just say it's in a safe place.'
'And why would you tell me?'
'Because I knew you'd be interested. Call it a wedding present.'
'And does this present have a price?'
'Sveta, Sveta, come now, if it had a price it wouldn't be a present.'
A silent 'but' hung in the air.
'Then is there a favour you need, perhaps?' she asked.
'Well, we do a have a small problem you could help with.'
'Which is?'
'My daughter.'
'Your daughter? I'm not sure that's anything I can help with. I have enough problems looking after my own family.'
'She wants to be a journalist, a foreign correspondent, would you believe?'
'Does she now?'

Svetlana was relieved that Dubnikov had not asked her to plant some story about a rival or politician he'd fallen out with.

'She's looking for some work experience – some contacts, perhaps.'
'Does she really want to do that?'
'Oh yes. I mean, she's studied in England and in Paris – speaks English and French.'
'You're serious, aren't you?'
'Mr Mendez must be able to help.'
'I know you... he doesn't.'
'My daughter is legit, a real student. She's very determined.'

'I'll ask him but he may have... reservations.'
'About my line of work?'
'Yes, Roman, about your line of work.'
'But you'll ask him?'
'I'll ask.'

Dubnikov sat back in his chair, apparently contemplating his hands, which were clasped together, before rising and walking over to a desk in the corner. He unlocked a drawer and reached inside for something, then returned to take his seat.

'Hold out your hand,' said Dubnikov.

Those words, and the tone with which he delivered them, reminded her of her form teacher at school who would speak the same words to nervous children before hitting their palms with a ruler for the most minor of perceived misdemeanours. She shivered at the memory before extending her closed fist and then opening it to reveal the flat of her hand. Dubnikov leant forward, compressing his not insubstantial stomach against his thighs and reached out to place on her finger a steel ring holding a small key.

'This is the key to a safe place, a present from me to you both. I know this is a present you will value.'

'The recording?'

Dubnikov smiled mischievously and nodded.

'Where?'

'Kursky Station, where else?'

She smiled and shook her head.

'And the number?'

'Eighty-three: my mother's age.'

'You're close to her, aren't you?'

'Are you not close to your mother?'

'Yes, of course but –'

'Your mother's child is not a gang boss?'

Svetlana didn't confirm his question.

'What does she think... about your line of work?'

'Mothers from Samara cannot help themselves, they always love their sons.'

'I believe they do,' said Svetlana, rising to her feet. 'Don't forget to let me have your daughter's CV.'

*

Nick couldn't believe their luck. The story, in the eyes of the viewer, would have stunk anyway but to have a recording of a poisons expert and a mafia leader taking tea together shortly before a bank robbery was just about as good as it got. Boy, it cut down the deniability. He knew from a moral point of view that the whole thing was a truth that needed to be told, but the pure journalist in him was excited that the elements they'd so painstakingly pulled together were going to mix into something explosive.

'I mean, come on! How good is that? It's about time something came easy on this one.'

'It's not easy, Nikolai, is it?'

'How do you mean?'

'Well, we need to get it to JF, right?'

'Yeah, so?'

'How easy is that going to be... undetected? You can't go to Madrid again. They probably won't let you back in this time and you'd be very likely to be stopped at the airport.'

'I'll transmit it.'

'Maybe, but everything you've got will be monitored now.'

'I'll find a way. It'll be more difficult getting it out of the railway station.'

'No, it won't. That's the easy part.'

He looked for an explanation but received only an enigmatic smile.

'Ahh... whatever. Come on, I'm in a good mood, you look hot, and we're going dancing. Let's go.'

Twenty minutes later, they stepped out of a taxi on Talalikhina ulitsa and headed for the Cuban restaurant that Kyle had told him about earlier in the week. As a kid, Nick's father had taught both him and his mother salsa and, though he was a bit out of practice, when the rhythms reached him as the door opened, he knew all he needed was a drink to be ready. In the restaurant, he talked her through the menu while they sipped at a couple of *mojitos locos*. They settled on Caribbean fish soup, followed by lamb with creole sauce.

'Have you done salsa before?' asked Nick.

'Never.'

'Nothing to it. You'll be great.'

'Like those girls, you mean?'

Svetlana pointed to a pair of young women, brightly dressed and practising effortless moves while they waited to enter the adjoining bar.

'Yeah, just like that.'

'I'm not dressed like them.'

'Don't worry, you're dressed just right.'

He looked down at her black skirt, which hugged her hips before flaring out from the top of her thighs. He nodded, then smiled at her.

After dinner, he was glad they'd eaten as he drank the remains of his second mojito, the alcohol knocking the edge off his timing but emboldening him as compensation. He stood and offered his hand, which Svetlana accepted, rising to follow him as he made for the entrance to the bar. They went in just as a trumpet solo, as if saluting them, jumped across the flowing river of salsa rhythm. The room was darker than the restaurant and thick with atmosphere as the showy bartenders lost out in the cool stakes to the excellent, driving band. The dancers, like rival gangs occupying their territories, stuck together. The beginners hugged the bar area, figuring one more drink would do it for them, so that they too could be like the regulars in the middle of the polished parquet floor, swinging their hips, joining and unjoining their bodies in exuberant turns while looks of intensity into each other's eyes promised later events worth waiting for.

'Can we watch for a minute?' asked Svetlana, as Nick's feet edged backwards and forwards, his hips moving involuntarily in time with the music.

'Sure, but just follow me. The step is one, two, three – then repeat – like this.'

He held her hands while she watched his feet and started to mirror his steps.

'Keep that step and swing your hips.'

She immediately trod on his toe, but soon had the hang of it when he introduced simple turns that allowed them to look far from beginners. He could see she felt sexy and was enjoying the rushing sense of freedom the dance was giving them. As the music stopped and the singer announced the band would be taking a short break, he kept his eyes staring into hers, pulled her to him and kissed her.

It was after one-thirty in the morning when they climbed into their taxi.

'That was brilliant. Can we go again?'

'So, you like salsa, yeah?' asked Nick.

'Fantastic. Do they have it in Boston?'

'Of course.'

'You're not leaving Moscow, are you?' interrupted the taxi driver, recognising Svetlana. 'My wife will be really upset if you do.'

'Nuh – no, I'm not leaving Moscow – just a holiday, maybe.'

She glanced at Nick, who shrugged and grinned. Eyes and ears were everywhere, it appeared.

*

'You've grown,' said Svetlana, the following afternoon, when she saw Sasha at Kursky station.

It did look like he was taller by a centimetre or two. Maybe he'd been eating more or less regularly, although she thought that unlikely. Or perhaps it was the additional black woollen jumper he'd acquired. She didn't ask from where.

'Has Richard been feeding you?'

Sasha nodded, then pulled the remains of a stick of bread from his back pocket and bit a chunk from it.

'Where's Marina?'

'There,' said Sasha.

He pointed over to a set of stairs across the concourse where, sure enough, his sister loitered. Svetlana waved to her, and received a sheepish acknowledgement, probably observed also by Marina's pimp.

'Is she all right?'

'She's okay, yeah.'

'I mean, no trouble with the *politsiya*?'

'No, she's been all right.'

'That's good. I need a favour, Sasha.'

'Does it pay?'

Svetlana was already a bit nervous and was not really amused by the young lad's graceless opportunism. However, she needed his help and figured now was not the time to have a debate about fairness.

'If you're successful. Come with me and I'll explain.'

They walked side by side to the café, where she ordered hot chocolate for both of them.

'Can you collect something from left luggage without being seen?'

'Of course: is that it?'

'Yes.'

'When?'

'When you've finished your chocolate. Can you bring it back here and pass it to me?'

Sasha gave her a look of incredulity, which was enough to give her the answer she needed.

'How much?' said Sasha.

She felt signs of panic as she thought he was trying to ransom the item, before she realised from his expression that he just wanted to know his proposed fee for the errand.

'Three hundred.'

He did her the courtesy of not haggling.

'Do you know the number eighty-three?' she asked.

'Yes.'

'What's it like? Can you write it for me?'

Sasha could have asked her for a pen, but instead emptied the contents of a sachet of sugar onto the grey plastic table top. Svetlana noticed how the dirt under his fingernails contrasted with the white grains as he traced out the two numbers with some hesitation, but nevertheless correctly.

'Good. Okay, here's a key to the locker. There'll be a small package inside. Make sure nobody sees you.'

Sasha left her to wait nervously. She looked in her purse and took out three hundred rubles in anticipation, so she would not be seen rummaging for his payment when he returned. The clock on the wall ticked on and she had to resist the temptation to look at it every fifteen seconds. A full six minutes elapsed before the young station dweller slipped back into his seat.

'Have you got it?'

'Yes?'

'Did anybody see you?'

'They never see me.'

Svetlana felt a plastic case being pushed into her hand. In return, she dropped the tightly folded notes to the floor next to Sasha's scuffed brown shoes, then sipped the remains of her now cold chocolate as he picked up his money.

'Buy some food, Sasha. Buy some food for Marina, too.'

'But it's my money.'

'Buy something for Marina, Sasha. I know life's not easy for you but she – well – she deserves it.'

'Okay, for you, I will. When are you coming back?'

'I'm not sure exactly... but soon,' said Svetlana, brushing the spilt sugar into her empty cup before standing to leave.

She walked towards the metro, her handbag tucked under her arm to protect its precious contents. Nick would be waiting for her at Sosunov's restaurant on Nikolskaya ulitsa, where it would look like they were just meeting up to further preparations for the wedding reception. Her journey west to Teatral'naya took only a few minutes. As she approached the restaurant, she realised that she was probably being followed but, in a strange way, was relaxed because of her ready-made reason for being there.

Inside, a waitress set tables with practised ease, glancing at Svetlana before returning to her work. Yevgeniya Sosunova arrived at the top of the red carpeted stairs to greet her favourite journalist.

Svetlana's Garden

Svetlana looked up and saw Yevgeniya, dressed in a black skirt and white blouse, a warm smile upon her attractive face.

'Svetlana Yuriyevna, welcome. Please come up.'

Svetlana climbed the creaking stairs and held out her hand to Yevgeniya.

'I am Yevgeniya Mikhailova. You are so welcome. Mark and I are thrilled you've chosen here for your reception.'

'Thank you. Nikolai has told me all about it.'

'Nikolai Ivanovich is already here, with Mark. Come on through, and if it's okay with you, please call me Zhenya.'

'Thanks, Zhenya – and I'm Sveta.'

Svetlana was impressed with Nick's choice. It was all he'd said it was. The facilities were fine, but above all, it just felt right. She smiled to herself.

'Svetlana Yuriyevna, welcome. I am Mark,' said the genial proprietor, shaking her by the hand.

'Svetlana,' she replied, taking in Mark's plump features and long moustache.

She glanced at Nick who was holding a glass of vodka.

'I see Mark has been taking good care of you, Nikolai.'

'Yes.'

'Of course I have. I've been telling him how lucky he is,' interrupted Mark. 'Svetlana, please, have a drink – vodka?'

'No, thank you, Mark, but some water, perhaps?'

'Certainly: no problem. Zhenya, would you mind, while I show Svetlana around. Nikolai, are you coming or do you want to wait in the office with your uncle?'

Svetlana shot Nick a questioning look that was met with a knowing smile. Whatever he was up to, it was okay, she figured.

'I'll wait,' said Nick.

The proud owner commenced a tour for his celebrity guest.

'We are great fans of yours,' said Mark. 'Thank you for all you do. It's great to have somebody who can speak out for the ordinary citizen.'

'It's nothing, really.'

Mark stopped and faced her, taking hold of both her wrists.

'No, Svetlana Yuriyevna, it's not "nothing". To Zhenya and me... it's not "nothing".'

At that moment, all the journalistic awards in the world could not have exceeded the value of these few honest words, spoken by a true, ordinary citizen of Moscow. She felt humbled.

'Thank you,' she whispered.

He released his grip.

'Well, that's the tour. I hope you liked what you saw.'

'It's excellent, Mark. I'm really pleased.'

'Good. Right, let's get you back to Nikolai and his uncle. He seems a nice guy but his accent is strange. I can't work it out.'

Back upstairs, Mark handed Svetlana a sheet of paper with handwriting on it.

'Here's the menu we've agreed with Nikolai, but you may want to check it over with him. If there's any changes, that's no problem at all. I hope you can read my writing.'

'Yes, thanks, Mark.'

'They're in there,' said Mark, pointing to his office door. 'Take your time and I'll see you later.'

She smiled and nodded before moving to the dark-panelled door to turn the handle.

Hubbard wore a tweed jacket and blue checked shirt with a fussy tie. The two men stood as she entered the small oblong room, one wall hidden behind a well-stocked bookcase and the others covered in beige paint, which looked like it had started as some other colour many years ago. Recently tidied papers sat in a stack on the edge of a light oak desk and in the corner was a television with video and DVD players.

'Svetlana Yuriyevna, pleased to meet you at last. I'm Peter Hubbard, and I've heard a lot about you.'

The introduction was delivered in grammatically perfect Russian but with an English accent. She looked at Nick who nodded his approval of the meeting. Svetlana stepped forward and shook Hubbard's hand.

'I take it you're here to help us, Mr Hubbard.'

'I think I can assist with what could be a tricky situation.'

'I spoke to Peter about it,' interrupted Nick. 'He can get the disc to JF.'

'How will you do that, Mr Hubbard?'

'Let's just say I have access to a route that is not likely to be inspected. Do you mind if I smoke?' he asked, taking out a cigarette and tapping it on the packet.

'I don't smoke,' said Svetlana.

Hubbard hesitated before putting the filter-tipped tobacco back.

'Nick says you have an interesting recording, which could further a story you've been working on?'

'Nikolai is correct,' she said, taking the disc from her handbag and handing it to Nick.

'Are you satisfied nobody saw you retrieve this?' asked Hubbard.

'Yes, as far as I can be.'

'Let's see what we've got,' said Nick.

He stepped forward and switched on the TV before watching the DVD player silently ingest the disc. There was no sound, but there was a date and time. The picture quality wasn't the best but it was possible to make out the features of customers.

'That's Grachev, there, sitting down,' said Svetlana.

'And that's Chernekov, in the background. Wait until he turns,' said Hubbard.

Svetlana and Nick looked at each other, somehow surprised that Hubbard would know Chernekov by sight, before returning their attention to the screen. Then, there he was, taking a seat opposite the mafia boss, representatives of the state and organised crime, like best buddies.

'I said you'd only have to tell the truth,' remarked Hubbard to Nick, in English.

'I'm not doing this for you or those you work for,' snapped Nick, in Russian.

He stepped forward, removed the disc from the machine and proceeded to rip and burn a copy on Mark's computer while the others silently watched. Nick then took the original, placed it in its case and handed it to Hubbard.

'You'll see this gets to Jack Freeman?'

'He'll have it tomorrow, dear boy,' said Hubbard, picking up his packet of cigarettes. 'Have a wonderful wedding. I hope you'll both be very happy together.'

Hubbard shook Nick's hand and bowed slightly to Svetlana before turning and leaving, shutting the door behind him with a respectful click.

'You trust him?' said Svetlana.

'Jack does – and Jack doesn't normally trust anybody. He said it would be okay and I respect his judgement.'

'Well, that's that then. No more to say on the subject. So, let's get married.'

'I can't wait.'

'Really, Nikolai?'

'Really, Svetlana Yuriyevna.'

'Okay, then let's celebrate. I think I'll have that vodka now.'

Chapter 30

Svetlana looked down the low platform at Kievsky station as the train from Kaluga disgorged its complement of passengers, including her sister, brother-in-law and Ivan's cousins who were hidden somewhere in the throng. She tried to follow every waving hand held aloft to the face below, hoping to see her relatives joining her for the celebration to come. Many anonymous faces passed by, until she saw coming towards her with arms outstretched her sister, hidden beneath a thick, brown woollen coat and fur hat.

'Sveta!'

The sisters closed the last ten metres between them and held each other in a lingering embrace.

'It's good to see you, Toma. How's everybody been?'

'Fine, fine. We're so excited about your news. He looks very handsome!'

Svetlana released her grip to greet her smiling nephews, hugging each one in turn, before offering her last greeting to Tamara's husband, whose benign grin didn't seem to have changed from the last time she'd seen him.

'How's Mum?'

'She's good... and looking forward to feeding you all!' said Svetlana

'Does she ever stop cooking?'

'I don't think so. Anyway, we'll take her out with us for the hen celebration. Aleksei, you're okay to go out with Nikolai and his friends from work aren't you?'

'Of course, no problem. How's his Russian?' asked her brother-in-law.

'He's fluent.'
'Is he a CIA spy?'
'No, absolutely not. Don't you think I'd know?'
'I guess so. We laugh about you sometimes, pretending Tenacity is your real name, not Dorenko.'

Svetlana chuckled at the slightly strange compliment. They made their way towards the exit as the sun sent down what she took to be the promising omen of rays of hope from the giant glass span of the arched roof above.

They struggled on Kievskaya metro's escalator with two large suitcases, which contained not only their clothes but food and wrapped presents for the happy couple. Her smug nephews exchanged knowing glances with each other as they hitched up the rucksacks on their backs, the only luggage they'd brought. Avoiding the rush hour, they completed the journey without further incident and were soon ascending in the lift to Svetlana's mother's apartment, from where they all emerged onto the partially carpeted landing.

'Can you smell what I can?' asked Svetlana of her sister.
'I don't believe it, it's like there's a bakery in here. I'm expecting to see a queue, any moment.'

As the door opened, the mixed aromas of bread and pastry swept over them like a wave, their creator standing there with a broad grin on her face.

'Come in, come in!' said the sisters' mother.

The small hallway hosted a flurry of hugs before cases were abandoned and coats removed.

'Come, sit at the table. I knew you'd be hungry.'

A still-warm loaf was accompanied by meats, rolled herring, salad and three types of *pirozhki*. Glasses for every eventuality stood guard by the place settings.

'What would you like to drink? Aleksei... vodka?'
'No, later thanks, Raisa, but a beer maybe?' he replied.
'Of course. Boys, what would you like?'

An hour passed as news both important and unimportant was exchanged, the males around the table having less and less to say as discussion about dresses and fabrics became ascendant.

Svetlana's Garden

'Come on, we'll clear up later. Sveta will show you the dress,' said mother to her daughters. 'But wash your hands first.'

'Can we watch the TV?' asked one of the boys.

'Yes, of course. The remote's on the table next to it.'

In her mother's bedroom, where the atmosphere was full of pride, Svetlana slipped into her dress and posed demurely for the onlookers.

'He'd better be prepared to pay a big ransom,' said her sister.

'Just what I said,' added her mother.

Svetlana swallowed and closed her eyes.

'What is it, dear?' asked her mother.

'I'm so happy, Mum.'

Tamara and her mother shared a glance. They stepped forward to embrace the now tearful Svetlana, still coming to terms with the realisation that she had a second chance to live life as her childhood dreams had intended.

*

'Yeah, show him in,' said Jack Freeman to Victoria.

Moments later, Peter Hubbard entered Freeman's office.

'Peter, come in and take a seat.'

The two men shook hands before Hubbard sat by the small rosewood table in the corner of the room.

'Coffee?'

'Thanks, Jack, that would be good.'

'How was the journey?' asked Freeman, as he filled two white cups from a handled stainless steel flask.

'No problems, really.'

'Good, good. Have you something for me, then?'

Hubbard reached into his jacket pocket, then placed a case containing the disc on the table.

'And it's clean?'

'As clean as anything from a diplomatic bag can be,' replied Hubbard.

'You know what I mean – nothing added or deleted?'

'You have my word.'

'You've seen it?'

'Yes. I think it – how can I put it – will add to your report.'

'How's Nick?'

'Happy, I think... and looking forward to his marriage.'

'What do you make of Svetlana?'

'If she was sitting here, I'd give her a job, if I were you.'

'That good, huh?'

'She connects with her audience. Isn't that what good reporters have to do?'

'The good ones, yeah.'

Freeman held his cup to his lips, then placed it back on the saucer in front of him.

'What will happen to them, Peter?'

'It's hard to say. There's going to be trouble, of course.'

'This Malenkov, what's he like?'

'Not good, I'm afraid.'

'Can you protect them?'

'Only if you don't broadcast.'

'You know that's not an option.'

'No, and we want you to broadcast, anyway. It suits our purposes at the moment.'

'We're not doing it for your purposes!'

'Jack, sorry, I didn't mean it like that. I respect our – our understandings.'

'I left a long time ago, Peter. I enjoy being a reporter and I enjoy the truth.'

'I know you do and we respect that, really. But, as we've talked about, sometimes what you're going to do anyway just happens to coincide with our view.'

'Surely you can do something for them?'

'The stakes are high. Ironically, that may help here, but on the other hand, maybe not.'

'What do you mean?'

'Directly accusing the Russians of experimenting on kids and developing a gas for foreign interventions in energy supplies is not going to be forgotten or forgiven.'

'The point being?'

'Enemies have been disposed of, on and off Russian soil. Yes, there's a stink kicked up but they reckon that sooner or later the need for oil and gas will have western governments talking again – and the Chinese are hardly going to complain. But, Jack, you know all this and you don't need me to tell you.'

'What about Langley?'

'Again, you know the situation. That's why you're talking to me, instead. The Brits already have bad relations with the Russians, so it doesn't matter.'

'I've known him a long time, watched him grow as a reporter.'

Hubbard stayed silent.

'He was pretty wet behind the ears when I first got him but he was keen – had an eye for a story – know what I mean?'

Hubbard nodded.

'He doesn't know it, but as the years went by it was almost like looking at my own son... not that I ever told him that. I thought this Russian thing would be good for him – thought Madrid was maybe making him a bit comfortable. But here, he doesn't get shot.

'Jack, it doesn't matter where... Look, we'll do what we can. I don't know exactly how they'll react.'

'Peter, does he understand all the danger, I mean really understand?'

'Do you know, I don't think so... but she does.'

*

At nine the following morning, Svetlana opened the curtains to look down on Lenskaya ulitsa where shadows were hiding from the golden light of the rising sun. The night out with her mother, sister, Polina and a couple of close friends had been a great success. They'd surrounded her with genuine affection and goodwill for her new future, beginning that day. She turned to see Tamara slowly stirring.

She smiled at her and recalled childhood memories from when they shared a room and secrets together.

'Wake up, sleepy.'

'Oh, Sveta, another few minutes.'

'I'll shower first, but boil the kettle, will you? We have to be at Mum's for ten-thirty.'

'Oh...'

'I mean it, Toma, we have to be ready.'

After she showered, Tamara emerged from the bathroom with a towel perched on her head to sit with Svetlana for breakfast.

'I'll miss you, Sveta.'

'How do you mean?'

'I think you'll leave here.'

'You do?'

'Yes.'

'Moscow's what I know.'

'And you know enough. Go with your husband and Ivan.'

It took them half an hour to reach their mother's apartment and they were only about five minutes late as she opened the door to greet them.

'Sveta, Toma, come in. Polina is already here. She's waiting to do your hair.'

'I want to iron the dress first,' said Svetlana, as she ran through the list of things she'd told herself not to forget.

'I've already done it, so just calm down. Here, take some tea for you and Polina. She wants to wash your hair before the boys get back.'

'Where are they?'

'Ivan wanted to buy you some flowers.'

Svetlana stood still holding two mugs of tea, and looked at her mother.

'He's never bought me flowers.'

'Looks like things are changing, then. Go on, hurry up.'

Later, Ivan breezed in with his cousins, carrying a large bunch of white chrysanthemums. He walked straight to Svetlana under the watchful gaze of his grandmother and handed the flowers over without a word but with half a smile.

'Vanya, they're beautiful. Thank you, so much.'

She stepped forward and hugged him closely. He wriggled in embarrassment as his cousins playfully mocked.

Over the next two hours, competition for the bathroom of the modest apartment was strong as its occupants prepared themselves. The bride-to-be enjoyed the fuss being made of her but declined help with her make-up, which was a flawless mixture. Right on time, her mother appeared in the doorway holding up the dress, with not a crease to be seen.

'Okay, young lady, let's get this on you.'

Ten minutes later, Svetlana emerged into the living room with her mother at her side and met her now immaculately dressed relatives and friend. She stood with effortless elegance in the beautifully fitted satin and lace dress, shining hair rolling over her shoulders. A collective intake of breath preceded a round of impromptu applause and the break-out of wide smiles.

*

'Come on, Nick. Cars are here,' said Konstantin.

'Coming,' replied Nick, slipping on the jacket of his expensive, blue wool suit, a wedding gift from Jack Freeman.

They made their way down to the ground floor and into the lobby.

'How's your head?' asked Konstantin.

'D'ya know, not too bad.'

'That's good.'

The automatic glass door slid open for them as they walked out to be met by bright sunshine and the rest of the guys, including Kyle Hughes, who leant nonchalantly on his crutches.

'Does this mean I can have my apartment back?'

'I guess so,' replied Nick. 'When do you lose those?'

'Couple of weeks, maybe; depends on the physio.'

Svetlana's Garden

Nick surveyed the scene of three black limousines and eight besuited men, some in sunglasses. They looked like a mafia gang from the movies and he chuckled at the sight.

'What's up with you?' asked Konstantin.

'Nothing, nothing at all,' replied Nick, opening the rear door of the first car. 'Gentlemen, shall we?'

The traffic was pretty bad, but the cars managed to keep more or less in tandem as they made their way to Svetlana's mother's apartment.

'You got plenty of cash on you?' asked Konstantin.

'Yeah. Am I going to need it?' replied Nick.

'Who knows?' said Konstantin.

Nick looked out on the great metropolis as they drove along and reflected on so much that had happened to him in the months he'd been there. He filled his lungs with air and realised that for all its Latin rhythm and nightlife, it was not Madrid but Moscow that had re-energised him and stripped him of any last vestige of complacency. Optimism flowed through him as he contemplated the blank canvas that he and Svetlana could now paint together.

The guys were in good spirits as the cars drew up, with Nick able to see a small party blocking the apartment entrance, including Ivan, his cousins and their father. They all alighted from the cars and strolled to the entrance.

'Are you Nikolai Ivanovich?' asked Aleksei, theatrically.

'I am,' said Nick.

'And are you seeking the hand of Svetlana Yuriyevna?'

'I am.'

'Then you will have to pass the tests... difficult for an American.'

'I have Russian blood.'

'Who was the author of Anna Karenina?'

'Tolstoy.'

'Name three other Russian authors... quickly.'

Nick's mind began to race and he took a deep breath to try to calm himself as the onlookers smirked at his predicament.

'Er... Chekhov, Solzhenitsyn...'

'Come on Nikolai Ivanovich, your bride awaits, if you can pass the tests.'

Who was that author Mum used to speak of? Damn it, he'd even read one of his books as a child, when his mum was teaching him. *What was his name?*

'Yevgeniy Zamyatin.'

'Well, well. Pass, Nikolai Ivanovich,' said Aleksei, opening an imaginary gate for him with the sweep of his hand.

More riddles awaited him on the third floor before he was allowed to advance to the sixth, where sentries, led by Tamara and Konstantin, had been posted.

'Halt!' ordered Konstantin.

'You're supposed to be on my side,' said Nick, slightly out of breath.

'He's on the side of love,' interrupted Tamara. 'And you must prove your love, for your bride has been kidnapped and a ransom has been demanded.'

Arms collectively folded in front of him as Nick considered his next move.

'And how much is the ransom?'

'How much is your bride worth to you, Nikolai Ivanovich?' asked Tamara.

Nick grinned, entering fully into the spirit of things. He turned out all his pockets until he arrived at the last one from where he extracted a wad of cash, all he had on him. He sank to one knee and proffered it to Tamara.

'Give her back to me, please.'

'I will see what I can do,' said Tamara, who turned and walked the twenty metres or so to her mother's front door, where she knocked.

Whispered words he could not make out were exchanged before he was beckoned forward to the doorway.

'Your ransom is acceptable, Nikolai Ivanovich. Close your eyes and wait.'

Nick did as he was told, anticipating the smell of her perfume. Suddenly, he was nervous and desperate to see her.

'You may open your eyes now.'

He did so but looked only at the empty doorway, his anxiety rising further. He looked around. The landing was now empty except for a lone figure at the far end, shadowed by sunlight streaming through the glass behind her, and which created a golden plinth upon which she appeared to stand. It was Svetlana. He walked towards her, his heart beating in his chest. As he drew near, her bowed head rose and her closed eyes opened, accompanied by a grin that seemed to keep on growing. She looked stunning and, above all, happy.

'Oh, Sveta, I love you.'

'And I love you, Nikolai.'

*

The cars glided to a halt on Butyrskaya ulitsa. Nick in the first one, accompanied by Konstantin and Svetlana, with Demchi in the second, now adorned with a pair of entwined rings on the roof. The weather was kind as a clear blue sky overhead allowed the afternoon sun to bless them.

As they entered the Palace of Marriages, family members came forward to offer the couple traditional gifts of bread and salt for prosperity. Svetlana clutched a bouquet of white roses as they stood together, making a truly handsome couple. Demchi cut in and Svetlana took his arm to follow the receptionist into the room where the ceremony was to take place, while Ivan, tugging at the tie he was not used to, accompanied his grandmother.

Nick took his place at her side, shifting nervously. She gave him a playful dig in the ribs with her elbow. Their witnesses and guests in the light oak-finished room with large oblong windows looked on admiringly. In turn, she looked at Demchi, standing in for her dearly missed father, his shoulders back and chest restrained by the snug-fitting waistcoat of his light grey suit. His face had acquired an expression she'd not seen before and she took a moment to realise what she was witnessing: it was special pride, in her. She looked him straight in the eye and mouthed 'thank you'. He closed his eyes and bowed his head in acknowledgement. Next to Demchi, her mother, dressed in a pale pink linen suit, was unable to wipe the grin from her face. A few office staff, well aware that it was famous reporter Svetlana Dorenko who was to be married, peeked round the door to catch a glimpse of her and the American. The registrar stepped forward and began the ceremony as Svetlana playfully pinched Nick's bottom, removing any remaining traces of nerves.

'I do,' said Nick, in reply to the enquiry as to whether he would take Svetlana for his wife.

The new Mrs Mendez heard the tiny phrase echo in her ears, delivered firmly and without a trace of doubt but, nevertheless, with a private whisper attached only for her. She resolved then and there not to forget that sound.

Nick took Svetlana's hand. She felt his touch, gentle but insistent, as the ring rose up her finger before coming to rest.

Photographs followed before rice and rose petals showered them as they descended the steps hand in hand to the waiting cars that would take them and their guests on a traditional tour of the city to pay respects to Russia's fallen heroes.

*

Two hours later, Mark and Yevgeniya Sosunov were waiting for them as they entered the restaurant and made their way upstairs, ready to meet their guests. A small guard of staff applauded in unison as they ascended the last few steps, one of them stepping forward with a tray of filled champagne flutes.

'*Za lyubov!*' announced Mark theatrically, offering his toast to love and unofficially declaring the two-day celebration open.

Soon, the toasts were rolling one into another, glasses celebrating their own impending demise before they were hurled to the floor to bring luck to the newlyweds. A feast followed as waitresses in crisp white blouses brought forward course after course and voices rose progressively in volume as the intake of alcohol climbed. The excellent band added fully to the occasion, belting out traditional Russian songs, rich in the sounds of accordion and balalaika. Guests, some more proficient than others, but all with enthusiasm, broke away from their places and took to the dance floor. An unceasing wave of euphoria swept backwards and forwards over the room.

'Come dance with me!'

'Well, Nikolai Ivanovich. So masterful! How could I refuse?'

Nick pushed back his chair and took her hand. Other dancers made way for them, forming a circle and clapping along as the smiling couple held each other and twirled in time to the music. Happiness made them light on their feet.

Dancing and singing continued late into the night, fuelled by copious amounts of vodka and wine as the guests demonstrated their enjoyment of this special event by becoming more and more intoxicated.

It was one in the morning when Svetlana threw her bouquet in the direction of the unmarried girls, closing her eyes to avoid the unseemly scramble that ensued amid more laughter. She and Nick left the revellers to it, until they would all meet again the following day to continue festivities.

*

The limousine whisked them through Moscow's streets en route to her apartment, where they would spend their first night.

'I hope you haven't had too much to drink,' whispered Svetlana.

'I'm fine,' he replied, winking at her playfully.

'Good... because it's bad luck not to make love to me on our wedding night.'

Later, they embraced and kissed through the whole of the lift's ascent. Nick stuck out a foot to prevent the doors from closing when, at the fourteenth floor, she initially refused to release him from her grip. With a sigh, she stepped back, took hold of his tie and led him to her front door while clutching a silver bag containing cards brought to the reception by well-wishers.

Once inside, she tickled him under his chin.

'You can have the bathroom first and then you can wait for me... but don't you dare fall asleep!'

Svetlana's Garden

'No chance,' said Nick, as he turned and removed his tie.

She could hear water running in the background as she looked at herself in the mirror, unable to remove the smile from her face and filled as she was by happiness. At that moment, everything seemed possible for them, and she could not wait to begin to colour in the life she'd formerly lived in shades of grey. She winked at herself, before reaching for the clutch of cards. The first one was from Mark and Yevgeniya, with a delightful little poem they had taken the trouble to compose. She stood it up on the dressing table and opened the next one, from which three photographs fell to the floor, face down. She read the pretty card, not recognising its author – "Kseniya" – before shrugging and putting it next to the other. Reaching forward, Svetlana picked up the photographs and turned them. The sound of the water disappeared. Suddenly, she could hear nothing as the shock of disbelief struck her. For some seconds there was a void as all senses were suspended. Then, a jagged knife seemed to be making its brutal way into the pit of her stomach. She dropped to her knees and reached instinctively for the wastepaper bin, the base of which drummed as it accepted her vomit. She retched before trying to stand, only to fall back as excruciating headaches launched themselves inside her skull. Stains ruined her beautiful dress as she vomited again. Then the tears came. She pinched herself to see if she had fallen asleep and had succumbed to a nightmare, but the damp patch on her dress confirmed she was very much awake. She looked again at the images of Nick and Victoria. The kiss hurt her terribly. The naked embrace in Kyle's bed, where she too had slept, was a hammer blow but the smile – a smile she'd seen before – was real, and unforgivable. She felt the turn of the knife as she looked down, her hands trembling.

'Okay, your turn,' said Nick jauntily, as he walked in, unbuttoning his shirt.

He stopped in his tracks.

'Sveta, darling, what is it?'

A trembling finger pointed to the kiss.

'Is this true?'

He advanced to see what she was looking at and gasped as the image came into view.

'It's not what it seems.'

'Is that true? Is that you?'

'It is me... but it's not what it looks like.'

'And is that true?' asked Svetlana, pointing to the clearly affectionate smiles Nick and Victoria were exchanging.

'Well, yes – but darling – listen –'

'And this?' she said, nudging the photograph of his own body with its forearm resting casually upon Victoria's naked breast.

'I'm – no – I don't remember.' Look, I love you. This just isn't what it seems.'

Nick moved towards her, offering outstretched arms, but now her shock was giving way to a growing wave of rage.

'Get away from me!'

'Sveta, please.'

'That's why you went to Madrid. You went to see her.'

'No!'

'Don't lie to me! I've seen the way you looked at her!'

'Sveta, please.'

Nick moved towards her again.

'Don't you touch me!' she shouted, a growl entering her voice as the anger really started to take hold.

'Please, Sveta, please. We can work this out.'

'No, you can get out! In fact, get out of my life! Go back to Spain and live with your whore!'

'Sveta, please –'

'Get out – get out!'

He held up his hands as a gesture of conciliation, backing out of the room towards the front door as she advanced upon him, screaming obscenities. He opened the door and stepped through it, his palms open, pleading to be listened to. She watched him through the doorway, while a momentary pause as she drew breath allowed him to speak.

'Sveta, you are my wife. I love you and I will not let it end like this. I will fight for you!'

'You'll fight for me?' she snarled sarcastically. 'Then you'll need your Russian blood!'

The frame shook as she slammed the door in his face, leaving him helpless outside and her, devastated, within.

Chapter 31

'You want more coffee?' asked the waitress.
'Huh?' responded Nick.
'Do you want more coffee?'
'No.'

With a grunt she turned away, leaving him, unshaven and dishevelled from his night walking the streets. Only when the rain started, at five-thirty in the morning, had he sought refuge in the café, alone at first before being joined by one or two night shift workers seeking sustenance before slumber. Right there and then, his clothes still damp, he had no idea when he would ever sleep again. He veered between bouts of self-inquisition as to what had happened and desperate longing to be with Svetlana. Again and again, he traced back over his movements with Victoria. He remembered Propaganda and her impetuous, alcohol-fuelled kiss, but taking her to his bed? He had no recollection of that, and yet there he was, in the naked company of a young woman who had already signalled the plausibility of such a situation.

Who had the camera? Who had that fucking camera? he asked himself. *Who wanted to harm us so much they'd resort to sending photographs on our wedding day?* He rapidly concluded Malenkov must be behind it and initially thought such a realisation by Svetlana would bring about a change of heart. However, he realised the problem was the content of the message, not that Malenkov was the messenger who'd delivered it. *How could I have been so stupid? How could I not remember doing something so absolutely idiotic?*

Without invitation, a tramp sat down opposite him despite plenty of alternative red, plastic-cushioned seats. Startled, Nick looked across to see the matted brown hair and unkempt beard of a dark-clothed street dweller whose time wandering aimlessly must have put Nick's adventure of the previous night to shame. The words reached him at the same time as the smell of sweat and urine.

'Got a smoke?'

'Sorry, I don't,' replied Nick.

'Got any change?'

'I don't have...'

Nick reached in his pocket where the tips of his fingers came across two coins. He'd forgotten them, too. He put five rubles and fifty kopeks on the table in front of him and slid them across, where they were spirited away without thanks.

'Twenty years I've been here – broke my heart – bitch!'

'Sorry?'

'Women – bitches – all of them. Stay away from them.'

The waitress came through the swing door from the kitchen.

'Nikolai, get out!'

Nick stood, unthinking.

'Not you,' she said, gesturing to him to sit. 'I've told you a hundred times. Now, out!'

His breakfast companion rose unsteadily and glowered at the waitress.

'Bitch – fucking bitch!'

'Yeah, whatever. Just get out or I'll call the cops.'

He shuffled towards the door, repeating his expletives as he went, the last one like a fading echo as the door closed behind him.

'You're Nikolai too, then?'

'Yeah,' replied Nick.

'And do you think I'm a fucking bitch, too?'

'I don't know. Are you?'

'Sometimes. That's sixty rubles, for the coffee.'

*

Her mother rocked her in her arms like she'd done when she was a child, while her sister looked on. Aleksei, who earlier in the day had teamed up with Konstantin to tell guests there would be no second day of celebration, put his head round the door but Tamara gestured to her husband to leave them be. He withdrew. Svetlana stared open-eyed but saw nothing, all other senses subservient to the aching sadness dragging her under water and threatening to drown her famous spirit. Her heart, so receptive to the misfortunes of others, had all but closed down for her own protection. Consolation was impossible: there was none. She didn't hear her mother's gentle whispers or the rain lashing at the window as it cascaded from deep, grey clouds above. Her skin, without make-up, was pale and drawn, eyes red from tears that had flowed from one hour into the next. She was still in the pyjamas her mother had insisted she wear when she'd arrived after Svetlana's almost incomprehensible but desperate phone call in the early hours. A discrete spray of air freshener had only partly masked the remnants of the smell of vomit.

'Do you want tea, Mama?'

'Thanks, Toma, that would be nice. Sveta, would you like some, darling?'

'I don't want anything,' whispered Svetlana.

Her mother held her hopelessly damaged baby a little tighter.

'There, darling, it'll be all right,' she said softly.

'Why, Mum? What have I done? What's wrong with me?'

'Nothing, honey, there's nothing wrong with you.'

'Why, Mum?'

'Humans are complex.'

'Was Dad complex, for you?'

'Yes, in his own way he was.'

'Am I not good enough?'

'Of course you are. You're beautiful and talented.'

'I trusted him... gave everything.'

'I know, darling. Maybe the two of you can work something out.'

'No!'

'I'm sure he loves you.'

'He doesn't. I thought he did... but he doesn't.'

'You'll have to see.'

'There's nothing to see. He'll go back to Madrid... or wherever. I could never trust him again.'

'You should speak to him, in a day or so.'

'No.'

'Really, I think you should.'

'No.'

Tamara returned with the tea. The pot and cups were not quite aligned properly, but today her mother let it go.

'He's called; said he'd call back,' she said, as she put the tray down.

'I don't want to speak to him. I just want to be left alone.'

'Just consider it,' said Tamara.

'I want to be left alone. Unplug the phone.'

'I don't think that's a good idea.'

'Just unplug it.'

'Okay,' said Tamara, leaving, only to return a short while later to pour the now brewed tea.

'I'll keep Ivan with the boys tonight. Mum, are you going to stay with Sveta?'

'I will, darling.'

*

When Konstantin reached Kyle's apartment, he found Nick sitting on the steps in the entrance lobby, head in hands.

'Kolya, come on, let's get up to the apartment.'

'What did she say?'

'I spoke to her mum. She won't see you.'

'I need to speak to her.'

Konstantin put his hand on Nick's shoulder.

'She won't see you. Better leave it, for now. See how things are in a day or two. Come on, let's get you upstairs. You look like shit.'

With resignation, Nick rose to his feet and followed Konstantin to the lift.

Once inside the apartment, he was met by reminders of what should have been as his eyes fell on cards from well-wishers, a bottle of champagne and the remaining three ties he'd lined up before choosing the blue silk one he'd worn at the ceremony. Konstantin began to discreetly remove them.

'Kolya, get a shower while I fix us something to eat.'

Nick sighed, then nodded before turning for the bedroom.

He closed the door behind him and stared at the bed, willing his memory to help him to fill in the gaps that were driving him to distraction.

After he showered, he rejoined Konstantin, who'd prepared tea and *bliny*.

'Eat those.'

'I'm not hungry,' replied Nick.

'I don't care. Eat them.'

Nick reluctantly did as he was told while he looked out at the traffic shuffling its way down ulitsa Pokrovka.

'Have you lived here all your life, Kostya?'

'Yeah, all of it.'

'I thought I was getting to know it, but does this city always have to turn round and shit on you?'

Konstantin, a slight curl appearing at the corner of his mouth, put his tea down.

'Always,' he replied.

Chapter 32

Demchi had told her to take a few more days, but Svetlana had insisted on returning to work. She and her mother had spent the past week at Konstantin Golovnin's *dacha* outside Moscow, which the *Izvestia* editor had been good enough to lend them, while Tamara stayed behind to look after Ivan and his cousins. The break had given Svetlana the opportunity to reconstruct the semblance of defences she needed to isolate her heart from further harm. She'd made straight for the office from the train as the last of the country air left her lungs and birdsong receded to memory.

She ignored the sympathetic but inquisitive glances as she made her way to her desk, casually dropping her shoulder bag to the floor.

'Hi, Vasya, where are you up to with the Novorublevo planning thing?'

Vasiliy, dressed as ever rather too brightly, turned towards her, a look of surprise on his face.

'It's, er... here,' he replied, handing her a small, bound booklet.'

'Have we got enough?'

'Yeah, should be a good story.'

'Have you done the draft copy?'

'Thought you'd be doing it.'

'You do it. In fact, from now on, I think you can do more front-line pieces.'

'If you think so.'

'Yes, Vasya, I do... and so does Demchi.'

As if he'd been announced, Demchi put his head round his door.

'Sveta, got a moment, please?'

She made her way towards him as he held the door ajar.

Inside, on his desk, two mugs of steaming coffee stood waiting for them. He shut the door and allowed a few seconds of silence to preface the moment. He opened his arms and she stepped forward into his embrace.

'Sveta, you know I care.'

'I know, Demchi... and I know I can always trust you.'

'He won't stop, you know. He'll come for you. I don't know what went on but he – I saw it in his face.'

'He's been here?'

'Told them to tell him you weren't here, but he's called many times.'

'Don't let him near me. I need to move on.'

'That's not the end of it.'

'Passion's not enough. At my time, I needed commitment. He had his chance,' she said, as she released herself and sat down.

Demchi perched himself on the edge of his desk and reached for his coffee.

'So, now?'

'Now we work,' said Svetlana.

'You don't want some more time?'

'No, I want to work.'

Demchi drew a long slow breath before nodding.

'What happened with the Petrov boy? Did you get to the bottom of it?'

'Yes, it was Chernekov's gas. They were just experiments for him: numbers, not names. It's the gas from the bank robbery and the pipeline attack.'

'Big story.'

'Yeah.'

'What are you going to do with it?'

'What can I do? Are you going to run it?'

'No.'

'So, it's finished then.'

'What makes you think so?'

'You can't run it and it's over with Nick. I can only do what I can do. Sometimes you have to leave it. You taught me that, remember.'

'I remember, but you can't drop this.'

'I have dropped it. Things have changed.'

'You better follow me,' said Demchi, beckoning with his finger.

Svetlana rose from her chair and walked behind him as he made his way along the corridor with its framed pictures of yesteryear's headlines. He led her to the modest journalists' lounge, where old linen-upholstered chairs contrasted with the big-screen TV Demchi had acquired when he'd upgraded the cable service.

'You'd better sit down.'

Svetlana lowered herself into one of the chairs and splayed her fingers out on its arms.

'I take it you haven't seen this?'

'Seen what? I've been in the country. The last thing I wanted was to watch television.'

'Hmmn.'

Demchi switched on the set. Its deep blue screen flickered slightly while he fiddled with the control of the digital recorder.

'Damn things. Never can seem to work these properly.'

The tail end of an airline advertisement played before an INN newscast began. Svetlana rose from her chair.

'Demchi, I don't want to watch this.'

'Sveta, sit down.'

She sank back into the chair and crossed her legs, petulantly turning her face from the screen. Within seconds, Nick had been announced and began to speak in English. To the casual observer, the tone of his voice would be familiar but while she would not look at him, unmistakably, there was an undertone of sadness. She thought about putting her fingers in her ears, but dared not in front of Demchi. Gradually, she could not help being drawn in as the story she knew so well unfolded from Nick's compellingly constructed sentences. He introduced the viewers to Chernekov and Grachev, two characters in their silent conspiracy played out at Starbuck's. Demchi winced, no doubt imagining the reaction in the Kremlin as one of their top poisons experts was seen to take tea with a gangland boss. When he introduced his interview with Katenin, she could not help but look up and now her eyes stayed fixed to the screen. The footage had been edited to intersperse the mural images of the gas chamber and Andrei Petrov with Katenin's subtitled voice-over. Finally, and chillingly, the photographs of the chamber filled the screen to the soundtrack of silence. Nick appeared, outside but in close-up, wrapped up against the weather but without a hat, exposing all his features to the lens.

'The story of Yakov Katenin has taken us from Moscow to secret trials in Siberia, to mysterious attacks on the pipeline in Georgia and back to Moscow again, where the young Katenin met a similar fate to his lost friend, Andrei Petrov. The Kremlin has yet to comment officially on our findings, but its reaction will be watched with great interest in major capitals around the world, given the implications for vital future supplies of energy.'

'Nick, it sounds like a number of people have been incredibly brave in helping to compile this story,' said news anchor, Dave Sullivan.

'Dave, in the nineteen years I've been reporting, I've never encountered anything like it, including some I can't mention. As the expression here, in Russian, goes: *I care only for my love's infliction, and let me die, but only die in love.* Nick Mendez, for INN, Moscow.'

The camera pulled back from his face and Svetlana's eyes widened in astonishment. Not only was he reporting from Moscow, but he was standing, of all places, in front of Lubyanka.

'Thanks, Nick. I'm sure that's a story we're going to hear more about – and we'll be reaching for our phrase books.'

Demchi switched off the TV and turned to Svetlana. Her heart had picked up speed at Nick's recklessness and at the unmistakable words of Pushkin with which he'd concluded. He'd been speaking directly to her.

She looked back at Demchi.

'Why has he done that from Moscow – from Lubyanka?' she asked.

'He's fighting for you.'

'It's too late.'

'He got your story out for you. Did he say he was going to do that?'

Svetlana's Garden

'Yes, but that was before. I mean, I didn't think he'd –'
'What? Keep his word?'

She looked down at her fingers as she often did when struggling for something to say. Demchi maintained the silence for a few more seconds.

'He's going to die for you. You know that, don't you?'
'It was foolish. He could have done that from anywhere.'
'From anywhere, Sveta. Yeah, from anywhere – but he did it from here – for you.'
'When was the broadcast?'
'The day before yesterday.'
'And...?'
'They've not heard from him. Vasiliy spoke to Konstantin Bereznity over at INN.'
'Has Malenkov got him?'
'Maybe; if not, he'll be looking for him.'
'He's probably abroad.'
'I don't think so. He could have left, of course – but he's here – waiting for you.'
'I won't take him back.'

Demchi sighed and knelt down in front of Svetlana, taking a hand in each of his.

'Look, Sveta, maybe he got drunk – he won't be the first guy – and maybe he screwed the Spanish girl, and maybe there isn't a future for the two of you. But he did get your story out – put his life on the line for you. You owe him that.'

*

Malenkov didn't even offer a handshake as he met Svetlana in reception at Lubyanka, his demeanour one of irritation. She followed him, a couple of paces behind, to the small room where he'd originally seen her.

'It's a good thing for you that he didn't name you or I'd be arresting you, right now.'

'Where is he?'

'I was hoping you'd tell me that.'

'We're not together, but with your wedding gift, you probably guessed that.'

Malenkov's mood visibly lightened and he smirked.

'Ironically, we were doing that for you, Svetlana Yuriyevna.'

'For me? How's that?'

'We felt that you were immersing yourself in a pool of trouble with a foreigner who was clearly out to damage our country.'

'He was doing his job.'

'Which does not involve sabotaging the work of our country's security services. We didn't want to have to take harsher measures and were hopeful that some distance between you and Mr Mendez would put a stop to this libellous nonsense. But unfortunately for him, he still chose a path of confrontation.'

'You could have done something else. You didn't have to tell me he'd slept with the girl.'

Svetlana was immediately annoyed that she'd allowed a display of emotion before this weasel-faced creep. He couldn't resist a triumphant laugh, it seemed, as he leant forward across the table and lowered his voice.

'It's a great irony that the two of you have been duped by the very story you were investigating.'

She looked at him, ignorant of the would-be joke he seemed to find so amusing.

'The gas – Svetlana Yuriyevna – the gas. It's difficult to make love to somebody, even one so pretty as Miss Santos, when you are unconscious. You of all people, a reporter, should know not to jump to conclusions without checking your facts.'

'But the kissing...?'

'Oh, a momentary present from a rather impetuous girl. We just struck lucky with that. It makes no difference now.'

Malenkov's words fell away as they were blocked out by the explosive realisation of what she'd done. Her stomach churned and her mind raced as remorse wrestled with elation. He was out there, somewhere, and a rush of longing to be with him swept through her.

Svetlana's Garden

The drone of Malenkov's voice returned as she looked at him, confidence returning to her.

'So, Mrs Dorenko, foreigner or not, he's broken our law and things are to some extent out of my hands.'

Svetlana stood, towering over Malenkov's diminutive, seated frame. She leant forward.

'Leave my husband alone! And my name, Captain Malenkov, is Mendez!'

*

She emerged from Lubyanka with fists clenched to see the city lights begin to twinkle against the darkening early evening sky. Her stride was purposeful and spontaneously she jumped onto the plinth of a bronze statue, hugging it as she surveyed her surroundings from her elevated position as if it would make him easier to see.

'Nikolai, hang on! Wait for me!'

She walked on, a grin upon her face contrasting with the blandness of the passing Moscow pedestrians. Suddenly, the normally annoying arguments of the city's traffic provided an uplifting soundtrack, an orchestra of hope driving out the silence of despair. Somewhere, out there, was somebody without whom there could not now be personal happiness for her, no matter how much time passed. She quickened her pace, anxious to find the man she now realised was quite simply the love of her life.

*

Nick pulled his coat tighter around him to fend off the cold seeping in from the concrete below. This had been the only place he could think of that would not compromise the security of those around him but still hold out the prospect of contact with Svetlana, if she would speak to him. Staying at the apartment had been out of the question and it would have been visited within minutes of his broadcast. So, here he was, in conditions probably worse than a prison cell, with only the clothes on his back and as much cash as he could raise – but at least here he was still free.

Suddenly and silently, Sasha was in front of him holding a blanket and some folded plastic sheeting.

'Here,' he said.

'Thanks,' replied Nick, who handed over the reward he'd promised upon Sasha's return from his impromptu shopping trip.

'Have you seen her?'

Sasha shook his head.

'Will you keep looking out for her?'

'Yes.'

In the next moment, the street child was gone, leaving Nick to improve his temporary dwelling amid the sound of dripping water and the background rumble of trains going about their business. He was grateful for the plastic as it would help to hold back the cold breeze that endlessly blew across the dirty floor but which at least moved on the smell of old diesel permeating down to basement level. He'd arrived just before the broadcast had gone out, so he knew there would now be a heavy FSB presence staking out all the main transport hubs to look for him.

Sleep had been very sporadic since his wondrous day had turned into a living nightmare. When he did sleep, it was fitful and invariably filled with dreams of the naked Victoria smiling at him, which exacerbated his anguish when he woke. Still, a clear recollection would not come to him and a final broadcast, to add to the material he'd given to Jack Freeman, had been the only plan he could come up with to reach Svetlana. He had no idea of her reaction or, as he huddled in his own loneliness, whether she'd even seen it. There was no option but to wait and see.

*

Svetlana had confided in nobody, wisely concluding that knowledge entrusted to others could only endanger them. However, the next morning she was about to place her faith in Roman Dubnikov, figuring he could look after himself and that, in any event, without help she would not find Nick. The mafia boss seemed to look at her almost kindly, stroking the underside of his chin with his thumb.

'I was sorry to hear the news,' said Dubnikov.

'You shouldn't believe all the news you hear,' she responded with a slight, sly grin.

He tilted his head in her direction.

'Malenkov set him up. He was unconscious from Chernekov's gas.'

'Sounds like Malenkov, the rat-faced little prick,' said Dubnikov. 'So, you still have a husband, eh?'

'Yes, and I need to find him.'

'Before Malenkov?'

'Can you help me?'

He drew breath and traced the rim of his cup with the tip of his finger.

'We've known each other a long time now, but I sense times are changing. If you leave, I'll still have to deal with the likes of Malenkov.'

She looked at the floor, realising his business logic was impeccable as usual. Their relationship had been built upon classic Russian lines of mutually exchanged favours and she was in danger of having no such currency. Right now, she had no promises she felt able to deliver on and just hoped that a small reservoir of goodwill might exist to be called upon. Her hands began to tremble slightly and under Dubnikov's gaze she clasped them to her knees. She lifted her head and looked at him through half-closed eyes.

'Please, Roman, please?' she asked, almost in a whisper.

He stroked his face downwards from his cheekbones and pinched his chin.

'Sveta, Sveta, I don't know. How do you manage to get yourself into these situations?'

While it seemed he was trying to be playful, she felt only growing anxiety as her pleading look would have revealed.

'Who last saw him?'

'His cameraman, I guess,' replied Svetlana.

'No, before that?'

'His assistant at the station – Konstantin.'

'And you've spoken to him?'

'He had no clue. Nick hadn't told him anything.'

'What about the cameraman?'

'Malenkov's got him, but he was freelance for that broadcast only, so he'll probably be okay.'

'Well, your husband is still thinking then – and that's good. Look, Sveta, we'll do what we can but no promises.'

Svetlana rose from her chair, buttoning her coat.

'I can't promise anything in return.'

'Well, it's a good thing I like you then.'

She smiled, then turned for the door, reaching for the handle.

'Oh, Sveta, if I'm right, I may not see you again. I hope it all works out for you.'

'Goodbye, Roman,' she answered, without looking back.

*

Malenkov fidgeted outside the office of deputy energy minister Leonid Kutaisov, checking his tie fitted evenly around his collar. He watched the handle turn under invisible influence and the door opened with two distinct clicks of its lock. An aide beckoned him in and he advanced across the rich carpet towards the substantial desk, behind which the minister sat. He took a seat.

'What news have you for me, Captain Malenkov?'

'Well, Deputy Minister, we believe he's still in Russia – in Moscow.'

'Why would the Americans not have removed him by now?'

'He's not CIA, Deputy Minister, and anyway, he has another motive.'

The minister's look invited further information.

'He married the reporter, Svetlana Dorenko.'

'I heard about that.'

'We think he's still here... for her. The broadcast told her he was still in Moscow.'

The minister's look hardened and he leaned forward, clasping his hands together.

'That broadcast, Captain Malenkov, was a disaster. Who knows what else he's got. We've explained it as an ill-informed deception, but any more such broadcasts are out of the question.'

'Yes, Deputy Minister.'

'I hope I make myself clear?'

'Perfectly.'

'You'll imagine there have been discussions further up from me.'

'I'm sure, Deputy Minister.'

'And I have to say, there has been little enthusiasm for the way things have been handled up to now.'

Malenkov looked down at his thumbnails and placed one over the other, before the minister continued.

'Nevertheless, you've been authorised to bring this to a conclusion.'

'A conclusion, Deputy Minister?'

'A final conclusion, Captain. This matter is considered so serious and its future implications so grave that we cannot afford to have this man re-appear. Do the Americans know we are looking for him?'

'Yes, Deputy Minister.'

'Good. When you find him, we will apparently continue to look. They can have his body in a year or two when things have calmed down.'

'And Svetlana Dorenko?'

'Get rid of her too. No, on second thoughts, perhaps not. The American will not be missed in Moscow, but we've been taking some criticism about the journalists. I'll leave it to your discretion, Captain, but I want her silence. Is that understood?'

'Yes, Deputy Minister.'

'That is all.'

Malenkov stood and took a small bow in the minister's direction, before turning to make his exit.

Downstairs, his driver was waiting to take him the short distance back to Lubyanka, where Malenkov pulled in his assistant, Il'ya, to see him.

'Any news?' asked Malenkov.

'No, sir.'

'It's only a matter of time. He's here for her and she's looking for him. With luck, we'll get the pair of them together.'

'What's the instruction, sir?'

'Get a small team together... three of you: you, Petlyuk and Marov.'

'Marov's in hospital with appendicitis. There's the new guy. He's been good, so far.'

'Okay, fine. When Mendez is found take him out with the gas.'

'The lethal version?'

'Of course... and drop him off a cliff in the Urals.'

'And her?'

'Leave her to me. I have an idea.'

*

Two more days passed, during which Svetlana visited every place she and Nick had spent any time together, her progress hindered by having to avoid her FSB tail whenever she could.

The last stop on her list was Poxoronka Cemetery, where his impromptu eulogy had first given her a hint that perhaps he was not the stumbling fool he'd first seemed. She found the graveside where he'd stood and longed to hear him speak again of love and honour. A stone now stood, bearing the name of the departed citizen. She spoke in a whisper.

'Comrade Valentin Sergeiovich, my husband spoke for you when there was nobody else. I have lost my love and have nobody to speak for me. Tell me where I should go now?'

The breeze took up her words and carried them away towards the setting sun, leaving her in advancing darkness with only memories and corpses for company. She bit her lip and turned for the exit, unsure where to go next.

On the train at Alekseevskaya metro, Svetlana watched the doors advance towards each other. When under way, she realised that instead of going the few stops to Babushkinskaya and her apartment, she'd boarded the southbound train and was heading for the city. She looked at the overhead map, her eyes falling upon Kurskaya.

'Sasha,' she said out loud, to the consternation of the *babushka* sitting next to her.

Sasha, of course: he will help me look. Why didn't I think of that before?

A short while later, the escalator delivered her onto the concourse and she looked for the young boy, the hood of her coat pulled up in an attempt to hide from the inevitable FSB observers. Her breath shortened with growing anxiety as she calculated the places she might find him. Ten minutes later, and on her fourth attempt, she saw him, deeply engrossed in a video game and apparently the recent recipient of some money.

She stepped into the small arcade and reached out to tap him on the shoulder. He glanced at her but only momentarily, his attention returning to the serious business of defending himself from the onrushing horde of cyber-monsters occupying the screen in front of him. Sixty seconds later, his game ended.

'I just missed my record score,' said Sasha.

'Sorry,' replied Svetlana.

As the screen went blank, Sasha turned to Svetlana and grinned at her before beckoning her to follow him.

'Sasha, wait!' she pleaded, anxious to tell him of her need for help. He didn't stop to listen.

As always, with Svetlana, the young lad took her along a variety of diversions. Eventually, forty paces or so after his own little abode, Sasha came to a stop and pointed to a void under a corrugated steel shelf. Svetlana saw nothing but darkness and looked to Sasha for explanation. Turning to leave, he jabbed his finger in the direction of the blackness, bidding her to look. She crept forward and knelt, her eyes slowly adjusting to the gloom. Ahead of her, some two metres away, was what looked like a piece of loosely-rolled carpet. She reached forward and stretched out one of her elegant fingers to check its texture. As she did, the object stirred as if brought to life from the energy of her touch, causing her to jump up with a start and hit her head on the steel above.

'Ow!' she exclaimed, rubbing her head.

An arm emerged, followed by another... then an unshaven and dirty face, with eyes blinking for focus. She stopped attending to her head and transferred her hand to her mouth to catch the gasp of her breath at the sight of Nick. He looked frightened, cornered as he was, and apparently unsure whether he had encountered friend or foe. His trembling hand came towards her and she knew the instant his palm fell into hers that the love she'd thought hopelessly lost had returned.

'Nikolai, oh, Nikolai!' she exclaimed, before falling forward into his arms, her body quivering and tears of joy overwhelming her ability to speak further.

'I thought I'd lost you,' he said, sniffing and wiping his own eyes.

'I'm sorry – I'm so sorry!' she said.

Nick held her to him, his arms vice-like.

'Nikolai, forgive me. I'm so sorry. I love you. Please forgive me!'

Nick released his grip and struggled to free the rest of his body from the rolled blanket and plastic. He reached for her again and kissed her deeply. He was unwashed and his teeth had not been cleaned in days but for Svetlana, right then, he smelt of expensive cologne, his taste like fine wine. She clung to him tightly, whispering 'I love you' over and over.

Later, Sasha enjoyed his role of temporary butler. He brought them a packet of *bliny*, some salami and orange juice for their supper, before leaving them for the night.

'You need a bath,' she chuckled.

'So do you, now,' he replied, poking her on the forehead with his finger.

'Do you think we'll have bad luck because we didn't make love on our wedding night?'

'Our wedding night was stolen. So, this is it, instead.'

'And you went to all this expense,' she smirked, theatrically sweeping her hand around their cramped quarters.

'Nothing but the best for you, my darling.'

Nick's smile fell from his face and he took her hand.

'I thought I'd lose you.'

'I know what happened. It was Malenkov,' said Svetlana.

'Of course... but I can't remember.'

'You were set up – gassed and unconscious – with her.'

'I couldn't remember.'

'I'm sorry I doubted you. I need you to forgive me.'

'There's nothing to forgive. Malenkov caused this.'

'No, Nikolai Ivanovich, I need you to forgive me for doubting you. I mean it.'

'Then, I forgive you,' he replied.

'And I need to thank you.'

'For...?'

'For fighting for me, Nikolai.'

She felt Nick's hand gently stroking her hair, until it touched her cheek and caught the particular tear that had taken two decades to fall from her eye.

'I'm learning to fight.'

'No, Nikolai, it's in your blood.

Chapter 33

The night before had thrown up no solutions as to how Nick could leave Kursky station without falling into the hands of the FSB. But, with a new morning, inspiration had come to Svetlana. It was Wednesday and Richard, as he always did, had been there feeding the children and tending to their ailments. There had not been a moment's hesitation from him when Svetlana had outlined the situation. At the end of his working day, he held open the side door to his old van as Nick emerged from a hidden exit under Sasha's guidance, then spirited himself aboard. Richard and his friend God, if he was so inclined, would look after Nick until his planned reunion with Svetlana, in three days' time. She'd reckoned that by then they'd have a plan for Nick to cross the border into Latvia, after which she and Ivan could follow on.

*

'Sveta, I was worried. I expected to hear from you this morning.'

'It's fine, Mum, nothing to worry about. Did Ivan get off to school okay?'

'Yes, but I think he'll be pleased to see you. He's been missing you since Tamara and the boys went back. Normally, he's fine here but I think he just wants to be back home.'

'I know, I've just had a lot to do.'

Svetlana put her finger to her mouth and signalled for her mother to follow her to the kitchen where she put on the radio and turned up the volume. She spoke close to her mother's ear.

'I found him, Mum.'

Svetlana's Garden

Her mother looked startled and stepped back. Svetlana signalled again for her silence before continuing.

'He was set up, to discredit him. The photographs are staged.'

'Who told you this?'

'It doesn't matter. I know the truth and I have my husband back.'

Her mother took Svetlana in her arms and reached up to stroke her hair.

'Oh, darling Sveta, I'm so pleased. He seemed such a good man.'

'He is a good man, Mum. I shouldn't have doubted him.'

'What will you do now?'

Svetlana stepped back, gripped her mother's forearms and looked straight into her eyes. From the radio, opening phrases of balalaika announced the famous old tune *Korobushka*.

'He's in danger, Mum. He did a very brave thing for me, a broadcast. He has to leave and I must follow him.'

No more than a hint of disappointment crossed her mother's face.

'You must be with him.'

They embraced for the duration of the song as memories of her childhood raced through Svetlana's mind, but a future without her mother close by beckoned.

'I love you, Mama.'

'And I love you, darling. I always will, wherever you are.'

'How will I live, without you?'

'You will not be without me. I will always be here,' said her mother, placing her hand on Svetlana's heart.

They had tea while they reminisced over old photographs and waited for Ivan to return, which he did shortly after three p.m. He put his rucksack down and hugged Svetlana, under the approving eye of his grandmother.

'Hi, Mum. Are you okay?'

'I'm fine, Vanya, just fine. Are you hungry? Do you want something to eat?'

'Can we just go home?'

'Granny's made us some *plov*. We can have it in front of the TV.'

'Great.'

They said their goodbyes and made for the metro. Ivan strode out at his mother's side instead of following on behind as he usually did.

*

'Tip your head forward a bit,' said Richard.

Nick did as he was told and then felt the cool steel of the battery hair clippers as they rested on the base of his neck. Richard would give haircuts to the children at Kursky, which also gave him an opportunity to check them out for nits or other parasites. Here, in the lounge of a cramped and musty one-bedroomed apartment above his lock-up garage in the Biryulyovo industrial area, south of the city, cutting hair was easier than outside the station at the tailgate of his van.

'Make it short, Richard. I need to look different.'

Nick's thick, slightly waved locks fell as Richard made swift progress across his scalp, leaving him with no more than a centimetre's length of hair as a backdrop to the fledgling beard he'd allowed to grow since his last broadcast. Within a few minutes, Richard had finished and held up a mirror.

'How's that?'

'You should be a professional,' said Nick, turning his head each way.

'When I go back, maybe I will be.'

'Where's back?'

'Montgomery, Alabama.'

'No way! Spike – my friend – Spike Ruskin, is from Montgomery.'

'It's a long way from Alabama. What's he do?' asked Richard.

'Navy: wanted to follow his dad.'

'And you, did you follow your dad?'

'No, he was a teacher. I wouldn't have had the patience.'

Richard swept some of the cut hair from Nick's neck with a tissue and removed the grey towel from his shoulders.

'They'll be watching for you at the border.'

'I guess,' replied Nick.

'God will keep an eye on you, Nick.'

'Even non-believers, like me?'

'Even you.'

'If... if anything happens to me, will you look out for her?'

'You've seen her. She'll be okay,' said Richard, walking round to face Nick. 'Okay, you'll do. Spread this out, while I make us some coffee.'

Nick took the offered map and unfolded it on a low wooden table, which displayed four beige tiles in its centre, each carrying a picture of a *matryoshka*. Richard returned.

'So, we just drive right down the M-9?' asked Nick.

'Yeah, right up to the border crossing – where you're arrested – if you get that far. Nah, we'll have to work out something else. Sveta's speaking to Dubnikov.'

'You know him?'

'Where do you think I get my supplies from?'

'The Lord works in mysterious ways.'

'He has to, Nick, to get things done.'

Nick shook his head, smiling.

'Probably go south-west to Smolensk and follow the Belarus border,' continued Richard. 'You can't use the normal crossing point.'

Nick took a sip of coffee and looked across at Richard.

'Why are you doing this?'

Richard gave an enigmatic smile before returning his attention to the map.

'Here looks good to me,' he said, pointing. 'After that, you can make your way to Riga.'

An hour later, they shared a tin of sprats and some bread, complemented by vodka.

'I don't cook much for myself,' said Richard.

'But you do for the kids.'

'Yeah, well they're the future aren't they?'

'What is the future for Russia – for those kids?'

'Even the Lord may struggle to answer that one, Nick. There is huge potential, but the corruption will probably kill it. Big ambitions have a habit of being disappointed. I learnt a long time ago to keep it simple and just get through each day.'

'And the future for journalists?'

'Like Sveta?'

'Yeah,' replied Nick.

'Uncertain – depends what you're saying. Better get some sleep, you might be short of it over the next few days.'

Chapter 34

They'd not spoken in two days, fearing that any communication would give Nick away. Svetlana, however, had not been idle. With a loan from Dubnikov, she'd bought a second-hand Ford and had arranged for one of his guys to meet them at Sebezh, the day after next, having found a suitable crossing point at the Latvian border. She'd left it to the last minute, but now it was time to tell Demchi she'd be missing for a few days. The last thing she needed was him sending out a search party for her.

'Hi, Vasya, is Demchi in?'

'In his office,' replied Vasiliy.

She knocked and Demchi beckoned her in.

'I need a few days off.'

'For a good reason, I hope,' replied her editor.

'A very good one.'

'Which is...? No, on second thoughts, don't tell me. It's easier to cover for you if I really don't know.'

She smiled at him while he stubbed out his cigarette in the overcrowded ashtray. With a wave, she turned and left, making her way straight to Belorusskaya metro.

Richard had picked up the car and left it full of fuel and provisions, near to Molodezhnaya metro station. As she approached it, Svetlana reached into her bag and let her fingers close around the spare key. She looked around for a final time, but could see no trace of an FSB tail. Reassured, she watched the car's lights blink as the alarm de-activated and then settled herself in the driver's seat, so supportive compared to the tired springs in her old Lada. The engine started first time. Soon, car and driver were heading south-west to the rendezvous point arranged with Richard, next to the woods at Izvarino. The wipers intermittently swept drizzle from the windscreen as darkening clouds above threatened something more inclement to come. Svetlana was apprehensive, but at the same time exhilarated that she was to be reunited with her husband and drive him to the border to begin a new chapter together. Constant checks in the mirror appeared to show nobody was following, and she thought of Richard who by now should be on his way back to Moscow to meet up with the street kids under his care.

As she approached Izvarino, a turn from Vnukovskoye shosse took her down a track towards the woods from where, at any moment, she expected Nick to emerge. Svetlana turned on the headlights to combat the gathering gloom and then slowed to a crawl while she peered out through the partially misted window. The car came to a stop and she waited. Save for the distant hum of traffic and the rustling of leaves, all was still. Then, there he was, stepping out from behind a tree trunk some fifty metres away, before striding towards her. She ran to him and flung her arms around his neck.

'Oh, Nikolai, I've missed you so!'

'And I've missed you, darling.'

They held each other tightly and shared a lingering kiss.

'We must go,' said Nick.

He took her arm and directed her back towards the car as the first drops of heavy rain from the forthcoming storm pattered on the sandy track.

Just as they'd enclosed themselves, the sky finally released its watery burden and torrential rain mixed with hail pounded on the roof of the car, as though demanding admittance. She was certainly glad not to be in the Lada in such conditions. While the heater began to clear the screen, they removed their coats and fastened their seat belts for the journey ahead. She switched on the wipers, only to be met with the sight of a large blue van, not more than five metres in front of them.

'Shit! Where did that come from?'

'Better back up, there's no room to pass.'

Unnerved, Svetlana put the car into reverse and gingerly reversed up the path towards the main road, the rear wiper struggling to provide other than interrupted vision under the rain's onslaught. Slowly, she covered the three hundred or so metres back to Vnukovskoye shosse, where two pairs of headlights grew larger and larger in the rear window. She glanced forward to see the van was still with them and holding its five metre distance.

'Nikolai, what is it?'

Nick lowered his window and stuck his head out. Then he pulled back in, water streaming down his nose and cheeks, his eyes wide with surprise.

'It's a trap!'

They were both frightened as they looked into each other's eyes, sharing the realisation that the bond between them was about to be forcibly broken by the FSB. Svetlana pushed the central locking button before looking forwards and backwards in a desperate search for any angle that might allow their escape, but it was clear there was none. He took hold of both her hands.

'Sveta, no matter what happens, I will always love you. Nothing – nothing will ever break us.'

His noble words were interrupted by the sound of smashing glass as a gloved hand, bearing a pistol handle, took out the rear passenger window and unlocked the door before holding it open. The sound of squelching footsteps announced the arrival of an unwanted visitor who slid into the rear seat, a brimmed hat pulled down to partially cover his face. The head rose and a thumb pushed back the hat to reveal the angular features of Malenkov, a grin upon his face.

'Mr Mendez, at last we have the chance to meet. I've heard so much about you.'

'Fuck off and leave us alone, Malenkov!' hissed Svetlana.

'Hmmm,' said Malenkov sarcastically. 'I see a change of name has not brought about a change of spirit, Mrs Mendez.'

'I'm an American citizen. I want to speak to the embassy.'

'Shut up, Mr Mendez! This is not Boston or Madrid. This is Russia, a country whose hospitality you have seen fit to abuse. Get out of the car, both of you!'

In the seconds it took to cover the twenty metres separating them from the FSB cars, Svetlana and Nick were soaked through before they were each put into a different car.

Svetlana shivered, not only from the freezing rain that made her clothes stick to her skin, but also at the thought that the Mercedes she was travelling in was probably the same one that had carried young Katenin to his death.

'Just expel him. I'll do whatever you want.'

'You're in no position to bargain,' replied Malenkov. 'I used to admire your persistence, but do you know, I've become rather tired of it.'

'He's just a reporter, an American.'

'He is a saboteur.'

'That's what journalists are to you, aren't they?'

'No, not at all. I'm in favour of the press reporting, but with the freedom to report comes responsibility.'

'To report what you want, you mean.'

'I suspect we're never going to agree on that.'

'Don't harm him. If anything happens to him, don't think I'll leave it.'

Malenkov bristled as he turned to look at Svetlana. For a moment she thought he might even strike her.

'Don't threaten me, Svetlana Yuriyevna! You are as deep in this as he is and you will have plenty of time to reflect that it would have been better for both of you if you'd not mixed him up in this in the first place.'

Behind the menace, Malenkov had a point. The gnawing background guilt she'd been feeling about involving Nick in the Petrov story came to the fore. She said nothing more for the rest of the journey.

An hour later, in darkness, they drove into Lubyanka and as the gate closed behind them Svetlana realised they really were on their own now. She struggled to hide the dread she felt inside, but realised that if there was to be any hope for them, it was imperative to retain the ability to think clearly.

Nick and Svetlana had been separated for several hours. She didn't know where he was or what had happened to him. For her part, she'd been placed in a cell without windows but with a light which was never extinguished. Her clothes had not had the opportunity to dry out properly and she shivered continuously in the damp, cold enclosure. Eventually, the door opened and a stern looking woman, dressed all in black, signalled to her to follow. Rising up a flight of stone steps, Svetlana emerged onto a linoleum floored corridor from where she was shown into an interview room, approximately five metres square, with a metal table and four chairs.

'Sit here,' said the woman, before taking station by the door.

Svetlana sat and contemplated the skin on the back of her hands, pale from the cold. Malenkov walked in, carrying two mugs that turned out to be coffee for him and hot chocolate for her. The irony of such a soothing drink being presented in such perilous circumstances was not lost on her. Malenkov put her mug down and she immediately wrapped her hands around it, seeking out warmth.

'I have a dilemma, Svetlana Yuriyevna. I have a job to do, and in this instance, I need to be sure that neither you nor Mr Mendez has any additional slanderous material. Your husband seems to think that his silence will in some way protect you, but it just places you both in more difficulty.'

'If you've harmed him –'

'I warned you, don't threaten me!'

Malenkov barely restrained the malice in danger of taking over his expression, before pulling up a chair opposite Svetlana and reverting to his sly tone of mock-friendship.

'Earlier, you mentioned the possibility of expelling him and I've been giving it some thought. Provided that – and I mean provided that – I could be sure no other material was about to come out, then perhaps an arrangement could be reached.'

'What do you want?'

Malenkov's tone hardened.

'I want you to talk to him. Tell him that reassuring us there's nothing else will save his life... and yours.'

Svetlana looked into his eyes and saw no sign that he was bluffing. For sixty seconds longer she looked but Malenkov didn't blink, not once.

'Take me to him,' she eventually responded.

As she followed the diminutive FSB officer down the long corridor, she imagined she had a hockey stick in her hand, which she'd use to knock him to the ground before smashing his skull. She felt no revulsion at the thought. Indeed, she looked forward to it. Malenkov stopped at the last door on the right and held out his hand to bid her to enter.

'Five minutes,' he said.

She walked past him and confidently turned the handle.

Nick rose from his chair the moment he saw her, his face strained and his haircut making him look like he was already prepared to spend time in prison. He rushed over and held her.

'Sveta, are you all right? Did they hurt you?'

'No, I'm fine. We don't have long. Sit down, Nikolai.'

Nick drew two chairs together and they sat facing each other, holding hands.

'He says he'll let you live if you tell him everything,' said Svetlana.

'And you believe him?'

'What choice is there?'

'The choice to save the lives of others,' replied Nick.

She knew then that he had made up his mind. There would be no co-operation and he would not sacrifice more lives to grasp at the slim chance of saving his own.

'But, Nikolai, please?'

He put his hand up to stop her protest and leaned forward, holding his lips close to hers before delivering a kiss.

Malenkov entered with three burly assistants.

'I've heard enough. Say goodbye, Svetlana Yuriyevna, because Mother Russia has had enough of this interference.'

Two of the assistants stepped forward and wrenched Svetlana from Nick's grasp while the third pulled out a pistol and pointed it at him, interrupting his move to help her.

'Get off me!' screamed Svetlana with venom. But she was dragged through the doorway as she shared a last desperate look with her husband.

'Nikolai, Nikolai!' came her plaintive shouts, over and over again, then fading until finally extinguished, leaving Nick with Malenkov.

'Then, your fate is sealed, Mr Mendez. But then again... it was the day you met her.'

*

It had been late when Malenkov finally went to bed but he'd slept particularly well. Next morning, sitting behind his desk, he had a smile on his face as his assistant, Il'ya, walked in.

'Congratulations, sir.'

'Thank you, Il'ya. I think it's fair to say we can all be quite pleased with ourselves.'

'Who do you want to deal with Mendez's disposal, sir?'

'Who's done it before?'

'Of the three of us, myself and Petlyuk.'

'Then give it to the new guy. The men need to build experience.'

'Are we cleared to proceed then, sir?'

'Straight away, Il'ya. Let's get that shit off the sole of Russia's shoe.'

*

They'd left Nick in a small room no more than three metres by four. Every surface, apart from the steel door, was covered in white tiles and there was no window, only a small vent in the centre of the ceiling. Over-tight cable ties held his arms to the legs of the fixed steel chair on which he was sitting.

He'd spent the time reconciling himself to his fate, having long banished the terror and racing heart that had accompanied him to this place. He marvelled at the sense of serenity that had befallen him now he had accepted his impending death as inevitable, and had visited the furthest recesses of his mind to pay respects to all his best memories. This was it. There would be no last request.

The large door opened with a wheeze as air sneaked in, before being followed by a large figure in a red boiler suit wearing a gas mask and pushing what resembled a golf trolley with two stainless steel cylinders strapped to it. Nick stared at them, well aware what they contained. Finally, he and the gas he'd so assiduously searched for across this vast country had come to meet. Malenkov entered the room, the white tiles reflected in his immaculately polished shoes, his face confident, proud even.

'Let her live,' said Nick.

'That is not in your gift, Mr Mendez, but I have already decided, subject to her silence, that she will live.'

'You cannot silence her.'

Malenkov reached into his pocket and took out a strip of gaffer tape from which he removed the backing before clamping it over Nick's mouth and smoothing it across his cheeks.

'I can... and I will. Goodbye, Mr Mendez.'

Malenkov turned and left, pulling the door closed behind him.

Nick had often wondered if his life would actually flash before him at the moment of his death, as many said was the case. Time seemed to slow as, frame by frame, images of a hand stretching out for the left cylinder reached his brain. Movements, resembling the progress of a second hand around a watch's face, were joined by the sound of gentle hissing as an invisible serpent of gas snaked its way towards him. There was nothing to taste, but the slightest smell of sweetness, like spring rose petals, caressed his nostrils before a floating feeling announced his short journey to another place had begun. Chest movements shallowed, fingers holding the chair's legs slowly lost their grip, and as Nick's neck surrendered in its fight to hold his head up, consciousness, like a cowardly lover, slipped away from him.

*

'Where is my husband?'

'In a moment, Svetlana Yuriyevna,' replied Malenkov, as he sat behind his desk and casually compared the length of his fingernails.

Svetlana had not slept at all in the cell to which she'd been returned the night before. Her face was pale and drawn, with tear tracks apparent and her manner agitated.

'I know you care much for your son.'

'Where is my husband?'

'Shut up and listen!'

Svetlana was taken aback by the menacing tone of Malenkov's rebuke. He continued.

'I'm going to let you live, but there are strings attached. Firstly, you will write nothing about this country again and, secondly, you must leave Russia.'

'But this is my home.'

Malenkov held up his trigger finger to indicate he wasn't finished.

'I'm past negotiating. I'm simply telling you. That is what will happen or you will find yourself without a son or a mother. You have three days to leave. You leave, and they live.'

'I cannot organise things for my son in three days.'

'Your son stays here, Svetlana Yuriyevna. In fact, we are looking after him right now. He'll be returned to his grandmother when you are on a flight out of here, but he stays in Russia to ensure your good behaviour. You can have him back in a couple of years if we've had no trouble with you in the meantime.'

'You can't take my son!'

'We can do whatever is necessary to protect this country from you and people like you! Just who do you think you are? Don't you realise you've brought all this on yourself?'

'Where is my husband?'

'Your husband is dead. He finally found the gas you've both been looking for.'

Svetlana tried to stand but was floored by shock, and she fainted.

*

Svetlana's Garden

It must have happened, but in the thirty-six hours since she'd been released from Lubyanka, Svetlana couldn't remember when she'd not been crying. She and her mother had frantically searched for Ivan but there was no sign of him. Malenkov had not been bluffing. Perversely, the urgency of Ivan's situation had given her a reason to function and held back the agonising grief waiting to visit her. As always, her mother had been a tower of strength, making her eat and trying as well as she could to offer reassurance that Ivan would be returned safely.

Meanwhile, Vasiliy had made the arrangements for her departure. Aware that he had a villa in Marbella, he'd approached Dubnikov who had agreed she could stay there for a while. She had been so distraught that a meaningful discussion about where she could go had been impossible, but her shrug of the shoulders and hands held to the sky when he'd suggested Dubnikov's place had been the nearest he'd got to a yes. So, it was a journey to Malaga that he'd booked for her.

She stared at the gaudy, red paper folder holding her economy class ticket, its promise of tourist bliss disguising its real purpose as the cruel instrument of her exile from the country and the people she loved. Her mother pressed a cup of tea into her hand.

'Drink it, darling.'

Svetlana's hand trembled as she took a sip of tea. Her mother had not been judgemental as her daughter had told her the story of all that had happened and all Ivan would need to know if he was not to feel abandoned by her.

'I should have listened to Demchi. He told me, Mum. I should have listened.'

'Sveta, I have something to tell you, something I have never spoken of before.'

She took her daughter's hand, closed her eyes for a moment, and then continued.

'Before you were born, before I met your wonderful father, I was very much in love with a young man from Kostroma. He'd travel to see me every week, no matter what the weather. I can still see his smiling blue eyes when I close mine. I desperately wanted to marry him, as he did me, but my mother told me to wait until he'd done his army service. My heart told me not to, but my head listened to her and we agreed to postpone our plans. While he was away, I'd wait for his letters, which would always arrive in the first days of the month, and my heart would fly when I read the things he'd say to me. On a spring day in April, his sister came to see me and told me he'd been lost in the forest on an exercise and had frozen to death, before they'd found him. Part of my heart died too that day, and wonderful as your father was, it was another man who taught me to listen to my heart, not always to my head. Demchi is wonderful and you know how fond of him I am, but you should never regret following your heart rather than his head.'

Svetlana threw her arms around her mother's neck.

'Oh, Mum, I love you – I love you – I'm going to miss you so much.'

Chapter 35

Demchi arrived at five-thirty the next morning to take Svetlana and her mother to Sheremetyevo. Svetlana seemed to have shrunk, no longer the tall energetic fighter that he was used to seeing but instead a little child, tearful, lost and alone, sitting on the edge of her suitcase. He coughed and turned away to compose himself.

'Thank you for coming over, Gregoriy. It's kind of you to take us,' said Svetlana's mother.

Demchi smiled and nodded.

'Would you like a drink before we set off?'

'No, thanks,' he replied. 'We can have something at the airport. We'll have plenty of time as the flight's delayed an hour.'

Svetlana spoke but they couldn't make out what she was saying, so soft and feeble was the sound. Demchi bent down to be close to her.

'What is it, Sveta?'

'The children – I want to see the children – at Kursky.'

Demchi glanced at Svetlana's mother and she nodded her approval.

'Okay, come on then. If we go right away, we'll have time before the traffic builds. Give me your case.'

Svetlana sat in the back of Demchi's car as he drove them to the centre. She said nothing. The winter was not quite ready to hand Moscow over to spring, as rolling grey clouds above released a fresh fall of sleet that danced in the gusting wind as it neared the ground. It was just after six when they reached Kursky station.

'We have to leave in about twenty minutes,' said Demchi, turning his head to look back at Svetlana.

'I won't be long,' she said, almost inaudibly, as she opened the back door.

They watched, as Svetlana's shuffling, laboured steps took her through the main entrance and out of sight.

'Oh, Gregoriy Maksimovich, do you have any contacts in Spain who can help her?'

'No, but I will speak to Mr Freeman at INN, I'm sure he will help.'

*

Svetlana didn't hear the early commuter ask the time as she reached the familiar steps that would take her down to areas of the subterranean level rarely visited by those other than the homeless and some maintenance staff. The skin of her beautiful hands, usually protected by gloves, lay open to the cold, but she cared not if the numbness overtaking her fingers joined the defeated ranks of her other senses.

At the bottom of the steps, one of Sasha's group greeted her as she made her way through the steel, rivets and concrete that played host to temporary homes of recovered cardboard and plastic. And then, there she was, looking down at the pathetic little shelter which passed as home to Sasha and his sister. She peeled back the grey plastic sheet that was draped over it and held in place by three broken bricks. They were both there. Marina was asleep, curled up in her old blanket, no doubt having been kept up working until the early hours by her pimp. She looked almost peaceful, although a fresh bruise on her cheek told of a recent unsavoury episode. Sasha was awake, sitting up and rocking slowly back and forth. His eyes were wide and staring, his mouth occasionally commencing then just as quickly dropping a silly grin. He was high on glue, a pastime that consumed him when he no longer wished to face the wretchedness of his precarious existence.

'Sasha, it's me, Sveta.'

She received no response other than a tuneless hum, which began to accompany his strange, seated dance.

'I have to go away. I wanted to tell you and Marina.'

Sasha stared blankly into the distance without acknowledging her. Tomorrow, he might reflect that he'd not seen her for a while, and look forward to his next treat of hot chocolate or doughnut. He would wait in vain.

'Goodbye, Sasha. Look after her.'

The grey cover slipped back into place, a grubby curtain falling on the finale to her relationship with these two youngsters whose courage deserved so much more but which would reward them with nothing.

She had almost reached the top of the stairs, when the lingering ghost of grief put its hand on her shoulder and forced her to her knees, crushing down on her with its burden of unbearable sadness. A strange reflex groan emerged from her throat as her hand grasped for the steel handrail to stop her from falling backwards. She tried to say his name, but found the breath that had been stolen from her dear departed husband had been taken from her also.

'Oh, Sveta, come here,' said her mother, as Demchi quickly descended the few steps to reach Svetlana and help her to her feet.

They both supported her as they made their way back to the car, where her mother sat in the back seat resting her sobbing daughter's head in her lap as the vehicle turned out of the station and headed for the airport.

*

Demchi accompanied Svetlana in the check-in queue at Terminal D, where a number of fellow passengers recognised her and gossiped about her obvious distress. Svetlana, normally so observant, was oblivious to the mutterings and pointed fingers. Dressed in black trousers and jumper, now with sunglasses covering her eyes, she shuffled forward until she faced the humourless Aeroflot clerk behind the counter who inspected her passport before glancing up to see if the bearer's image matched.

'Remove your glasses.'

Svetlana reached for the frame of her spectacles, dragging them to the bridge of her nose to reveal red, puffy eyes that advertised her distress.

'Boarding is at nine-fifty.'

Without further ceremony, the attendant slapped her passport and boarding card on the counter, and then crooked her finger to beckon forward the next passenger. Demchi ushered Svetlana sideways towards her mother.

'There's two hours to wait. We have time for a drink before you go to security,' he said.

He and her mother each took an arm and guided Svetlana to the nearby escalator in search of the food court. She watched the metal steps align and then separate, a machine carrying her one step closer to her impending expulsion.

The whole area was busy with jostling travellers, brand names clamouring for their attention while offering them routine fare at inflated prices. A quiet corner was out of the question.

'Sveta – here – sit here,' said her mother, beckoning her to follow to a just vacated table.

'I'll order,' said Demchi. 'What do you want?'

'Coffee, for me, Gregoriy. Sveta, what about you?'

'What?'

'What do you want to drink, darling?'

'Just water,' mumbled Svetlana.

She held her hands to her ears in an attempt to block out the noise of surrounding voices, all rising to be heard above the others. The sunglasses did a good job of hiding her face but failed to protect her from the gesticulating, agitated crowd, when all she wanted was to be alone. She shut her eyes tightly, but there was no relief as she found herself looking at the vision of a deep, black well into which Nick and Ivan were falling while reaching out desperately for her to save them. *Was insanity and the imposition of daytime nightmares to be added to the insult of her exile?* She punished herself for her fate by imagining the alternative scenarios that had been available, but which she'd rejected. Her head throbbed and it felt as though sharp needles were prodding the back of her eyes, a first instalment of the many physical tortures to be meted out in the hell to which she was descending.

The familiar stroke of her mother's hand on her hair caused Svetlana to open her eyes.

'I love you, Sveta. Nothing will ever break that. We will all be together again... I'm sure of it.'

Svetlana managed a feeble smile and squeezed her mother's hand.

'Mum, what about Ivan?'

'He will be fine. Nothing will break his love, either.'

'He didn't deserve this.'

'He loves you, exactly as you are. I will let you know when he's back. He will be fine with me, until we are together.'

'I'm so sorry, Mum'

Her apology was not allowed to go further as her head was drawn to her mother's shoulder and into the familiar comforting embrace that had been there since the beginning of her memories.

'Here you are, girls,' said Demchi, putting down a small plastic tray. 'It's busy today. I'm just going to check what the queue's like for security.'

Demchi turned away, picking up his ribbed paper cup of coffee.

'What will I do without Nikolai, Mum?'

'In time, darling, there will be somebody special, again.'

'Not like him – not like him.'

'Queue's pretty bad. Better go,' said Demchi, returning.

Svetlana's steps on the way to security were laboured, condemned as she was to the waiting exile. It would have been disrespectful to make small talk, so they said nothing. At the front, a stern-faced security officer checked documents, unconcerned at the jostling back down the line. She turned first to Demchi who opened his arms to embrace her, while she pulled at the lapel on his jacket.

'I'm sorry, Demchi. I should have listened to you.'

'It's because you never did that I'm here now. You were always the special one. I just never told you.'

'If I can ever come back, can I have a job?'

'You can be the editor and I'll write for you.'

'Oh, Demchi...'

She sniffed, trying to hold back tears while she gripped hard upon his jacket. He kissed her on the cheek and then nodded to Svetlana's mother that it was time to hand over to her. She held her daughter. Svetlana snivelled and wiped her nose on her sleeve, a sudden sense of panic rising from the pit of her stomach.

'I don't want to go, Mum. I'm scared.'

'I know, darling, but we'll work this out. We will.'

'When will I see you?'

'Before long... and, we can speak by phone. I can even see you, because Ivan will teach me to use the internet.'

'Mum, I'm scared.'

'Be brave, sweetheart. Everything will be all right,' she said softly.

Svetlana shuffled to the front of the queue, her shoulders hunched and hands trembling.

'Next!' barked the security guard, grabbing Svetlana's passport and boarding card.

Her bag started the journey before her as it silently disappeared into the X-ray scanner, while she stepped through the metal detector. Her possessions recovered, she looked back over the heads of those following her, where she saw her mother and Demchi, straining on tip-toes to catch the last glimpses of her, their smiles showing signs of strain. As she retreated slowly towards the departure lounge, Svetlana removed her glasses to better see her mother wave goodbye. She offered a feeble wave in reply and watched as the elderly lady's elegant fingertips finally sank into the sea of people in between them. Now, she was alone, with no way back and an unknown future.

'Gregoriy Maksimovich, what will happen to my baby?' sobbed Svetlana's mother to Demchi.

'I don't know, Raisa, I don't know.'

He could only hug her as hard as he could to offer some comfort, while tears welled up in his own eyes as he too realised that part of what made his life worth living was lost to him. He would not go to the office but would ring Jack Freeman, in Madrid. *After that, I'm going to drink vodka, lots of it*, he thought.

*

It wasn't cold on the plane, but Svetlana nevertheless shivered slightly as she sat in a window seat over the wing. Lack of food and sleep were taking their toll on her and she wished she'd brought something to send her into slumber. A bleached blonde, aged about thirty and wearing expensive but vulgar jewellery and a tight fitting cream suit, sat down next to her. The woman's husband wore T-shirt and jeans, and carried too much weight for his years.

'Can I get a drink?' he enquired of a passing stewardess.

He received a less than warm stare at his idiotic question.

'When we're in the air,' replied the attendant.

Svetlana, sensing the possibility of conversation from her travelling companions, looked out of the window, knowing that somewhere her mother would still be waiting and watching. Above, a worker, wrapped up against the morning cold, stood on a gantry and directed a de-icing gun at the wing. The window was suddenly opaque as thick green fluid was sent in Svetlana's direction, and she recoiled from it.

'Fasten your seat belt, madam,' said the stewardess, her voice stripped of emotion by years of routine.

The blonde had mixed up the belts.

'I think you've got mine,' said Svetlana.

Her neighbour took this as an accusation and bristled as she followed the line of the belt to its root, only to see Svetlana was right. She undid it, her face softening, and offered it up.

'Sorry,' she said.

'No problem,' replied Svetlana.

By now, the captain had started the engines and the rocking of the plane disguised the shaking of her own body.

'Are you going on holiday?' enquired the blonde.

'Not really.'

'We are. We've got a place in Puerto Banus. Do you like it there?'

'Never been.'

Her tone, which signalled a lack of enthusiasm for further conversation, was ignored.

'Oh, you've got to go. I mean, the yachts and the shopping. It's just great.'

Svetlana looked out of the window as the plane began to taxi, hoping for a last glimpse of her dear mother before this machine lifted her from Russian soil and placed her down somewhere far away, as a stranger.

'And I got this ring there. What do you think?'

'It's lovely,' lied Svetlana.

'Anyway, as I say, you need to – Are you okay? You don't look so good.'

'Just tired,' replied Svetlana, closing her eyes and putting her head back.

*

With the time difference, it was still only lunchtime as the plane commenced its final descent into Malaga. Svetlana had not been able to sleep, but had kept her eyes shut most of the way to avoid contact with anybody, opening them occasionally when it was necessary to escape the cruellest episodes of her daydreams.

She looked down at the mountains with their red-tinged soil, and the blue sea, which became larger in the near horizon. There should have been hope in this new beginning, but as the ground came towards her she felt only approaching despair. The plane made its way out over the sea and then turned for the runway, landing a couple of minutes later with a thud, which shook the passengers before their seat belts restrained them against the fierce braking. Outside, the spring sun shone brightly from a clear blue sky as the wing turned in the direction of the terminal, closely followed by its shadow on the tarmac.

'Bit of a heavy landing, that one,' said the blonde.

Svetlana's Garden

Svetlana nodded and managed a weak smile before closing her eyes again. Moments later, she felt her hand being taken and looked to see be-ringed fingers press a blister pack of pills into her palm.

'Take two of these, no alcohol mind. They'll help you sleep. Looks like you need it.'

*

Outside, she shuffled towards the front of the queue, her eyes once again hidden behind large sunglasses. The temperature had reached twenty-two centigrade. A few posters in Russian had led her to believe that maybe the taxi driver could speak her language, but she received only a blank stare in response to her enquiry as he placed her case in the boot of his car.

'Here, please,' she said, in English.

She held out the handwritten note that Vasiliy had given her, which bore the address of Dubnikov's place.

The driver inspected it, frowned, then punched coordinates into his sat-nav, watching it intently as it plotted a route.

'No problem,' he said, turning to hand her back the note. 'You Russian?'

'Yes.'

'Many Russians – good for business.'

She nodded as he eyed her in the mirror. She didn't feel like talking, especially in English.

Ten minutes later, they were on the autoroute heading into the mountains from where she could look down upon the coastal towns and the glistening water beyond. Svetlana could hardly remember when she'd last seen the sea. It had been many years before, when she'd had a week in Sochi with her mother and Ivan. Her phone bleeped to indicate an incoming message. She opened it with trepidation and turned the screen away from the sun to better read the text.

Ivan safe with me. Have explained and told him we will be together. Call when you can darling. All my love, Mum.

Svetlana's Garden

Svetlana gasped in air and covered her face with her hand as a wave of relief swept through her. She shut her eyes, recalled her son's last embrace, and longed to feel it again, but realised that moment would be a long time coming. Malenkov had kept his word – and retained his power of life and death over her family to ensure her good behaviour. She opened her bag and removed the simply-framed picture of Ivan that her mother had taken from the sideboard in her apartment. She pressed the image to her lips. There was relief in his safety, but hope was too distant to yet be real. They drove on.

'Marbella,' said the taxi driver tapping his thumb on his window.

Svetlana looked down on the town whose name she'd heard many times but which she knew little about. It was supposed to have charm, she'd heard, but if it did it was not obvious from her elevated view. Soon, they left the motorway and headed higher up the mountainside following the female-voiced directions of the sat-nav that led them to the electronic-gated entrance of a palatial property, which was surrounded by a three-metre-high whitewashed wall. Clearly, crime paid well. The driver let out a low whistle as he surveyed the property his meagre income could never hope to afford.

'Yours?' he asked, in English.

'No, a friend.'

'Eees special friend,' he responded, counting imaginary banknotes with his fingers.

Svetlana paid him what he asked. It seemed a lot compared to Moscow, but she had no idea whether she'd been conned or not, although she presumed so as it would have been unthinkable for a Moscow taxi transporting a stranger to a dacha outside the city not to take advantage. A dust cloud, thrown up from the departing car, obscured the view of the town below and she was left standing alone next to her suitcase. Through the gates, immaculate lawns stood either side of a long tree-lined driveway, which led to a large white villa. Columns held up the roof of an open marble porch and balconies fronted every upstairs window. She rang the bell on the gatepost and waited, looking down at her feet to see her shoes lightly dusted with fine sand. With a slight shudder, the giant gates separated and whirred as they opened. Svetlana moved forward, pulling her suitcase behind her, which rocked uncertainly as its small castors rumbled across the red tarmac drive. The Spanish sun touched the back of her neck with warmth, but her heart remained in the grip of a cold Moscow winter as her laboured steps took her nearer to the carved oak front door, which began to open.

Svetlana stopped at the edge of the porch, then looked up to see a woman, somewhat older than herself and not so tall, but slim. She had perfect olive skin, which complemented her immaculate, highlighted, dark blonde hair. She wore an elegant knee-length maroon dress and no jewellery, save for gold stud earrings.

'Welcome, Svetlana Yuriyevna. I am Rosa,' she said, in accented but correct Russian. 'I am Roman Dubnikov's housekeeper.'

'Hello, Rosa. Please call me Svetlana, or Sveta, if you prefer.'

'I was very sorry to hear of your loss. Roman has asked me to help you in any way I can.'

'That's kind of you.'

'Come on in, you must be tired.'

In the circular entrance hall, five doors faced a sweeping staircase, which separated at its summit and lead onto a first floor balcony.

'Would you like something to eat?' asked Rosa.

'I'm not really hungry, but could I have a bath?'

'Of course. Leave your case and I'll bring it up.'

Svetlana followed Rosa somewhat unsteadily up the stairs.

'I thought you'd like this room. You can see the sea and the lights of the town look good at night.'

Shutters over the windows were partially open and net curtains, swaying in the breeze, brushed against the heavier lemon drapes that accompanied them. A gigantic bed was covered with a gold spread above crisp cream sheets and an antique dressing table played host to fresh spring flowers.

'In here,' said Rosa, opening the door to the en-suite bathroom. It was bigger than Svetlana's living room back in Moscow and must have cost more than her whole apartment was worth. 'There's a robe for you on the back of the door. Run the water and I'll bring your things up.'

A little later, Svetlana slipped into the warm water and draped her arms over the side of the bath while the built-in Jacuzzi began to gently massage her tired limbs. A long soak was something she normally relished as an occasional treat, but her aching heart would not let her enjoy it, as her mind wandered to images of Nick's pale body, lifeless and stripped of all its dignity. Guilt nagged at her that she could not even kneel at the graveside of her husband and whisper to him of her desire to be reunited with him in death, one day. Her eyelids were heavy with fatigue, but every time she closed them there were images of Nick's dying breaths, his eyes rolling backwards as the gas finally took him. She missed him utterly and feared for her sanity.

*

Later, as Svetlana descended the stairs, she could smell garlic and fish wafting up from one of the partially open doors below. She wore a pair of loose-fitting linen trousers, which Rosa had pressed while she was bathing and had laid out on her bed, along with a matching top.

She peered nervously round the door and Rosa turned.

'Come in, Svetlana. I have made paella. Do you like it?'

'I've never tried it,' replied Svetlana.

'Then you must. Come, sit on the terrace. It will be ready in fifteen minutes.'

'Can I ring my son, first?'

'Of course... I'm sorry, I should have offered.'

Rosa showed Svetlana into a study and left her sitting at a desk bearing a computer and a telephone. Her hand trembling, she reached for the receiver and began to dial. Malenkov would undoubtedly have his people listening in and would also know where she was, but it didn't matter any more. All he would hear was family sentiment, just as he wanted.

'Mama, it's Sveta... I'm okay, Mum. I'm safe. I've arrived at the house. Are you all right... and Ivan?'

'Yes, dear, I'm fine. Ivan is here and waiting to speak to you.'

'Mum, are you all right?'

'Ivanushka, is that you? Darling I'm so sorry. Has granny told you...?'

'I miss you, Mum...'

'I miss you too, but I have to stay here for a while...'

'Will we be together again, Mum...?'

'Yes, Vanya, we will, I promise...'

Svetlana did her best to reassure Ivan, securing his word that he'd look after his grandmother while they were apart and concentrate on his studies. Ivan told her that they were going to purchase a webcam the next day and when she called again they would be able see each other. She put the receiver down, relieved to have heard her son's voice and distracted by it, but she still carried the feeling that something was wrong. Nick was dead and this breath of fresh air was expelled as she was pulled back under the waves of despair.

Svetlana heard a soft tapping on the study door, before Rosa's face appeared.

'Come, Svetlana, it's ready.'

'Really, I'm not hungry.'

Rosa stepped fully into the room and folded her arms.

'Roman Stepanovich said you could be difficult. If you faint with hunger, I have to pick you up, so eat, please.'

Svetlana, shamed at the prospect of being not a guest but an imposition, sighed, stood and followed Rosa to the terrace at the back of the property. She sat in a white cast-iron chair and took in the patterned orange tiles, interspersed with large potted plants, while a substantial sun umbrella cloaked the table in semi-shade. Rosa returned with two plates of golden paella and placed them down next to a bottle of Coma Blanca, well chilled, as evidenced by the condensation clinging to it. She sat opposite Svetlana and nudged a plate towards her.

'Come on, eat,' said Rosa, as she poured them each a glass of wine.

Svetlana picked up a fork and brought a few grains of rice to her mouth. She had to admit the taste was delicious as she scooped up some more under Rosa's watchful eye.

'Delicious.'

'All Spanish girls can make this. Our mothers teach us.'

'My mum taught me to cook.'

'Of course. Do you speak any Spanish, Svetlana?'

'I'm afraid not.'

'I will teach you. You can get by in English here, but you miss so much. There are English people here over twenty years who still don't speak Spanish. It's crazy.'

'Where did you learn Russian?'

'Moscow. I studied mathematics at Moscow State University. It's where I met my husband.'

'What does he do?'

'Nothing: he's dead.'

'I'm sorry.'

'So, we share a loss. I should have known – should have stopped him. He worked part-time for Roman's father to supplement his income while he was studying, just errands and stuff like that. I wanted to come back to Spain, so we moved here and Eduard – that was his name – started to work full-time for the Dubnikovs, managing their connections here.'

'So he was part of the gang?'

'A criminal, yes, but I loved him, so there was no choice. Anyway, one day he didn't come back, and that night I had to drive all the way to La Linea to identify his body.'

'I'm so sorry.'

Rosa lifted her head and looked at Svetlana, who held her gaze.

'We choose our men, Svetlana Yuriyevna, but after that love chooses our fate. Come, eat some more.'

*

It was after eleven when she woke. The night before, and despite the wine, she had taken two of the pills her air travel companion had given her. She didn't know what was in them, but combined with her increasing fatigue they'd certainly done the job. The sound of a piano reached her. She knew the piece well: Tchaikovsky's *Reverie du Soir*. Her father had played it many times when she was a child, before they'd had to sell his treasured Krasniy.

The cool tiles soothed her bare feet as she made her way down the stairs to seek out the source of the music. Rosa was sitting at a pitch-black baby grand, her fingers deftly moving across the keys, managing emphasis where required but seemingly without applying pressure. She saw Svetlana and stopped playing.

'Did I wake you?'

'No, not at all. My father played this.'

'Mine too,' responded Rosa. 'I don't usually stay but I wanted to see you were okay.'

'I'm fine.'

'Come on, I'll show you where everything is. Do you want coffee?'

*

Over the next month, Rosa drove down every day from her house in Antequera, invariably finding Svetlana sitting on the terrace with tracks of recent tears that evidenced an ongoing struggle with her melancholia. Nevertheless, out of respect for the housekeeper, Svetlana practised Spanish with Rosa, and made good progress.

She spoke to her mother and Ivan every day, mindful to pick her words carefully as Malenkov's men would undoubtedly be monitoring their communications. Jack Freeman had flown from Madrid to see her the previous weekend and had assured her that when she was ready there'd be work for her, although that was the last thing on her mind. She'd put it off for a while, worried they might blame her for their son's death, but Svetlana had eventually gathered the courage to email Nick's mother and father to tell them where she was. Their response had been instant and reassuring, helped by the fact that Jack had filled them in on the situation, at least as far as he could. They'd flown from Boston to Madrid without hesitation, before catching a connecting flight to Malaga.

Svetlana didn't know how long she'd been standing behind the door, nervously examining her rather ragged fingernails, but when the bell sounded it startled her. She reached for the handle and pulled it towards her. Bright light from the setting sun behind them left the faces of Juan and Larisa Mendez in shadow, but as they stepped forward at Svetlana's beckoning she could instantly see Nick's eyes in those of his father. He was a tall man, with a moustache and swept-back greying hair, while his wife was still blessed by good looks built around high cheekbones and framed by immaculate, short blonde hair. Larisa spoke first, in Russian, her Samara accent still noticeable.

'He told us all about you and we're so glad we came. I'm Larisa and this is Juan, although he likes "John" these days.'

Svetlana felt her composure cracking, before she was smothered in the embraces of her new in-laws, their grief collective and raw.

When the tears had dried, she took them to the terrace for tea and orange juice.

'He was always a bit of a rebel,' said Larisa.

'But in a good way,' interrupted Juan.

'Yes, dear, in a good way, of course. We brought you some photographs. We had copies made,' said Larisa, placing them in Svetlana's trembling hands.

She looked through them one by one, each a stepping stone to their eventual union and the fate their love had now delivered.

'I will treasure them,' said Svetlana softly.

She and Larisa made supper of sea bass and salad, while Juan sat outside holding the smoke from his cigar in his mouth, as if fearful that once breathed out his memories might float away with it. His wife and Svetlana looked at him through the window.

'John misses him terribly. He feels guilty for being ill at the time of the wedding.'

'That wasn't his fault,' said Svetlana.

'Of course not, but it's just that – well – he still had conversations. They didn't always get along so well when he was younger, but later they were close... still things to say.'

Svetlana nodded and shut her eyes before opening them again when she felt Larisa squeeze her hand.

'Mr Dubnikov, the man who owns this house, says mothers from Samara cannot help themselves and that they always love their sons.'

'They do, no matter what,' replied Larisa.

They swapped reminiscences from Yaroslavl and Samara over their meal, a clear moonlit sky and cheery background music of cicadas failing to lift the solemnity at the table.

'Would you like coffee?' asked Svetlana.

'It's late and we'd better get back to the hotel,' said Larisa, putting her hand on the back of Svetlana's hand.

At the door, they exchanged kisses and promises to keep in touch, before her two guests turned to leave. Juan looked back.

'What will you do, dear... in the future?'

'I don't know,' said Svetlana, 'I haven't really given the future much thought.'

Chapter 36

The natural stoicism that was part of the air in Moscow was not there to help her in Marbella. As the weeks passed, Svetlana spoke and thought mainly in Spanish, as Rosa had encouraged. She took to wearing black most of the time, despite the summer heat, and ate sporadically unless her housekeeper friend was around. The lustre of her hair had begun to fade and the corners of her mouth looked permanently turned down, whenever she looked in the mirror. An aching heart accompanied every conscious moment and listlessness affected her limbs.

She was sitting on the bottom step of the stairs, elbows on her knees and head in hands, when the doorbell sounded.

'Go away – please just go away,' she muttered.

It rang again. It seemed the visitor was particularly insistent. Wearily she stood and slid her feet across the marble hallway to open the door.

'Mrs Mendez, I wonder if I might come in?' said Peter Hubbard, removing his straw hat and holding it to his chest.

She was surprised to see who it was, and stood silently before collecting herself and waving to him to enter.

'Mr Hubbard, why are you here?'

'I'll explain. Perhaps there's somewhere we could sit?'

She led him through to the terrace, bidding him to take a chair.

'Would you like coffee?'

'Tea, if it's not too much trouble,' replied Hubbard.

She looked at him through the window while the kettle boiled, half expecting him to disappear in front of her eyes and return to his life in the shadows, where he and those like him seemed to live. *What does he want?*

'That's very kind,' said Hubbard, half rising from his chair as Svetlana put down his tea with milk, followed by a cup with lemon for her.

'What can I do for you?' she asked.

'I'm most terribly sorry for the loss of your husband. He was a fine man.'

'He was, but forgive me, Mr Hubbard, you didn't come here just to pass on your condolences.'

'Indeed.'

He rubbed his chin and then placed his hands together palm to palm, before continuing.

'We really are very grateful to both of you for what you did. There was denial and a lot of bluster, but the Russian authorities are being a lot more conciliatory now in their energy dealings.'

'And Andrei Petrov and Yakov Katenin – are they being conciliatory towards them?'

'I'm afraid not.'

'They are playing a game with you.'

'Perhaps: international relations can be complicated.'

'Is there something else, because I'm quite tired?'

Hubbard drew breath.

'Nick had a house – a villa – near Seville. It was registered to an offshore company and it's now effectively yours. We've taken the liberty of checking it for devices, but it's clean. If you have time, I could take you.'

For a moment Svetlana sat in stunned silence.

'A villa? Why didn't he tell me?'

'He told Jack Freeman he wanted to surprise you.'

She looked at Hubbard, unsure whether she should feel betrayed or excited.

'Take me there.'

Soon she was ready to leave, energised at the prospect of a connection to her departed love. Hubbard held open the door to his hired Mercedes as Svetlana slipped into the passenger seat.

'It's in a little place called Los Arrayanes, about twenty kilometres from Seville,' said Hubbard, releasing the handbrake.

Svetlana willed the car to go faster, anxious to be there. She thought that Hubbard's sedate driving style contrasted with the danger that she supposed was attached to his profession.

'How long will it take?' she asked.

'We'll be there by lunchtime.'

They climbed up through the mountains that looked down on the coast, passed Ronda, and then began their descent to the gently rolling land below. As they drove, the coastal breeze that had followed them receded. The air fell still and the temperature outside rose to over forty degrees. Vast splashes of colour from sunflowers, lavender and irrigated green fields rolled out before them like a giant, living canvas shimmering under a fierce sun.

An hour and a half later they were on Seville's outer ring road and crossed the Guadalquivir River before turning south for their destination. Svetlana's sense of anticipation grew stronger as they approached. Her hands gripped the seat and her eyes peered out, determined to be the first to catch sight of the place her beloved Nick had so frequently stayed.

'Down here,' said Hubbard, pointing.

He turned the car into a dusty track, then drove on for another two hundred metres through trees that towered overhead, until they reached a sand-coloured wall topped with pale, red coping stones. She wound down the window and listened to the tyres pressing into the gravel below, surprised by the wave of heat, which overwhelmed the air conditioning. Hubbard pulled the car to a stop.

'Is this it?'

He nodded and in seconds Svetlana was making for the round arch that framed double wooden entrance gates, just too tall for her to see over. She tried the round cast-iron handle but it refused to budge.

'Here... your keys,' said Hubbard, stretching out his hand.

Svetlana almost snatched them from him, straining to identify the correct key. She tried one in the large lock and then another that with a slight, grating protest turned under her hand's guidance. This time, the handle lifted and she pushed open the gate just wide enough to step inside, before glancing back at Hubbard.

'I'll wait,' he said.

There it was, an elegant white house with a terracotta roof, a monument to her husband – and now her home. She stood to view it all, her palms pressed flat against the gate behind her. In front of her, almost the entire area leading to the house, some thirty metres away, was covered with large, inlaid octagonal tiles, a jigsaw that depicted a field of vibrant sunflowers. At intervals, the tiles gave way to islands of earth allowing at least ten olive trees to stand and cast their intricate shadows on the ground. Her eyes widened as she took in the scene, accompanied by the insistent afternoon heat.

She stroked the leaves of the first tree while advancing towards the house, a rustling welcome greeting her in return. She felt quite light-headed in the heat, not helped by having skipped breakfast once again. A bead of perspiration slowly traversed her temple as she neared the building and caught sight of the grounds beyond. A lawn, in need of cutting but apparently watered by a sprinkler system, led up to a kidney-shaped pool, which was overlooked by a marble terrace and still more olive trees, hemmed in by a high hedge. Svetlana carried on, stopping by the water to look at her reflection. She reached in and swept her hand from right to left sending ripples to the far side, like emissaries carrying news of her arrival. Something beckoned her towards the hedge, where a shadowed opening invited curiosity. Her nostrils twitched. She held her blouse loose from her chest as sweat threatened to make it cling, as she stepped through the gap in the hedge. Despite the heat, she shivered, because facing her was a garden, just as she'd imagined it as a child: a swathe of wild flowers allowed to run free below a host of fruit-laden orange trees, their sweet scent pervading the air and filling her lungs. Ahead lay a clearing with a crescent-shaped wooden bench and a stone table, stained by blossom long departed.

She sat down, closed her eyes and remembered childhood Yaroslavl, the sound of her mother singing Rybasov's *None But You* fresh in her mind. She began to sing it, now knowing where her mother's extraordinary emotion had come from, as Svetlana too serenaded a lost love. The last few words tailed away as the sunlight sneaking through the leaves danced upon her eyelids.

A short while later, the front door opened with a groan from its hinges, to reveal a large living room with rich ochre tiles and two large settees covered in natural linen. A wood-burning stove sat under a close-brick chimney and in the corner was a modest flat-screen television. Svetlana entered and moved to the first window. She pulled at the cord and raised the shutter, releasing waiting light to reveal a small scorpion scurrying for cover. She ran her finger across the top of a settee before turning and opening French windows to the terrace outside. Behind her, a corridor revealed other rooms, the first of which she instinctively knew, as she touched the handle, was his bedroom. Inside, were a large cast-iron framed bed and a bamboo chest of drawers, on top of which sat a porcelain tray, which held sets of cuff-links, all covered with a fine layer of dust. She slid open the louvered door of the wardrobe and saw a selection of his clothes, relieved to see nothing indicating the previous presence of another woman, although she realised he must have brought them there. She removed a white cotton shirt from its hanger before pressing it to her face as she sat on the edge of the bed. She drew a deep breath through the fabric and into her nostrils, sure that there was a lingering trace of his scent to add to her memories. Svetlana clasped the garment to her and lay on the bed with knees drawn up towards her chest.

'Oh, Nicholas, I love you and I miss you so much.'

Chapter 37

In the months that passed, Svetlana did some freelance research for Jack Freeman about Russian expat communities. He would occasionally come to visit her, with his wife. Back in Moscow, Ivan had done well with his studies, anxious as he was to please his mother and, in his own way, to look after her. Their collective adversity had apparently given him a new set of priorities: his surly, monosyllabic conversation was no longer evident. They spoke and saw see each other daily on the internet, and a new sense developed between them to compensate for the loss of close-quarter communication. Svetlana regretted the burden that she watched him carry, even though he did his best to disguise it.

Ten minutes of conversation had already passed between them that day.

'How's Misha?' she enquired.

'He's good, but I beat him in the maths test on Monday.'

She smiled her approval.

'Granny said you'd been very helpful with the shopping.'

'There's new bags at the supermarket. I think they're a bit heavy for her.'

'How's your English coming along, Vanya?'

'There are so many rules, it's difficult. Is Spanish easier?'

'Rosa – you know, my friend – she comes here most days and teaches me.'

'Will she teach me?'

'I'll ask, but I'm sure she'll be okay with it.'

'I miss you, Mum.'

Ivan was looking straight into her eyes as she caught her breath, and fought to keep some composure. She reached out her hand to touch the screen, stroking his cheek.

'We should be together soon, Ivanushka. I'll ask Granny to speak to them.'

'I know where to go. I'll ask.'

'Vanya, no, I don't want you going there.'

'I'm not afraid.'

*

Ivan was stubborn, just like his father, but she'd made her mother promise to talk to him and try to keep him away from Malenkov. The FSB captain had said a couple of years had to pass without trouble and she didn't want anything antagonising him, even though it had been fifteen months since she'd left Moscow.

The bell sounded. Svetlana opened the door to see Rosa standing there.

'It's Saturday. We're going into Sevilla for food and flamenco,' she said, in Spanish.

'I don't really feel like it,' replied Svetlana, also in Spanish, as Rosa had insisted.

'Sveta, enough! We're going. Get changed... and don't wear anything black!'

'I've got work to do,' said the reporter, pointing to a pile of papers next to the computer.

Rosa walked over, sorted the papers into a pile and then stuffed them in the desk drawer.

'Tomorrow.'

Svetlana capitulated and turned for her bedroom. Once there, she opened the wardrobe and let her hand skip one by one across the hangers of her small collection of clothes, stopping at the deep-red cotton dress she'd bought as a reluctant guest at the wedding of Rosa's niece, earlier in the year. She slipped into her bath robe to put on some make-up, only to find that her mascara had congealed, so long had it remained unused.

'You got any?' asked Svetlana, looking through the doorway and holding the dried-up brush for Rosa to see.

Her Spanish friend shook her head and then smiled as she reached into her handbag before following Svetlana into the bedroom.

'Here,' said Rosa, handing over her own mascara. 'What are you doing with your hair?'

'Is there time to wash it?'

'You don't need to. It's fine. I'll do it for you.'

Rosa picked up the patterned hairbrush from the dressing table. She stood behind Svetlana, who watched as with slow, steady strokes, Rosa smoothed then gathered the thick, black hair together before pulling it back and forming a tight bun at the back.

'Put your dress on,' said Rosa, turning for the door.

She returned moments later, carrying a cream lace shawl, which she put round Svetlana's shoulders.

'It's a present, for you.'

'I can't do that.'

'Be quiet, it's done now, anyway. Now, let me look at you. Not bad – not bad, at all.'

Svetlana sat back on the dressing table stool to look in the mirror. She was surprised to feel Rosa's hands on her head.

'Stay still, Sveta. I have something else for you,' said Rosa, clipping a small, red silk carnation to the hair above her friend's temple.

While she had largely avoided the sun, time in Andalucía had inevitably brought some colour to her previously pale complexion, and while her skin didn't have Rosa's olive tint, Svetlana could nevertheless blend in with the locals of Seville on that late summer evening.

*

Forty minutes later, the two young widows walked arm in arm along the banks of the Guadalquivir, joined by citizens promenading before dinner. A handsome middle-aged couple came towards them and passed by, the two women sharing a glance without speaking of what might have been. They stopped for a drink and watched the evening light change while they sipped water and picked at a small bowl of green olives. Around them, the city geared up for a long night ahead.

As the hour approached ten o'clock, they entered Tablao El Arenal, in Calle Rodo, where Rosa had made a reservation. Hanging lanterns and wooden beams looked down on rows of square tables below, which led up to a stage at the head of the room. Giant painted portraits of flamenco performers shared wall space with more modest prints, while knowing locals distinguished themselves from the tourists occupying tables in the corner. They were shown to their seats and Rosa ordered some wine to accompany the forthcoming meal.

'It's time you came out more.'

'I don't feel comfortable,' replied Svetlana.

'Then drink some of this,' said Rosa, filling their glasses.

They'd barely started their first course, when the sound of strong chords from a guitar announced the start of the show. The guitarist stepped alone onto the stage and sat. Svetlana watched his fingers flow backwards and forwards across the strings, bidding the passion within the instrument to reveal itself. Rhythmic clapping accompanied a troupe of dancers who swept in. Over dinner, Svetlana watched as colours, movements and sounds blended together to deliver their stories of passion, tragedy and of love, lost or stolen. She saw faces in the audience rise or fall, as music and the aching longing of the soloist's voice broke down defences to allow the soldiers of joy or sorrow to break through. She saw it all and understood what was happening to them but her own heavy heart would not stir beyond the merely functional role it had assumed.

'Look,' said Rosa, tapping the back of Svetlana's hand and pointing across the room.

Two men, smartly dressed and standing, stared at them.

'They look okay,' she continued.

Loud applause greeted the end of the show as waiters in black bow ties swooped on tables to clear away abandoned dishes.

'I'm going to the ladies',' said Svetlana, rising from her chair.

Her path took her straight towards their admirers and she fixed them with a stare as she approached.

'Go home to your wives,' she said coldly as she passed by, leaving them to work out the secret behind her accent.

*

She wasn't to know it, but Raisa Dorenko had picked a good day to plead her grandson's case. Malenkov was distracted, puffed up with pride at his promotion and, in his own mind, now moving to higher things than dealing with the likes of Ivan.

'Captain Malenkov, it's been a while, now.'

'Actually, it's Colonel.'

'Excuse me?'

'It's Colonel Malenkov, now.'

'I see. Well, congratulations, Colonel.'

'Thank you. So, Raisa Konstantinova, what can I do for you?'

'The boy misses his mother and it's been so long since he's seen her.'

'And you want me to let him go to be with her?'

'He's so young.'

'He can go. She seems to have learnt her lesson. But, if there's any more trouble – any more slanderous material – I may have to reconsider.'

'There won't be, Colonel, trust me.'

'I hope you are more trustworthy than your daughter. However, as a little insurance, you will stay in Moscow. Is that understood?'

'I understand.'

'I'm glad you do. Well, if you'll excuse me, I have a meeting to attend,' said Malenkov, as he held the door open for Raisa to leave.

As Raisa left, Malenkov's assistant stepped in to speak to him.

'I know you're in a hurry, but I thought you might like to know about this.'

Il'ya handed him an envelope, which the FSB colonel opened, and drew out a photograph.

'Well, well, interesting indeed, Il'ya. It seems Colonel Chernekov continues to have some dubious friends. When was this taken?'

'Last night, sir.'

'Hmmn... Okay, let's file it for now, but I have a feeling that might be useful before too long.'

Malenkov smiled, grabbed his jacket, and made his way down to his driver who was waiting to take him to the Ministry for Energy.

A short while later, he once again faced deputy energy minister Kutaisov.

'Thank you for coming over, Colonel. Would you like some coffee?'

Malenkov was surprised to be offered this courtesy, feeling that on previous occasions his presence could best be described as tolerated, rather than valued.

'Yes, please, Deputy Minister.'

Kutaisov signalled to his aide to bring coffee.

'We were quite impressed with your efforts to help us clean up the problems we had in Georgia last year.'

'Thank you, Deputy Minister.'

'We have another issue that's – well – delicate.'

'How can I help?'

'For some months now we have been in negotiation with our friends in Kiev about gas prices, but I cannot say our efforts are being met with the appropriate measure of respect.'

'I'm sorry to hear that.'

Kutaisov raised his hand to silence Malenkov.

'There are elections coming up and it might be to the advantage of the citizens of Ukraine to have a government which was more constructive in its dealings with Russia. If that was the case, we could perhaps be more sensitive in our approach to the price of gas.'

'You want me to deal with a politician?'

'No, no, Colonel, if we deal with Trublayevskiy that way, there's a danger of a sympathy vote for his party. Leave that to us, but we want to learn lessons from the affair with Svetlana Dorenko and Mr Mendez. We don't want that kind of publicity this time. It's bad for business.'

Malenkov nodded, cautious about speaking again until he was invited. The deputy minister continued.

'Trublayevskiy has a press secretary, Bogdan Goncharenko, a former newspaper editor. Unfortunately, he's unusually well informed about energy matters and feeds not only his boss but his foreign political contacts too. There will be an argument about energy for the voters to consider, while they struggle to keep themselves warm, and Trublayevskiy's argument will be considerably weaker without that man.'

'I will deal with it, Deputy Minister.'

'Timing is everything, Colonel. I don't want them having time to regroup and I want us distanced from it.'

'It's perfect for the gas: there will be no trace. I will make the arrangements. Is there anything else, Deputy Minister?'

'No, thank you, Colonel, that is all.'

Malenkov rose from his chair and half turned.

'Oh, thank you for the coffee, Deputy Minister.'

*

Rosa had stayed over and the sun was already high when she and Svetlana rose for a late breakfast. They took to the terrace outside, where, even beneath the sunshade, the temperature had climbed well past thirty degrees.

'Juice?' asked Svetlana, holding up a jug of freshly squeezed orange, the product of her beloved garden.

Rosa nodded, as she pushed the balance of a glazed pastry into her mouth, sign language indicating that conversation would have to wait a while. She finished chewing before taking a sip of her drink.

'Roman Stepanovich is coming next week.'

'Yeah?'

'On Friday... he's just sent me a text. Do you want to see him?'

Svetlana felt the familiar sense of ambivalence towards Dubnikov that she'd had right from the beginning. He'd made profit on the back of the misery of others, but in a strange way she missed him.

'Not really.'

'He did help you out.'

Rosa's logic and tone were both compelling. Svetlana smiled in defeat.

'Will he come here? You know I hate driving on that coastal road.'

'I'll bring him.'

Rosa took another drink, waving away a small wasp with the back of her other hand.

'Those guys last night looked a bit shocked. What did you say to them?'

'Told them to go home to their wives.'

'They would do. They'd probably just stopped off after work, anyway.'

'Stopped off?'

'For recreation... at Tino's or Salvador.'

'Huh, I wouldn't be surprised if Dubnikov owns those places too.'

Rosa smiled.

'Is that what they do here?' continued Svetlana.

'Some of them.'

'Your husband?'

'No.'

'You sure?'

'I'm sure, Svetlana Yuriyevna,' said Rosa, switching to Russian.

Rosa carried on, reverting to Spanish.

'I have to take my mother to her sister's in Albacete next week. Will you be okay?'

'I have work to do for Jack Freeman,' she replied, pointing in the vague direction of her desk.

'It does get a bit better, you know.'

Svetlana looked at Rosa, whose shoulders the sun was beginning to touch as it moved round. She shaded her eyes with her hand to better see her Spanish companion's compassionate face.

'You develop a way to cope,' said Rosa. 'You know, a not too bad way of dealing with it.'

'Right,' said Svetlana, examining her nails.

*

'Hello, darling, how are you today?' said her mother, as Svetlana looked back into the webcam.

'I'm okay, Mum.'

'I went to see Mr Malenkov. He's been promoted – a colonel now. He says Ivan can leave.'

Svetlana's eyes widened and she reached forward to grab each side of the screen, shaking it, willing it to reveal more.

'When, Mum? When can he leave?'

'In eight weeks, at the end of the school term.'

'You can bring him then?'

Her mother looked down, suddenly silent, and bit her lip.

'Mum, you can bring him – right – in eight weeks?'

'I cannot come, dear,' replied her mother, in a voice barely above a whisper.

'Why not?'

'Colonel Malenkov says I must remain. It's for the best.'

'No, no, it's not for the best!'

'Ivan will return to you and that is the most important thing.'

'You're both important. Mama, I miss you so much.'

'And I miss you, darling, but your father was right and we simply can't have all the things we wish for.'

'Why, Mama? What is so wrong about wanting to have my mother and son together? What is such a threat to the state, to Malenkov and all the pigs that work with him?'

'Darling, I don't think it's wise to talk like that,' said her mother, putting a finger to her lips to call for silence. 'I assured Colonel Malenkov there'd be no more trouble.'

'I'm sick of this.'

'Darling, please... for Ivan!'

Svetlana let go of the screen and sat back on the chair, frustration once again suppressed by the implicit power that the FSB, in the form of Malenkov, could wield. She drew a breath and then sighed.

'I'll look for a school for him.'

'Good, Sveta, that would be good. He can learn Spanish. Look, dear, I can see you're upset. Be happy for Ivan and we can speak again tomorrow, when you'll be feeling better.'

'Mum, it's not right.'

'Enough, darling, let's speak more tomorrow. I love you. Bye, for now.'

'Bye, Mama.'

Svetlana stared at the screen, her mother's image now gone. Her already beaten and bruised emotions struggled, as relief that Ivan could join her wrestled with despair that her dear mother, a hostage of her own motherland, could not. She looked across the room where she saw the bottle of Rioja that Rosa had brought as a gift, the night before.

The second glass saw her slow down, although, right then, as she sat cross-legged and watched a moth repeatedly throw itself at the siren lamp outside the window, she had no wish to hold back the temptation her first husband had found so irresistible as a way of escaping his woes.

*

Roman Dubnikov's mother sang to herself as she prepared *pirozhki* in the kitchen of her *dacha* on the outskirts of Samara, bought for her by her son some years before. She glanced at the clock on the wall, calculating that they would still be warm when he arrived. She was proud that he was taking the trouble to visit her, instead of flying straight from Moscow to Malaga as he usually did.

Her gardener stepped through the back door and removed a pair of working gloves.

'I've fixed the fence by the second field and trimmed the trees behind.'

'That's great. The whole place looks better since you started working on it. Do you want some *kvas* or a beer?'

'When will Roman be here?'

'In about an hour.'

'Some *kvas*, then... I'll have a beer with him when he arrives, if that's okay.'

'Help yourself. You know where it is,' said Rozaliya Dubnikova, putting a baking tray in the oven and closing the door.

She busied herself by setting the table and then made up the room for her son. Later, from the top of the stairs, she heard a key in the lock and made her way down as quickly as she could.

'Roman!'

'Mama!'

She put her arms around him in a tight hug.

'I'm so proud of you. You're such a good boy.'

Chapter 38

'I'm sure your son will be very happy here. We've had a lot of foreign-born children, including some Russians and they've all settled well.'

'Thank you, Señora Aido, that's good to know.'

'Would you like to see the rest of the grounds? We have quite an emphasis on sport here.'

'Ivan is very keen on that.'

'Good, come on, please follow me.'

Svetlana followed the principal as she took her on a tour of the school, the fifth she'd seen in four days and, she was relieved to feel, the one that Ivan would be attending when the new term started.

'Would Señor Mendez also like to see around, do you think?'

'My husband was killed last year, I'm afraid.'

'I'm so terribly sorry.'

'It's all right, Señora Aido, I understand. Just so you know, Nick was not Ivan's father. He was a journalist, posted to Moscow.'

'Of course: Nick Mendez, of INN?'

'Yes.'

'The students would watch him as part of their English lessons.'

'It is a tragic loss and I'm very sorry.'

'Thank you. He and Ivan didn't really have time to get close.'

'We will handle it sensitively. That is, I'm assuming you think we'd be right for Ivan.'

Svetlana surveyed the impressive, white painted *cortijo* rising up behind the principal and the expansive grounds surrounding it.

'Yes, Señora Aido, that's what I think,' said Svetlana, extending her hand.

*

She'd shopped the day before, so there was food and drink on that Saturday when Rosa was due to bring Dubnikov down to Los Arrayanes. Her friend had insisted that she would cook, determined as she was to provide some authentic Spanish cuisine. So, Svetlana had merely to set the table for a late lunch and put some rosé in the fridge to chill, along with one concession to Dubnikov – a bottle of his favourite Saproshin vodka.

Rosa had been right – and wrong. It had become easier to function superficially with the benefit of routine, but just below the surface time had healed nothing at all. Svetlana's desperate sense of loss was as raw as ever and bouts of deep melancholia could take her at any time, as they had that day, exacerbated by the prospect of unending physical separation from her mother. At such times she took refuge in the garden, where she could close her eyes and recall childhood dreams of a place where everything would be special, removed from Soviet hardship.

She'd not gone so far as to give the trees names, but it felt to her as she walked through the hedge that each one had become a friend, greeting her benignly as she passed. The sun beat down relentlessly, hanging on to the last of the season's heat, and the leaves, kept short of water, had hardened the tone of their rustle as the wind brushed them against each other. Her limbs felt heavy, seemingly unable to support even the weight of the simple, brown cotton dress she was wearing. In her mind, deep clouds rolled overhead, even as the sun shone. Placing her hand down to take her weight, Svetlana lowered herself to the wooden bench where she'd spent so much time since her arrival. Normally, with eyes closed and sense filled with the smell of oranges, she'd have the power to direct her mind back to dreams formed in childhood – but today was different. She feared she was finally losing the last vestiges of strength that had somehow allowed her to repeatedly ward off thoughts of a selfish suicide. She tried to revive those Yaroslavl imaginings, but after a few seconds images of Nick failing before her eyes and of Malenkov's malevolent sneer would break through. It seemed that despair had chosen this date, at this place, for a final battle over her sanity, cruelly not waiting for tomorrow, when she might have felt a little better. With eyes clenched tightly shut, she imagined her mortal body slipping from the bench to disintegrate, blown away by the wind as particles of sand, and merging with the surrounding carpet of flowers.

She was suddenly startled by a hand on her shoulder. She opened her eyes as Dubnikov took a seat on the bench beside her.

'Svetlana, long time no see. I thought you were in a trance there,' he said, in Russian.

She rubbed her eyes, adjusting to the light, and then focused on his pale unshaven face, a slight smell of alcohol on his breath.

'Roman – sorry – I was daydreaming.'

'So, are you pleased to see me?'

'Of course. How's Moscow?'

'Busy.'

'And, your journey?'

'From Samara... went to see my mother. You know how mothers from Samara love their sons. Sveta, you don't look too good.'

'I've not been very well.'

Dubnikov sat back, slowly shaking his head from side to side.

Rosa appeared at the archway in the hedge.

'Come and get a drink, you two.'

'In a minute,' said Dubnikov, waving her away.

He turned his attention back to Svetlana.

'Sveta, do you know a man called Vitaliy Kanatov?'

She didn't want questions and just wanted to be alone. She looked at Dubnikov who kept his eyes upon her, apparently insistent upon an answer.

'I don't think so. Wait a minute – FSB – lived near me in Moscow. A little boy was ill.'

'That's him: he works for me now.'

She fleetingly saw something she'd never seen before in the face of this gangster – compassion.

'He took care of a special thing for you and has sent it as a present.'

She looked down to see his hand press something into hers. It was a gold ring, the one she'd given to Nick at their wedding. She froze as her eyes took it in, the sun casting its double as a shadow on her open palm. A long pause followed, before she pressed it to her lips. She held it there with the tips of her fingers, before she slipped it onto her own finger to rest next to the ring he'd given her.

'Tell him thank you, please.'

'I will.'

'Did Rosa know about this?'

'No, nobody knew.'

'Roman, I want to be alone, for a while. You understand, don't you?'

'You're not the old Svetlana, are you?'

'How can I be?'

Rosa appeared silently, before speaking to Svetlana, in Spanish.

'You have a visitor.'

'She wants to be alone,' said Dubnikov.

'Rosa, I'm sorry, do you mind?' asked Svetlana, also in Spanish.

'Suit yourself,' replied her friend, beckoning to her employer.

They left Svetlana with her garden and thoughts. She watched the rings, side by side, and then turned them slowly together with her thumb and forefinger. In that moment, a lone cloud passed across the face of the sun and the light fell away, following her mood. She felt totally alone, her fantasy as a child turning out to be no more than a picturesque prison for her memories. Oh, how she longed to be that young girl again and to re-write the story of her life so that its theme might instead be hope realised. But no, here she was, a castaway on her island home where she would live out her days, separated from the mother who had carried her and visited occasionally by a son long since gone to tread his own path through life. There was no reason to hold back the trembling of her lip, or the tears forming below her closed eyelids. The wound that refused to heal shot a spasm of pain through her as she clasped the rings to her bosom, while her throat let out a low moan to accompany the faltering exhalation of her breath.

'Oh my darling, forgive me – forgive me,' she implored.

A gentle gust of wind brought forth a polite round of applause from the leaves around her, recognising that when it came to the representation of tragedy, like ballet, the Russians were the masters, whatever the language.

'I see you learned Spanish. Your accent's not bad,' said a voice.

For her, time stopped. All sound fell away and there was no movement at all, while a blanket of shock draped itself over her. Her eyes remained firmly closed, she knew not for how long. Then it began. Somewhere in the distance, where animal senses were alerted to events long before their human cousins, an embryonic wave began to form. The first she heard was a far-off whisper, but this quickly turned into a rumble, the ground beneath her toes seeming to shake as the tidal mass gathered to sweep over her. She opened her eyes just as the sun re-emerged, its blinding light mottled by the leaves and obscuring her view of the tall figure she struggled to make out, but who was now standing over her. The wave's rumble had now become a deafening roar as it broke over her, forcing the air from her lungs and carrying with it her ecstatic declaration.

'Nikolai!'

She stood up quickly, but immediately fainted as her arms dropped limply to her side and her knees buckled. Nick lunged forward, arms outstretched. Her body rolled as it tried to escape his grasp, but his left hand was steadfast under her shoulder blades as his right scooped up her failing legs. He drew her towards him and planted on her waiting lips the kiss he had carried for so long. Her eyes flickered open, consciousness returning, fleetingly at first. She reached out and touched his face with her fingertips.

'Am I dreaming? Is it you? Is it really you?'
'If I dropped you again, you'd know.'
'Then, don't drop me.'
'Once was enough... never again.'

Svetlana reached up and put her arms around his neck as he stepped forward to place her back on the bench, before sitting beside her. She clung to him, stroking his hair, tears of unrestrained joy rolling over both cheeks.

'Oh, Nikolai, I love you. I couldn't bear it without you.'

'Sveta, every day I wanted to tell you.'

'Nikolai, where...? Why...?'

'I've been back in Samara, a gardener for Roman's mother. She hid me, until it was safe.'

'But you could have –'

'No, Roman was right – no contact with anybody, including you – until I was forgotten about. Malenkov would have had me shot, without a doubt.'

'But he didn't... and you're here,' said Svetlana.

She drew the fingertips of both hands from his ears across the stubble of his face to the point of his chin. A mischievous smile crossed her face for the first time since she'd left Moscow. Svetlana slipped from the bench to the flower-covered ground below and tugged at his arm, beckoning him to follow her. They lay side by side in the shade of a tree, locked in each other's arms and at last sharing the same orange-scented air.

*

Dubnikov and Rosa had considerately disappeared. A simple note on the dining table, made damp by the condensation from the chilled bottle of champagne they'd left, promised a call, the following day. Delicious aromas drifted through from the kitchen, where Rosa had left them a prepared dinner of gazpacho and lamb stew. Nick sniffed the air as Svetlana read the note and smiled.

'Put that in the fridge,' said Nick, pointing to the champagne. 'Let's have a shower, first.'

As she walked down the corridor, the sound of water reached her. Nick was already standing under the falling jet, his forearms folded as he rested his elbows on the deep blue tiles. Svetlana slipped off her dress and joined him, put her arms around his waist and pressed herself to his back. They stood for a long while as the tepid flow cooled the heat from their skin and cleansed away insidious memories to make way for a new beginning. He turned and she stepped into his open arms, stretching to meet his kiss as it descended.

A little later, Nick opened the wardrobe.

'Whoah... there's a lot of black stuff in here.'

'I didn't feel colourful. But tomorrow... I'm going shopping!'

'I'll buy you lunch.'

'I'll look forward to that.'

'And we can discuss the honeymoon.'

'Nikolai...?'

'You didn't think I'd forgotten, did you? Every day, while I waited, I planned it out.'

'We're going? We don't need to hide? We're going to Venice?' she asked.

'I promised. We have to keep a low profile, but we can go.'

'Oh, Nikolai, thank you,' she said, hugging him tightly.

*

'So, you see, he did repay you – my life for his son's life. I didn't know he'd switched the gas and thought I was dying. All I could think about was you.'

'What will happen to Vitaliy?'

'Depends if they find I'm alive. If they do – well, another reason I had to stay hidden.'

'Malenkov will find out.'

'We'll go to America, at least for a while. I'll speak to Jack, he knows people. New identities, maybe. We'll work something out.'

'And for Ivan?'

'The same – of course.'

'He's coming here in a few weeks.'

'Rosa told me.'

'And she can cook, yeah?'

'Fantastic,' said Nick, taking another mouthful of stew.

They sat on the terrace long into the evening, moonlight taking the place of the sun's embers. Their conversation was interspersed with interludes of fulfilled silence, when Svetlana would hold his hand to reassure herself he would not slip away again. The fading aromas of their meal allowed in occasional traces of the smell of oranges. The air was kind to them, carrying an atmosphere of contentment.

Later, she cleared their plates and immersed them in a sink full of water to await attention in the morning. Nick stood in the doorway to the terrace, looking up at the star-filled sky. She approached him and closed the doors before turning to embrace him.

'C'mon, husband, we have things to catch up on,' said Svetlana, leading him in the direction of the bedroom.

*

It was eleven-thirty the next morning when the phone rang. Svetlana answered it.

'Hi, Jack, how are you?'

She winked at Nick.

'I have somebody here who wants to talk to you.'

She handed the phone to Nick.

'Hi, Jack. If there's anybody with you, get rid of them.'

Silence apparently met him from the other end of the line.

'Jack... are you there?'

The conversation was brief. Nick replaced the receiver.

'What did he say?' asked Svetlana.

'He's on his way, and asks if you can do the paella?'

Svetlana sniggered.

'Have you still got a job?' she asked.

'Yeah... as a ghost reporter,' he joked.

She stood and smiled at him, before brushing his face with her hand.

'Right, I have nothing to wear for my honeymoon. Are you coming shopping?'

'I'm looking forward to it. I'll get the car keys.'

*

Jack Freeman opened the drawer to his desk and took out his passport. He phoned through to his assistant and asked her to book him on the next flight to Seville as he glanced at his spare suitcase in the corner of his office, always packed and on standby.

At heart, he was a reporter through and through. He knew now that he was sitting on a story he couldn't reveal, at least not for a long time. He wanted to tell Malenkov and his crummy friends that Nick and the truth he'd told had survived their best efforts to silence him, but for now he'd have to keep his own counsel. His phone rang.

'Great, that gives me three hours. Can you get Pepe to pick me up...?'

'Sure, no problem. Also, Bogdan called for you, from Kiev,' said Freeman's assistant.

'Oh, yeah? Get him back for me, please.'

Freeman waited only a couple of minutes to be put through to Bogdan Goncharenko, press secretary to President Trublayevskiy of Ukraine.

'Bogdan, how's it going?'

He listened intently while Goncharenko outlined the pressure being applied to his boss by Moscow in the run-up to the forthcoming elections. He was anxious to counter the implicit message that citizens voting for the incumbent would find themselves cold in the forthcoming winter, as the Kremlin took its revenge for failure to support its favoured candidate who was perceived to be more sympathetic to Russia's interests.

'We can tell it, but we can't slant it any way.'

'I'd expect nothing else,' said Goncharenko.

'Have you spoken to Kyle Hughes? He's on his way to Kiev to cover it. He could do an interview, but we'd have to offer the same to the other side...'

'Friday would be good, Jack, if Kyle could do it then.'

'Right, Friday it is. Where do you want to do it?'

'The Energy Ministry.'

'Nice – like you're style. Kyle and the crew will be there at three in the afternoon...'

'Thanks, Jack. All the best, my friend.'

'You too. Take it easy Bogdan.'

Freeman put the phone down and placed his passport in his jacket pocket. This was going to be an interesting election.

*

Malenkov had travelled under his false Estonian EU passport and tossed it on the Wedgewood-blue cover of the king-sized bed as he looked around his room at the opulent Hotel Opera in Kiev. He was taking no chances and had decided to supervise the operation locally. The small team he'd picked, including Il'ya, had booked in at rather less palatial accommodation a few days before. A knock at the door announced their arrival to report on Goncharenko's movements and traffic to his mobile. Malenkov let them in.

'So, let me have your update.'

'Security's not really a problem. He has a bodyguard if he's with the President, but otherwise not. Works irregular hours, which is not so good, but tries to be home by twenty-two-hundred if he can. Lives in an apartment overlooking Mariinsky Park. There's underground parking and the camera can be taken out easily enough.'

'Good, Il'ya. Anything else? What about his car?'

'Drives himself, usually – black Mercedes – but uses his wife's Renault some of the time.'

'Right.'

'There's one more thing,' said Il'ya.

Malenkov gestured to him to continue.

'He's meeting Kyle Hughes of INN for an interview on Friday afternoon, and after that he's doing the national stations here.'

'Is he, now? Right, that decides our timing. Ideally, we'd have waited until Saturday, but we don't want those interviews being recorded. So, it's Thursday night or Friday morning. Work out the details and let's pick it up tomorrow.'

Svetlana's Garden

'What about Hughes?' asked Il'ya.

'What about him?'

'Do you want to deal with him too?'

'No, absolutely not. He doesn't really cause us any trouble in Moscow, so let him go back. It's better him than some interfering bastard, like another Mendez. Right, if that's all, I'm going to catch up on some sleep.'

*

Svetlana gave Freeman a hug and kisses on both cheeks as he emerged from the arrivals hall at San Pablo.

'You look better,' he said.

'I feel better.'

'How is he?'

'He's alive, Jack – he's alive!'

'I'm happy for you. He's a good man and an even better reporter since he met you. But, you – you're dangerous.'

'I haven't felt dangerous.'

'But you're feeling it now?'

She grinned and raised her eyebrows.

'Are you hungry, Jack?'

'I ate at Barajas, so I'm all right for now.'

They made their way to Svetlana's car and soon the barrier rose at the parking area exit to release them in the direction of the city.

'Thanks for the piece on Krasnodar, it gave us all kinds of leads.'

'Good,' replied Svetlana.

'I have something a bit more challenging for you, if you're up for it?'

She took her eyes off the road, just long enough to give him an inquisitive glance. He continued.

'You know there's an election coming up, in Ukraine?'

'Uh huh.'

'I had a call from Bogdan Goncharenko. Do you know him?'

'No, but Nick will.'

'Yeah, he does. Anyway, he's Trublayevskiy's press man and his strongest card on energy stuff, which the President's pretty hopeless on. The Russians are leaning on them with big price rises – threatening to turn off the tap. You know the sort of thing?'

Svetlana nodded.

'He wants to put his side of the argument and Kyle Hughes is coming in to interview him on Friday. I figured you and Nick would be the best people to give Kyle some different bullets to fire, as questions.'

'Did you know Malenkov's been promoted to colonel?'

'You didn't mention it.'

'Funny, thought I had.'

'What's he got to do with it, anyway?'

'How big are the stakes?'

'Big: if the people think their granny's going to freeze, a freedom mentality only goes so far.'

'I'll give you a question,' said Svetlana, her eyes narrowing. 'How do you interrupt a message?'

'Huh...?'

'Shoot the messenger. Do you know if Malenkov's in Moscow?'

'How would I know?'

'Find out. Ask one of your guys to speak to him about something – anything.'

'And if he's not there?'

'Then, he's in Kiev.'

'Nah... I can't see it.'

'He's done it before. If the stakes are high enough, he'll do it again – won't take the risk of leaving it to others.'

'Should I pull Kyle out, you mean?'

'I didn't say that. It's his call – and yours – but you'd better protect him. Malenkov didn't hesitate with Nick.'

'I still can't really see it.'

Svetlana pulled the car over and stopped the engine, before turning to Freeman.

'Do you believe in experience?'

'Of course.'

'And, in me?'
'Yeah, but you've been out of this for a while.'
'You remember Yushchenko – poisoned – lucky to survive?'
'Yeah.'
'What makes you think the Kremlin will just leave things to the arguments? How many other reporters didn't get to tell their stories?'
'I'll warn Kyle.'
She started the engine and pulled away.

*

Nick was waiting for them, leaning on an olive tree at the front of the villa with a glass of water in his hand. Freeman stepped out of the car and for a few moments looked at Nick before stepping forward to embrace him in a tight bear hug.

'Jesus, son, now I believe in miracles.'
'How've you been, Jack?'
'Helluva story... one day?'
'One day.'
Freeman released him.
'You want one of these?' asked Nick, holding up his glass.
'Shit, no. Get me a beer will you?'
Nick grinned and signalled to him to follow. Svetlana took Jack's hand and led him into the house.
'Put your case in the end room. Your beer will be out on the terrace,' she said.
Relaxing with their drinks, Freeman repeated the issues for Nick's benefit.
'Sveta's right, they won't leave it alone,' said Nick.
'We should be there,' said Svetlana.
'You're dangerous again,' said Freeman, laughing. 'Sorry, but there's no way. I have big plans for you two in the future, but right now, I need you to stay out of sight and... alive. Kyle's a big boy and can handle things, but I could do with those killer questions for him.'
'When are you going back to Madrid?' she asked.
'Tomorrow night.'

'We'll work on it. You'll have them to take back with you.'

Freeman swigged the last of his beer and then picked up the second one Svetlana had opened for him.

'Mr Demochev sends his best.'

'Demchi, you've spoken to Demchi?'

'Yeah, Svetlana. He says it's okay for you to call him if you want to, but just don't mention the military.'

'Is he okay?'

'What counts as okay for a grumpy old Russian editor? Call him yourself.'

She smiled at Freeman.

'And you two, what's your plans now?'

'We're going to talk about it on honeymoon,' replied Svetlana.

'Honeymoon! Now we're talking. Are you going to Venice?'

'Venice,' confirmed Svetlana.

'Get your butts over there. You deserve it.'

Chapter 39

Two days later, they sat at the edge of St Mark's Square in glorious sunshine, sipping pleasant but outrageously priced Pinot Grigio. The house band, in immaculate white jackets and black bow ties, serenaded them, while in front of them a horde of insistent pigeons delighted and frustrated the milling tourists in equal measure. Nick glanced at the bill that was clipped down on a small stainless steel tray.

'Jesus, look what you pay for the band!'

Svetlana looked elegant in a white dress with vibrant blue patent leather belt. She pulled her sunglasses to the bridge of her nose.

'Am I not worth it, then?'

Suddenly, he had a new context. It reinforced in him why he was here with this beautiful, complex woman who had brought him a different life of passion and danger. He laughed as she pushed her glasses back into position.

'Every cent.'

'Good, then take me for a gondola ride.'

Nick left money, including a tip, as they rose from their table. They strolled, in air made from oxygen and coffee, through winding streets where it seemed every fourth shop window displayed masks showing the full range of human emotions. Arriving at the Rialto Bridge, they turned down Sestiere San Marco towards a row of gleaming black gondolas where a group of men in traditional blue and white hooped shirts chatted as they waited for custom.

'You will choose me, señora?' asked a handsome young man, in his mid-twenties.

Svetlana's Garden

Svetlana turned to Nick with a mischievous smile. She was not asking him, but was telling him that the choice was made. He smiled and nodded.

'I am Pietro,' said the young man as he helped Svetlana step into the gondola while holding on to her hand just a little too long.

He waved to Nick to take his chances, by stepping in on his own.

As they moved away, the gondola began to rock in the swell created by passing boats. Later, Pietro expertly kept his balance as they made sedate progress alongside ornate buildings that had no right to still be standing but somehow did. Nick put a protective arm around Svetlana's shoulders, catching her smile from the corner of his eye.

'Eees the most romantic city in the world, no?' asked their host.

'Perhaps,' replied Svetlana.

'No, eees magic place. Here you will be very happy. I am always happy here.'

Svetlana looked at Nick and kissed him.

'You're right,' she replied.

*

The FSB team saw Goncharenko's wife drive out of the garage, taking their two children to school. The choice of car was now easy. Malenkov had made the call that simply gassing him there in the car wouldn't do. Given voter sensitivity and the Kremlin's need for the right result, a bona fide-looking accident was required. A thin smile crossed the FSB colonel's face as he saw the first piece of the day's jigsaw fall into place.

After ten minutes, Malenkov watched Bogdan Goncharenko emerge from the pale green door, which lead from the apartments above. The four corners of his Mercedes blinked as he blipped the key on his way across the ribbed concrete floor. He settled behind the wheel and then started the engine.

Traffic was heavy on the main city roads, but light in the surrounding streets. Goncharenko pulled up at a set of traffic lights.

Before he could react, Malenkov had shut the passenger door and lowered himself into the passenger seat.

'What the —?'

The putative protest was cut short as Malenkov placed the barrel of his gun against Goncharenko's ribs.

'Do you know Borysohlibs'ka Street?'

'Yes.'

'Drive there.'

'What do you want?'

'Shut up and drive!'

Malenkov held the gun firmly enough to act as a reminder, but not so hard as to cause bruising. He'd been through all the details and within ten minutes they were under the trees, seventy-five metres from the junction with busy Naberezhno-Khreshchatyts'ka Street.

'Stop here.'

He looked round to see his FSB men pull to the side of the road in the following car. Traffic lights in the distance held back the next flow of traffic, giving Malenkov the opportunity he needed.

'Are you a betting man?'

'No.'

'Pity, because if you drive really quickly, your odds are fifty-fifty that you can make it to hospital before you die. Goodbye, Mr Goncharenko. I'd hurry now, if I was you.'

In one movement, Malenkov donned the gas mask he had tucked inside his jacket and directed a short spray at his hostage's face. In less than five seconds, he was halfway to his colleagues, the mask once again hidden. Gratifyingly, while he briskly walked, he heard the screech of tyres as Goncharenko accelerated away. He climbed into the rear seat, just in time to see the now dead press secretary drive into the path of the passenger coach that would provide a host of witnesses able to confirm a terrible accident had taken place. His pulse quickened, but the moment was special for him, one of immense pride in his country and in his own professionalism. Il'ya selected first gear, turned in the road and drove steadily away.

Svetlana's Garden

*

Svetlana surveyed the ornate restaurant. Coloured murals were set within scrolled panels and old chandeliers threw layers of complex light upon them. In the corner, on a raised stage, a pretty Chinese girl, probably late-teens, played flawlessly on a jet-black grand piano. Svetlana wondered what had brought her here. *A student perhaps, earning some money towards her fees?*

'Nikolai, do you remember the first time you took me to dinner?'

'Yes, at Café Pushkin.'

'Will we ever have dinner there again?'

'I was nervous.'

'I remember. You were trying not to look at my bottom as we went up the stairs.'

'How did you know that?'

'Nikolai... please.'

'It's difficult not to look.'

'Is the right answer. It's funny how you learnt to say the right things. I gave you no chance, in the beginning.'

'You were right to be tough on me.'

'That's not what I meant. I just thought you were hopeless.'

'And now...?' he asked.

'Don't fish for compliments, you know how I feel. But thank you for bringing me here to Venice.'

Nick reached forward and topped up her glass with wine, before lifting his own.

'I want to make a toast,' he said.

She returned her eyes to him.

'To the future,' he proposed.

Their glasses gently touched, before each drank a little of the rich, red Chianti. His toast implicitly spoke of a past and her face fell as she remembered those who had helped them to be here now but for whom there was no future.

'To our friends, present and departed,' she said, closing her eyes for a moment of respectful reflection.

'Our friends,' said Nick.

Svetlana's Garden

After their meal, they walked arm in arm towards Hotel Danieli to which their booking had been switched, at Jack Freeman's insistence, as a present from INN. On the roof terrace, Svetlana asked if it was possible to just have a drink. The head waiter showed them to a corner table from where they could look out on the city and its magnificent lagoon with tethered boats, silhouetted by the moonlight. In the distance, giant cruise ships in the port boasted of epic voyages completed and of those to come. They sipped Amaretto from cut glasses, finely shaped ice cubes tinkling an accompaniment.

'This is perfect, Nikolai, just perfect,' she said softly, reaching for his hand.

*

Next morning, Svetlana opened her eyes in their room at the fourteenth century gothic Dandolo Palace, which comprised one of three in the hotel. She felt herself a royal character in a novel as she looked at the opulent surroundings, with tapestry wall coverings and exquisite antique furniture. No doubt, some of the Italian influence of St Petersburg had originated here, although she hoped with less tragedy in its history. The sound of running water told her that Nick had risen, unseen by her, and was taking a shower. She went to the window and looked out across the lagoon to Murano Island, which seemed to her to wake and stretch as it was warmed by the new morning's sun.

Nick strolled through in a white towelling robe, his damp hair tousled but his chin neatly shaven. Svetlana kissed him on the cheek as she made for the bathroom.

She looked in the mirror, framed in Italian marble, and drew a brush slowly through her hair, which was once again shining luxuriantly. Putting the brush down, she noticed that her nails had recovered their shape, now enhancing the long slender fingers that her mother had assured her would one day point to the man she'd love. She made a private promise to her reflection that one day she would be reunited with her mother, however and whenever that could be.

When she returned, Nick had turned on the television and was watching the INN headlines while pouring out two cups of the coffee he'd ordered.

'Come and get your coffee. It's going cold.'

Nick's words tailed away. Before them, Kyle Hughes appeared on screen.

'He's okay,' whispered Svetlana.'

INN's Moscow correspondent, temporarily stationed in Kiev, began his report.

'While turnout has been steady, it's too close to call the result with any certainty, although early exit polls do seem to show a slight lead for Moscow's favoured candidate, opposition leader Oleksy Cushko. Cushko has sought to reassure voters that he's best placed to end the simmering row with Moscow over gas prices that threatens to leave Ukraine short of vital supplies, with winter just around the corner. The incumbent, President Trublayevskiy, is known to struggle with the detailed arguments in this area but his highly articulate, western-educated press secretary, Bogdan Goncharenko, was due to conduct a series of briefings, before he was killed in an apparent car accident. Some have their suspicions, but it's fair to say not even the President's team have been able to come up with any evidence of foul play. The next twenty-four hours are going to be pivotal in seeing whether Ukraine keeps its recent western-facing policies or if, once again, it turns east and into the waiting arms of the Kremlin, hoping for easier relations with its powerful neighbour. Kyle Hughes, for INN, in Kiev.'

Nick lowered the sound and turned to Svetlana. Images from the screen danced on their faces as they looked at each other.

'Should we have been there?' asked Nick.

'Your Russian blood troubling you?' she asked.

'I can't go back to where I was: it's all changed for me.

'Do you think we can make a difference?'

'We have to try... They won't stop, will they, Sveta?'

'No, Nikolai, they won't stop. Truth is an inconvenience, and messengers like us are easily erased.'

'But we'll go back to the fight, won't we? You know we will?'

'It's in our blood. Yes, Nikolai, we will fight again... for the truth.'

'And us? You – me – what will happen to us?'

'I chose you, Nikolai Ivanovich... Now, love will choose our fate.'